American Oz Maker

by

Warwick Gleeson

DEL SOL PRESS.

PIPER ROBBIN AND THE AMERICAN OZ MAKER.
Second Edition
Copyright © 2025 by Del Sol Press and Warwick Gleeson.
All rights reserved.
Printed in the United States of America.
Del Sol Press, 2020 Pennsylvania Avenue,
NW, Washington, D.C., 20006.

www.delsolpress.org
ISBN-13: 978-0-9998425-4-6

Cover Art by Scott and Mila

Our books may be purchased in bulk
for promotional, educational, or business use.
Please contact Del Sol Press by e-mail at
editor@delsolpress.org

Second Edition: August 2025
10 9 8 7 6 5 4 3 2 1

For Melly

Acknowledgements

For their insight and influence, special thanks to Joe Hall, Richard Hacker, Kara de Folo, Ryan Ringdahl, Gerrit Hansen, Saul Rip, Walter Cummins, Gardner Browning, Shami Stovall, Theodore Roethke, Jayne Anne Phillips, Peter "Rings" Jackson, Kayla Hardy-Butler, Audrey Woods, Leonard Cohen, The Flying Monkeys of Des Moines, Frank Baum, Brandon Sanderson, and the best canceled TV show ever, "Emerald City."

Books in this Series

WORLD MAKER (prequel)

AMERICAN OZ MAKER

Author Bio

Warwick Gleeson has lived in both LA, D.C., and NYC, and worked many different jobs, everything from waiter to small business owner. Screenplays verge on option, but short fiction published in many national journals including *North American Review* and *Quarterly West*. He lives in the Seattle area on an island with a most wonderful wife who is a popular historical mystery author.

.A

From the 16ᵗʰ to the 21ˢᵗ century, the War for Utopia was fought between two great magical cities, London and Kathmandu, to determine the destiny of humanity.

London valued a universal perfection of human form, the fusion of magic with science, and rule by benevolent sorcerers known as World Makers, whereas the followers of Kathmandu preached cultivation of virtue, harmony with nature, and a Bodhisattva-led democracy.

After numberless casualties over many time streams, London emerged victorious, and the Primal World Maker decreed a Grand Human Transfiguration. An elite new species was thereby created and tasked with a cosmic destiny.

But peace and destiny availed them not.

A dark and alien intelligence lurking among the stars had already condemned the inheritors of Earth to a fate both deadly and inescapable.

TABLE OF CONTENTS

➢ GLOSSARY

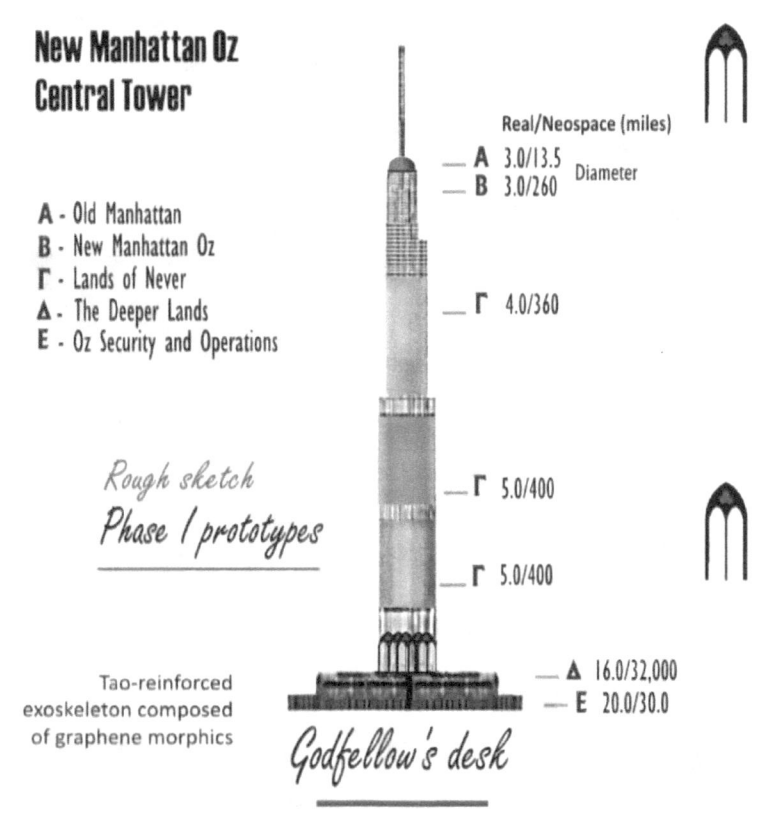

New Manhattan Oz
Central Tower

Real/Neospace (miles)

— **A** 3.0/13.5   Diameter
— **B** 3.0/260

A - Old Manhattan
B - New Manhattan Oz
Γ - Lands of Never
Δ - The Deeper Lands
E - Oz Security and Operations

— **Γ** 4.0/360

Rough sketch
Phase I prototypes

— **Γ** 5.0/400

— **Γ** 5.0/400

Tao-reinforced
exoskeleton composed
of graphene morphics

— **Δ** 16.0/32,000
— **E** 20.0/30.0

Godfellow's desk

Chapter I

Mongkot's Fear – Ragamuffin God – A Sky Full of Corpses

SINCE THE AGE OF BRONZE, Piper Robbin had outlived many nations and empires, and in her various guises, dethroned her fair share of tyrants, gods, and dark magicians. But by the year 2058, she'd grown bored. To remedy this bout of existential ennui, she sold her beach house in Oceanview, and intent on remaking her life, flew east for the promise of an American jazz renaissance in New York, not to mention a role or two in a real Broadway musical.

Jazz and the theater. All will be well, she told herself.

Upon arrival, Piper found a cheap apartment in Brooklyn, landed a barista job, and began auditioning for bit parts. She also adopted a few sensible habits to assist in her rejuvenation, among them an energetic consumption of the local cuisine. Therefore, every Friday evening, rain or shine, she'd stroll to the corner of Westcott and Prospect to visit the popular local street chef, Ms. Chariya Song, and pick up an order of her favorite Cambodian khor stew with caramelized palm sugar, fish, whole eggs, and a healthy scoop of trotters.

During such intervals of culinary bliss, the jovial Chariya loved to regale Piper with crazy stories, her favorite subject being her unique Cambodian family. For her best customer, she'd don her red headscarf and sauce-splattered white apron, cherry picking the tales while preparing the steaming bags of takeout.

"Didn't you say your family would be flying in from Phnom Penh this month?" Piper asked Chariya one cool autumn evening. She welcomed the fresh new air of October, always a promise of relief and the *auld lang syne* melancholy she'd learned to cherish.

"Yes, they are here now," Chariya said, "but I think New York is too big for them. They are restless and wish to move."

"To where?"

"Seattle, or Ventura. I'm not sure. They are scientists, engineers, and they want to change the world."

"I see, well so does my violently obsessed father who just landed in town. In his case he's fixated on the concept of utopia. Once he even remade the entire city of London into a quirky version of the Oz Emerald City."

"Emerald City? Oz?"

"Long story... So how can I help your wise children with their noble mission?"

Chariya laughed as her tongs snagged the best trotters. "But Piper, they're young enough to imagine they know everything."

"Chariya, I'm pretty old and I know just *one percent*."

"And they've pulled along from Cambodia my funny-headed single nephew, Mongkot, who shouts every day about a great evil coming to the world."

"Gods, don't we have enough evils already?"

On the verge of completing the take-out order, Chariya leaned forward across the metal counter, close enough that Piper could feel the woman's breath like fingers gently poking her face. "Mongkot bought a strange object from a street vendor in Phnom Penh, who told him that if he placed it beside his bed at night, he would have dreams of the future."

Enough to drive him mad, Piper thought. She suddenly felt a surge of concern for Chariya and her family. "You should take heed, Chariya, I've heard the Cambodian black-magic underground can be dangerous."

"Ohhh, Piper, I don't know. Many people say magic is not real, and if untrue, Mongkot is still mad as a drunken weasel, and his dreams... God, so horrible."

Piper couldn't help but be curious. If her friend was in danger, perhaps she could help. After all, despite her current passive appearance, she was still the daughter of a World Maker, as well as the most powerful sorceress to ever walk the soil of Europe, much less the new world.

"Chariya, do you recall his latest dream?"

"A real scary movie. Something about a woman's face in a bright halo spinning around in the sky, and apes with great wings covered in blood... oh and the cries of people screaming in terror."

"That's *so whack*. And apes with great wings. Perhaps related to the Hindu monkey god, Hanuman?" Chariya didn't reply, only chortled nervously while Piper watched her put the finishing wraps on the takeout. Chariya then placed the order in a bag and handed it to Piper across the counter. Piper thanked her, and said, "Magic or no, Chariya, I hope you don't move. I would not wish to lose you."

Piper turned and began walking home. She retraced her steps down Westcott, carrying dinner for herself and her Oz-obsessed father who had just reappeared in New York without warning, and while engaged in this activity, she ruminated again on Mongkot. Given the dark origin of his artifact, she could not readily dismiss his nightmare vision despite her desire to remain happy, at least temporarily.

: /

THE BROOKLYN STREETS QUIVERED AND PULSED with ribbons of carnival light, by turns festive and dark, and the neighborhoods brimmed with every manner of oddly glowing creature, Japanese droid pal, and anomalous street crime. Humans of many species, both real and artificial, jostled each other for attention while flashy face-drones, jazz poets, and other bodies both aerial and ethereal whispered overhead, all competing for attention with the corner street comics who belted out their lines from portable "air speakers."

It was the best of times, and the worst of times.

Where had she heard that line before?

Regardless, another question to consider. Was New York in autumn not the perfect place for her to forget her true identity? To lose herself and unwind as someone she never knew: a young American girl fresh out of California and seeking an acting job on Broadway. She could sing, dance, do cartwheels, soar and swoop like Peter Pan, whatever it took.

Her jovial co-baristas at Tempestuous Times Coffee affectionately termed her the "Brooklyn putz" and said she appeared too pixie-like (5' 1") and barely fourteen years old. That fact alone might hamper her dreams, though she didn't care. There truly was no business like show business. She'd even been auditioning for parts in *The Lion King* and *Book of Mormon* (both having run in NYC for over 50 years); and besides, she could always look older anytime she wished.

Though I don't wish to.

The role of a naïve mango pixie suited Piper for now—a self-imposed lesson in humility coupled with a need for a rush of new impressions. She'd sectioned off her old recollections of lives and times long ago with a simple spell spoken in Galician, her favorite magical language, *"Deixe só que os novos recordos sexan os primeiros"* (*Let only new memories come first*), thus allowing only her most recent memories to compete for attention. In this way, she easily lost herself on the bigger stage of New York without, for example, feeling compelled to compare busy sidewalk fruit carts in the boroughs to Constantinople market stands during the reign of Emperor Justinian.

: /

LATER THAT EVENING, PIPER AND HER OZ-OBSESSED father, Edison Godfellow, devoured Ms. Song's khor and streamed their favorite schlocky movies on TV as they reclined on a tacky flower-print couch in the living room of a grimy apartment—one complete with sputtering ceiling light, several score cockroaches of varying size, and a single window overlooking an inauspicious and sullen sliver of Manhattan skyline.

Piper turned to her guest and said, "So dad, whaddya think of my grand skyline view?"

"Impressively depressing, my darling." He was using the remote to locate a suitably ridiculous movie on Flick-a-Zon. "Rather like a termite mound in comparison to the magnificence of London."

Though a Primary World Maker, and as such, the most powerful magical being on the planet, her father had now devolved to a frail, ragamuffin god in worn jeans and torn white frock. He appeared to Piper like a starving version of his former self, hardly capable of making a bowl of cereal much less a world, but still, his old macho Greco-Italian look was evident: hair thick and shaggy black, dripping in ringlets down his neck; nose and chin of a Renaissance prince; earlobes pinned with dozens of tiny silver-metal insects—each capable of growing to fully animated, house-sized magical violence in seconds.

Piper rolled her eyes. "Your old Emerald City, eh?"

"Yes, so to speak" he said, followed by a whimsical smile. "I spent years engineering every molecule. Even the emerald towers gleamed in seventeen different shades."

"And filled with silly straw scarecrows?"

"Don't be absurd, Piper."

"Isn't designing an entire city with seventeen flavors of Oz already kinda absurd, dad?"

"No. I assert that it stood as a brilliant work of art blending cinematic motifs of a fond utopia with the core need for a wondrous new world that by its very presence… yes, by its very presence culls forth the best in human beings. If nothing else, I am a utopian, yet also a romantic idealist."

"But what does it matter now?"

He paused a few moments before verging on gloom. "Very little. London has forgotten me, and I'm still not certain the War for Utopia is over."

"And how many whack-o-tons of magic did it take to erect those gargantuan towers?"

"Enough to reforest Europe from Normandy to Sicily, as well as resurrect the Neanderthals."

"And how many British subjects did you piss off?"

"Hundreds of thousands, but they saluted me with tankards of ale once I created flying cars."

Piper gave him the Bronx cheer.

"Daughter, how is it you can behave so immaturely after more than twenty centuries?"

"Dad, sometimes *it's you* who act like a child. Think of the good you could have done in the world with all that magic… And you've spouted off about London Oz *at least five times* over the past week. Do you really need to rabbit-hole your shit?"

"Psychotherapy is a long dead pseudo-science, Piper, and you should know —"

Enough was enough.

She interrupted him with her signature "snap": small white hands palm up above her mango head, arms elbow out and pushing high, her expression a big smiley face—all achieved in a quarter of a second.

In reaction, Edison's eyebrows pinched ever so slightly

as if feeling a twinge of migraine. "I loathe that silly snap thing," he said. "Must you further evolve your role as a fool American?"

"I'm having fun, father, and for the first time since jazz was invented."

"But your speech, the language you damage is—"

"Brooklyn is my dumb *muther-f'n jazz*, and don't you *sass my ass*."

"Please, Piper. You attempted a farcical identity restart many years ago in Hawaii. It failed miserably."

"Was it my fault that King Kamehameha went on a rampage and slaughtered half the island?"

Edison stood to his feet and faced Piper, and when he spoke, his tone was sharp with impatience. "Search your memory, daughter. Recall that you once lived as Grand Sorceress of the Holy Roman Empire. You commanded *every room* you ever entered with power and magnificence. Magicians feared you. Kingdoms groveled before you."

"Yeah, yeah, and I can return to those *groveling moments* whenever, but it all bores me now, kinda like a plate of cold putz and cheese."

"Putz and cheese?"

"How many times can you watch the same movie, dad? … No, it's really about the New York skyline now."

"What are you blathering about?"

"One of your smelly malignant narcissists just blocked the view." She pointed out the living room window at a nearby corpse floating about ten feet away. "A refugee from Phase I of your Grand Human Transfiguration?"

Edison turned to see what appeared to Piper like a

bloated purple bag in a business suit—no doubt a Wall Street banker drifting over from Manhattan. She knew he'd either died of hunger or exposure, just like the rest of them, and *good old Dad* had to take full responsibility.

The city skies swirled with these "white collar corpses" as the news called them, and as fate would have it, a few dozen were TV news executives of one kind or another, their identities soon evaporating as they mixed with the thousands of nameless others from Central Park to Yonkers, the mass of them like flocks of black geese camera-frozen in time.

"An *insufferably bad movie*, darling Piper," Edison said. "But an autumn storm front down from Canada will move them over the Atlantic by tomorrow evening."

"Shark food, eh Pops?"

"The cretins will rain down beyond the major shipping lanes, at least 100 miles out."

"Of course!" Now Piper was angry. "You knew this dark circus was coming. You and your London bunch planned it decades ago after winning the war. And now you've triggered your *Grand Transfiguration* spells this past week without hesitation. It's taking place all over the United States, and across the world."

"Yes, yes, however, it's Phase I only, and just one of those arguable atrocities you must endure when you wish to forever change the world for the better."

"Just one of *those arguable atrocities?*"

"The entire human race has been forged on the anvil of atrocity going back over 70,000 years. Intellectual honesty demands—"

"I thought you were a *sentimental idealist*."

"Damn it, Piper."

"But you swore that this initial mass termination of undesirables would be put on hold until we could discuss alternatives. So why did you lie to me?" *I might look like a young girl, but I've lived a score of lifetimes, and he knows I love him despite his evil... Seriously though, does he think I'm stupid?* "You can't possibly imagine I'm even a bit gullible. And what else have you lied to me about? When is the next atrocity?"

Piper flared her Grecian-blue eyes so wide her father could bore straight into them. And that's what she wanted—for him to see her lives like small pinpricks of white island in the Aegean, down from 15,000 feet to the grinding millet wheel and her hands carving monsters in beach sand even before the Greeks saw the first performance of *The Birds* by Aristophanes.

"No next atrocity, no Phase II, I swear it."

Piper's mind stuttered as she noticed how her father's ember-soft eyes of swirling nebulosity were suddenly scanning out to horizons she could not see, gazing at a myriad of locales at once across time and space.

Or perhaps even further. She never knew exactly.

Following a long pause, he refocused on her, took a deep breath and said, "Can we both simply admit the world will be a delightful and much preferable place without the perpetual twittering of offended narcissists, borderlines, sociopaths, and the like? Can we not simply term them *Despicables* and be done with them?"

"No, we cannot. Who are we to decide?"

"Who do we have to be, Piper? Life is not fair. More than two thousand years have taught you that."

Her mind yearned for a quick fix, a way to rehabilitate the many thousands of life-poisoning mental defectives and gently restore them to gravity. Unfortunately, she did not possess the power to defy her father, nor the wisdom to find a lasting solution.

Would she ever?

Perhaps one day, I will go back in time and fix this.

She rejected the idea of launching purification of the human species by terminating legions of annoying freaks, even though she could not deny the one simple and cruel truth. *They unquestionably make life relentlessly miserable for everyone else. And what do my co-workers at Tempestuous Times Coffee say when they get a real bastard or total bitch for a customer?*

"Chuck that clucker, motherfucker!"

Regardless, she would never forget the sight of the "Despicables" all kicking and screaming as they shot upward to finally halt about two hundred feet or so above the ground (from across the U.S., coast to coast, the highest per capita levitations occurring in Washington, D.C. and Los Angeles—worldwide in Moscow, Tokyo, and Riyadh), and no one could touch them, not even Piper, as if a field of hot magic negativity surrounded each one.

Even water from fire hoses turned to steam.

: /

FOUR DAYS PREVIOUS, GODFELLOW HAD FOUND his daughter working as a barista at Tempestuous Times Coffee on 8th Avenue in Chelsea. He appeared in line one morning around 9:30 AM, ordered a mocha caramel 16 ounce with whipped cream, and though she stood off to one side, operating the espresso machine, and though he appeared to be a shriveled and distraught version of his former self, and though she hadn't seen him in the flesh since the Battle of Jutland in World War I, she recognized him immediately.

"Padre?" She gasped at the burning horror in his eyes as he turned to stare at her.

The sight relieved her of motion. She'd never witnessed him in this state, not once, not even in early Greece when she herself was feared by the tyrants of Thebes as the "cursed daughter of Archimedes."

Since late Neolithic times, her father had existed, born of a black magic leviathan by the name of Ahriman who fell to Asia from the stars more than ten thousand years ago; and in later eras he was known by many names (not just Archimedes, but Paracelsus, Da Vinci, Diderot, and The Wizard of Menlo Park). Regardless, he was always an inventor supreme and the most powerful sorcerer this side of the Milky Way.

So what in freezing hell could have terrorized him?

The forgotten child in Piper Robbin, for the first time that day in the coffee shop, knew the meaning of real panic. Crushing a stone to powder or throwing a javelin half a mile wouldn't fix anything (and neither would anyone in New York care) like in the old days of Alexander. Muttering spells that made deserts bloom or the oceans boil meant less than cooking burgers on a grill. Mortality for all, even the gods and greatest sorcerers, might be just around the corner.

People think just because you're a great magical being

that you have it easy. No assumption could be more mistaken. Your hopes and dreams are spit on, your happiness ruined, your friends killed, and you lose sleep at night, worrying about shit just like everyone else.

And besides obligations you really don't want, you face mega-dangerous freaks way too often because you're expected to, you're the official bad ass. You can even die in lots of ways, and after all that trouble, sometimes you don't come back.

Piper had felt the need to spell-fashion a *memento mori*—a small half-face, half-skull ebony stone that hung from a thin iron chain around her neck—there to remind her that she too, in the final hour, could not escape mortality.

Once done, she confronted Edison Godfellow with a most basic question. "Just tell me, dad, quite simply, why are you here?"

She'd asked him while on her break, standing outside on the sidewalk and jostled by the mob. He answered with direct eye contact, penetrating loud and clear into her mind:

"I have come from the future to do whatever is necessary to prevent the current version of myself in this time stream from ending all human life on Earth as we know it."

: /

THE CURRENT VERSION? PIPER WAS SPEECHLESS. She tried to get emergency time off, but her TTC shift supervisor, Ms. Francine Axelrod, erupted with "Mon Dieu! No way! No how!" so Piper quit, leaving a long line of customers behind to curse and fume.

She escorted her father home to her apartment, and once there, he exposed the full horror story. Awed by his confession and visions of a doomed world, she listened intently as he explained in feverish detail what was supposed to take place in the coming days via the eyes and memory of a perpetrator recalling his dark past.

Following the final victory of London over Kathmandu, the Grand Human Transfiguration was declared and began to take shape. Viral spells conceived, crafted, and tested over the years by his Sorcery Enhancement Teams were timed to erupt like a chain of volcanoes from pole to pole along every major Earth ley line; and if humanity had one voice, it would have terror-screamed nonstop as the world about them dissolved into nightmare and chaos.

"In truth, the Phase II magical transfiguration wave bands trimmed and forged the planetary morass of human flesh into remarkable new beings," he said, as though in a daze of once-fond memory. "I dubbed them, *Superna Humanitas*, and the evolution was fascinating, strange, unprecedented, but also irrevocably deadly. Many millions died, good people too, but even so, my current version made no attempt to fathom the depth of his villainy. He denied even the concept of it. All was for the greater good."

At that point, only one inevitable goal remained.

A mass migration from Earth to the stars.

To Piper's alarm, her father collapsed at this point. He cried out like a trapped animal as she trembled with a consciousness of his agony and fear. *A monstrous being deep in the star nursery of the Orion Nebula saw them coming, set its trap and waited*—a thing far more evil and powerful than any child of Earth could ever have foreseen.

It attacked with a "mouth" of cosmic energy nearly a light year in length. Only that metaphor came close to describing the ineffable nightmare that engulfed his ultimate dream of new humanity.

Piper gasped. Though a light year was a miniscule measure of distance on a cosmic scale, still, the comprehension of an intelligent entity that enormous immediately became a mind-numbing task, even for a being such as herself. She knew she would obsessively dwell on it for many centuries to come.

Its presence in Orion must have suited its appetite. The nebulous alien monstrosity drank from oceans of stellar radiation, cosmic rays and hot gases, perhaps even feasted upon rogue planets to maintain its energy level.

But no time for contemplation. Another gasp by Piper followed upon learning it had swallowed whole fleets of colonizers and military class dreadnoughts—many of them bigger than Long Island and strong enough to punch a hole through the sun—consumed and channeled lightyears per second into a black gullet of hellish dimension wherein no escape was possible.

Thus did *Superna Humanitas* perish, and in a manner inconceivably malefic, and the story concluded as the mighty and once invincible Primary World Maker fell into fits of sobbing, repeating again and again:

"*Mea maxima culpa!*"

Piper felt both rattled and amazed. Never had she seen her father more inclined to expressions of actual guilt, and that horror in his eyes she'd noticed earlier flashed into being once more. Nevertheless, upon recovery minutes later, his composure returned, and he continued with his surreal and frightening story.

"Before I approached you at the coffee shop this morning, I had attempted to meet with my current deluded self and plead with him to listen, to tell him what would happen if he went forward with his madness. However, he would not take the slightest chance on me being a trick or trap connived by his enemies... besides, he saw me coming. He'd met with me only once before, in a prior century, but after only minutes he cursed and hurled a spell at me."

Edison Godfellow would nevertheless strive to halt the upcoming disaster of his own making.

But how?

The ultimate resolution depended on a makeshift radio telescope he'd built and set up on the roof of her tenement building—currently concealed in a towel-covered box of cardboard beneath an old water barrel. And though she wished to marvel at the boldness of whatever plan he had in mind, he could not or would not reveal details.

"We have so little time in which to act," she said.

"In truth, far more than you would believe possible," he replied with a puzzling wink.

Chapter II

Chiseled With Myths – A Taste of Glock – A Glitch of Spell

PIPER CEASED HER DEBATE WITH EDISON and left him alone with the Flick-a-Zon remote and khor takeout so that she might check on her motionless little buddies living in the apartment bedroom, namely, her box turtle, Alcaeus, and her dwarf Komodo dragon, Cleon—each in their own special terrarium with rock and plants, water drips and bugs.

She'd known them both since the Bronze Age, and every now and then, her spell craft gave them a bit of true consciousness plus a means to vocalize, and they would always stare up at her, blink, and ask the same question:

"When will you free us of this prison?"

How odd to hear such a question from such a little mouth. *So ripe for existential dilemma. Small things in glass boxes are better off with tiny brains that don't allow for memory or questions.*

Come to think of it, strong magic such as hers should be constrained by rules, but who would ever enforce them? For example, who could have prevented her from taking Cleon back to paleolithic Turkey and spelling him big as a jet airliner just for fun?

Around 42,000 BC, and she assumed only a few human sapien clans chipping out spearheads might be mulling about, though *how wrong she was*. Stone-walled cities, grand plazas of polished terrazzo tile, and tall black temple columns ideo-grammed with myths could be seen sprinkled throughout the countryside, reminiscent in her mind of the author Robert E. Howard and his novels about the "Hyborian Age."

The people there called themselves the *Kunglah Ju*, and the lumbering mass of Cleon scared them into new religion. On her part, she crushed rocks for the gaping crowd and hurled a boulder or two at least half a mile, and as a reward they chiseled her into a god and gave her a name, *Channa La* (which meant "wonderful strength"), though it mattered not, for the future human world of archaeology would never know these people as anything other than meaningless slashes on crumbled stone.

In truth though, will we not all share that destiny?

Piper's stream of consciousness was interrupted by the start of the movie her father Edison had chosen. The musical theme for the Mystery Science Theater 3000 selection blared like old acid surf-guitar from the TV: *Son of Hercules vs. Devil of the Desert*. And as she began to sing along to the funky lyrics while returning to the living room, her father pawed at the white bags of khor stew atop the coffee table. He rummaged for a moment, looked up at Piper with a frown, and said:

"Where's the plum sauce?"

"Uh, *plum sauce?*"

"I asked you to bring it."

"No, you didn't. Since when do you want bloody plum sauce for khor stew?"

No reply. She watched his eyes stare through her and beyond. But at what? As she looked on, his other eyes retracted from their planetary orbits, and in the room of his mind, became a swarm of vision on every side, focusing to search for one phenomenon, one inevitable and omnipotent force becoming a bigger threat by the moment.

"Dad?"

He spoke to her in his daze of watching—his voice cold and neutral, yet vibrant as an echo of fallen idol. "Piper, I want you to go to Ms. Song and return with the plum sauce... *Now.*"

"Bullshit. What are you not telling me?"

"GO NOW!"

What the hell?

Suddenly outside on the street, she stood facing in the direction of the Cambodian take-out, her entire nervous system tingling and her hands shaking as if with Parkinson's due to the abrupt teleportation against her will.

The night fell black and shattered with garish light. She looked up to see the Wall Street corpse directly above her, and she swore it was staring down with an oafish mocking expression as if he knew something she did not. Then the ground quaked, and like membranes filled with molten glass, every window in her apartment building exploded. Burning people began shrieking. How many she did not know, though she knew she must save them.

Before Piper could act, a whip of turbulent energy uncoiled like a rogue sun flare from her living room window eight stories above. She observed the Wall Street corpse disintegrate into a memory of burning sparks, and at once she understood the nature of the force—a Tao magical wavelength strong as a thunderstorm, yet contained, compressed into a small vortex and potent enough to kill or kidnap half of Brooklyn.

Only a master black sorcerer, or a World Maker, could have executed the spell.

After considering the totality of the event, and its target, she had a pretty good idea who.

And if correct?

I am destined for the fight of my life.

:/

IF YOU WERE UNLUCKY ENOUGH TO BE EDISON GODFELLOW at this particular moment, dangling from the roof edge of the La Mancha Tower in London nearly two miles high—damp, chilled, and gagging as a sunset of soft golden cloud wafts past you while the god-murderous eyes of Catherine Romanova drill into your brain like white-hot pokers and the 60 mm barrel tip of her black-plasma Glock pushes into your throat—you would understand that less than a minute remains in which to convince your homicidal tormentor of a few reasonably important things.

First, that you're really on *her side*.

And second, that killing you, here and now, will not save the human species, or the Earth.

Quite the opposite.

However, as you might expect, conversion to a lenient viewpoint proves difficult.

"You will not find eternal peace after I pull the trigger," she says with a voice like two centuries of glacier grinding four miles of granite. "I will seize your soul and condemn it to a hell you *cannot* imagine."

With your tongue on the barrel tip of the Glock you taste the carnage wrought by the weapon in years gone by. It tastes of charred flesh and metallic toxins in tiny amounts, detectable only by you and instruments of hybrid magic technology.

It's times like this you wish you were less perceptive.

If only you could return to New York.

But your tormentor is not finished.

"And if you believe that pulling this trigger will not sufficiently end your malicious and abhorrent existence," she says, "I happen to know the entire roof and upper third of this London cloud tower of yours will blow right off three minutes from now in a maelstrom equal to well over several hundred megatons."

Since you cannot talk because the Glock is now shoved against the back of your throat, you send your words clear and less than profound directly into her forebrain. *"Yes, I know what will happen. I lived through this already, remember?"* She does not answer, only glares and shoves harder on the Glock. *"You could have executed me by now. You did not have to allow me these minutes, and it's because you are still hesitant, because something informs you that my true demise will allow a creature even more terrible to rule this world."*

"Yes, damn you three times, but I've never wanted anyone deader than you!"

"Look into me, Catherine. I am not the current version of myself on the verge of obliterating humanity. I am from the future and have returned to prevent my worst crime."

"What nonsense is this?"

"Look into me."

"So you can trap me in a hellish mind prison of your making? You must believe me a fool, Godfellow."

You stare at her, and even in this awkward position, you cannot deny the core biologic truth of it.

You still love her.

She gleams like a golden kiss of magical Tao, the timeless wave of the cosmos, magnificent with determination and power, her long chestnut-auburn hair blowing glossy in the high-altitude winds, shot through with tendrils of white vapor, and her eyes like fiery oceans of war at twilight.

Must she appear so mercilessly mesmerizing?

Nonetheless, her prediction is accurate. A titanic shaft of pure energy equal in fury to an Earth-shattering asteroid will disintegrate the top of the La Mancha Tower in London, thus resulting in a toppling fall that will kill many tens of thousands.

You know only minutes remain.

You picture this scene because it happened in your past, part of the War for Utopia. Your enemies had planned a way to relieve you of your finest and most unique weapon in the struggle against them—a brilliant device known as "War Tracker" (only seconds beneath your feet).

So here you are again. How many times must you return to this unavoidable humiliation?

A tear rolls from your eye as you begin to suffer traumatic stress. The last time, things were good, fine and happy. Only several miles away, you danced with your old wizard girlfriend Mandukai to the tune of "You Make me Feel so Young" by Sinatra. A sudden blinding flash, a singe of hair, your pinot noir heated to bubbling, and you watched the La Mancha cloud tower topple in the misty distance like a dream.

Endlessly falling.

"You do look *different*," Catherine says with suspicion, expelling a small cloud of frosty breath as she continues to dangle you with one hand in the air over 10,000 feet up, examining you like an alien specimen, "More pathetic than usual, disheveled, even sad… And now, crying?"

"*I have been humbled.*"

"So you claim you are no longer worse than any tyrant who ever lived?"

"*You must have seen the other version of me, the current one. He is in New York, in a magical bubble of bunker miles beneath Central Park, preparing for his end of days.*"

"No, I saw only YOU in this pointless lab coat and preparing to eat that disgusting stew with your Greek imp of a daughter. My spell led me to you quite easily."

"*Listen, please, I know how to prevent the catastrophe that will soon occur.*"

"And I can prevent it *now*, by allowing you *to perish*."

∶ /

PIPER ROBBIN FELT ANXIOUS OVER THE EXPULSION of so much Tao from her apartment. Her little buddies, Cleon and Alcaeus, might have been hurt, burned to crispy wontons, or worse, atomically disintegrated. On top of that, the moans of the poor tenement people burned by molten glass increased in volume as they began to move or douse their wounds with water, mixed too with the screams of mothers and fathers discovering the bodies of their dead children. Father had vanished to God knows where and Piper knew instinctively that an extreme act of violence loomed in her future. Why? Because only one being possessed the kind of reckless audacity and sheer power required to kidnap him just before his favorite dinner: World Maker Catherine Romanova. His strongest and most dedicated foe.

A fidgety Piper knew she would need all her wits and skills to locate, much less battle such a being.

First though, I must set things right.

One smartly spoken and powerful Galician spell invoking Ahriman would not only save the people disfigured or killed by the molten glass, but restore all things to what they were a moment before the torrential energy of pure Tao intruded into their world:

> **Por todo o poder de Ahriman,**
> **Volve este lugar que vexo,**
> **De arriba a abaixo e en todo,**
> **Ao que sabía que antes cambiara**
> **Á vida, á enfermidade e bágoas coma á auga.**

> (*By the power of Ahriman,*
>   *Return this place of slaughter,*
>   *Top to bottom and all around,*
>   *To what I knew before it turned,*
>   *To life, disease, and tears like water.*)

No sooner did the spell reboot the dark and grimy tenement building to its former desperate self, filled with sick, sad, and impoverished people unburned by molten glass than it also restored the Wall Street corpse. Oddly enough though, a quirk of the spell had spawned a side

24

effect of spontaneous magical animation. Piper could not have foreseen it. Never had such a circumstance happened to her—a little like flipping a light switch that punches a big hole in the wall.

The corpse had renewed itself, yes, like all else, though instead of floating in place above, it stood in the street, its back to her, weaving drunkenly on two legs and tittering like a mad man.

But how?

Piper hated the distraction of pondering what might have caused it. The Galician chrono-restoration spell was spoken perfectly, and it should have acted perfectly. It only focused on a single building, one small amount of space, such a little thing.

So what glitch of spell has possessed this damned corpse?

The hideous, two-piece-suited, Wall Street creature turned to stare at her, only ten feet away from where she stood. It appeared to recognize her. Its purple bloated face tried to smile, but the force of the smile lanced it like a boil. The face exploded onto the sidewalk, and a moment later, a hanging sliver of lips opened onto a hole of glistening bloody teeth. The thing spoke to her with a voice painful and shrill:

"*Already, I am here.*"

"And you are?"

"*Your father's worst nightmare.*"

"He has more than one, these days."

"*Know this, sorceress, at such time the many-lived fool speaks these three words, American Oz Maker, your fate, and that of this human infested world will be fixed.*"

"American Oz Maker?"

The half-faced corpse remained silent. It levitated into the air, up to where it had floated just before the burst of Tao destruction, and as it rose, it never ceased to stare downward, its bloodshot eyes determinedly fixed on her.

As if chilled by an oncoming disease, and for the first time in centuries, her entire body shook with a quake of genuine fear. She embarrassedly pictured herself as a terrorized cat on a wobbling branch. Her palms beaded with cold salt water and her breath expelled long and deep clouds as she recalled her father's story about the ineffable galactic entity that had consumed the cream of *Superna Humanitas* in the Orion star nursery.

And now, her worst nightmare also?

I must face the truth of this corpse. It's a manifestation of the genocidal Orion entity my father fears, and it has already arrived on Earth, decades from now, then followed his trail into the past where I now stand. Perhaps my restoration spell, or Catherine's explosion of Tao guided it, and soon enough, it absorbed the passive aggressive bitterness of Brooklyn and found language.

But first things first.

My next step is not debatable.

26

Chapter III

City in Her Eye – *Caixa de Mundos* – A Million Years of Tao

SIX SECONDS BEFORE THE LA MANCHA TOWER in London evaporated into a hot cloud of sub-atomic particles, Catherine's feet flew out from under her and she somersaulted forward into airy cold space, her accursed captive, Edison Godfellow, violently yanked from her grasp. She reflexively pulled the trigger on her Glock. The magic plasma discharge thumped in her ears and shook her body like a nearby sonic boom, and she heard Edison shout, "Piper, no!" as the world spun and blurred to a horizon of pure darkness upon which rose a dim blue sun.

Flat on her stomach and inhaling a mouthful of jet-black sand, Catherine coughed. Her eyes fumbled for her missing Glock. *What in Beelzebub's name?* she said to herself as she stood and turned to see that her body had skidded like a flat boulder for hundreds of yards over a black sand beach, and one that stretched for miles to either side.

A miserably gloomy and depressing ocean lapped at the shore, and the freezing cold air, near zero in her estimation, drizzled down in icy gray sheets. Clouds in the far distance collapsed to the barren earth as if too heavy to float, and like shadows made whole, various tower shapes and blocks broke the horizon.

Ancient creations or natural formations?

A moment later, Catherine recognized this hellishly cold lump of volcanic stone upon which she stood as Iceland, though the exact moment in time eluded her. Edison must have roused from his feigned paralysis and hurled her to this place like a discarded toy. Strangely enough though, even until the last he appeared willing to die, to allow her Glock to fry him to a radioactive marshmallow soup— almost as if he'd told the truth for once.

Might he have?

But then, his final shout to that annoying daughter of his, *Piper Robbin*. The last thing Catherine needed now was that self-righteous little mongrel from Greece interfering in any way. Whether the ancient crone-child loved her father or not, the world must be saved from his destructive dreams of human transformation; and depending on her next moves, she knew the War for Utopia might be finally decided in a matter of hours if not minutes. However, before she could verge on decision, a whispering voice in the cold, dark air found her ear.

"Look to the ocean, Czarina."

Catherine turned and saw a pair of enormous eyes fading in above the dark waves, blending with the hazy blue sun of Iceland. The eyes floated towards her, becoming smaller and fleshing out on all sides to a face, and farther down, to the dim outline of a female human body. A whirlwind of black sand whipped up from the beach to meld with the apparition and give form as it drew closer and whispered once more:

"No more games. We must talk."

Catherine blinked and there stood Piper Robin only three feet away, though not looking like a foolishly small coffee shop employee. Instead, she'd chosen a classic manifestation far more overwhelming, that of the Grand Sorceress of the Holy Roman Empire—Countess Bianca Elise Cappello—a hum of radiance and righteous power, an archetypal life and death symbol.

The old Piper in her utmost glory.

She wore a shimmering, black velvet gown, over which fell a dark gray cape to her waist, gold-chained at the collar and edged with a wide scarlet band pointed every few inches with magical "spontaneous life" medallions that appeared like moon-silver ducats, each one inset with a single primary war symbol: dragon, fire, meteor, goliath, kraken, and more—monsters and primal forces that were hers to command. Sufficient, Catherine knew, to level every city in Europe. A Medici scarlet collar flared up behind the head of the Grand Sorceress, at least a foot high, broad and circling around to part a cascade of dark lustrous hair that fell to either side of her shoulders. Around her neck hung a half-skulled *memento mori* amulet, and about her waist, a six-inch wide girdle of polished red leather inset with strips of black-ion Tao battery, as well as a dozen or so silvery trinket-like devices serving various secret magical purposes, plus twenty sorcerous "sun rubies" big as thumbs and each worth a Byzantine Emperor's ransom.

Catherine absorbed the full power of this display.

It matters not. I will bring this woman to her knees.

Catherine stared into Piper's eyes, attempting to subordinate her by force of will, but the distractions and magic of those eyes made the task impossible. The Aegean-blue of the irises swirled with currents and floated tiny pinpricks of white. Catherine stared more closely, focusing down into the swirl. The pinpricks became small islands of white beach in a blue-emerald sea, and upon those beaches human figures moved. She saw them as if she were a gull, gliding above, soaring high to finally arrive at a vast black gulf of pupil, and deep into that dark abyss, she peered. Something was alive down there, she felt it in her skin— slight vibrations of human-like industry.

Unable to resist, she dropped straight down. Half a minute later, finding herself upon the floor of the pupil pit, she entered an illumined space like an enormous cavern and glimpsed in the misty distance a huge and magnificent city with spires and towers below a strange purple moon an hour from horizon.

The scene naturally came as a huge surprise. Apparently, the mega-ancient Grand Sorceress was far more diverse, far more complex than she could have imagined.

"Pardon me for interrupting your trot through my eyeballs, Czarina, but you dropped this," Piper said, withdrawing the Glock from her cape and handing it to Catherine.

"What's this I see?" asked Catherine, phasing from her vision and taking the Glock. "The daughter of Archimedes here to protect her father. Now I know this universe must certainly be askew."

"Always a smarty pants, you are," Piper said. "I haven't seen you since the Battle of Lepanto... You haven't told me if you like my *bling*." Piper spread her arms and bent her hands at the wrist to point at herself.

"*Bling?*"

"Never mind. It's an American thing."

"And I do not recall giving you the slightest permission to interrupt my interrogation of your father," Catherine stated coldly.

"Don't need it, Cath. I'm not one of your Russian palace flunkies. I am still a Grand Sorceress. Know that I stand here, before you, and on the battlefields of old Europe, battling sorcerers of the East and West at this very moment."

Catherine snorted. "What matter to me your petty time feuds with amateur magicians?"

"Listen. I was simply trying to restart my life in New York when you smashed in and kidnapped my father… And you almost killed my turtle and pet Komodo."

"I care nothing for your pathetic life, your psyche, or your Greek pets. My only concern is the utter and lasting extermination of your father."

"But you need him now. Please *listen to me*."

"Listen? To the daughter of a genocidal psychopath?"

"Just hear me out instead of mindlessly playing this role of self-righteous Nemesis."

"Hear the lies you and your insane father invented?"

Piper took a deep breath. "You must have noticed something *very different* about him… The way he behaved was erratic, unusual, unlike the past."

"For once he did not look at me with rape in his eyes. I will grant you that," Catherine said.

"It's *way more*. I know you're not stupid, Czarina. You must see—"

"I see only a foolish game played by fools."

"And I see only one fool," Piper said, her own face darkening. "Will you let your hate blind you while the human race borders on complete annihilation?"

"I will kill your father. That will end the threat."

"Enough! That is *enough*."

"If he meant well, as you say, why did the abomination hurl me to the black sands of Iceland?"

31

"He didn't. I did."

Catherine's eyebrow raised. Here was something new. She had not guessed the Grand Sorceress capable of such a bold and powerful feat.

Piper continued. "It's quiet here, desolate. I want no deaths because of our quarrel."

Catherine rammed a left fist into the open palm of her right hand. "If we fight, Countess Coffee Beans, there will be but *one death* on this island."

Piper grinned like a Grand Sorceress high on ego. "Don't be so cocky, Cathy. I was hurling bolts and boulders long before you were born."

"And I conquered the greatest black sorcerer on Earth when only fifteen—*Temujin Gur*," Catherine snapped.

"I know, I know. You are the missile silo of sorcerers, more raw power, yes, but your Mother Yarrow, Maria of Pozzuoli, is no longer with you, and my *bling* is formidable, not to mention my own magic and wealth of Tao."

Catherine was shocked. "How do *you* know of Maria?"

"Never mind. It isn't important as the fact that—"

A fire-golden aura of Tao abruptly flared from Catherine's head and shoulders for a moment before receding to a simmer, rather like a corona of solar eclipse. "NO! I must understand. How does a bratty little barista know of my Mother Yarrow?"

"Just a guess... You confirmed it," Piper said, the currents in her eyes gaining in intensity. "Brooklyn and Europe taught me to be shrewd."

"*Curse you!*"

"Curse all you want later. A thing far worse than me exists. The real enemy, our common enemy."

Catherine clenched her fists and calmed herself, the part of her brain that prepared for battle planning the first move. She knew she must rid herself of the barrier of Piper Robbin. The daughter of Godfellow stood in the way of ending the War for Utopia with one bold stroke. And if one bold stroke did not suffice, then more would follow, again and again, for as long as it took. She would never give up. The price of surrender was too great.

I must be stronger than ever and not waver.

With the voice of a haughty Czarina, she said to Piper: "Tell me Countess Barista, what are *those strange cities* at the bottom of your eyes? Those islands in your irises?"

Piper laughed. "I'm like a whale who collects colonies of life while swimming about. I have cities and villages within me, places out of time, places so small you cannot see them without knowing where to look."

"So you risk the lives of all these sad little civilizations?"

"They are protected with so many layers of spells it would take you—"

"Consider your children now hostage, barista!"

"What?... You've gone *insane.*"

"I will strip them from you."

"Back off, Czarina! This is pointless. You must—"

"I must kill your father by any means necessary."

"You must not. You need him. *Goddammit listen!*"

"I will listen to *nothing,*" Catherine snarled. "You are the one wasting time. I will hold the peoples of your body hostage, thereby removing you from my path."

"NO YOU WILL NOT!"

Catherine witnessed Piper's entire body flaring with rage and force of Tao, growing in size, taller and taller as the black sand of Iceland swirled at her feet. "THEN REAP THE WHIRLWIND, COUNTESS!" Catherine shouted back, also adding volume and rage to her form.

"Then quite simply, *FUCK YOU!*" Piper bellowed with an acutely weaponized voice. It caught Catherine off guard, booming loud enough to not only be heard across the sea in Greenland, but enough to topple castle towers and pulverize all bones to jelly within a radius of a hundred miles.

Though sizzling with hot tendrils of buffering magic and grown to the height of a young fir, Catherine gasped in pain and stumbled backwards. But only for a moment. The sonic pain she answered with a potent spell: *Polo obsequio máxico de Tao, Deixe que a miña forza suba motto antes que eu!* (*By the magical gift of Tao, Let my strength surge well before me!*), and by jabbing forward with both fists she ignited invisible blocks of magical striking force possessed of enough concussive power to floor a mad herd of charging bison.

They struck the Grand Sorceress, hurling her backwards, rolling and skidding her body over the Iceland beach in much the same way Catherine's own body had been treated.

The Czarina grinned with satisfaction, though no time to gloat. Never allowing foes a chance for breath, she soared at meteoric velocity through the gray, drizzly air directly at Piper, intent on pummeling the woman into a humiliating submission; but halfway there, she met a warm and hairy wall of flesh. It grunted upon impact. An enormous paw swung and whacked her to the black shore a hundred yards away as if she were a small bird. A half moment later, feeling dazed, her clothes ripped and muddy, she heard a horrific roar like a tall building collapsing and gazed up to see four gigantic dragons diving straight at her from the low-hanging fog—and not mediocre dragons, but mythical, devil-faced, bronze-black behemoths big as navy destroyers and fully scaled, their four bellows of iron melting flame simultaneously cascading down on her with enough combined heat to vaporize half of Iceland.

Piper's accursed bling!

Just as the first flames licked Catherine's face and body, crumbling her clothes to embers, she noticed a huge dark object out of the corner of her left eye. She pivoted to see an Iceland boulder the size of a house whistling towards her. For half a moment, she glimpsed beyond it and saw yet another ominous threat—a cyclops no less than twenty stories tall.

No doubt the flesh wall I struck.

Though no time to ponder.

Catherine burst like shrapnel from beneath the shadow of the massive stone just before it struck. As she soared into the bleak Iceland sky, she ripped the Glock from her smoking waistband and squeezed a round. The boulder exploded with a sun-bright blast that hammered the air. Like a bat-smacked ball, Catherine's body was hurled backwards in an arc, hitting the nearby freezing surf at least a mile out and vanishing deep beneath the waves—the blast also launching scores of spinning rock chunks like white hot missiles at the oncoming dragons, thereby scattering them with great howls of pain that echoed and rolled in the fog.

Only now, where is that twice damnable sorceress?

Undaunted, Catherine shot to the surface and levitated above the dark waves like a prophecy of doom. Rivulets of fresh blood coursed down her torso and dripped into the foamy red surf—her skin torn with gashes and cuts still in the process of closing, her right hand still clutching the Glock.

She strained her magically enhanced senses and probed with telepathy, but her enemy remained invisible. "ARE YOU IN HIDING, SORCERESS OF COFFEE BEANS?" she shouted to the barren grey waste.

The answer arrived immediately.

An icy wave of sea over fifty feet high slammed into her from behind, knocking her forward and enveloping her, gripping her like a gigantic fist. No ordinary water though, its texture had been transformed to a substance like liquid steel, and it squeezed her tighter and tighter, focusing enough pounds per square inch to pancake the entire city of Reykjavik. Moments later, the mass began to spin her around in its dark prison. It thrust itself into her screaming mouth and down her throat until she could not even choke.

Her Glock was lost in the tumult just before the entire volume of it lurched high into the air. It rose to become the head of a demonic waterspout that sucked hundreds of thousands of gallons from the frigid Atlantic before shrilly discharging itself onto the shore, skipping and hugging into a mile-high raging tornado of black sand and liquid metal.

Catherine panicked.

She thrashed and twisted like a mad animal within the black womb of tornado head until the situation worsened. From out of nowhere, a pure beam of blinding electric force drilled into the vortex, and as if several hundred thunderbolts were relentlessly striking one spot, it persisted, causing the entire whirling mass to glow and howl. Catherine felt herself being electrocuted, squeezed, and suffocated all at the same time.

Spinning into the misty dark atmosphere above Iceland, beginning to lose consciousness, she channeled by force of will every bit of her remaining power, mind-spelling until it erupted from her eyes with a crackling beam of intensity hot enough to vaporize the crushing liquid steel that cocooned her. Like a torch, her radiant eyes cut away at the tentacles of murderous fluid. The blister-red beam sliced more and more from the head of the thick metal tornado, thereby creating huge gaps until she was inevitably hurled away by the kinetic momentum, her body skyrocketing above the clouds, flipping head over head at hundreds of miles an hour.

While struggling to regain control, she gagged, and with a loud groan, ripped the last scraps of suffocating substance from her mouth, then refocusing on the immediate future, knew quick action was necessary before the accursed Grand Sorceress could check her once more. She uttered an effective and familiar stealth spell: *O tempo é lento, O meu formulario non visto* (*Time be slow, my form unseen*), and within moments, dove down beneath the cloud cover.

As a golden eagle soaring for prey, she searched once more for her enemy (who she admitted to herself was far more adept than she had believed possible). Though the Czarina's energy was nearly drained, she retained enough, she knew, to strangle Piper Robbin for a full week if necessary.

Seers of Kathmandu, show me her throat!

Catherine flew down and around the area where the fight had been taking place, gliding like a silent ghost, scanning carefully. The sorceress was there, somewhere, disguised, or even invisible. She hoped for a clue in the sprawling scene of frozen time.

Then she saw it.

Hundreds of yards away, in a shadowy corner of rock near the base of the dissolving black tornado, the sand blew a form in the air: the slight curve of a face, and a few feet lower, half a hand, dim and passing in that still moment, though unmistakable.

I have you now, little barista.

Catherine swooped silently onto the phantom from behind. She felt the substance of her foe, knew she could probably snap her head from her shoulders and burn it, but out of sympathy for the many innocent beings she harbored—and given that her father Godfellow might intercede at any moment (for even though now pathetic, he was still a World Maker possessed of power beyond description)—she believed it best to drag her prey into the time closet with her.

Catherine locked one arm tight around Piper's neck, her legs lifting to scissor the waist of her fellow giantess. She then summoned her aria power because she wished to not only slow the clock but also weaken her foe enough to render the struggle brief. Within three blinks of an eye, she felt the warm hearth of magical aria deep within herself, and two blinks later, sang with an operatic voice her spell:

Polo poder de Tao,
Faga o seu tempo o meu,
ea súa fora só a metade,
Ata a morte ou a miña vontade
Permita o seu Descanso.

(*By the power of Tao,*
  Make her time my own,
  Strength halved by strife,
  Until death or my will
  Return moments of life.)

Upon conclusion, their two bodies fell back into the black sand. The world of storming winds and dragons suspended into still shots. Catherine heard Piper cough and felt her hands frantically gripping at the chokehold, her body bridging backwards, writhing and struggling to pull away. But it was no use. The Czarina held tight and squeezed with her ship-crushing legs until Piper let out a strangled shriek, and then, using her free hand, she repeatedly drove a sharp fist into Piper's ribs, each blow forcing a muffled cry of agonized pain from Piper's throat. There was no escape, especially not for a world class sorceress whose strength had been severely sapped by spells and battle.

"You will cease this struggle, or I will snap your neck." Catherine spoke calmly into Piper's ear. "Your resistance was brave, but now it is done."

"*Fuck you.*"

"You will submit TO ME." Catherine tightened her hold, forcing Piper to struggle harder for breath.

"I'd rather die."

"And what of your precious cities? Your islands and peoples? What of them?"

"You cannot—"

Catherine twisted Piper's head until their faces were only an inch apart. She locked eyes and bored once again, down through the deep craters of pupil darkness to emerge onto worlds with strange suns, purple moons, and gleaming towers, and as she stared farther, she observed streets and plazas, uncountable numbers of beings and their shadows going about a business she could not fathom.

"I see them," Catherine whispered coldly, "I can murder them in their thousands. You doubt me?"

"Monster!"

"I will demonstrate, Grand Sorceress of coffee beans."

"Noooooooooooo, they are innocent!" Piper's hot tears rolled down her cheeks, her muscles straining to their utmost, body thrashing desperately.

"You should never have dared me to battle!"

Like a vengeful goddess, Catherine hovered and sensed the denizens of Piper's worlds as they felt vibrations like small quakes becoming more intense. She surmised from their surprise and panic that in the centuries of their existence they had never felt such tremors, not while dwelling on the lands and seas huddled in a God-flesh they believed forever divine, harboring, and invincible.

Chapter IV

George M. Cohan – Ushering Dust Mites – First, Manhattan

SUNLIGHT FLICKERED BEYOND PIPER'S EYELIDS. An autumn breeze chilled her face. She smelled the aroma of Chariya Song's Cambodian cooking, and heard music, very close, as well as the distant sounds of horns and general human pandemonium she knew so well.

Brooklyn.

Her body reclined, her mind sleepy with a dissolving dream of a roaring tsunami washing over the Long Island. But why that dream? She didn't know. The dream had caused her to flee, chased to the Statue of Liberty.

She moved. Pain in her side made her wince.

Yes. I remember. The fight, Iceland, and what of my places, my children?

She searched into her eyes for her micro-visible nations. She soared through and over their cities and villages like a phantom, tapping minds and pinging masonry until she knew they were fine, only a little shaken by tremors felt earlier, as if an evil god had prepared to annihilate every atom of their existence. Piper blew a soft, Brooklyn-like autumn wind over them and through their hair, over their fields and seas, so they would know their Protector had returned and safety was assured once more.

Upon completion, she opened her eyes to thin slits. Shapes and colors darted before her. All was blurry. She then heard music again, even louder than before, and this time with lyrics:

Give my regards to Broadway
Remember me to Herald Square
Tell all the gang at Forty-Second Street
That I will soon be there...

She recognized the old song by George M. Cohan—one her father used as a tease. She lifted her head, opened her eyes wider, and inevitably focused on a single object as the song continued: a television monitor about a foot high. It sat upon an apple crate, obviously arranged to be the first thing she would see upon awakening. On the screen was an image. She realized immediately that it originated from deep space, no doubt a radio telescope image. A deep black background with a star-white dot in the center, and to either side, a hair-thin line of glowing energy, both lines elongating 6.09541 centimeters before widening to big fans of nebula.

A human finger lowered itself into her vision and pointed at the star dot. Next, she heard her father's voice, subdued and respectful. "That, my dearest daughter, is a billion solar mass black hole, and those jets to either side are sub-atomic particles several million degrees hot and stretching for over ten lightyears before finally expanding into cooling clouds... Even for a World Maker, such a thing is incomprehensible."

Piper turned her head and gazed up to see Edison Godfellow, exactly as she'd left him before his first bite of khor stew—raggedy dark and mad-scientist-looking with big and brown remorseful eyes. He smiled down at her with a look of genuine love. His hand stroked her hair as he bent to kiss her on the forehead.

The first time he has kissed me in centuries.

"So shines a good deed, father," Piper said and smiled, suddenly aware of how acutely exhausted she felt, almost as if recovering from a fever, aware also they were on the rooftop of their tenement building around 10 AM and that she'd been transformed into her pixie-like Piper self.

She glanced up and saw no floating corpses littering the sky (most likely blown out to sea), and that triggered her memory of the Wall Street corpse last night.

Or was it last night?

Then out of nowhere, Catherine Romanova's voice rudely interrupted her musing:

"*Ahhhhh.* Such an ironically tender moment between the destroyer of cities and the childish curator of them."

Piper sat up and strained her neck to look around her father's torso for the purpose of glaring at the snotty Czarina. And that turned out worse than she expected. The woman lay on a patio recliner, wrapped in a big beach towel and wearing gaudy sunglasses. In her right hand she held what appeared to be a Bloody Mary with lime.

What the living hell?

At first, Piper was flabbergasted, but within seconds she wanted to spit the image from her thoughts. She'd tried so hard to free her life from negativity and hate, and a new identity in New York reflected that desire, only now she admitted to herself that she hated this self-righteous World Maker more than she'd ever hated anyone.

When will the sun melt her flesh cocoon to reveal her true self? A giant fucking wasp.

Piper understood she should display and practice more discipline, but she had so many reasons to hate the

43

arrogant royal troll. The woman humiliated her in Iceland, threatened and terrified her little cities for no good reason, and last, though not least, remained perpetually obsessed with murdering her father.

"Catherine has already witnessed this," Edison said, gesturing to the screen. "I waited for you to awaken before explaining the rest."

"Why is this ridiculous Russian diva wearing a towel?"

"Well, she—"

"In truth, I am Prussian, and I took a shower," Catherine said with a stoic voice. "That accursed black sand settled in places I would not have it."

"So she's showering here and hitting up our liquor cabinet. What's next? Shouldn't she return to the 18th century and rule some peasants?"

"I would take you and your damnable father to task, coffee beans, but for the fact I am sorely drained," Catherine said. "I believe to save himself your father spelled me into a weakling."

"This is a new age of reconciliation!" Edison proclaimed, looking back and forth, his eyes begging Piper to understand. "And no bickering. There is no time for petty rivalries."

He took a step back, fished a remote out of his right lab coat pocket and clicked at the small TV screen. The clouds of sub-atomic particles turned a light golden red. "This is what we might have seen from a starship if sufficiently close billions of years ago, but now, observe what happens when I scan for a unique wavelength." He clicked again and the clouds on either side interlaced with threads of light blue. "What do you see?"

Piper observed Catherine lowering her sunglasses and appearing surprised. "In Beelzebub's name, *it's Tao energy*," she said.

"YES!" Edison shouted. "An incalculable mass of Tao created in the sub-atomic maelstrom of a black hole and birthed into the universe… These hair-thin blue tendrils entwine with the heated gases and radiation of the cooling subatomica, and each is at least a few million miles thick. This too, I must say, is unimaginable."

Piper could not move. Like Catherine, she was stunned by the sight and conception of it. Here was enough Tao to easily create an entire galaxy, or obliterate one.

"Feeling a bit microscopic?" Edison said.

Like a worm giving rides to a dust mite.

"Now fill your thoughts *with this*." Piper had never seen her father more excited or vigorous. He clicked the remote again and a large patch of amorphous white-golden cloud filled the screen. "We are viewing the core of the Orion Nebula, part of the complex wherein the entire fleet was dissolved by that monstrous cosmic entity. And now… *this*." Another click and Piper witnessed small blue streaks appearing here and there in the cloud mass. Not nearly the mass of the black hole nebula, but still, amounts far beyond any concept of the term "enormous."

Edison continued. "I used a small radio telescope I invented here on this roof to find these images and test for Tao wavelength, so it was no surprise when I discovered large deposits in Orion, enough to…" His voice became distant. "Enough to *destroy us all*."

After a few moments of awed silence, Catherine spoke. "Edison, you must tell me. What in plain truth happened to your grand armada? Or will happen years from now, should I say?"

Edison turned to face her. "My most precious Czarina, you have no conception. We were more than a fleet, you see, 884 fleets to be precise, over a thousand ships each and totaling well over a billion members of..."

Piper watched him carefully.

A stumble of emotion again?"

"We were drifting through Orion to observe the primary star nurseries at close range. Then it came upon us." He pushed both hands through his dark locks, apparently steeling himself for more memory.

Piper knew that Catherine, like her, could see without doubt that here was a being, the ultimate World Maker, forever changed and truly humbled. It hardly seemed possible, and though she'd heard this story once already, she thirsted for more details.

Who wouldn't?

Edison continued. "My chief astrobiologist argued it had followed us from somewhere beyond Orion and simply chose its place of ambush within the Nebula corridor. I tended to agree, for we were constrained in that place, disallowed the broader freedom of maneuver, but as the thing grew larger and ships in proximity began to go dark, we fired on it."

"How did the apparition appear?"

"As I told Piper earlier, from our viewpoint it appeared like a mouth, emerging from the wall of the Nebula, opening wider, and wider still, over five trillion miles from left to right, perhaps more, but I am uncertain because it appeared to fluctuate from moment to moment...

However, whatever its size, or origin, or reason for being, it would not tolerate the presence of our humanity. I tried to reach out and only felt its implacable desire to annihilate us."

Catherine gasped. Piper too was speechless.

"By the dark face of Ahriman, it was like nothing else to have ever touched my thoughts. I tell you truly, I nearly became insane on the fringe of it. And it came on relentlessly, leaving no choice, so we unleashed the full power of the fleets, enough to dissolve a star cluster to a cloud of helium.

"What types of armaments?" Catherine asked.

"Everything imaginable. Black hole cannons, war spells, particle beam weapons, dark plasma, nova mines. Never have I seen such a rain of fire and blinding energy, but it all proved useless against it. *All useless.*" He took a deep breath. "More and more ships went cold as it engulfed us. I ordered those furthest away to escape, to accelerate and leave the rest of us behind, but they could not. It struck at a multi-light speed I would have thought impossible, and it proceeded to swallow us, along with whole convoys of military class dreadnoughts big as Long Island."

"How did you feel?"

"Helpless... and afraid, *very afraid.*"

Though her father appeared ready to shut down, Piper had to know. "What happened to you then?"

Edison walked a few feet to a small wooden chair and sat down, the look on his face sliding to a state somewhere between mindless trance and misery.

"We drifted into the mouth, or what appeared as such. The stars and nebula vanished, and within moments we resurfaced, two years later in the Magellanic star group beyond the Milky Way."

"Portal-launched *that far*?" Piper felt both mystified and terrified as she dared to comprehend the sheer amount of power needed to relocate that many ships such an enormous distance.

"Outside our viewports we saw the whole bloody big galaxy, many times brighter than the full moon... one of the most amazing sights I have ever witnessed. But the intermission of incredible beauty was short lived." He put his arms on his knees, hands clasped, head pointed down. "Our ships wallowed in place, and the hulls were penetrated. Nothing prevented them from entering and consuming our people within the inner sanctums and quarters... That's when the terrible screaming began. Combat Sorcerer teams and Hell Drone security units were dispatched, but no use. We watched the carnage from the command deck, on the monitors... difficult to describe, like swarms of bloody red insects surrounding their victims and biting them down to nothing."

Catherine appeared genuinely anxious, if not terrified. "*Beelzebub's name!* How did you escape this horrid infection?"

"I joined with a platoon of Black Class combat sorcerers, and with all the power we could muster, spelled my escape through time and space back to Earth's past. And I vowed to set things right so the disaster would never take place."

I must ask him.

"Do you feel guilt for having lived, Dad?"

"Yes."

"And where is your *Caixa de Mundos*?" Catherine said.

A Box of Worlds? Piper noted that her father appeared surprised, and he hesitated, enough that she knew a lie was coming. And what the hell was a *Box of Worlds?*

"There was no time for such things," Edison said.

"Dad, I'm old enough to know after a few thousand years that you're lying again."

Edison stared only at Catherine. "Alright, yes, I have it. But you cannot fault me. No one can fault me for possessing it."

"So what in the name of Hera is it?" Along with being insanely curious, Piper was irritated by her current state of ignorance.

Edison paused and looked down.

Catherine grew impatient. "Do you wish me to answer on your behalf?"

Though obviously annoyed, he turned to Piper. "A *Caixa de Mundos* preserves and protects objects, securing and suspending them in time. *Caixa de Mundos* will work with an original, or create a copy, whatever is required."

"And you made a copy of the entire armada?"

"Parts are copies, though most is original."

"You mean, you—" Piper stammered for the first time since the sack of Samarkand by the Mongols in 1220.

Edison reached through his shirt and pulled forth from around his neck a silver chain with a black amulet. *But no.* Piper realized it was not an amulet, rather a dull black cylindrical object, perhaps half the size of a lipstick tube.

Just as she began to open her mouth, Catherine interrupted. "The entire sum of the fleets, flesh and all. By the Lords of Light, sir," she said with a respectful voice, staring intently at the object. "A masterful act of magic. I

49

truly have *never seen* the like."

"Yes," Edison said, scrutinizing his daughter far more than necessary.

"Okay, sooo when will that cute little bunch of *bunnies* get to escape?" Piper had to know, even if it pissed him off.

"Whenever appropriate. There is no rush, and I assure you, they will never be used to attack the Earth, or its people, in any way. I swear it."

Must I have faith?

:/

WHAT HAPPENED NEXT THAT MORNING struck Piper as event stranger than a bizarro *Box of Worlds* containing a few giga-tons of *Superna Humanitas*. Her father informed her and Catherine that "the best is yet to come." His final solution to prevent the imminent problem of his other self—as well as the next and most ugly phase of Grand Human Transfiguration scheduled to occur within 24 hours—would be demonstrated.

Edison went downstairs for a few minutes to get breakfast and coffee while Piper ignored Catherine, that is, until deciding to break the awkward silence.

"I am sorry for kicking your *fat ass* in Iceland."

"You *what?*" Catherine pulled her sunglasses down and stared in disbelief.

Edison appeared with a large tray of food just before Piper could start another brawl that might have leveled whole city blocks. He handed them each a plate of scrambled eggs with chorizo, cilantro, tomatoes, and cheddar cheese, two slices of bacon, one crabcake, and a slice of dark rye with pepper butter, plus two clay-fired mugs of steaming coffee.

Piper ate like a starving animal, stuffing down the hot food and gulping the coffee, watching sideways as her enemy did the same.

Edison grinned as if pleased. "While you partake, I will present my plan for solving the major issues. Prepare to expand your imagination." He fished a small clump of grey metal out of his side coat pocket. He held it out on the palm of his hand so they could see. "Melted spoon," he said. "I collected the Tao energy radiating to us from Orion, as an experiment, and after 24 hours I was able to store enough to melt this common tablespoon with a primitive cluster laser I devised." He smiled big as a carnival clown at Piper. "Do you not see the implications of this event?"

"So you melted a spoon," Piper said. "Too bad…"

Then it hit her. *Of course.*

"We go back in time," Edison said, "We collect as much as we need. At least a million years of Tao from Orion should do it."

"A million years with one primitive dish?" Catherine appeared incredulous as she wiped her mouth with a napkin.

"Upon phasing far enough into the past, we station ourselves and begin the construction of giant collector dishes. I have legions of multi-purpose drones remaining from the renovation of London. We will dispatch them to mine Ganymede and Callisto for materials, and as that process continues, engineer creations more magnificent than even the Very Large Array in New Mexico. Once done, a few thousand of them will hug the dark side of Jupiter and remain there for the duration. The massive radiation and magnetic field of the planet will keep the entire complex safe from detection."

"Let me guess," Piper said, "Because—"

"Thereby disallowing any opportunity for my other self, or an alien hostile to stumble upon them in the distant past and wreck our plans."

"Your other self is a source of limitless annoyance," Catherine said. "But I see—"

"The plan is brilliant, Dad," Piper broke in. "When do we leave for Jupiter?"

"Once you finish your coffee."

Catherine cleared her throat. "And once *you* are done with your dishes, Edison Godfellow, you will possess the ultimate divine power you need to kill that star kraken. More than *sufficient* I would say?"

"We will use its own Tao from Orion against it, as well as retain enough to render my deluded counterpart powerless and thereby save this sad world we love," he said without emotion.

It was plain to Piper that her father would not dodge or disguise the fact that a supreme cosmic revenge figured into his plans. Could she blame him? Despite his callousness in seeking utopia, he truly cherished the new people, the Great People, the *Superna Humanitas*, and Piper herself knew what it was like to feel maternal towards a large population, to be adored by them, trusted by them.

Narcissistic thinking? *Of course.*

She then realized she'd failed to inform him of the Wall Street corpse, and she proceeded to explain what had transpired, and what it said. Edison listened to the anecdote and frowned, long and hard. "My *worst enemy*," he said, rolling it around in his head. "Most likely the oversized mouth from Orion."

"Wrong. Your worst enemy *is still here*," Catherine said with a wry smile.

"*Shut up,*" Piper said to Catherine. The Czarina quickly turned and glared. "The Orion alien, no question."

"Yes," he said, "though here, in the past and far from Orion, its power must be greatly diminished. Whatever its true intention, we must assume it is hostile. However, it must not be allowed to interfere with our Jovian master plan."

Piper nodded. "Devil hang the corpse."

Edison continued. "We remain in Jupiter orbit long enough to set things in motion. Next, we jump forward, a few tens of millennia at a time for the purpose of checking Tao storage levels, then we return to Brooklyn later this afternoon in time to prepare for the upcoming Transfiguration circus."

"And how will this unspeakable power from Jupiter translate upon our return? In phases? In parts?" Catherine asked, narrowing her eyes at Piper as if daring her to issue one more command. "What will be our primary objectives in the days to follow?"

"We will utilize the Orion Tao to create a strategic and populated defense network of invincible new city-worlds. Together they will unite, and with assistance from the fleet, harass and drain our alien foe until we can kill it."

"And our very first steps?" Piper still wasn't clear.

In response, Edison unleashed his "thousand-year stare" (as she termed it whenever he suddenly appeared half crazed), and in a deep baritone voice replied with a statement that totally perplexed her:

"First, we *take Manhattan*, then we *take Berlin*."

Chapter V

The HMS Phaeton – His New Love Monster – S.C. Vampire

IF YOU HAVE NOT EATEN REAL FOOD in many months *there is nothing quite like the taste of a perfectly cooked khor stew.* Piper mused on this as she took yet another delicious slurp of Ms. Song's yummy concoction.

Earlier that afternoon, upon returning from helping her father and that overbearing cretin of a Czarina construct and install the Tao collection dishes on the dark side of Jupiter, Piper had voted for an early dinner, feeling quite starved, and though she hated to admit it, still trembling a bit from her exposure to the inexorable and vengeful power of Catherine Romanova.

So now, once again, Piper reclined on the roof of her tenement building next to a small table upon which sat her dinner and reheated coffee. It was late October, around 4:30 PM in the afternoon, the autumn sun low on the western horizon. The last gasp of sunlight on the buildings and white-washed floor reminded her of the light in classic Edward Hopper paintings—pale and melancholy.

To her right sat grizzly old Alcaeus, and Cleon also, both in white bathrobes, both feeling relieved to be restored to humanity, if only for a short time before having to later resume their cold and slow identities.

Following their initial discomfort with Piper's mango yellow hair and smallish size, they compared memories. The last thing the two of them recalled was the Battle of Jutland in the North Atlantic. The year, 1916. They stood on the badly rocking deck of the HMS Phaeton near nightfall, hearing fire-hot German shells sizzling overhead, as well as the curses of the desperate crew, their attention suddenly distracted by a British battle cruiser two miles away on the dark sea bursting into a geyser of flame like a volcano blowing its cap.

Next, the fearful shout of a sailor nearby, "Torpedo!"

Then nothing.

"You didn't think I'd leave you to be blown to bits?" Piper communicated with the two of them in English before taking another sip of coffee. She toned down her usual attitude for their benefit.

"No, though it was clearly terrifying," Alcaeus said, able to speak English because Piper had spelled it so. "Why were we there in the first place, Macaria?"

"Yes, why?" Cleon asked, squinting into the sunset.

"Your break from the animal kingdom was overdue, and I was aiding the British Empire to win the battle in order that we might restabilize the course of World War I. The Czarina and Paganini's forces were helping the Germans, but at the time, I was still working for my father—"

"You mean, Archimedes?" Alcaeus said.

Cleon gaped and spoke as if bewildered. "Doing what, perchance? Helping him purchase the heads of Persian nobles at the market in Thebes?"

Alcaeus guffawed and Cleon followed in kind.

"Gentle philosophers," Piper said calmly, "No such thing. It is hard to explain, but a war across time was taking place for the future of Earth. We called it The War for Utopia. My father was on one side, together with London, and those who defied him on the other, under the banner of Kathmandu. Conflict occurred at critical junctures, points where history could be changed to meet the goals of either side—depending of course on who was victorious... Besides, the battle of iron ships was exciting, wasn't it?"

They both nodded vigorously in affirmation.

Piper continued. "You must have known I was protecting you. I will always *protect you.*"

Alcaeus reached out and squeezed Piper's hand, then sat back, cleared his throat and spoke. "What do you they call you during this period of Earth, Macaria?" he asked.

"Piper Robbin."

"How odd," Cleon said.

"I prefer Macaria, your Grecian name, if you will not be displeased?" Alcaeus said.

"No, I will not."

"In all this time, Macaria, have you not yet conceived a spell to relieve us of our wretched fate?"

Piper felt embarrassed and found it impossible to hide. "The spell leveled by the Wizard of Corinth, Dardanos, to destroy you was strong and mysterious. As you know, I keep you alive the only way I can, by allowing your humanity only once every century or so, then returning you to primitive form before the magic virus can deal you a horrible death."

"Alas, only a *beastie solution,*" Cleon said with great exhaustion.

"But you also know I will not stop trying to solve this, and as I have reminded you both a dozen times, living in such a manner is preferable to dying for many days in the jaws of that virus. It is worse than Black Plague, slower onset and more violent... I know. I've seen it at work."

"Such is our fate for daring to defend you at the Corinth royal court," Cleon said with pride in his voice. "But in truth, dear Macaria, I would not have had it otherwise. We are faithful to you, now and forever."

Alcaeus chuckled and slapped his knee. "Would that we now held goblets of fine Athenian wine to toast that truth! … Well then, since we only have a few short hours to make use of our senses, please tell us of your adventures."

"I would love to. Where should I begin?"

"Alright then, who do you love, or hate? And what worlds will fall at your feet like stars in the night?"

:/

PIPER ROBBIN ENTERTAINED HER OLD FRIENDS Alcaeus and Cleon with stories of her adventures. She updated them on everything including her death struggle with Catherine and the great end-of-days war which would begin on the morrow, as well as the solution to it predicted by her father. Though the final and precise form that such a solution would take was still a worrisome itch to Piper, and though Edison Godfellow was changed, and for everyone to see, still, for a being such as he on the verge of true morality to now possess near absolute power?

A million years of Tao in his veins.

After she'd needled him earlier, he claimed his "invincible new city-worlds" would be bases of power, "focus points and energy dispensers" that would dampen and firewall the incredibly powerful Phase II spells set to soon erupt by his misguided other self. What these city-worlds might actually look like, he would not say, though the words of the Wall Street corpse stuck in her brain and renewed themselves at least half a dozen times per day:

American Oz maker.

Though she never saw him watch the film, she knew of his obsession with Oz, his design and creation of a new London to suit that obsession. She'd ribbed him about it only a short time ago. Perhaps it would somehow play a role in defeating the new evil from the stars? But how exactly?

Super powered Munchkins?

Back to old Alcaeus and Cleon. They were nevertheless spellbound. So much had happened since the Battle of Jutland. World Maker war stuff, new coffee franchises, the phenomenon of Broadway, khor stew, bad Italian movies, and much, much more. And as usual, the curious Greeks wanted updates on Piper's bizzarro private civilization collection.

"Do you hide new tribes upon yourself?" Cleon asked.

"Oh yes, please tell us!" Alcaeus said, loud as an excited little boy.

Piper smiled. "Very little, my old friends, not a lot since I saw you in 1916, just a dozen or so towns and villages in Sicily such as Catania and Ortona, both targets of mass destruction in a conflict known as World War II. Now they're on the coast in my left iris."

"Praise to you, Macaria," Cleon said. "What would the world be without your museum?"

"And what of Thebes? And Argos?" asked Alcaeus.

"On the iris coast, like I've told you each time you ask."

"And how do they fare?" Cleon asked.

"They are prosperous, but I have to break up fights."

"By the gods, Macaria, where do you find room? I know you magically shrink them to sizes the eye cannot see, but still…" Cleon shook his head, mystified.

Piper could not answer in a way that made sense to them. Nonetheless, the two feisty ancients made it clear they dearly wished to be conscious in the most human way imaginable when reality imploded and things went boom. Piper desired it also, though she worried the virus might creep up and fever them with a vengeance if they did not return to their beastie forms soon enough. Whatever. She swore not to deny them the chance to see the beginning of a new world, to be present during the first hour of the rest of human history, one very unlike any gone before. Piper also had to admit to herself:

It feels good to hang with old friends when on the brink of Armageddon.

An experience of context and balance, and on a far less intellectual level, she was also ecstatic to have escaped the social claustrophobia present on the Jupiter array platform caused by her father and his new love monster.

Miss Wasp Face. Catherine of Arrogant.

Piper truly believed she might hate Catherine less if the relentless imperiousness of the woman ever subsided, even just a little. Perhaps one day? At least, the pathological need to kill her father had evaporated like stale cyanide. But at such a cost! Witnessing the Czarina not only in retreat but grinding to the opposite pole by torrentially balling her father while in Jupiter orbit a million years ago had propelled her into an emotional state of rage she was not prepared for.

By the American gods, I went bat shit!

Weeks of working together to mine and manufacture the scores of Tao dishes, as well as conjure the titanic orbital platform necessary to properly array and aim them at Orion, brought the two closer together—way too close for Piper's taste. After only a week she spotted Catherine stroking her father's hand for a few seconds. But Piper held her tongue even though an unexpected anger flared within her—a dark emotion that surprised her, and within only hours, made her feel ashamed.

Am I a child to behave in such fashion?

Regardless, she cornered Edison one night as he rode a small construction shuttle. He'd been directing a brigade of London drones that were mining the last of the metal ore on Ganymede.

"Dad, you are *hooking up* with Catherine?"

"I was hoping you would be relieved."

"I want to be, but how did it happen?"

"One day, as we spelled a row of dishes into order, I told her I finally believed something her previous mentor, Niccolo Paginini, had told me hundreds of years before. He said that what made a being truly ideal wasn't power, immortality, or strength over objects, but wisdom, compassion, and the courage to make moral choices over selfish ones."

"Yes, and…?"

"Upon saying that, Catherine kissed me on the lips, and kissed me again, and—"

"Okay, Dad. Don't need more film."

Though of course, it didn't end there.

Weeks later, Piper caught the two of them returning from a time pocket, a place in the past they had slipped to for purposes of being alone. And no words of reason could have prevented her from confronting them both upon detecting their re-entry to the Jupiter platform control core. Piper felt possessed, unhinged, the entire universe gone red. She appeared before them like a nerve-shattered Tinkerbell sputtering out of thin air, just in time to choke at the sight of the promiscuous Czarina sucking like a Santa Cruz vampire on her father's neck.

"Overthrow a few empires for a hotter sex?" she asked, eyes narrowing them to targets. Piper observed Catherine pausing, her sense of having been insulted beginning to germinate.

"Our affair is none of yours, sorceress of *coffee grinds*."

"I say differently, empress of the *besotted*."

Before Edison could intervene, Piper's vision filled with Catherine's eyes glaring murderously. She could see or sense nothing else. In Piper's mind, the flames of the World Maker's eyes churned like galactic arms of cosmic rage, and though Piper hated to admit it, she began to tremble like a child before a bullying mother. Once more, her little cities and peoples were threatened with extinction, and her hate mixed with fear, one attempting to antidote the other.

Moments later, steaming mad and frustrated, Piper vanished from the Jupiter core platform. She left her father with his beloved Catherine and found a small dark corner in the station to be alone with her humiliation. Then she wept, long and hot, for herself and those she held dear, and for the first time in centuries, she wished for a mother's comfort—a wish that could never have come true in any era. Her mother, a former queen of Sparta named Arachidamia, would simply have said to her:

"Draw your sword, Macaria, and let the gods decide."

Piper wasn't out of options though. She might hide in the past, return to the Holy Roman Empire, or even ancient Greece, but the war for the future of Earth was being fought now. She would not run from the conflict for any reason, and at the same time, there was no avoiding the stark realization that the hour would come, sooner or later, when either she or Catherine would perish, finally and absolutely, and regardless of what the future held for anyone else.

This universe is too small for the two of us.

Faced with inevitability, preparations must be made.

Her first step? To discover a haven for the innocents.

Her second?

More Tao, more magic power by any means necessary. I will draw my sword, but not until the time is right.

Piper's father once tried to explain to her the true limits of her power at such time she lived as the Grand Sorceress, but his explanation provided no real numbers. He simply said, "My daughter, if you desire, you can divert a moth from its flame, even though on the other side of the Earth, or open a mile-long crevice in that same Earth and send an entire army to its doom."

Moths and armies. Not good enough.

Chapter VI

The End of Days – Memory of Earth – The Emerald City

TOO EXCITED TO SLEEP, ALCAEUS AND CLEON stayed awake for much of the night on the rooftop patio of Piper's building. They soaked up as much consciousness and life as possible, until not able to prevent it any longer, they napped in their chairs, heads leaning back against the old brick wall.

On this day of Armageddon, Alcaeus was first to attain true wakefulness, yawning and rubbing the back of his stiff neck at 9:30 A.M. The morning was bright and long-shadowed on the roof, the skies streaked with fading combs of cloud. A mug of hot coffee with cream and sugar sat beside him on a small wooden end table. Piper explained the purpose of coffee, and Alcaeus, his old hands shaking, put the cup to his lips and sipped.

"Ahh, unusual taste. I like it, Macaria" he said in a husky voice. He laid the cup back down as if too weak to hold it and glanced up to see Piper's worried stare.

She bent forward to examine a spot on his upper exposed chest. "It has begun," she said and frowned while reaching out to touch the area he could not see, though once her fingers pressed down he felt a bruise-like pain. "The size of a small egg, and darkening… I must return you and Cleon to—"

"No, I beg you, not yet. How unfair to deprive us of this fateful day."

Piper sighed and rolled her eyes.

Alcaeus was determined. He let out a hacking cough and

upon recovering asked, "How much longer, until the end of all things?"

Piper gripped the top of the white bathrobe he wore and gently pulled it down to his waist. Probing with her fingers, she knew Alcaeus felt at least twelve more egg sacs of pain growing on his body. She sensed him chilling, a bit feverish, and he sought to warm himself with the strange coffee drink. But no sooner did his lips near the brim than the answer to his last question arrived from a source he did not expect—a male voice, deep and resonant from about twenty feet away:

"IT WILL BEGIN NOW."

A puzzled Alcaeus glanced around until he saw a big man fade into being from the blinding glow of eastern sun. He walked straight at Alcaeus, close enough to eclipse the light, the features of his face and form softening to a shadowy blue. The old Greek thought he recognized the fellow despite the odd clothing. Certain aspects stood out—the stature, commanding eyes, unruly black hair, and big toothy smile.

Then he knew. Bolts of Zeus, he knew.

"By the gods! Archimedes!" Alcaeus shouted and struggled to stand.

A pair of hands reached out to steady him as he tipped backwards, too weak to remain erect. The old philosopher was lowered back into the chair only to see Piper's worried face once more.

She rose to her feet, faced her father and said, "Alcaeus wishes to see the end-of-days fireworks, and he's stubborn enough to kill himself because of it."

"The curse of Dardanos?"

"Devouring him like a starving dog."

"His wish will come true then. Shall we proceed, Grand Sorceress?"

"Just the two of us? Where is your waspy love toy?"

Love toy? Alcaeus had never heard such a term. It made him want to heave up his coffee, and he did, loud and long onto the roof, his head beginning to burn as if twenty candles had been lit and placed beneath his neck.

Cleon, stirring awake, called out to Alcaeus and he too began to heave; and over the sound of ancient guts spewing their contents, Alcaeus heard a second woman's voice, cold and proud, speaking with an accent he did not recognize:

"If you mean me, then *I am here*."

: /

THE BROOKLYN MORNING CLIMAXED WITH HORNS, seven different kinds of music, shouting humans, the aroma of cooking meats, the hum of billboard drones, as well as the morning itself, cool and crisp with a swirl of autumn leaf.

As the Dardanos curse forced the Greeks to vomit, Piper turned from her father to see the Czarina standing directly behind her. Back to her old stunning self, she appeared haughty and commanding as usual. She spoke to Piper with a calm voice:

"You best transform to the garb and look of the Grand Sorceress, and with all your magical arms and accoutrements, for once your *homicidal other father* sees his plans gone awry, he will surely take wing with every manner of war engine he can muster." Catherine then reached behind her back and pulled out a black-plasma Glock, tossing it to Piper. "Perhaps you can make good use of this. Just one round was sufficient to disperse your acrimonious bling dragons."

Piper frowned as she looked at the big weapon, and before a snarky response could become reality, the air pressure plummeted enough to pop her ears.

Edison grinned, and his grin waxed to a bigger smile, like that of a delighted boy chasing mean dogs with his favorite drone. Catherine's mood, in contrast, turned dark and apprehensive. Piper decided to attend to the burning heads of Alcaeus and Cleon who had both collapsed into a fetal position. She knelt, cradled Cleon's head and passed a hand over his face while whispering a cooling spell as he sputtered in agony. She did likewise with Alcaeus.

"The hounds are released, and it begins," Edison said. He stepped around Piper and pointed west. "There, on the Jersey ley line... BEHOLD!"

Piper rose to her feet and scanned over the desolate factory badlands of northern New Jersey. She glimpsed what appeared to be sun-golden dust devils, or whirls of gleaming fog hundreds of feet high thrusting up and evaporating to nothing, as if carried away by great winds.

"Just as I once planned it," he said with a tone of regret in his voice. "And now the antidote cometh... Wait! Piper, I must ask you."

"What is it, Dad?" She wouldn't look at him because she was generally disgusted.

"Today will be difficult, to say the least. Have you safely secured your peoples and cities?"

She didn't answer, only noted that Catherine was watching her with a stoic face. A moment later, the Czarina spoke.

"Hopefully, you have secured them, for on such a day as this we might surely perish."

Piper gaped at her in disbelief. "You would have destroyed them, Miss Empress, so why the sudden compassion?"

Catherine lowered her eyes. "In truth, I would not have harmed them. I was consumed by temper and determined to frighten you. You have my apology."

"It takes the end of days to make you apologize?"

"Take it, or *leave it mad*, as you say," Catherine snapped.

Piper reconsidered her tongue and chose her words carefully. "Those under my wing are safe," she said, and in an eye blink, stood before the Czarina, attired once more in her finery and radiant splendor as the Grand Sorceress of the Holy Roman Empire. "For the sake of alliance and good nature, I accept your—"

Her last words vanished to conjecture.

A loud and distant cracking sound overwhelmed them all, as if Earth itself had begun to split open like a melting glacier. *Perhaps ley lines widening to fiery canyons?* She wasn't sure, though the steadiness and depth of the noise was terrifying. Following a deadly sounding echo, daylight itself flickered like a light connected to a bad fuse.

Rounds of screaming erupted from the streets. Reality was now in question and wholesale panic evident in the tenor and persistence of the voices.

Piper overheard her father say quietly to himself:

"*And now the wheels of Heaven start, you board the*

Devil's riding cart, get ready for the future, it is murder."

Was he going mad at last?

"No, my darling daughter," he said, having heard her thoughts. "I am perfectly sane. Prepare yourself." And he added, directly into her mind so none could eavesdrop, "*I know your desire to be without mortal fear of Catherine Romanova, and once this day is done, you no longer will be. In truth though, I love you both.*"

Piper stammered inwardly and searched for a reply, only to be distracted by Alcaeus heaving onto the floor of the roof again. She bent down on one knee to tend to him, and old Cleon as well. "You wanted to see, now see this," Piper said, pulling them up one at a time. She placed them in sitting positions on the roof lounge chairs and faced them west. She wiped their faces and lifted a cup of water to their lips. The poor things were beyond hope. Haggard and black-boiled, sagging and shivering like pitiful newborn pups.

"You have minutes left, my little turtle and dragon. I cannot allow you to die."

Piper lost sight of her father on the roof, but saw the Czarina a few feet away, staring west, her breath deep and her aura of golden Tao fanning out from her, humming a dark and eerie tune, and all the while that frightful, Earth-sized cracking sound grew more ominous.

Will half the planet break off into space?

Piper had never felt more helpless.

Might as well join the street mob and go bat shit.

Daylight itself, having already flickered, became blinding. A shriek of white light consumed New York for a full two seconds. More shrill screams erupted from the street. The blinding light then faded in the eye to a night full of stars and a crescent moon in the western sky, as if time itself had moved hours beyond dusk. The screaming notched up from terror to hysteria. That's when Piper saw it from afar, a wall of translucent purple light at least a mile high, stretching unbroken north to south and racing towards them from the west at incredible velocity.

What the flaming fuck?

"That light…" Alcaeus gurgled.

Catherine spoke. "A wall of Tao force, a very difficult *Gravar e Almancenar* spell to create a memory of everything in this moment, and store it, atom by atom."

"Like the *Caixa de Mundos.*" Piper said.

"More powerful. I believe this spell is creating a memory of Earth itself."

"The *whole thing?*"

"Yes."

"But who would—"

"Your father is my best guess."

"Macaria!" Alcaeus said with the last of his strength, pointing to the sky.

Catherine, gazing upward, shouted to Piper, "The moon is being eclipsed, but not by Earth!"

"Then what?" Piper asked, distracted by Alcaeus.

"Ahriman's soul… *it's Mars.*"

"War god *of Rome,*" Cleon croaked. Blood ran from his eyes and nose. The lumps on his body, and on the body of Alcaeus, had turned an ugly black and oozed an evil thick liquor that clung to the flesh, and as they did, the sky above New York saddened to a dark and bloody twilight.

Mars appeared at least three times larger than the

moon, and its illumination streaming into the Earth's atmosphere affected the wisps and streaks of cloud above New York, turning them a deep and chilling Martian. And before another breath could be drawn, the onrushing wall of violet light passed through them in a soundless millisecond and sped away east across the ocean.

Piper's instincts told her to flee, and quickly, but she held her ground and clutched the *memento mori*, more afraid than ever in her life.

Game over, Brooklyn.

The borough shuddered next with a quake, at least 6.9 Richter, and another round of terror broke out, this time followed by the sounds of stampeding humanity. Scores of horns blared and sirens whooped frantically. Piper heard shots and glimpsed police tracer rounds in the eastern sky, scores of them, as if aimed at a monstrous Titan crushing its way into the city. Her eyes followed the rounds higher to view a sight that made her almost faint from shock.

I don't believe this.

The premier World Maker herself let out an astonishing, animal-like cry, and Piper will never know who clutched at who first, but only a moment later and she and the Czarina were hugging each other in a state of mutual shock, for Edison Godfellow now appeared as an impossibly huge colossus a few miles away and at least half as tall as the tallest skyscraper in Manhattan.

He'd dressed for the occasion too, with a huge and multi-colored striped scarf cascading down over a long black overcoat that billowed in the wind. His skin glowed a Tao-like gold in contrast to the dark Martian twilight. His black hair fluttered around his face and his wild, entrancing eyes stared towards Manhattan while his voice, telepathically loud enough to be heard in the ears and minds of the entire Earth, spoke these words in over 6500 languages:

TODAY IS THE END OF HISTORY.
A NEW HUMANITY IS BORN.
AND FROM THIS DAY ON, WE TAKE WHAT IS OURS,
THE COSMOS ITSELF OUR MEANS OF ASCENSION.
NO LONGER FEATHERS IN THE WIND,
RATHER WE SHALL *BE THE WIND!*

Following these words, the specter of the clamoring, gigantic Godfellow vanished, and the glacial, Earth-cracking sound abruptly ceased only to be replaced by a humanlike groan. It throbbed up from a place deep in the silent planet and rose, beyond the stratosphere to the border of space, and Piper imagined that the world itself had acquired one mouth and pain was its lonely voice.

A slight breeze passed over her.

The Earth groan faded.

An eerie quiet followed.

Conscious of Catherine's breath and closeness, and the strong yet soft hands of the World Maker gripping her arms, she swiveled to face her nemesis, and Catherine did the same. Both women stared into each other's eyes, feeling each other's breath, hostility and rivalry vanished for the moment and replaced by end-of-days tears. Both were amazed, yet neither spoke. They stood, clasped together as if entranced. Piper could not avoid an inexplicable desire to kiss Catherine. She knew Catherine wished it also, though not for long. Pulling away, the Czarina took a deep breath, and Piper heard her speak, mind to mind:

"*I hated you because you nearly killed me.*"

"*Must one of us eventually die?*"

"*There is no way to predict.*"

Piper did not reply. She lacked perspective, felt dazed. The whole thing was surreal. No sense of wrong or right, and in the eternity of moments that followed, silence between them endured.

Within moments, the silence ended.

Another powerful quake rattled Brooklyn for several seconds, and before it was over, a freezing gust of air hit the tenement roof, knocking the coffee mugs off the table, followed next by an even more ferocious and howling gale that tore between the buildings and would not relent. It shook Piper to consciousness, and a barely audible choking sound caused her to glance down and see Alcaeus and Cleon shriveled to dry figs.

Less than a minute of life remained.

What in the name of Artemis is wrong with me?

As the wind rearranged the tacky roof furniture and Catherine looked on pensively, Piper spelled the old Greeks back to their little homes before teleporting them deep beneath a pre-selected crater on Mercury—a secret place where her cities and peoples would reside until danger no longer threatened.

The next voice Piper heard issued not from her own mouth, but from her king of *what-the-fuck* father.

"Much as I hate to interrupt, my darlings…"

She turned and there he was, standing on the roof again,

only a few feet away. Piper and Catherine instinctively gasped in surprise before launching themselves at him. They struck out with their fists and shouted, their voices dissolving in the violent wind that rattled the borough.

"What *in Ahriman's name* possessed thee?" Catherine bawled out and impaled him with a fierce glare.

Edison smiled in response with his big Greek teeth. He still appeared in the outfit of brilliant scarf and gleaming black overcoat. The maddened wind disheveled his hair, but angry fists bounced from his chest without harm, and an instant later, three or four golden autumn leaves blew straight through him, as though he were a phantom. The whole magic act so irritated Piper because it reminded her of a certain god whom she'd always hated for being a supreme narcissist.

"*Goddamn it*. Stop acting like that asshole Zeus!"

Edison only smiled again and said, "We have things to do, my cosmic goddesses... Oh, and here come my old personal guard, my hungry God Soldiers."

"The accursed *Dio Soldati*," Catherine said with ire.

Piper glanced up to see hundreds, no, thousands of evil-looking black specks swarming near Mars, scores of them passing before the looming red planet before diving towards Earth, vanishing within the dark blood clouds above New Jersey only to reappear without mercy. She estimated them to be fifty or more miles away.

The air quivered as if with a distant explosion of force, followed by ear-blasting peals of massive thunder, as though the *Dio Soldati* units had already begun firing. *But at what?* Every cell of her being felt war approaching, and with determination to devastate whatever it touched.

The pipes are calling. I'll die with honor. How ridiculous, but I want it to be true.

"Never have I beheld so many in one place," Catherine said with profound darkness in her tone.

"More than enough to crumble and flatten every mountain range on this planet," Edison proclaimed with a dramatic flourish. He reminded Piper of King Macbeth and his arrogance prior to demise.

Macbeth got what was coming to him.

Piper refocused on the danger at hand and observed them closing in. "Why such a large swarm in New York though? Just a squad of those evil super pricks could finish us off."

"Because, my daughter, your maniacal other father is hellishly confused, and his Tao sensors inform him that something bigger is arriving to thwart his Phase II plans... Something *much much* bigger."

Catherine drew her Glock. "Your daughter and I will eliminate as many as possible before we perish. Will you be joining us, dearest fool?"

"AND WHAT ABOUT THE PEOPLE OF NEW YORK?" Piper shouted over the thunder and wind now strong enough to suck bricks out of walls and spit them like bullets.

"Though I hate Brooklyn cab drivers, you know I am a servant to you both, however, NO NEED FOR IMMORTAL HEROICS," Edison said. *"LOOK ON HIGH!"*

Piper did so and saw what appeared like a great torrent of Milky Way, the galaxy itself seen edge on and forming a hazy-soft path in the night sky, only this flow of Milky Way spread itself east to west, not north to south, and it moved, yes, almost imperceptibly, and as Piper tele-focused her eyes she realized she beheld not stars, but many tens of thousands of shimmering machines—the hulls and sides of enormous starships reflecting sunlight as they passed above Earth.

"The great fleet reborn," Catherine said in awe.

And as if that revelation weren't enough, an eerie wave of pure emerald light, like a curtain of Aurora Borealis, faded into view and unfolded on high, and to the amazement of all, began dropping towards Earth from the atmospheric vicinity of the fleet. Within less than five seconds, it fell to become a massive wall separating Manhattan from the aerial brigades of *Dio Soldati* farther west, and as it continued to fall in undulating waves like gentle surf near the shore, Piper's eyes resolved the light into a fog-like mass of magical emerald particles—a haunting and sorcerous mist.

She blinked for the first time in years.

A brick flew past her.

Within the womb of that emerald mist, the skyline of Manhattan evolved to an indistinct and glowing phantasm. Focusing closely, she believed she saw human beings hurling themselves from the tops of buildings, though she couldn't be certain. Next, a brief burst of golden light, and in contrast to her open-mouthed astonishment, the mighty emerald curtain bizarrely reversed itself, and it rose, scooping out a big chunk of New York and leaving behind a silent black abyss.

So much for Book of Mormon.

In a manner Piper could not grasp, the light curtain, now returned to its Aurora Borealis appearance, seemed to shudder for a few moments before collapsing towards earth once again, but this time far more rapidly. The many miles of it cascaded down like a pour of dark emerald molasses, roaring and booming as it broke the sound barrier until it resolved to a turbulent pooling disk where the old Manhattan once stood.

Edison Godfellow smiled with enough teeth to crack six chestnuts at once. "Impressive? The process is complete. Now my loved ones, observe the true rewards of our timeless and brilliant Jovian labors."

Piper noticed that the wind had died to a breeze, the thunder to a rain patter. She stared at her father's teeth—the undeniable product of simian evolution. *Should he not become a being of light and energy? Has he not transcended masticators?*

"Not at my bloody teeth, Piper. Look there!"

The plummeting of Aurora molasses had completely ceased and from the core of that mad swirl rose an emerald sky spire like nothing ever seen, not even in London. To say that Piper was utterly astonished by the vision would be an understatement.

As it continued to grow taller, she noted how it tapered gently towards its crown. Segmented vertical protrusions began to appear at intervals and cast long shadows down the trunk. *Five miles thick at least, but how much higher?* Relentlessly it thrust upwards, seeking to rule the heavens beyond the Martian clouds.

Piper was never sure how long it took (utter fixation making calculation difficult), though at the conclusion, a new and grand cosmic world was born—the central tower a full 60 miles in height and the base a perfect circle, 26 miles in circumference, though half a mile taller in the center due to the base gently stepping upward.

The invincible city-world. So gleaming and wondrous.

Overwhelmed by it all, Piper tearfully smiled.

Along the rim, through her watery eyes, she viewed a row of illuminated ports, ship bays, and windows of various sizes.

A military command and operations center.

Catherine, on the other hand, appeared rather dazed. "The Emerald City was your blueprint?" she said to Edison.

What? Even she has seen the film?

He nodded. "You may certainly draw that appropriate comparison, however, we are indisputably safe now."

"What became of the original Manhattan?"

He laughed. "Oh, up there!" He pointed towards the crown of the central tower, lost now in the mist. "At the very tippy top, snug in its own little bubble."

"Wasn't it always?" Piper said.

Chapter VII

The Daze of Broadway – *Ka'oi Aina* – New Guinea Pygmy

Catherine Romanova's Post Finem Journal
Year 1 PF - First Entry

So begins the end of days.

Predictably, I feel no guilt about not returning to the Golovin Palace in Moscow from whence I departed in 1778, decades after gaining my powers at Castle Anhalt in Prussia. Moscow past is suspended there, and it has played its role, come and gone. I owe it nothing. Living here in the dark excitement of this cosmic revolution reduces the walls of Golovin to those of a frigid and stale prison, and its many servants to naught but lonely wraiths wandering the myriad halls of Hades.

Regardless, I have also realized on this 'end of evenings' that no longer can I shirk the task of creating a new journal of thoughts, rumblings, and memories, especially now that the next stage of humanity has forced itself upon our innocent and confused planet.

Will things improve for us? Will final victory be ours? If so, what will be left to fear other than our own hubris and impetuous nature? However, a few items before I travel down that path.

First, I almost died at the hands of Godfellow's daughter, the former Grand Sorceress of the Holy Roman Empire and an ancient demi-god who in this century goes by the ridiculous name of Piper Robbin. She even shrivels to a pixie on occasion and serves hot beverages to the thankless and foolish of New York.

I thus find her behavior odd.

No matter, I should thank her because she has truly taught me the limits of my power by challenging me in ways I have not experienced in a long time; and though these challenges both disturbed and irritated me, even to the point of violence, I have developed a strange attraction. I hate her, and yet, I have warmed to her at the same time.

I do not know if time will allow us to become friends, for we are both elephantine in our stubbornness as well as terribly powerful beings who roam this little Earth; and speaking of power, I now understand how little I truly possess in comparison to what has transpired during this end of days.

In the past, during critical junctures in the War for Utopia, I often felt useless or weak in the face of events I could not begin to control. I recall the Battle of the Somme. I sat in a German bunker, enduring an Allied shelling of many hours and feeling preposterously foolish for believing myself to be a powerful magical being. In truth though, compared to what I have lived through recently, the Somme was naught but a dying candle.

As thousands of Dio Soldati formed in the sky above New York like a cosmic plague and the entire planet Mars drifted into view, I could do little else but clutch my small weapon and condemn myself to immediate mortality; and though I survived the carnage and insanity I must again confront the need to choose my raison d'etre—now more than ever.

Centuries ago, my mentor Niccolo Paganini provided me with a true purpose I craved, and though over the years we bickered and I began to conflict with his methods to win the

War for Utopia, I believed in his cause and focused my will on its achievement, even until most recently.

Niccolo and I eventually parted, and I can live without him, most certainly, but he took a good friend away, Maria of Pozzuoli, my Mother Yarrow—the most wise and magical companion I have ever known. I will not fill this page with my sorrows and grief on this matter. This is not the place, though I confess that even now, I am halved by her loss.

In general, my will to do the best for humanity has not wavered, therefore, I must keep this in mind until the general becomes specific; and I have no doubt this will take place. Though Edison has conceived and created a source-well of pure magical power like nothing I could have predicted, I know the universe has stubbornly placed a counteragent within our midst—thus has it always been.

Edison, however, envisions his seven new and omnipotent city-worlds—Manhattan, Berlin, Istanbul, Kinshasa, Shanghai, Jakarta, and Buenos Aires—as solutions near perfect, especially insofar as hostile circumstance and his primary fears dictate, and perhaps he is correct, and perhaps not. Though I should hate him with every breath, I must be honest with myself and admit I have fallen in love with the magnificent dark bastard.

May history and the universe forgive me.

: /

ONCE THE PHASE II GRAND TRANSFIGURATION had fizzled away its carbonation and been replaced by the new *Terra Oz Infirma* (as its creator dubbed it), Piper Robbin reverted to her mango-yellow hair, pixie stature, and latte-with-two-shots smile.

At first, she felt relieved to be back to her old self, especially since recent memories located and defined her as the hopeful Broadway actress, part-time coffee whipper, and full-time heroine of the streets. She'd longed for this, of course, her new life, her new start in old New York; but after a few hours of looking around, up and down at the ethereal creation of her father's New Manhattan Oz—now floating like an emerald sky world off the Atlantic Shore just above Block Island—she realized with a sudden surge of depression that her Piper self, as a whole, was no longer realizable.

Am I useless or just foolish?

Her barista days were irreversibly over, and the daze of Broadway was fading. That tiny old island now fixed in the glass attic of New Manhattan Oz had breathed its last. Besides pastrami being thrown to the cats, *we've got people zombie-walking out of their pointless jobs*, doom preachers every few blocks, a baffled and beaten police, public transportation shutdowns, power blackouts, chanting mobs, no khor stew, and other chaos-driven insanity like that—the kind you'd expect now that a paradisiacal mother of redemption was drifting just offshore, radiant and beckoning with a promise of wizard-like wonders and New Order Oz bread for all.

Was the whole island fated to become nothing but a museum, and the Met, only a museum within a museum?

Not to mention the miserable fact that no one needed her to be a heroine any longer, underground or otherwise; and though she possessed the powers of a god on nuclear overdrive, even that fact dulled to insignificance. In the confines and gleaming spaces of *Terra Oz Infirma* she would be no more powerful or influential than a crippled street urchin attempting to be heard over the crowd noise at Madison Square Garden.

Will I be just a nothin', head all full of stuffin'?

So what's next?

A return to old New York seemed possible, but already, now that the "Despicables" had been culled and breezed over the Atlantic, the grand remainder of humanity qualified (according to her father) to ascend to the "warm and dreamy spaces" of the seven magical sky worlds seeded by him around the globe, for they contained sufficient "neo-dimensional space" to "house and nanny" the population of a hundred Earths, and perhaps more, though Piper could only guess. The magical physics of Oz space were beyond her. The raw Tao force siphoned from Jupiter had elevated reality to a truly bizarre magical plane.

She admitted to herself that old pops had pulled out the stops for the New Oz Order that now dominated Earth. Following the mind-numbing act of creation that fateful night, he'd lifted her through the air for miles, and like that colossal emerald tower, she levitated into the Martian-tinted dusk over New Jersey, feeling with her eyes the jade-smooth, wave-gleaming surface of that same tower, noting the otherworldly rainbow aura that clung softly to it, then higher still to the very crown of Manhattan; and from that height, she gazed down through the transparent roof bubble covering the island, her vision settling a few stories above the streets.

She saw thousands of Manhattan denizens scrambling and screaming and darting about like the classic ants of a stirred mound while above them, in the Mesospheric darkness, the stars fiercely glowed, many more millions and more intense than ever.

Piper pondered their condition—a human populace juxtaposed to a new infinity.

Will the stars make them humble at last?

"Doesn't look like they quite get it," Piper had said to her father as together they observed the crumbling body and soul of Manhattan.

"They will," Edison said somberly, floating in the frigid Mesosphere like a merciless idol. "It will come to them in their dreams, and their dreams will be a bridge to Oz."

Piper could not prevent her next thought.

Poppies, poppies.

: /

AND PIPER COULD NEVER FORGET WHAT HAPPENED NEXT. Drifting down through the twilight dark below the Manhattan crown, she and her father faced the great celestial tower of Oz and an enormous milky-jade door set in the outer wall over sixty feet high and inlaid with magical Tao symbols that glowed crimson as they drew near.

"The city must be overjoyed at our presence." Edison grinned mischievously at Piper as the huge door cracked open and swung inward.

"Really? A door built for giants?"

"Meant to accommodate a wide variety of sizes," Edison said. "But of course, not the only entrance. There are scores of them."

"And I've never known the complete answer to this, but

why the strange Oz obsession in the first place? What is the true origin?"

Edison paused, and said, "The theme of Oz was first encouraged, in truth, by my old enemy in the War for Utopia, none other than Niccolo Paganini himself."

"What? You cannot be serious."

"As you know, I had dismissed his ideas for centuries, believed him a sentimental and unrealistic fool, then one night I saw the film, the Judy Garland version. Its statement of primary virtues as necessary to a genuinely advanced civilization was nothing revelatory, however, the manner whereby the message was delivered resided within me and never left… The power of film, I suppose. We've spoken of this before, have we not?"

"I am still amazed."

"I required a model, a theme if you will, for a new and omnipotent utopia on Earth, therefore, why not Oz? London was the first experiment, and a good one, but now we have an array of supernal emerald cities even more glorious and mind shattering, and every one of them, over the rainbow."

Piper grinned and shook her head. "Dad, you're both *amazing* and seriously damaged."

"Aren't we all, my daughter?"

: /

UPON CROSSING THE OZ THRESHOLD and gliding through a lavender whiff of rainbow, she and her father immersed within *Terra Oz Infirma* itself. At once, she felt an odd surge of vertigo. Everything before her appeared upside down. Despite her wooziness, she glimpsed a whole new and magnificent city, one growing beneath the old Manhattan, though far larger, rather like a sprawling bulk of dense root in contrast to the smaller tree above it.

A moment later though, suddenly rotating 180 degrees, she found herself standing in a field of windy scarlet grass on the brink of sunset, and only then was she able to fully appreciate the vision of the New Manhattan Oz-scape— not a variation on the old one, still ensconced above them like a slowly crumbling corpse, but one astonishingly different.

On a side note, Piper could not imagine the current citizens of New York actually fitting in. She even found the concept a bit comical.

Like resettling Homo Erectus in a Manhattan penthouse.

Overall, the vision couldn't help but remind her of London, her father's original Oz super-city, though this version was far more ambitious: immense and shimmering starscrapers of dark-emerald glass haloed by drifting clouds and orbiting sky islands that looked like pale water lilies, and bathing all these magnificent creations a ruddy crimson hue? Nothing less than the Oz sun waning to dusk on the horizon.

Though hesitant to goad her suppressed narcissism to life, Piper nevertheless indulged herself, and this act consisted of a single frank admission:

We burn with dreams and turn our dreams into history.

She turned to her father. "It's way huger than the original Manhattan sputtering at the crown. How did—"

"Neo-dimensional space," he said, anticipating her puzzlement. "It supersedes normal dimensional reality, and it begins here on a small scale."

"A small scale?"

"Approximately ten to one ratio. The furthest border of this land is over a hundred miles from here in either direction."

"And what's out there?"

"Oh, lots of things... poppies, scarecrows, cowardly lions, you know, such as that."

"Give me a break, *please*."

"Alright then... We have great conifer forests, toadstool paths, fireflies and dragon lizards, sapphire lakes of every size, green hills and golden meadows, roaring rivers and steaming geysers, grand eagles the size of pterodactyls, huge lions with British accents, and a few miles of snow-topped purple mountains taller than Shasta... ah, and mysteries too, *lots of mysteries*, twin peaks and dark shadows, talking owls, as well as hidden portals to the Deeper Lands—"

"The Deeper Lands?"

"*Kaʻoi Aina*. At the base of our glorious Oz tower-city where the neo-dimensional ratio becomes enormous... one to 1,000."

"Wait. You're telling me a land mass exists at the base of this thing that's *20,000 miles* in diameter?"

"Close enough I believe, yes." Edison's face morphed to a look of self-absorbed transcendence (akin to his "thousand-year stare") and he telepathically whispered, "*Strangely enough, daughter, I do not yet possess sufficient knowledge of the new forms of flora and fauna swirling about down there.*"

"Eh? How could you not know?"

Edison visibly rebooted himself to a semblance of normalcy. "Upon our return from Jupiter, I completed the invention of a wonderfully new and unique piece of magical technology. I call it the *Apparatus Creaturae*. It allows me to fashion and channel the flow of Tao from Jupiter into the neo-atomic structure that comprises all the worlds of *Terra Oz Infirma*."

"I have wondered just how you engineered this sprawling mass of new matter in such detail, and so quickly."

"Ingenious, truly, my best invention... In a real sense, even better than my old War Tracker device. With the *Apparatus Creaturae* we have turned a corner and become creators, not destroyers."

"Don't doubt it for a second, dad, but—"

"I really feel good about it, Piper. I do."

"I'm glad you're playing God in a cool ass way, but—"

"Until recently, I was in a state of haste, and frustrated for ideas, so I allowed the *Apparatus Creaturae* enough latitude to, let's say, *become inventive...* And I daresay the beast snapped the leash." He laughed, though momentarily regained his composure. "A trifle *tres bizarre*. At the very minimum, it required general parameters, a foundation from which to build, so I provided it with the Oz books by Baum, as well as one of my favorite novels, Bradbury's *The Martian Chronicles*, plus liberal doses of Picasso and Dali, clips of the original *Bladerunner film*, holograms of Earth's most curious geography, and not least, a final dose of creation in the form of one of my favorite old movies, *Hell Boy* by del Torro."

"*Hell Boy?*"

"Let the land give birth to heroes and the monsters they must slay!" he said with a grand wave of his hand.

"*Hell Boy?*"

"And speaking of Mars, I have yet another revelation. With assistance from our eons worth of Tao I invented the first interplanetary tele-walk bridge. A place exists at least several kilometers in diameter in the Deeper Lands of each Oz city-world that appears identical to the rocky Martian plain of Tharsis."

"You mean—"

"Yes, it is the actual surface of Mars. You simply step from the soil of the Deeper Lands onto the Tharsis plain and you are officially walking on Mars. And you can continue from there to any destination on that planet."

"Mars sounds way saner than your Deeper Lands... Could *Frankensteinus Creaturae* be the better label?"

"Be positive, Piper. We will fully comprehend the Deeper Lands sooner or later, and I personally love surprises, but look at what we have right here. This brave new world!" He turned in a circle, spreading his arms wide. "All the nature and fantasy therapy you could wish for, and without blood loss."

"Shit, no *blood loss*. Now *I am* depressed."

"This entire mass of geography is a transitional space for the Manhattan types, as well as other crossovers coming up from Earth, a place of relative calm wherein they can recover, perhaps even with a glass of wine or beer, and share their wild adventures."

"Recover? I don't—"

"Consider what surrounds us right now as the warmer water of Oz, a wading pool prior to diving into the deeper and more predatory ocean... And daughter, Oz beer is served in yard-long glasses."

"Shut up. You know I'm a beer nerd."

"Belgian beer, my darling scourge of Europe. A sweet and tart Flanders Red, among others."

"You're trying to distract me. *That's evil*, dad."

Edison laughed.

Piper continued. "But these crossovers, as you call them, are humans. Are you planning on them getting killed as they wander around like foolish children in these Deeper Lands? If it's half as weird as it sounds—"

"No. As the Manhattanites and other citizens gradually filter down to the new city they... Let us just say, they are transformed."

Piper paused and folded her arms, staring at him, her face an odd twist of both annoyance and amusement. "Ahh, okay, so you still succeed in creating your super people, just like you always wanted. You knock off all the worst assholes and force-filter the rest. A plan with far less destruction than the old Grand Transfiguration, though essentially the same results."

Edison paused, and said, "In a sense, that is so."

"Isn't that what the Paganini hated?"

Paganini believed that cultivation of the spirit as well as adoption of principles meant more than corporeal evolution. I've never disagreed entirely, but...

"Niccolo never understood," Edison said. "That is why we fought. Our world, and our future, demands that humans be smarter, stronger, faster healing, telepathic, and more. Now, forward to the god city, *ma jeune fille!*"

Before she could object, Piper found herself sitting on a

tacky couch in a small and dingy one-bulb apartment exactly like the old one in the original Brooklyn. Outside the window she viewed the cityscape of New Manhattan Oz: the long, twinkling threads of flying cars, the cloud-like sky islands, the starscraper titans of frozen black electricity.

"Any Tao left? Just curious."

"Approximately 72.6%."

"You mean you created *seven flaming-ass-big Oz city worlds*, dragged the planet Mars here, reversed the *Caixa de Mundos* spell and restored the thousands of *Superna Humanitas* ships, as well as defeated the Grand Human Transfiguration, not to mention walloping however many battalions of *Dio Soldati*, and you still have *that much left?*"

"The *Dio Soldati* battalions are redistributed in the seven cities and 50% are with the orbiting fleet now in slow time."

"How slow?"

"Approximately one minute fleet time for every week of Earth time."

"The amount of Tao it takes to—"

"Insignificant. However, you have left out one major event," he said, clearing his throat and grinning like a child with a funny secret.

"What *is that*?" Piper asked suspiciously.

"Earth, the moon, and Mars have taken a little trip to another part of the galaxy."

"You—"

"A precaution. I considered teleporting the total mass of us to Andromeda, but it would have cost dearly in terms of Tao currency."

Piper looked stupefied. "I don't know what to say."

This definitely raises the what-the-fuck bar. He seems to

be containing himself though, using the new power quite wisely and not egomaniacally. The threat of that Orion thing must be a check on his old narcissism.

"We need more time to investigate our enemies in this galaxy. We need intelligence. The fleet never threatened that apparition in Orion. We simply paused to observe."

"And you're afraid you have may have doomed us all by engaging it."

"Yes."

: /

WORLD ASTRONOMERS CLAIM EARTH HAS MOVED

WASHINGTON (Reuters) Astronomers from the United States and 17 other nations including France, Britain, China, and Japan, held an emergency meeting this Thursday at the National Science Foundation (NSF) in D.C. to share findings they say that confirm that Earth, along with the moon and Mars, have been relocated to the other side of the Milky Way Galaxy. Several prominent astrophysicists were also in attendance, including Dr. Jay Gupta and Dr. Sarah Obajian from the Stanford Astrophysical Institute.

A press conference was held the following day at NSF despite objections from the White House. The mood in general was one of disbelief mixed with intense curiosity.

"This is just too world shattering and obvious an event to justify any muzzling of findings or opinions as dictated by the White House, or any other extant world government," said Dr. Gupta, one of India's leading astrophysicists.

Dr. Obajian added, "Though it certainly seems quite impossible, we have ascertained that the Earth and two other solar bodies have been physically moved to a distant quadrant of Milky Way, and judging by the star density in the night sky, closer to the galactic core by as much as 3,000 light years."

Chief astronomer at NSF, Dr. Mildred Cannon, fielded a barrage of questions from reporters as best she could, flanked and supported by five other scientists.

All were unanimous in the belief that the superior technology necessary to affect such a relocation to the orbit of another star, nearly identical in gravitational mass and energy to our previous one, must be related to other phenomenal events that have occurred around the globe, and in nearby space, not least of which was the recent relocation of the planet Mars.

According to Dr. Cannon, the extraterrestrials who accomplished such amazing and various feats, whoever or whatever they may be, possess a technology far superior to that of humanity.

"If you compare, for example, AI robotics to Paleolithic tool chips, you have some concept of the gap we're talking about," she said. "But the real question is, why did they interfere in human affairs in the first place?"

Dr. Gupta agreed, and added, "It appears they are attempting to protect us, perhaps even assist in our evolution, but right now, conjecture is the order of the day."

: /

"IS THIS ITCHY SUFFOCATING APARTMENT part of my

transition?" Piper said to Edison who now sat on the other end of the couch while lifting the TV remote out of a small box. "And by the way, how in Hera's name did the crazed people of Manhattan migrate down here so quickly?"

"My apologies, I meant to tell you. You drifted five days into the future when you passed through that big smiling Oz door."

"What?"

"I desired for you to see the post climax state of evolution, not the raw product."

"Is this ugly apartment an illusion or real?" she asked, spreading her hands.

"Oh, real, my daughter, way too real."

Piper scowled as best she could. "Promise to *never pull that time effect shit* on me again without my knowledge."

"Yes, yes, of course, but something else took place, a real change within you."

"What do you mean?"

"You are now as powerful as a World Maker. You have nothing to fear from Catherine ever again."

"Serious?"

"I piped several gigajoules worth of Tao into you—a little gift from Jupiter."

"I… thank you, uh, father," Piper stammered.

He's done this for me. He really cares.

"Now, time is of the essence, so I thought we could watch an abysmal flick. How about *Son of Hercules vs The Evangelical Spider People*?"

Piper sighed, suddenly nostalgic. "Without khor stew? I'm not sure—"

"Ahhh, I considered that also. *Voila!*"

Edison snapped his fingers like an old stage magician, whereupon Piper heard a knock at the door. She jumped up and answered. There stood Chariya Song in her favorite stained apron, grinning ear to ear and holding a white-bag order of khor stew.

"Piper, I missed you," she said and smiled.

"Chariya!"

Piper gazed at her and quickly realized she was different. A bit taller perhaps, slimmer, the signs of age vanished, and her overall being brimmed with vigor and strength. *The filtering process of transformation, of course.* Obviously, she'd submerged beneath old Manhattan along with the mass of refugees fleeing the boroughs of New York.

"You look radiant, my dear friend" Piper said.

"I have never felt better," Ms. Song replied with delight in her voice. "And my khor stew is better than ever. Here, sniff a little nose." She lifted the bag up to Piper, and hands down, it was truly the best khor she'd ever had the pleasure of sniffing.

"And how is your family?"

"All of us will emigrate to the Deeper Lands. We want to live there together. The new city is just too big for us, just too flashy. I feel like a little germ. It scares me."

"I understand, Ms. Song, I do. It is a little much, even for a strange magical pixie like me. But do be careful down there, please?"

"I will see you again, Piper," she said and smiled like a human being who cared and was grateful for Piper's concern. "I will still make khor stew in the Deeper Lands. You will smell the aroma of my cooking and find me," she said and laughed.

"I promise I will. Love you, Chariya!"

Following a last goodbye, Piper found the aroma and taste of the khor to be irresistible. She wolfishly chewed the trotters and drank from a yard-long glass of premium Belgian beer conjured by Edison as the two of them watched the *Son of Hercules* movie.

They both laughed long and well.

Chapter VIII

Picasso Guernica – Lands of Never – The Witch Empress of Earth

Czarina Catherine's Post Finem Journal
Year 1 PF – Entry 2

Last night I slept in an apartment located in the Berlin version of Terra Oz Infirma. Edison joined me at 2:43 AM. We accomplished a long bout of quite passionate love, and he thrilled me more than anyone I have ever known. In truth though, given his power, he would have to be intentionally lazy, or unfeeling, to leave me bereft.

Just as the sun rose on New Berlin, he departed. My last sight of him was his hand on my cheek. He opened the door upon his shadow and vanished in the sunlight with a whisper of "I love you" that sounded like soft breeze through a tree bough.

An hour later, I went for a tour. Like Manhattan, the core of the old city existed in the crown of the central New Berlin Oz tower. I was told the city-world could comfortably contain at least 200,000,000 people, or perhaps more. Theoretically, there was no limit to the amount of neo-dimensional space achievable with proper Tao spelling—or so Edison claimed. I personally do not know. In theory then, all of Europe could be contained in this one place, though even now I cannot imagine the French crowding into a German Oz.

I returned to New Manhattan by early afternoon, and with plans in my head to visit the other city-worlds but still intrigued by the possibility of new life forms in the Deeper Lands, I decided to take myself there by rising from the city and pushing well beyond the middle spaces of the Oz central tower. I can only say that as I rose I found the universe surrounding me to be surprisingly stunning and eerie, and in a most ineffable way.

However, I will endeavor to explain.

To either side of me floated enormous islands like dark stone mushrooms having taken root in the purple ether of the atmosphere. They varied in size. I found it hard to judge without closer examination since distances in neo-dimensional space, baked into the grander Oz pie by Edison, could be confusing, though each supported its own small world of one type or another. I extended my vision to see dangerous beasts lurking in a black leaf jungle, and on another, humanoids morphing in and out of spider-like forms as if composed of a strange organic putty. Still others in the farther distance appeared like glowing planets wreathed with lightning. Whether created of highly reflective substance or producing their own light, I do not know, though I became so curious I wished to investigate them all.

After more than an hour, I found myself plummeting straight downward once gravity in the tower had reversed itself. I fell towards a cloud streaked, planet-like surface I assumed to be my destination.

As I learned, the crown of every Oz tower simulated normal Earth gravity, whereas everything beneath the old city existed in reverse gravity until reaching the very bottom where gravity reverted to normal once more.

I entered the Deeper Lands on a curve, flattening myself out and soaring above a long row of snowy mountain peaks like a condor. Once beyond, I descended onto a sunlit plain of golden grasses that from on high appeared dotted with very large trees casting long shadows. However, as I drew closer to the surface, I realized that the sunlight, or what appeared as such, could not be sunlight since no sun was visible above *me or to either side. It puzzled me, and in another half minute I landed with both feet upon the plain, and what I witnessed there beggars my feeble attempts at description.*

The things I had believed to be trees were in fact monoliths of a sort, only well over a few hundred feet tall as if created by giants, even larger than the monstrosity unleashed on me by the Grand Sorceress in Iceland. Besides their baffling size, they were not simply faceless blocks, rather unique and intricately sculpted works composed of a material comparable to red canyon stone on Mars.

I gasped upon realizing their surfaces were a macabre buffet of elements vaguely resembling twisted limbs and portions of skulls fusing and entwining in collaged succession, one writhing mass atop the other, and so on, as if the demented creator had attempted to sculpt the most grotesque totem poles imaginable.

Over a dozen of these disturbing monstrosities thrust from the landscape in all directions for over a distance of several kilometers, and a line of them, apparently a variant species of monolith, stood frozen on the horizon like Medusas, but as I gazed at one of the more bizarre monoliths nearby, examining its parts, a chill gripped me. The thing moved. The mass of it twitched and rippled ever so slightly, like an animal shivering.

Had I imagined it? No.

The movement was subtle and unmistakable. I thought it disconcerting that my psyche had reacted with actual fear. Why? What did a World Maker have to be afraid of here? A pile of grotesque body parts pretending to be stone?

Then, as if in response to my thoughts, the thing moved again, this time with more vigor. I cannot explain it well, suffice to say it shrugged, and at the same time, the distortions of human mouth yawned at me. I felt yet another chill.

To bolster my failing courage, I yelled at it.

Warwick Gleeson

"Am I boring you perchance, oh monstrosity?"

Whereupon it answered. I heard a telepathic voice. The damnable thing slithered into my mind and sounded ever so much like a demon chewing rocks as it uttered these strange words:

"We speak with a voice of extinction."

Within moments, tears formed in my eyes, and a growing sense of dread filled and exhausted me like a sickness. Whatever the origin of the thing, I knew it possessed the power to burn my soul. Such a power I had only faced once before while in the thrall of a magical being known as Ahriman, the creator of the World Makers, and in a dream wherein he entrapped me deep within his insect-like eyes.

As I now pondered the power of whatever assaulted my psyche, that horrible megalith nearest me, and of its own accord, began to plough through the very rock itself and draw closer. I understood it was coming for me. I knew its dark thoughts. It would eviscerate me and absorb my essence into itself.

I shouted a sonic spell at it, powerful enough to shatter the walls of Constantinople at their thickest, but the monster slowed not a bit. The spell rippled its hide like a breeze on water, and that was all. I began to shake so badly I felt humiliated. I called out with my mind to Edison, a psychic shout, though I knew not if he heard, and nothing could have relieved me more than a dozen Dio Soldati swarming to my defense. I have always hated that violent military arm for their arrogance and brutality, but now, even their sad clown faces on the brink of mayhem would be a welcome sight.

Unable to contain myself and think clearly, I flew upwards at extreme velocity, and as I did, pulled my black-plasma firearm from my waist and in a state of rage shot round after round into the exact place where the monolith had stood.

Whether the unholy abomination was destroyed or not in the conflagration, I do not know, for the land exploded with a force of nearly 60 megatons that soon resolved to a flaming stew many thousands of degrees hot, though not until I was so far away that the impact site appeared like a flaring nova many light years distant.

Despite that terrible destruction, I felt relieved to be free of it, and alive, and hoped I had done the universe a favor by eliminating that evil—though it shuddered me to dwell on the potential of my efforts coming to naught, and disturbed me even more to consider what an entire force of those things might achieve if unrestrained.

: /

FOLLOWING SEVERAL YARDS OF BELGIAN BEER (Duvel Tripel Hop), Piper found herself being escorted by her father to the rooftop of their tower. After stepping out into the breezy cool night and glancing around, she noted its enormity when compared to her old tenement building still nestled in the noisy and odorous maelstrom of Brooklyn.

Simple, scuffed, and real.

The rooftop of this insane new starscraper appeared to be at least several acres in size, looking like a fantasy park in a dream. She felt genuinely awed by what she saw. The place was covered with rippling scarlet and lavender grasses, honey-engorged yellow hibiscus, tropical palms, sequoia groves, orange and fig trees, cobble-stone cool creeks and crystalline springs, jazz-whistling parrots, globes of softened light hovering in the air like unblinking fireflies, as well as several black marble-tiled patios with brassy Babylon torches over seven feet high, each one aflame and licking high enough to cast wild shadows.

Piper's father led her to a far corner of the roof where a few chairs on a small slab of patio overlooked the rolling darkness beyond the city. They sat down. Piper stared up to a sky filled with ten times the number of stars, as well as wisps of crimson and amethyst nebulae, and above all, the planet Mars on the eastern horizon, big and deep red as four moons.

"A fluid projection of the sky outside," Edison said. "As real as can be." He paused, and added, "We human-like beings need stars to rule above and provide inspiration. Do you believe that, Piper?"

"Yes, for the most part," she said, craning her neck to stare at the zenith. "But if you rise straight up in this tower, what's the next stop?"

"You rise higher as you simultaneously drop lower towards the base. And there, at last, you find the Deeper Lands... Of course, other things exist betwixt and between as you ascend, *or descend*, depending on your point of view."

"Such as?"

"Sky worlds, floating flowers of stone with stems, scores and scores of them, from a few miles in diameter to well over a hundred. Each are unique and fascinating, drifting on light winds in a swirling, nebulae-like ether, one upon the other like ascending steps to a final sky of dark violet."

"Sounds different... and what's on these, um, *sky flowers* as you call them?"

"Varying environments from barren to rather bizarre— vacation and creation communities, alien habitats, and such as that."

"Creation communities?"

"Yes, places where the new humans can easily harness portions of Tao and create things with their imagination. And there is no place I know that compares with your imagination."

"That's a *Willy Wonka* line."

"Also, one of my favorite films, next to *Wizard of Oz*."

"You're so eccentric, dad."

"And now, it's here, along with so much more," he said wistfully, gazing into the starry sky."

"Just a total mind fuck. Congrats."

Immediately following her snarky comment, Edison jumped to his feet as if shocked, faced Piper, and exclaimed, "And now, daughter of mine, an even bigger one!"

"By the American gods, what?"

"A last big surprise."

"*Oh shit.*"

"I present to you," he said, extending his left arm and open hand as though introducing a major celebrity on stage, "None other than…" He paused for a few moments. Piper saw a strange and small human being step forth from a stand of palm trees behind them, its body flickering with shadows and barely illumined by the soft light globes and stars. "None other than one of your best friends and allies."

A being on two legs, not more than four and a half feet tall, walked closer.

What the ?

Its naked body was smeared from face to feet with what

appeared to be a form of grey ash. A large penis dangled beneath a belly slightly distended from malnutrition, limbs gnarly and caked, face narrow, and most unique of all, huge and inscrutable eyes of black obsidian.

"A Yali pygmy from New Guinea?" Piper said with a look of amazement.

"Yes, and so much more."

The small ashen pygmy spoke with a gentle, woman-like voice, staring intently at Piper, expression never changing:

"Macaria, it is I, Alcaeus."

Piper gasped and sat up. "What? ... Alcaeus?"

"Yes, I am he."

Edison cut in. "I can only restore one Greek at a time, and the first is Alcaeus. His radical new form is the only way we can circumvent that hellishly irritating Dardanos curse. It's a fix, for now. I am still working on a better solution."

"Please pardon my shame," Alcaeus said, glancing down to his huge and ungainly penis.

Piper stood and walked to him. Despite her Piper stature, she towered at least five inches higher. Alcaeus stared up and blinked for the first time, blinked again, and a tear formed in his left eye like a little bead of polished obsidian. Piper reached out with both arms and hugged him tightly.

They both wept.

: /

YOU ARE ON TOP OF THE WORLD, AND YOU KNOW IT. You consider what you have accomplished, and with very little loss of life or limb. The daily narcissists, borderlines, bullies, sociopaths, and selfish manipulators are no more.

The human race is in the process of evolving faster and more efficiently than it ever could have, as well as dwelling in grand supernal environments of your own creation, and with ample evidence of peace and goodwill. The *Superna Humanitas* fleet is restored, in orbit, and more powerful than ever, perhaps even strong and versatile enough to face that relentless humanity killer in Orion.

In addition, Mars has joined with Earth and its moon to form an effective defense array in a distant pocket of the Milky Way. Meanwhile, the old corrupt governments of Earth are in the process of swift decay as millions every week join one of the seven city-worlds of Oz.

Now that the universe is doubtlessly unfolding as it should, you wish to entertain the concept of recreation. You desire to have some real fun. Yes. But where to start? You have heard the many and relentlessly threatening radio communications aimed at New Manhattan Oz by the latest acting U.S. president and her idiotic Pentagon generalissimos. They have become ever more dire and false and desperate as your great creation drifts over the American heartland in the direction of Chicago, inspiring awe and desire in all those who lay eyes upon it. Many of the onlookers, though fearful, feel they must follow the Oz Pied Piper wherever it may lead.

In the distance, you see the dark trails of humanity over a hundred miles long lumbering and pushing forward, growing ever closer to the biggest miracle in recorded history. State police and National Guard units have attempted in vain to prevent the hungry human mass from crossing over to paradise, though to no avail. The refugees always find a way, even trampling barbed wire and scattering cattle, whatever it takes.

As the masses ascend like choirs of windswept angels, higher and higher to the gates of *Terra Oz Infirma*, they communicate the frighteningly fabulous wonders they witness for at least 24 hours until their cell phones die and their voices are silenced. They say things like, "It's so big and strange. We love it, in a way we can't explain." And word of these tens of thousands of calls and texts spreads like a vision of God.

The Internet news and televised media, however, swallow and regurgitate the vision into an evil alien ploy. They try to make people afraid because that is what they've been doing for decades and cannot change.

Social media influencers agree.

News media personalities agree.

Government experts agree.

Psychologists agree.

Business leaders agree.

No one should go. The U.S. will defeat the green thing.

You know these whining and hollow beings of straw belong to a new human hive. They stumble and grope about in their dark tunnels, blindly following each other's scent.

Regardless, you decide to seek recreation by traveling to the White House, the abode of the current and so-called President of the United States. You materialize suddenly at the front door, well past the guard stations and terror-proofed steel.

You knock loudly.

While waiting and yawning, you see your appearance reflected in the nearest window. You muse on the fact that you really do resemble a 1970's character on British television—Doctor Who, played by the actor Tom Baker. You are wearing a dark, trench-like overcoat and a red-and-gold scarf around your neck that hangs down to your waist on either side. You also have a wide brimmed hat on, slanted to the left on your head. Your hair appears a bit wild, and your features are jutting enough to be remarkable—very macho now as befitting an old and debauched demi-god from Greece.

"Dr. Who calling!" you shout, growing impatient.

Within seconds, a team of dark suited Secret Service people answer the door with their spit guns pointed at you. You speak to them.

"Hello. I am Doctor Who. Where is the president?"

"DOWN ON THE FLOOR!" they shout in unison.

"Is the president at home?"

"DOWN ON THE FLOOR NOW!"

You sigh and mutter an old spell. *Tornouse o gusano, quente e con fame* (Become as the worm, hot and hungry). Upon utterance of the final syllable, the Secret Service raptors collapse and begin to squirm, eyes blank, mouths opening and closing like frustrated zombies. You know that upon recovery they will make haste to the nearest lavatory with severe bouts of diarrhea.

Wearing a wry smile and stepping over the silly vibrating bodies, you stroll towards a West Wing meeting room, singing with a reasonably good tenor voice:

There'll be blue birds over, the White Cliffs of Dover, tomorrow, just you wait and seeeee.

In a very short time, your eyes pierce the White House inner walls to observe a group of befuddled politicians sitting at a long mahogany table facing the new U.S. president who happens to be the former Assistant Secretary of Education.

How low the mighty have ascended, you say to yourself.

Before entering the conference room through the locked door, you spy a silver tray of *hors d'oeuvres* atop a cart to the right. You pluck a few toothpicks worth of smoked mussel with Havarti, consuming them with a zest born of pure bliss.

Without further hesitation, you then pass through the locked door like an irresistible spirit of Christmas past, and without even a special spell to enable it. You can just do it, like so many other things. You disobey the laws of physics as easily as eating mussels with Havarti.

Upon entering the room, a few of the political primates gasp and the remainder turn to gape at you like frightened seals. You say to them with a calm voice:

"So few of you left these days, eh?"

Not one speaks. They appear utterly terrified. They have seen the news videos of you when you were big as Godzilla and shouting about "feathers" over Manhattan.

You continue, nonetheless. "Washington, it appears, was quite suddenly vacated... Lots of sociopaths and narcissists going up like balloons, eh?"

A few gulps and nods. The rest remain paralyzed.

"I heard that the skies over D.C. were dark with skirts and suits, enough to blot out the sun. I guess that means there were far more Despicables here than anywhere else on Earth? Perhaps anywhere else in the universe?"

Silence. More nods.

You next glance at the former Assistant Secretary of

Education, and you wave at her and smile again. Her name is June W. Maclean. She smiles back fearfully, her hands shaking, eyes averted.

You talk to her. "Amazing, eh Jane? Every possible president in line down to you, just up and floated away. How many? ... Ahhh, how I love their demise."

Just as you are about to deliver a few words of wisdom and caution, you hear Catherine Romanova within you, and she is shouting with a terrified voice:

EDISON! EDISON!

She sounds as if far beneath the earth, her desperate telepathic call exhausted by its climb upward through miles of stone and darkness.

Catherine! By the lords of light, what is it?

No reply. You hear nothing.

You quite suddenly feel like the roomful of politicians who are watching you.

Fearful, uncertain, and on the verge of panic.

: /

PIPER AND ALCAEUS ROSE HIGH IN A CRAFT that she had selected from a pool of gleaming and sleek-hulled airships parked in her New Manhattan tower. In her mind she compared the likeness of the craft to others she'd seen long ago on the covers of American sci-fi pulp from the 1960's. Her father's idea, no doubt—again, another facet of his personality she'd not realized. Nevertheless, she wished to tour the upper atmospheres of *Terra Oz Infirma* and hopefully enjoy a glimmer in the eyes of her old Greek philosopher friend (now a New Guinea pygmy) at such time he beheld the next step in evolution.

At last, a chance to relax and explore after the insanity.

She looked over at Alcaeus, reached out and squeezed his little ashen hand as they rocketed upward at a velocity he'd never experienced. Less than half a minute later, they found themselves well beyond the miles-high spires of New Manhattan Oz, and inside of three minutes they entered a dark-violet sky of magnificent starry islands—all separate worlds of varying sizes crafted with a meticulous sense of detail and glowing with imagination.

Piper glanced at the features of several as they flew past. Among so many other things, she saw gleaming ice volcanoes, Saturn-like rings, Phobos-sized moonlets, wildly colored flora, colossal striding beings, and brimming bowls of ocean.

She heard Alcaeus gasp, not once but many times.

"I hereby dub these, the *Lands of Never*," Piper said.

"This is far preferable to death, Macaria," he said. "At first, upon seeing my reflection in a pond on your roof, I was uncertain, but at this moment, in this incredible vehicle, soaring like Hermes into the ether of another world, I would even choose to be a turtle again, as long as my consciousness could behold this."

But now, the awkward question.

"Alcaeus, you know, the New Guinea pygmies, who you closely resemble, were cannibals at one time," she said matter-of-factly.

He turned to look at her, his eyes widening. "By the gods, you jest, Macaria."

Piper paused for a moment, and said, "No, no, it's true… You don't have any urge to, um, chew a bit of human flesh, do you? Not that it would be bad."

"No, not at all. Such a thing is barbaric."

"Yes, yes, it certainly is. I would think—"

"Macaria, I must ask you. After all these centuries, how does it feel to possess the powers of a god?"

Piper paused again. "It feels confusing, in a way. I'm not sure of my destiny any longer. In Greece, I was certain."

"And what certainty became your actions in Greece?"

"I followed father's example. I wished to protect others, serve a greater good, and seek to unite Greece."

"In the name of Zeus, they certainly needed you."

"Over the centuries though, I became less considerate. The dark side of human nature controlled me."

"Yes, you are still ruled by your humanity. I see your father is no different, and that is to be expected."

"True."

"However, you command great forces. How do you compare yourself to the lesser beings of this world? Do you feel superior or have you learned humility?"

"I've been exposed to so much heartache, Alcaeus, and even more futility. I've learned that moral choice and wisdom are far more important than the ability to cook soup with your eyes or control the actions of fools. I judge my powers good only if they help me achieve something good. To tell the truth, I get more satisfaction out of simply observing the Milky Way on a clear night than anything else."

"Stars, endless worlds, my mind still rebels."

"Time and space make a mockery of power, old friend."

"That is so, Macaria, and you know that—"

Before Alcaeus could finish, the airship banked suddenly

and sharply starboard, slanting down at least 15 degrees and aiming towards one Land of Never several dozen miles away: a mass the size of old Manhattan, and leaving an unusual, comet-like trail behind it in the darkness. Piper quickly scanned the anomaly with her eyes and mind. She observed a covering of immense fir trees twice the size of California redwoods, and the island itself, cut lengthwise through its center by a rugged granite valley. Hidden on its surface, and for no good reason Piper could ascertain, were two magical beings with minds so powerful they could resolutely block her probes.

Who or what in freezing hell is way out here?

Piper wrestled with the airship's controls, cursing under her breath. Alcaeus vomited on his lap as the ship wobbled and bucked against the inexorable force pulling it downward. And just as Piper began to spell the plummeting craft to turn aside, she heard her father's voice whisper.

"Allow the ship to land."

: /

WHITE HOUSE VIEWS NEW OZ AND MARS AS ALLIES IN WAR ON HUMANITY

WASHINGTON (Reuters) In a press conference at the White House that included the president and Joint Chiefs of Staff, all parties on Monday confirmed their belief that the inclusion of Mars in solar orbit near Earth is linked to a mysterious new super technology that has also produced what are known to the American public as the Seven City-Worlds of Oz.

"The alien parties responsible originated on the planet Mars. They are, to all intents and purposes, Martians," President Maclean stated in her opening remarks.

In subsequent questioning, the president admitted that scientists could not state with any certainty whether the Martians were natives to that planet or possibly settlers from elsewhere in the galaxy who assumed control for the purpose of staging an Earth invasion.

"Some scientists disagree regarding the ultimate intent of the Martians," the president said, and further, "They obviously possess the power to destroy life on Earth but have not chosen to do so. Instead, they appear to be attempting to assimilate our citizens."

The Joint Chiefs presented a unified front in the belief that regardless of method or appearance, the totality of phenomena argued for a "war on Earth," and one that must be resisted by all means necessary.

Pentagon Chief, General Hamalcar Diaz, told those assembled, "Scientists agree that any superficial resemblance to the Emerald City in the Wizard of Oz is purely coincidental."

Reporters asked if further measures were being taken to prevent more citizens from leaving the United States. The president responded that all measures necessary were being taken especially in consideration of the fact that huge atrocities, or wholesale incarceration, or both, had been taking place. How else to explain the permanent disappearance of many millions of people, as well as their subsequent lack of communication?"

In response to a final question, neither President Maclean or the Joint Chiefs could comment in any detail on the finding by U.S. and international astronomers that

Earth itself has been transported to a new location in galactic space, except to say they believe it to be a transparent Martian trick.

"The so-called evidence of relocation is a Martian deception being used for the purpose of sowing panic and confusion in the minds of the American public," said General Tyrone Bradley. "Nothing could possibly have the power to do what Japan and France are claiming. We utterly reject this concept and call upon scientists to stop playing into the hands of the enemy."

: /

PIPER HAD WITNESSED REFUGEES from the crumbling American heartland, herded fast and crazy as shark-frightened beach goers into the bowels of New Manhattan Oz—falling through to discover wisdom, epiphany, and godless humanism, not to mention critically smarter brains and greatly improved internal organs.

Following a night or two of drinks and dancing in the New Manhattan, many fell even further, down to the Deeper Lands where they sought salvation, redemption, and a total life reboot free of debt and taxes, as well as the many other flaws of "civilization."

For the love of Jeeves, these crossovers can even mate!

Never once would they face the kind of financial and psychological corruption that the Despicable club of narcissists and sociopaths had always forced upon them; and as a bonus, no human being would ever be enslaved or forced to "bend a knee" again.

Social hierarchies based on riches, gender, or race were obsolete; money in any form bought nothing, health was assured, and Piper's favorite Belgian beer was plentiful.

True utopia, I'd say.

This is what Edison told Piper after she landed with Alcaeus. The two of them, along with Edison and Catherine, now standing in a small circle, eyes bulging like owls in the long shadows of the gigantic trees, bodies tiny and unimportant beneath a violet-black sky of swarming island stars.

"Why are you telling me this now, dad?"

"Because you must know the full reality of what we have established in order to understand the importance of what I am about to relate to you."

"You've won the War for Utopia. Right? I know."

Piper glanced at Catherine and noted how dire and focused she appeared, staring intently at Edison. Something serious had happened, something not so good. This wasn't about the War for Utopia after all.

Or was it?

Edison continued. "Humanity is evolving, even—"

"And now *threatened*," Catherine interrupted.

"That remains to be seen," Edison said with a calm voice, turning to face her.

"Are you fool enough to think me foolish?" Catherine said, beginning to anger.

"No, of course not. I just—"

"You have introduced a bad strain, Edison, and it is *violent, malicious, and frighteningly powerful.*"

"How could that be so, Catherine?"

"I cannot answer, but it exists. There is no question."

"All we know with certainty is that you became frightened and unleashed enough rounds of black plasma to incinerate Portugal."

"For good reason, and I am still not certain I killed the damnable monstrosities."

Unable to keep quiet any longer, Piper spoke up. "What fresh Godzilla are we talking about?" She glanced around like a five-year old, blinking, looking back and forth at them. At her side, Alcaeus let out a strange whistle. He appeared to her in the darkness like a surreal gargoyle.

A frustrated Catherine turned to Piper and gave her an account. Using human words interspersed with the cinema of magic telepathy, she pictured for Piper the hyperbolic massive monoliths with distorted faces and dark thoughts. Piper felt Catherine's fear through her eyes and witnessed the horrible stone-like monster growing closer, cutting through rocky earth as easily as a ship's prow through water. She then heard its evil words slither like a worm of hot acid into her own mind.

Catherine might be a scorpion bitch from hell, but she would never invent such lunatic shit.

Alcaeus put his small arms around Piper's waist and hugged her close. This situation had scared him to the point of needing a mother. She knew he was ashamed, but his fear was greater.

Catherine finished and turned back to Edison, stating with a voice of dark determination, "You have hundreds of thousands, if not millions of refugees, migrating even now to the Deeper Lands. They are unprotected and potentially exposed to these new nightmares... The monolith thing spoke of extinction, and its intent was demonstrably deadly."

Piper felt a surge of horror deep in her soul.

Might Chariya Song be one of the threatened migrants?

Edison appeared a bit dazed, uncertain, then he said after a pause, "The Deeper Lands lie above the New Manhattan operations center at the very base of this structure. Our crack security division is down there with thousands of *Superna Humanitas* personnel, a full Robotic Vigilance Force, as well as two battalions of *Dio Soldati* armed with enough black weapons to dissolve Neptune."

Catherine wasn't impressed. "So you say, but where were these magical forces and Neptune dissolvers when that grotesque behemoth charged me?"

"Oz security informed me that you fired the plasma and quaked the Deeper Lands from rim to rim, but they observed nothing before that, no anomalies or unusual activity."

"Then they *are fools*, or their devices have been compromised. Are you suggesting I am delusional?"

Edison's mouth moved as he stared at Catherine, but no sound came out. He was authentically speechless, while Alcaeus, still holding Piper, raised his head and said to him with his soft voice, "Your deeds are great, Archimedes, greater than all the gods combined, and thus, a little strife or taint must surely be the order of the day."

Ah, the diplomat in Alcaeus. I'd forgotten.

Edison smiled, apparently relieved by the comment, and said to Alcaeus, "Your effort to encourage perspective is certainly appreciated, good sir."

Alcaeus continued. "Nothing is without flaw. You have created this Oz, as you call it, here in this America, and no wondrous world like it has ever existed in the memory of humanity."

"Yes, Alcaeus. the *American Oz maker*, that's me," he said with a tone of defeat, lowering his head.

Piper scrutinized her father's voice and demeanor.

He knows Catherine is right. His utopia has been slimed already... But wait a minute. He just called himself... American Oz maker.

Shit!

Before Piper or anyone else present could light the match of another thought, it came to them from every direction—born of the shadows and wind in the branches, born of the Milky Way ether, born of the smoking dark land beneath their feet and possessing voice like a distant rumble of avalanche:

"HAVE YOU NOT YET GRASPED YOUR ULITMATE FATE, GODFELLOW?"

Piper felt paralyzed as she watched her father. He stood silently, in a state of both apprehension and amazement. The mysterious voice spoke again.

"IN ANSWER TO THE QUESTION IN YOUR MIND, I FOLLOWED YOUR CORPOREAL FORM TO THIS PLANET IN A WAVE OF MAGICAL LIGHT SUMMONED BY YOU."

"But your ultimate origin?" Edison's face now bordered on actual fear.

"YOU WERE THE GRAVITY OF MY CREATION LONG AGO."

Piper winced.

The gravity of his creation?

She glanced once more at the *memento mori* hanging from her neck. Would she face death bravely? She wasn't sure, though she'd kicked the habit of self-delusion at least six centuries ago. But her father Edison, as she might have guessed, wasn't quite ready to expire.

He sighed, cleared his throat, smiled ever so slightly, and said, "I am afraid, my mysterious nemesis from Orion, that I cannot comprehend your claim to my gravity."

"*I AM NOT THE TOTALITY OF BEING WHO CONSUMES YOUR FLEET IN A FUTURE NOW EXTINCT, BUT I AM PART, AND ALL OF IT.*"

"Part, and all?"

"*EVERYTHING IT IS AND WILL BE. AS SUCH, I AM THE EXTINCTION OF YOU AND YOUR KIND.*"

"I see… But tell me, why must you devour us? Why this terrible hate? Way too human of you, old sport."

"*I ONLY CONDUCT AN ACT OF PREVENTION.*"

"As you suggest, we can be dangerous, but the denizens of this world have imagined destruction at the hands of space aliens so many times that—"

"*POWER WILL BE GATHERED. YOUR CITY WORLDS WILL BE SLAIN BY THE DARK HOUSE OF OZ.*"

"Are you mocking me?"

"*THE BEINGS YOU CALL DESPICABLES, MURDERED BY YOU, WILL RETURN TO JOIN MY VANGUARD AND ASSIST IN MAKING YOUR FATE.*"

"No. No! I will not allow it!" Edison Godfellow's rage was finally surfacing and withering the nearby flora.

"*AND NOW THE WHEELS OF HEAVEN START, YOU BOARD THE DEVIL'S RIDIN' CART, GET READY FOR THE FUTURE, IT IS MURDER.*"

Piper almost choked in astonishment.

Scary shit, and we're just getting started.

Moments later, only wind was heard in the Land of Never. The alien had vanished like a dark soul leaving cold flesh, the lifeless body discarded, forever tainted by a memory of possession.

: /

CHARIYA AND HER FAMILY GASPED IN AWE as they soared in their aerial carrier, skirting the snowy peaks and gleaming lakes of the Deeper Lands. Known affectionately as "Jaguar Mom" to her grown children—daughters Chivy and Chanlina, nephew Mongkat, and sons Kosal and Kiry—Chariya closed her eyes and let a long and shrill noise escape from between her teeth that sounded like *eeeeeeeeeee* as all surfaces of the carrier, outside and in, even the seats, faded to total transparency.

Half-way into the flight and the Song family found themselves flying, soaked in sunshine, and with only their clothing left as a symbol of normalcy. Like great emperor dragons of old they flew, on and on, soon following an immense, white-capped emerald river as wisps of gleaming fog lifted from the dark forests and the sounds of creation became a low and soothing hum.

The world belonged to them.

Aside from blurts of astonishment, everyone remained speechless until the carrier landed ten minutes later upon a rolling plain of golden, California-like grass.

Chariya and her family disembarked from a ramp in the rear, feeling more grounded because color and substance had returned to the structure of the vehicle upon touching down, thus preventing passengers from feeling disconcerted about walking in airy space.

Once outside and ceasing to tremble, achy chests calming, Chariya and relatives glanced around to see hundreds of other people leaving the carrier, and like them, walking unsteadily into the sunshine of a new world. Many races and cultures were represented. And of course, this fact made sense to Chariya, for so many had been oppressed by the world's foolish and selfish governments, no matter their origin.

Now, here they were, free at last.

"The yellow brick road!" a young girl only a few feet away shouted excitedly to her parents.

She appeared to be from India. Chariya saw the girl pointing into the distance and followed her finger to observe the wonder of it. A yellow brick road. *An actual yellow brick road*, thought Chariya, and wider than the original, wide as her entire family stretched head to toe; and it gleamed a soft, maize-like yellow in the sunlight, streaming to a surreal and misty horizon.

High above the road, she glanced up to see dozens of shimmering specks in the sky—more aerial carriers, visible ones, ferrying migrants down from New Manhattan. How many would eventually land, she could not say, but hundreds of thousands were coming.

"The air feels good, and I am strong," her son Kosal said.

He stood over six feet and the transfiguration filter of the wonderfully magical New Manhattan Oz made him glow in his mother's eyes. Never had she seen him more strikingly handsome.

In days before, he'd been a sickly boy of 38 with a diagnosis of Lupus. Every few months a new disease overtook him, from rheumatoid arthritis to migraine-like headaches, but that changed thanks to Piper Robbin's father, Mr. Edison Godfellow. Kosal was now free of disease.

Chariya knew she could never thank Mr. Godfellow enough for what he'd done to restore her family and provide them with a new life. Indeed, how could anyone ever thank him enough? He'd saved the world. He rescued humankind. He righted wrongs and fulfilled dreams even before they were dreamt, and towering above the skyscrapers in New York that night, he presented himself as a true and terrible godhead.

Will humanity ever forget, or become ungrateful?

She would never allow anyone to say an unkind word about him. And before another word about anything could be uttered, the gathering crowd sounded suddenly startled.

A few shouts echoed the word, "Look!"

Chariya glanced up to see a sight quite beyond a daydream. A strangely beautiful woman hovered in the sky. She was about fifty feet above the ground, enough that people on the plain and road saw her almost immediately, and yet, no one witnessed her materialize. She was just there. Thousands more, leaving the aerial carriers and moving into the grasses spotted her also, their eyes and mouths widening in awe; but if they could have slowed time, enough to witness her evolution, they would have seen a dark pinch in the air, like a tiny crack, followed by the substance of her exploding from it like fluid under pressure, expanding and snapping to perfect form.

Chariya's nephew, Mongkat, began to panic. He pointed up and yelled:

"It's her! She is the one my dream foretold."

The apparition hung in the air like a glowing spike of ice,

feet together, arms at her sides, silent, as if waiting for more crowd to gather before speaking. She appeared to be observing the many aerial carriers landing, some of them fading into observable reality before touching softly down to earth. Though her face was sullen, and her eyes inscrutable and dark (*rather purple*, thought Chariya), her mouth spread in a bright smile.

A hostess smile of welcome.

To Chariya, she looked ever so much like a glossy white angel-doll wrapped in a one-piece gown of shimmering satin, the length of it from shoulder to knee haloed with a honey-gold umbra as if she were a Christian religious icon. Her hair, blonder than her gown, flowed to her waist and whipped gently in the breeze. Oddly enough though, the air blew right to left, yet her hair blew left to right, and her gown blew not an inch, constricting her legs like a tight bandage; and the white doll's feet were not visible because the gown fell several inches below them.

So unnatural and inappropriate, thought Chariya.

Then she noticed a very strange thing. What seemed to be a stream of nearly invisible, gnat-like specks jetting from the woman's eyes into the air for a few feet before veering sharply and flowing on behind her.

"Do you see that stuff, coming out of her eyes?" Chariya whispered to her oldest daughter Chanlina on her left.

Chanlina squinted into the bright air, turned to her mother and said, "I see something. It's blurry, like waves of heat... I can't see where it's going."

Chariya began to get a very uncomfortable feeling about what was happening. Her initial awe and exuberance discolored into mounting anxiety. She thought of Piper and wanted to see her. She wanted Piper and her mythic father to be there. Everyone would be safe then, no matter what this angelic fever dream of ice and eye gnats might do.

While Chariya ruminated on the potential of danger, the many thousands in the gathering crowd gasped as one. Mongkat groaned and began to shake. A new event was taking place. The honey-gold aura of the floating woman went nova. In less than a second, it had expanded to a hundred times its former size, jetting forth rays at ninety-degree angles to create an enormous, honey-gold star with four points; and in sync, the angel doll raised her arms perpendicular to her sides and flattened her hands in such a manner as to mimic crucifixion.

Wearing that same welcome hostess smile, she began to rotate, slowly at first, and as she did so, her body drifted towards the ground in a very disturbing and leaf-like manner, swaying left to right in broad dipping arcs.

"What the bloody hell?" said Chariya's son, Kiry. "She's like a Jesus second coming."

"It's going to kill us!" yelled Mongkat.

Normally, she would have shot them both a stern warning for such behavior, only now, that wasn't possible. The spinning apparition moved its lips and from the mouth issued a distorted human voice loud enough to be heard for many miles. It sounded feminine, yes, though one force-filtered through a wall of turbulent water:

"I AM THE WITCH EMPRESS OF EARTH."

No one present could process this. They only stared and gaped. Chariya no longer saw the hive of gnats shooting from her eyes and had no time to consider the matter further for the angel creature began changing color to darker and deeper shades of black and purple that throbbed and waved over her form like the blade shadows of a fan. And as this Witch Empress drew closer to the paralyzed crowd, now stretching nearly a mile, the bottom ray of the honey-gold star dipped low enough to begin skimming the mob of human flesh.

Chariya witnessed the insanity from a short distance, her attention compromised as screams erupted—a few at first, then increasing in number. Before she could act, the air imploded once more with the booming voice:

"FOLLOW THE YELLOW BRICK ROAD."

And again:

"FOLLOW THE YELLOW BRICK ROAD."

The crowd surrounding her groaned like a wounded beast and began pushing forward. Chariya heard even more screams and turned to see the Witch Empress only twenty feet or so behind her, spinning closer to the ground, the honey-gold aura like a thin blade, and whenever it touched human flesh that flesh began to glow like a translucent container of brilliant white light. Little head bulbs like stars began popping up everywhere as the air filled with short shrieks of pain.

"They're burning!" Chariya heard a man shout, and a true stampede began, lunging in the general direction of the yellow brick road. Many people stumbled and fell, tripping others behind them. Those farther ahead broke into a run. Chariya, frightened in a way she'd never been before, reached back to grab the hands of her children and shouted at them over the growing roar, "Hold each other's hands! Hold on!"

Piper, Piper, please hear me! she cried out in her mind.

Mr. Godfellow, help us! Oh God, help us!

Their feet soon felt the harder texture of the yellow brick road, and yet, the bricks softly massaged their feet—magical and soothing in this world of madness and death.

How could this be?

More pockets of space appeared nearby, due to others having fallen and formed clumps of madly thrashing bodies. Chariya turned again for a moment to locate the inexplicable monstrosity, and saw it, far off to her right, spinning close to the ground within a chaotic mass of shrieking humanity.

She and the rest of her family continued running, faster than ever, their newfound stamina and strong legs propelling them forward at a rapid pace for several minutes until Kosal shouted behind her:

"Mom, she's gone!"

Like most others, they slowed to a walk, breathing heavily and disheveled by the ordeal. Chariya searched for evidence of the evil floating creature. She saw nothing, only a perfect blue sky and the darker human confusion amidst the golden grasses.

She took account of the whole family. Miraculously, everyone had survived the gauntlet. A few began to weep, and she took them in her arms, and others in the family joined to form a hugging circle, thereby releasing a good portion of the suffering and shock.

And they weren't the only ones.

Those who had fled in hysterics were now halting to cry and regain breath. Emotionally and physically, the entire herd felt exhausted, and who could blame them?

Still breathing hard, Chariya's daughter Chivy said to no

one in particular: "We come here and are healed of sickness, freed of cares, and bred for paradise, but now we are hunted by the Witch Empress of Earth… What is happening? Can *anyone tell me?*"

"Destiny is all," Mongkat said in a daze. "This is our doom, and we cannot prevent it."

The rest of the family simply breathed and stared blankly. No one attempted to silence him, Chariya least of all.

Like one mind, the mass around them sighed and began to move forward again. The yellow brick road shivered to the tramp of many thousands seeking salvation. Chariya's family imitated them. Was there another alternative? Of course, they might wander into the grass on either side, seek the crest of the next hill, but what would be the point? Everyone was now effectively marooned in this place, abandoned to the whims of bizarre and potentially homicidal beings. Nevertheless, the wonder of Oz beckoned in the misty distance. Would protection exist? Would there be an actual city? Some form of redress or New Manhattan authority to answer for the hostile ballistics of the Witch Empress?

The answers to these questions would never come.

A loud, echo-rolling thunder slammed down from far above. Everyone raised their heads to see a jet-like contrail that streaked half-way across the sky and abruptly ended in a frozen burst of smoke. Many black specks spread out from the smoke and began dropping towards the ground as if hurtling at a speed greater than what gravity allowed.

People began pointing again. A few yelled. Chariya could not make out what they said. She focused intently on the specks, now becoming larger objects, and she understood. They were human bodies, hundreds of them, falling at extreme velocity towards the milling crowd.

Recognizing the danger, people on the flanks began scampering off the yellow brick road, fleeing into the surrounding grassland, though in some cases no escape was possible. Like meteors of smoking black flesh, the bodies hit the living at nearly two hundred miles an hour, instantly killing whomever they fell upon. One of the corpses struck two people near Chariya: a young Caucasian man and his red-haired wife. The plummeting body exploded into spray and bits of bone, showering Chariya and her children, but the actual victims vanished in a microsecond, their parts flying in all directions—no memory remaining other than a huge splatter of blood and intestinal shreds.

"One of the aerial carriers exploded!" her son Kosal cried out, wiping the blood from his eyes.

From all sides people began to howl, traumatized by the gory impact of the human hailstones and the death they brought with them. Only Chariya's concern for her family prevented her from doing likewise.

"Shot down? How?" a frightened Latino woman turned and asked Kosal, still wiping blood from his face. "My children are coming down in one of those machines."

But no time to consider.

The Dark House of Oz announced itself.

Chapter IX

Despicables Return – Battle of the Deeper Lands – The Therapist

CATHERINE ROMANOVA WATCHED EDISON TREMBLE. She saw it in his hands. She did not believe he even realized it. His face was a mask of shock, apparent even in the darkness beneath the giant trees. Would he break down and weep before her?

Piper and Alcaeus stood off to the side, scrutinizing him and looking perplexed. Everyone accepted that he'd known changes, frights, and ordeals, especially after the transformative massacre in Orion, only now he actually shook. She knew he was afraid, and who wouldn't be? His utopia, all he'd struggled and fought for, and perhaps even tens of millions of beings, now faced annihilation at the whim of this vengeful Orion monster.

She took two steps closer and placed her hand on his shoulder. He turned to her and said: "Catherine, I have a special gift for you. I should have accomplished this earlier, but I was greatly distracted."

"A gift?"

"I have used a portion of the Tao from our Jupiter collection efforts to undo the vengeful spell that Niccolo performed that permanently disallowed the presence of your Mother Yarrow."

Catherine felt stunned and taken aback. It was way too wonderful to believe. "You mean, Mother Yarrow Maria? Maria of Pozzuoli?"

"Who else could I possibly mean?"

"Where is she?" Catherine asked, more excited than

she'd been in years.

I am here, a voice in her mind said.

Maria's voice. It was her, no question.

Catherine then knew and felt her warm presence, as though Maria were hugging her and whispering gently. Catherine began to weep. She could not restrain herself. The separation from Maria had been unendurable at times. A terrible punishment.

Alcaeus appeared bewildered. "What is happening? I do not understand."

"Her Mother Yarrow," Piper said matter-of-factly. "She is a being, a famous warrior woman from Earth's past magically linked across time to a companion host, and in this case, our imperious Czarina."

"What purpose does she serve?"

"She advises her, enhances her power—"

Catherine cut in. "She provides me with strength and wisdom. She calms me and loves me."

Maria heard and said to her host, mind to mind:

I do love you, darling Catherine. I am sorry to have left. It only seemed like an hour to me, though I know for you it was many years. Niccolo would not listen. He was determined to punish us both for turning against him.

Piper rolled her eyes at the last comment by Catherine, put her finger over the lips of Alcaeus before he could ask another question, and said to everyone, "This is all really grand *as a circus in the middle of the Pacific*, but you said yourself, Catherine, the Deeper Lands are threatened. We need to move on this. I cannot locate or see my friend, Ms. Song, no matter what I do. She might be down there, even near death at this very moment."

Mother Yarrow Maria took note.

Cathy, who is this upstart?

Catherine wiped a few tears from her cheek, looking annoyed with Piper, and said, "I realize you have a friend who cooks a strange stew for you and your father; however, you do not understand the import of this. Maria will help us defeat this cosmic kraken."

"Soooo let's *get to it*," Piper said impatiently. In a tenth of a moment, she transfigured herself into the Grand Sorceress, manifesting a magnetic field that drove compasses mad. "I am no longer an upstart. Do you hear me, oh Maria of Pasta Fazool?"

She is powerful Cathy, and prideful.

"Do not *insult* Mother Yarrow Maria, barista of beans," Catherine said.

"Then do not *test me* again," the Grand Sorceress replied. Her sudden hot gush of irritation seemed almost inexplicable to Catherine, and much as the Czarina was loathe to admit it, a bit hurtful.

The Grand Sorceress continued. "My power is greater than when you fought me last, and you almost died."

This last statement was made with such steel-eyed conviction that Catherine shot a surprised glance at Edison. Had he betrayed her by making his daughter stronger? And if so, why? It certainly was within his scope of power now to have accomplished such a task. But did he believe she really threatened his daughter with death?

Did Piper believe such a thing and convince him?

Edison met Catherine's eyes. They displayed no emotion. With all of utopia and *Superna Humanitas* now threatened once more, such tangents were of no matter to him. She knew it. She understood.

Still, the issue would be resolved.

It will be settled, Cathy. She cannot threaten you.

With a dry voice, Edison said to Catherine and his daughter, "Enough. There is no time for this, no time—"

His voice was cut off by a low-toned warbling. He reached in his side coat pocket and extracted his personal chronocom, a device engineered for a large variety of space-time communication purposes. It resembled a wafer-thin disk of gold about the size of his mouth. It floated up from his hand and levitated to within a few inches of his eyes.

Catherine heard a voice issue from the chronocom. male or female, she could not say, though it mattered not:

"Sir, we lost contact with one of the aerial carriers from New Manhattan while in transit to a Deeper Land base point. Three scout craft were dispatched to investigate. They reported a range of matter disruption on strong Tao wavelengths, enough to cause serious harm to the refugees. We surmised that an unknown force had masked our ability to detect it sooner. Do you wish us to dispatch a *Dio Soldati* unit to investigate?"

"What are the scouts reporting back now?" Edison said to the chronocom floating before him.

"They will not respond. Connection ceased precisely 67 seconds ago."

"What was the nature of the violence?"

"Unknown. We have no data to—"

"Dispatch a war battalion."

"An entire battalion of *Dio Soldati*, sir? A team would—"

"NO. As I direct. Full weapons array. Now."

Catherine's eyes sought those of the Grand Sorceress. The unexpected fire of hostility had been replaced by grim resolve. Both were mature and fearful enough to know that petty personality friction must be set aside. Whatever the true essence of the Orion entity, it possessed the power to sidestep Edison's sensors and spells in the Deeper Lands.

Catherine considered the circumstance.

Another bad sign, a very bad sign.

The coming conflict might well be prolonged and supremely violent. As before, Catherine held the hand of mortality close to her heart, only this time it was different. Her timeless and stalwart Mother Yarrow would stand beside her once again, no matter what came.

:/

ON EITHER SIDE OF THE MULTITUDE, something very strange was happening. Triangular shapes resembling giant black fins at least fifty feet tall were ploughing through the golden fields. A chorus of frenzied noise had announced their arrival, everyone turning to see the fins kicking up rocks and swirls of dust, as well as disgorging a scent of decayed carrion, and though it seemed like forever, it took hardly a minute for the macabre parade to halt.

Chariya watched them gathering about a hundred yards distant and directly in front of the human migrants, as if to block their passage on the yellow brick road.

What came next was truly bizarre.

At the point where the onrushing columns of black fins veered inward to meet, a large dust cloud billowed up. Despite this, she still observed several of the fins moving inside the cloud, flapping and shimmering. Next, a loud noise like a metallic screech erupted, blasting out waves of strident sound that only tweaked the onlookers into even more confusion.

Seconds later, as the dust began to settle, it became obvious to those present that the black fins were fusing, though in a puzzling and jumbled manner. From the earth they rose to stretch and morph into sheets and wall-like shapes, groaning painfully as they mounted one another, curling and twirling and thrusting into each other's gleaming black flesh while simultaneously giving birth to acts of buttress and tower.

"Parts of it are... copulating?" Chanlina said.

"It's humping itself," Kiry said.

"But what about *that*?" Chivy fearfully asked, pointing.

Ms. Song forced herself to turn away from the sexualized coil and thrust. In the direction indicated by Chivy's finger, another phenomenon was taking place. She saw what appeared to be the gnats that a short time ago had flown free of the Witch Empress eyes—thousands of them from north to south, low to the earth and shivering with mirage-like effect. She shot a glance to her other side and observed the same phenomenon. And in a manner precisely like the falling bodies from the aerial carrier, the gnats grew larger at unnatural speed, leaving no doubt as to their final destination.

"Where will we sleep tonight?" Chanlina was woozy

with psychotic break.

Before a reply could be realized, the eerie voice of the Witch Empress echoed over the Deeper Lands.

"BEHOLD THE DARK HOUSE OF OZ!"

None could see the Witch Empress, but everyone stared at the eerie tumult of creation erected before them. As they looked on, the structure, hundreds of feet tall, released a long and deep sigh. Scattered trails of bluish smoke curled up from thin cracks in the exterior and clusters of small bubbles surfaced and popped. Major acts of birth and division devolved into nothing more than slithers of flotsam.

The tower itself appeared solid enough, though the overall impression was that of a piecemeal sculpture composed of enormous black sheets and oblong shapes, twisting tubes and coils, and in several places, warped windows opening onto the black vacuum of space. It appeared both light and heavy to the eye, whimsical and indestructible, and effectively, a product of alien insanity. The human brain could not contain, explain, or refute it.

Mongkat curled into an embryo and began howling.

Chariya felt helpless. Was this salvation? Was it doom?

The voice of the Witch Empress blared forth again:

"YOU ARE HERE TO BE WELL AND HAPPY."

The crowd said nothing, just stood there breathing, splattered, and traumatized.

"BEING PRETTY FOXY, ARE YOU NOW?"

Dropped jaws and puzzled faces.

"TRYING TO DECEIVE WITH LOOKS OF INNOCENCE?"

As Chariya stared, a decapitated head of Witch Empress faded into view like an ethereal crown. It floated just above the peak of the Dark House—a hideous, ghostly vision wide as the tower itself, displaying that same phony smile; and though translucent and gleaming, Chariya could see deep into the terrible and evil purple eyes.

Becoming dizzy, she felt a sharp stab in her head.

"Your eyes, mother!" daughter Chanlina cried out, "They're *bleeding*."

Chariya felt the blood trickling down her cheeks. She looked around to see her family, as well as unknown others beside them, all bleeding from the eyes.

Thousands upon thousands bled out their misery, for having absorbed the malefic eye-purple of the Witch Empress, blood was the only response the human body could make.

Would she bleed them all dry?

"THE LAST ONE TO GO WILL SEE THE FIRST 126,984 GO BEFORE HER!"

Upon that pronouncement, and even louder than the Witch Empress, a girl of thirteen years let go a ripping shriek of terror in Chariya's ear.

"NOW HOW ABOUT A DOSE OF DESPICABLES?"

In response, a chorus of animal-like roars in the thousands shook the air at once, as though an old jet turbine nearby had suddenly revved to life. The mob once again panicked and fled in every direction. People knocked heads and tumbled to the earth, others shoving violently at each other, shouting and cursing as they did so.

Before Chariya could gather her family or even think, she looked up to see the gnats on the horizon grown to monstrous size, closing in and howling a war cry that sounded like:

MOM BEEEEEE COOOOOO!

She saw their unclothed bodies, seven feet long or more, sheathed in brownish-grey fur and sprouting enormous bat wings, and their snarling mad faces looked like those of fanged gorillas.

"YOU IGNORED THEIR DEATH, BUT YOU CANNOT IGNORE THEIR NEW LIFE!"

Chariya and her family ran through the waving golden grasses, seeking the horizon, though they knew not where to go. Another chorus of savage roars erupted. The flying ape demons were creating a series of large vulture circles above the plain. Hundreds in each circle, they barked shrilly like tortured hyenas while raining a putrid defecation down on the mob of terrified humanity now flooding off the yellow brick road in ever greater numbers.

A big splat of stinking feces hit Chivy. She screamed as it crackled and dripped from her head to her chest, eating away at her flesh like mustard gas. Others screamed too, only the screams this time were more pain-filled and desperate. Just as Chariya reached out to her daughter's smoking body a gooey lob smacked her right hand and burned it to the bone in seconds. She recoiled in white hot agony, and instinctively lifting her face to the sky, saw dozens of growling, ape-faced beasts diving towards her to end the pain.

Her last thought was the momentary realization that the face of the closest Despicable snapping at her with blood mad fury, and only a few feet away from ripping her to shreds, resembled a former neighbor in Brooklyn.

He'd always been such an intolerable asshole.

: /

THE GRAND SORCERESS PIERCED THE AIR of the Deeper Lands, along with her father, and Catherine—who had believed it best to first reconnoiter the situation from on high rather than materialize into the thick of it.

They all agreed.

Down to five thousand feet and Piper passed through a cloud to spot a flying platoon of *Dio Soldati* dispatched from New Manhattan Ops, and not more than half a mile in front of her. Though she'd viewed them before, the sight of her father's fierce and destructively powerful god soldiers encased in layers of magi-tech armor and looking like humanoid black spiders was always a cause for awe, if not outright terror. Once before in history, a World Maker with aria power, like Catherine, had met her end at the hands of seven of them working in unison. Hammering relentlessly at her with enough force to vaporize Cambodia, they burned her down to salt, and later, in a spirit of jest, sprinkled her on their fish dinner down to the very last grain.

A full battalion of these super bitches should make this a cake walk.

Could she have been more of a fool?

The first sign of disaster consisted of pummeling waves of sound striking her body like clubs of steel, each loud enough to powder every building in NYC. Moments later, the second sign became obvious. From about twenty miles away, Piper spotted a macabre structure towering up from the golden plain below. It appeared patchwork and twisted, the color of a dark iron asteroid. Several platoons of *Dio Soldati* were already in the process of bombarding it with the devastating force of every weapon in their arsenal.

Piper knew instinctively that it was alien.

The Dark House of Oz?

She adjusted her eyes to shield them from the bursts, blinding flashes, and jolts of grinding beam weapons cutting like torches at an invisible blister protecting the insane-looking structure. She couldn't help but glance over at Catherine who flew close at her side.

Her face appeared alarmed.

Communicating telepathically, the Czarina said to Piper, "*Down below us, those American crossovers have been butchered. They perished before the Dio Soldati could assault that monstrous structure.*"

A cold surge of panic seized Piper Robbin. Chariya and her family might well have been part of this immigrant crowd. She must know. She tried to find her with a mind probe. She called out to her, but it was a little like communicating in static through a wall of static. Eerie alien energy radiating from the Dark House scrambled com links and probes on all magical and non-magical frequencies. Piper's anxiety increased and she very nearly broke formation to search among the bodies.

I must know the truth, whatever the cost.

Sweeping over the ground with her vision, she focused in closer, enough to view the true and ugly sweep of the carnage: many tens of thousands of people burned, mangled, and chopped into a hash of parts; and even more shocking, hundreds of corpses in the process of being devoured. Ape-like, bat-winged beasts squatted in the golden grasses on their haunches, hundreds of them, chewing like lions on bloody hunks of human meat.

Servants of the Dark House?

"New Manhattan Oz is quaking!" her father yelled. "They feel it to the very crown!"

Catherine shouted back even louder:

"WE MUST CURE THIS DISEASE NOW!"

Piper saw the raging Czarina draw her Glock and begin squeezing off round after round at the Dark House. The hyper-velocity shells struck its accursed blister shield almost instantaneously, each one creating a blinding burst and a noise loud as July 4th in Disneyland compressed to one second. Meanwhile, above and below Piper, nearby and far away, the flying lines of *Dio Soldati* unleashed salvo after salvo of world-killing fire—the likes of which she'd never witnessed. But the alien creation did not buckle or dissolve as the grand assault intended.

However, all was not lost.

As Piper flew closer, she noticed that the crackling Dark House shield, saturated now with a multi-hued patina of destructive energy, seemed to wobble, even implode in places.

Like a giant bubble being hit by a stiff wind.

She could resist no longer.

Upon hurling her own bolts of blazing cosmic Tao, coupled with a rain of electron particle beams—each at least a few million volts strong—a gigantic holo-projection popped into reality above the structure.

What fresh hell is this?

As if in answer to Piper's violence, a translucent and

spooky-looking face now hovered above the Dark House. It stared straight at Piper. The apparition closely resembled a human woman, or what pretended to be one. The hair was white as fresh frost, eyes huge and simmering a bitter purple, facial features overwhelmed by a gigantic phony smile that appeared almost comical.

Piper surmised it existed within the protective blister of the Dark House since bolts and destructive energies of various kinds had no effect other than to create an interruptive strobing, the face like an old silent film with select frames cut out.

The mouth then opened. It spoke to Piper:

"I AM THE WITCH EMPRESS, RULER OF THESE LANDS."

The Witch Empress?

Piper was baffled, and upon completion of that absurd and laughable proclamation, the entire Witch Empress face peeled back and gaped to a black tunnel that emitted a shrill banshee howl loud enough to terrify the thousands of rats still left miles above in old Manhattan. The next thing heard was Catherine's telepathic voice, frantically calling out.

"By the eyes of Ahriman, look at what comes!"

Before Piper could adjust her own eyes to focus through the swirl of light and distraction of the strobing Witch Empress face, a distant and swelling chorus of bestial roaring overwhelmed the background noise. She blinked and spun around to behold tens of thousands of winged flying shapes on the horizon, their size increasing as they drew closer, and at a pace hard to believe much less explain.

More Despicables, and moving at Mach II.

141

The scavengers, still munching corpses on the plain, answered the roar with one of their own. Piper watched as the *Dio Soldati* battalion present, at least six hundred soldiers, turned about to direct a hellish fire at the oncoming minions.

Flame-red whips, spurts of annihilating Tao energy, and black-plasma flack spread out for miles and crashed into the ranks of the flying beasts. Whole lines of them either went down in smoke or incinerated to cinders where they flew. Others barked like mad hyenas and soared in great arcs and circles to avoid the killing energies. Still, they came on, as though being manufactured endlessly. *Dio Soldati* farthest out from the Dark House were already drawing their graphene sonic-swords and deploying deadly flanker drones while maintaining full weapons fire.

It's now or never.

Knowing her father and the Czarina Romanova might well disapprove, the Grand Sorceress nevertheless dropped downward and within moments flew less than ten feet above what remained of the newest American dream. Seven or more of the monkey demons, in succession, bared their fangs with a snarl and rose to challenge her. They didn't stand a chance. She immediately down-sliced them into bloody filets with the spell sword of her vision, her *Espada do Ollo*—twenty feet long and slashing out mercilessly before her with enough shimmering Tao to carve blocks of carbon steel. But despite her own contributions to the growing massacre pile, she could not locate Ms. Song, or any part that resembled her.

Piper slowed her velocity and killing pace to exercise patience and thereby make her task easier. But the interminable *whump-whump* pummeling in the air caused her to gaze beyond the nearby carnage.

The Deeper Lands conflict was quickly intensifying and spreading out. It astonished her to see new scores of heavy particle-beams ripping thunderously at the sky and brilliant suns of nuclear airburst rising into the atmosphere at a distance of 200 miles or more. The defense forces of New Manhattan Oz were ramping up to maximum pressure, holding back nothing short of calling in a fleet warship from Earth orbit.

This much firepower for a mob of monkey bats?

Piper's feet hit the ground. Impatient and anxious, she ran among the strewn corpses, and as she did so, began to weep. Less than a minute later, she stopped to vomit, for never had she immersed herself in such a sheer amount of grotesque and pointless murder. She'd viewed gory fields of battle in times past, from Marathon to Normandy, and beyond, but this was worse. The eyes of the dead were mad with terror, whole families tearfully holding each other close as they died, many of them burned down to acid-eaten skeletons.

As she struggled for self-control, her *Espada do Ollo* waved into being of its own accord and decimated eleven more hideous monkey things, each one enraged that she'd interrupted their grisly feast, and each one barking savagely until the last possible moment.

Then Piper found what she was looking for, puzzled together with other grisly human remains. At first, only a fragment of face.

Chariya?

Her eyes were closed, half her mouth open in a scream.

Gods, most of her is gone.

Her right shoulder and arm were attached, the hand clutching onto a shred of clothing. Whoever belonged to the shred had vanished, most likely torn away. If any family remained, they would be unrecognizable now. Piper's only chance was a time reversal spell, like the kind she'd used in Brooklyn to restore the tenement building:

Polo poder de Tao,
Devolver estas vítimas de masacre
A forma completa, bo corazón,
E esencia da auga.

(*By the power of Tao,*
 Return these victims of slaughter
 To full form, good heart,
 And essence of water.)

Nothing… No change.
She repeated the spell. Still, nothing.
This isn't possible.
She repeated it once more, and again, louder each time, until interrupted by a voice that pounded the earth:
"SHE WAS THE LAST TO GO AND SAW ALL OTHERS GO BEFORE HER."
A distraught and shaken Piper glanced up to see the head of the Witch Empress hanging in the air nearby. It had departed the crest of the Dark House and lowered itself to stare at her. As the endless booming of battle continued, the Grand Sorceress of the Holy Roman Empire defiantly scrutinized the giant gloating face, her thoughts beginning

to fill with overwhelming rage.

It smiled that sick plastic smile, unnatural and motionless, its evil purple eyes become a glistening mirror filled with mangled corpses strewn to a dark horizon, but undeterred, Piper bellowed out with a cry that rivaled the ground shaking power of the alien:

"PREPARE FOR DEATH, OH GENOCIDAL BITCH!"

And if anyone still alive could have watched from a distance, they would have witnessed only a half second of blur, straight and true, directly into the mouth of the Witch Empress.

: /

WORLD MAKERS AND MASTER SORCERERS NEVER BLINKED, because they didn't have to. The image of the Witch Empress in Piper's eyes morphed in a millisecond to another face. A face in a quiet place. And curiously enough, the new visage resembled the so-called Witch Empress, as though one had morphed into the other.

Piper paused and stared.

Where the fuck am I?

She sensed she was sitting up, her back against a yielding and comfortable material that felt cool. As the Grand Sorceress she could easily divide her consciousness into parallel tracks, and then some, only now she focused solely on the alien.

Its eyes appeared purple. Piper knew that a cheap coloring process called "iris tinting" made them look that way. The eyes of this smaller apparition appeared sleepy, even sultry, and they blinked in a human manner—eyeliner and lashes dark, though highlighted by a rainbow on each eyelid that occasionally strobed to reveal a different color combination.

Tacky shit for a Witch Empress bitch.

Its hair was dyed a green-hued platinum, down its shoulders and back, thick and straight. Nothing imaginative about it. Facial features average, and the fatty lips, a glistening hue of pinot noir—the source of this obvious as it lifted a glass of red wine and sipped. Following the wine glass, a black Russian cigarette in the other hand came next, glowing brighter as the alien inhaled.

Piper glanced down to examine the rest of it.

Overall, the humanoid disguise emitted a look of exhausted resignation, as though tired of fruitless endeavor. Nevertheless, garment wise, it decked out in a hot red organza gown, a black halter, and to top off the swank, a flashy diamond choker.

Dressed for a glam and sexy evening. Insanely cliché or just insane? I'm not sure whether to laugh or gag.

The alien lifted her left forearm so Piper could see the underside of it. On the pure white flesh appeared a dark flying monkey tattoo. Piper flinched. The alien grinned, lowered her appendage, and said with a deep voice tinted sarcastically Russian:

"Comfortable?"

"Of course I'm not... And you look ridiculous."

Piper tried to stand. Following her astonishment at being riveted, she gritted her teeth and strained until the veins on her neck were ready to burst. She spoke three different spells to counter. No effect. Only her head and neck muscles functioned.

She noted that her butt rested atop a black leather couch, and the small office she found herself in was simply furnished with a gray-ash theme. A single framed painting by Picasso (his hideous and prophetic portrait of Gertrude Stein) hung on the wall, and the Witch Empress sat on a reclining chair, learning forward into Piper's face.

"Let *me up!*"

"No, please, I desire my patients to be *comfortable.*"

"I'm not your patient, space gas."

"We are having a session. I inhabit the body and mind of a Berkeley psychoanalyst."

"You what?"

"Her name is Nina Cohen. Humans claim that Berkley therapists comprehend the human psyche better than anyone else, so I chose her. She is well regarded by her peers in the Bay area. As a bonus I learn so much about human delusion, pride, selfishness, and other weaknesses. She's a bridge into your world, and if not for her, I'd have no baseline, *don't you know?*"

"So let me get this all straight. You're the analyst Nina Cohen, a genocidal Orion alien, and the Witch Empress of Earth all rolled into one. *A fucking trinity?*"

"Not to mention, a malignant narcissist."

"Then you prefer the baseline of an asshole?"

She laughed and gave a little wave of her hand. "Tell me now, do you like my Despicables? Aren't they precious? They enjoy having that little space beneath their ear scratched."

"Those bloody ape creatures?"

Nina grinned and took a drag. "Yes, yes. So very Ozzy."

"By the way, *Nina*, what happened to your narcissistic

twaddle? That bullshit about the *wheels of heaven* that you threw at us a little while ago?"

"I was indulging myself… mmm, special effects."

Piper chortled. "What can you or Nina *possibly know* of special effects?"

"Nina knows about special effects, yes, yes."

"And I know far more than Nina."

"And I might possess you also, as you must realize, but it takes a lot just to keep you here. Plus, I'm still resisting daddy's sad little forces outside."

"I'm surprised you admit your insufficient power."

"Just have to be careful, don't you know?" she said and took a drag off her black cigarette.

"Where in hell are we?"

"My therapist office in the Dark House. I'll soon be opening branches in New Manhattan Oz, lots of them."

"In hell." Piper glared at the ersatz alien analyst. "So this whacked out therapist you've possessed dresses like a retro sex toy and smokes black cigarettes during sessions?"

"Oh, no, no. She fantasizes it. I'm just helping her out, and by the way, she wants to scissor-shag you despite the fact you're an annoying bitch."

"Exciting."

"Nina finds you powerful and sexy, what with your lovely dark hair, super body, and magnetic aura. We can feel it, both of us, really, we feel your interference. Nina's compass points north to the Grand Sorceress," the Witch Empress thing said. Her moist tongue protruded out to massage her upper lip.

For the first time, Piper noticed the shimmering quality

of her lavender eye shadow. She laughed derisively. "Ha! This entire circumstance is *soooo idiotic*. You jump through time to arrive on Earth and begin a slaughter rampage, make threats to destroy everything, then sit here helping a warped Berkeley therapist act out her fantasy sex shit?"

"Theater, darling. I've inherited a human idiosyncrasy for theater. While inhabiting this grotesque flesh puppet of Nina I find it relaxing and oddly rewarding. After all, throughout her life she's been a drama queen, filled with special effects since a child." The alien took another hit of the cigarette before releasing a long sigh of smoke and sound. "Yet another reason to eradicate your species."

"How many reasons do you need?"

"Only one, *don't you know?*"

"Won't you *illuminate me?*" Piper asked with murderous venom in her voice.

The alien executed a barracuda smile. "Your father said it. The answer lies in your culture. It's a reflection of the suppressed guilt you carry with you, because deep inside you know the most important single truth—the fact that you're a bunch of evil little trolls. So, of course, star aliens decide the human species is much too dangerous to be allowed into the galaxy."

"You killed my friend, and her family, bitch witch, and they weren't going into space. So what is— "

"All humans carry the potential to seed themselves, sooner or later, don't you know?"

"If you say *don't you know* one more time, I'm going to rip your—"

"Even if you did, I'd grow another one in seconds."

"And if you really had the power to wipe us out you

would have done so before now, and without a pack of raving monkey asses."

"Yes, but only if I had not occupied the life of Nina Cohen. She likes to toy with people she hates, and she hates nearly everyone, so now I toy with you. That's why I've been mocking and playing with this dark Oz disease residing in the subconscious of your ancient daddy... Tell me now, as your therapist, are you aware that he raped you in Thebes when you were one year old?"

"I'm sorry, psychopath-alien Nina, but repressed memory diagnoses were debunked by real psychologists many decades ago."

"Oh, no, it explains so perfectly why you're flirting with danger and trying to protect others. It also explains why you allowed yourself to be stretched and entered by so many Theban warriors when much younger... all a reaction to being raped by daddy." It said this matter-of-factly and puckered Nina's lips as if desiring to kiss her patient. "You only must admit it, and if you do not, you'll remain a pointless savior all your life... I mean, with what little life you have left," the analyst added with a snarky *you-are-so-dead* grin.

Piper paused long enough to watch the grin leave the face of the Witch Empress whereupon she stated with perfect calm, "I am going to split you apart until not even a solid molecule remains."

Focusing every bit of magical power and will that belonged irrevocably to the Grand Sorceress—as well as to a true demi-goddess of ancient Greece—Piper strained with all her might to snap and scatter the molecular bonds that held the accursed Witch Empress together. The possessed body of Nina Cohen, whatever subconscious or personality bits were left of her, would explode into steam and later fall to the Earth as rain—a small price to pay for saving the world.

"You cannot run from your past. I'm simply trying to help you." Nina raised her lip on one side while observing her patient's throbbing temples and reddening face.

Had it learned that irritating lip raise from its host?

In the face of her enemy's psychoanalytic smirk, Piper spoke the most potent disintegration-and-relocation spell she could imagine, invoking Ahriman himself:

Criatura das estrelas,
Deixe o vapor de auga a átomos
e as sales e os metais
Estoupan no fondo de Marte,
En nome do Ahriman.

(*Creature from the stars,*
   Shall your water now steam to atoms
   And your metals and salts
   Burrow deep beneath Mars,
   In the name of Ahriman.)

At first, the spell didn't appear to work. The Nina Cohen alien face remained calm. The power it possessed dampened the effect, as it had outside. Then Piper heard a strangely familiar voice in her head:

"*Grand Sorceress, I am Maria of Pozzuoli, Catherine's Mother Yarrow. Your father and Catherine have empowered me with their magic to probe the veil of the star alien and find you. The vibrations of your spell led me to you."*

Piper remained focused on the Witch Empress. She knew that between using enormous amounts of alien Tao to thwart the forces attacking the Dark House and holding a powerful magical being hostage, precious little remained to accomplish feats like also piercing the defenses of Piper's mind—which would require force equivalent to blowing the side out of Mount Baker.

"Catherine and your father, along with his army, will focus a new barrage on the Dark House in precisely six seconds. This might allow your spell to hurt the star alien or destroy it. Be brave and concentrate your will."

Four seconds. Three. Two. One.

The face of the psychoanalyst twitched. A small one, though no mistaking it. Within another second, it twitched again, precisely the same way. A replay of time? Piper wasn't certain, but following three more cycles of this twitch, a trickle of blood ran from Nina Cohen's nose and the Russian cigarette painfully singed her pale fingers. As if in response, her eyes flared a ghastly purple and her mouth opened wide and black. She then let out a scream of insane rage that sounded like a cross between a wounded Gila monster and a mad Despicable.

"YEEEEEEARGGHHHHHHHH!"

Following this violent release, she sobbed, as a defeated and humiliated psychoanalyst might sob, and as Piper stared, the Nina thing stood up from her chair and took two steps, still sobbing, tears and blood now running in streams from both eyes.

She bent forward, grasped her patient's face in both hands as if to squeeze it. Her black nails dug deep until

Piper felt her own hot blood running down the sides of her face to her neck, and like the great god of howler monkeys, the alien screeched at her with a head-splitting sound.

"WHERE ARE YOUR LITTLE NATIONS? WHAT HAVE YOU DONE WITH THEM? TELL ME NOW."

Piper smiled and said nothing.

"DO NOT PLAY PASSIVE-AGGRESSIVE GAMES WITH YOUR ANALYST WHO WISHES TO CURE YOU!"

Though the face of the horrid creature quivered and bled, and though the evil purple eyes glared like homicide, Piper realized the disintegration spell had stalled. She was about reboot it when Maria of Pozzuoli interrupted once more.

"Your father says the Dark House is ready to fall. Reach out to me. Let us deliver you from the star alien's lair."

Piper, not wishing to appear helpless, and acting out of pride, deliberately ignored Mother Yarrow's direction and instead refocused her will and magic on a single medallion of her dragon bling:

Dragon volar,
Queimar e engulir agora,
Todo mal e oc.

(*Dragon fly forth,*
burn now and swallow,
all evilness and hollow.)

With the Orion abomination at her weakest, Piper gambled she could unleash just enough scaled chaos to escape the insanity.

Her hunch paid off.

Within a moment, an eclipsing mass of writhing mega-dragon roared to life. The teary and bleeding face of the alien-possessed psychoanalyst vanished behind a crushing wall of dark scales. Two seconds later, a whip of dragon-tail sent Piper whooshing through the back wall of the office like a slapped hockey puck.

Downward she fell into a chasm-like void, throbbing with a splitting headache, and while falling, she could have sworn that from somewhere far away she heard the Witch Empress ragefully shriek:

"I WILL TURN EVERY ONE OF YOUR CHILDREN AGAINST YOU, MACARIA!"

And those were the last words Piper could ever recall from her first and only Dark House therapy session.

Chapter X

Magical Goddesses – Post Finem Confession – Hegemony

AFTER PIPER BLACKED OUT AND AWAKENED in a large and well-lit medical exam room deep in the Operations and Security Center of New Manhattan, she lay on a white bed, looking up and blinking at the shiny med-tech devices pointed at her. She was alone. No alien-possessed analyst or writhing dragon to be seen. Just enough peace and security to render recent events a bad dream.

A turn of her head to the right revealed her monitor read-outs and body analysis graphics. She examined them. All appeared normal. No concussion. Nothing missing. Nervous system untouched. Tao levels spiking high without fever. A pint or so of blood loss due to the black dagger nails of Nina Cohen piercing her face, but that was it.

A turn of her head to the left revealed a large floor-to-ceiling window that looked out over the waters of a small sea a few thousand feet below. Or one of the Great Lakes? She wasn't sure. Hadn't she heard that New Manhattan Oz was drifting slowly towards Chicago? Nevertheless, she remembered soaring though the clouds, thumped by air turbulence along with Catherine and her father on their way down to fight what would be known in future years as the Battle of the Deeper Lands; and this in turn reminded her of taking flight for the first time above the Aegean Sea more than two thousand years earlier, using magic to defy gravity in a way that filled her with awe and wisdom.

Piper closed her eyes and recalled that in her journeys

above the Greek islands in search of heroes, villains, and monsters, she learned compassion for the peoples of Greece, despite their flawed humanity, and vowed to keep them safe.

No longer must they fear the windy seas of forever.

As her thoughts returned to what had taken place hours ago, *or was it days?* Again, she felt confused. Too much humanity, so much death, madness, and violence.

I'm tired. Dammit, tired. I just wanted a new life on Broadway, a few friends, some funny bad movies, a reasonable paycheck, khor stew and beers now and then. Was that too much to ask? It's no surprise Dad returned from the future with an insane genocidal alien on his tail to ruin everything. This kind of situation is nothing new, I know, but after so many centuries, I still haven't lowered my expectations enough.

Her thoughts then turned to Ms. Song.

I listen to my own petty complaints, but my friend Chariya and her darling family were murdered and eaten by savage beasts. What is wrong with me? I don't want to imagine their fear for themselves, and for each other, all fusing into one major horror scream. We promised them utopia and all they found was the worst killing field imaginable.

The voice of a woman clearing her throat distracted Piper. She opened eyes-wide to see Catherine standing at the foot of the medical bed. Her face appeared determined, jaw set, eyes stirring with a need for violence. Her honey-hued hair fell upon her shoulders, and she wore a simple white blouse and black jeans.

"Feel better, Grand Sorceress?"

Piper still existed in the corporeal form of Europe's most

feared master of the dark arts. In her state of reverie, she hadn't thought much of it. Her body had been stripped of clothing and she was naked beneath a white linen sheet. She sat up in the bed, holding the sheet to her neck, and her pounds of brunette locks tumbled down to either side. In truth, she felt grateful for the temporary distraction.

Catherine continued. "We found you unconscious and bloody atop a heap of broken corpses. You have just recovered from a coma."

"How long?"

"Your father brought you here two days ago."

"Where is my bling, and clothing?"

"Hanging in the closet," Catherine said dryly.

"What finally happened in the Deeper Lands? I lost touch during the therapy session."

"Therapy session? Are you now behaving like a foolish comedian?"

"No. You tell me what happened, and I'll explain, okay?"

Catherine took a deep breath. "The Despicables were driven from the skies. Many thousands perished, and most just vanished. Your father assumes they are hiding in a parallel dimension, or in nearby space."

"But I saw megatons of mushroom cloud as far as a two hundred miles away. I don't get it. These Despicable things were just stupid monkey fur. I killed a few dozen myself."

"Groups of them combined in the air to create scores of magic circles."

"Magic circles?"

"Yes, it was odd. They would hold hands, facing out from the circle, and a magic blister shield formed and protected them. Nothing less than our strongest weapons

157

compromised their physical nature."

"And what of the Dark House?"

"Destroyed. Edison was forced to summon one of the ships from the fleet to administer the final *coup de grace*."

"Which one?"

"The *Gallipoli*. A sustained bombardment for less than half a minute relieved us of the Dark House. It shriveled like a burning weed and puffed into nothingness."

"Amazing. Please, let me view in your mind. I want—"

"I will consider your request, though not until you answer a few questions." Catherine looked grim.

"Oh, here we go with the imperious Czarina routine?"

"Your condition does not entitle you to insult me."

"I've told you before, Cathy, I'm not one of your mud-caked peasants or court suitors, and in case you've forgotten again, I'm two thousand years older than you."

"We have already been through this. I have traveled the centuries, fought in a time war, and I am a World Maker. Your mere age is of no consequence."

Piper paused, feeling herself flushed, and said, "Don't poop your pants, but I now have the power of a World Maker. You already know that."

She knew she'd struck home with that comment. The Czarina's eyes flared and cooled again as she struggled for self-control.

"Yes, and yet, you *have not* the power of magical aria." Catherine walked around the bed and drew closer to Piper until only a few feet away.

"But I am as powerful... sorry."

"Perhaps we should test your opinion and powers, Grand Sorceress?"

"Perhaps *we should*, ego maniac Czarina."

Catherine paused, glaring murderously. "Why? Why did your father bestow you with such power? Do you wish to kill me? Did you whine to him I might kill you?"

"I didn't whine. He just knew."

To Piper's surprise, this comment triggered Catherine into becoming teary, and yet, her tight jaw proved that anger fought to reassert itself.

Was she suddenly jealous?

Or was it a tear of ego rage?

Catherine breathed deep several times, chilling herself, and said to Piper, "Mother Yarrow Maria placed herself at risk in attempting to save you. The force that besets us possesses the power to reach down through the centuries."

"We're all at risk, Cathy. None of us are immortal."

"Why did you ignore Maria when a captive in the Dark House?

Piper laughed out loud in a mocking tone. "Because I don't need your putz mother *telling me* what to do."

Catherine dropped all pretense of maintaining control, her blood pressure once more volcanic. "Fool! You are fortunate to even be alive, and your reckless attack and capture are evidence you require a nanny."

"What?" Piper jumped from the bed to face Catherine, holding her bedsheet before her, her breathing deep and furious. "How dare you. I have no need of your mother or you! FUCK YOU!"

Though she often ignored it because it rarely emanated through her Grand Sorceress attire, her "rage halo" now distorted the air into a wavy and translucent scarlet light that haloed her from head to toe. In contrast, Maria of Pozzuoli's war symbols formed—rune-like glyphs in various hues of blue and green, several feet wide, shimmering to either side of Catherine Romanova.

Maria's voice intruded into Piper's head yet again:

"You shall not harm Catherine. Cease your child-like temper."

But this just made Piper angrier. On the brink of catastrophic violence, the locked eyes of Piper and Catherine radiated enough opposing force to melt glass and wither flowers—the core of the effect concentrated south of Chicago—and as in Iceland, a rippling violence seized their limbs and bodies, their flesh furrowing as if battered by wind.

"Tell your mommy to wipe your nose and go home. I'll hurt you on Mars," the Grand Sorceress said.

But before Catherine could reply in kind, an interruption occurred. "Magical goddesses of Oz!" Another woman's voice emanated from the other side of the room. "Please look my way and feel fortunate to be so grand and immortal."

Piper turned to see Alcaeus standing in the doorway. He looked pitiful and downcast.

What was wrong?

Alcaeus continued, "I am sad, dear ladies, for though I treasure life, this new form is wearing on me, and yet, look at the two of you. So powerful, so beautiful, so perfect, and now quarreling like children. Yes, *children*. Please forgive me for being so blunt. I love you both, and worship you."

: /

Czarina Catherine's Post Finem Journal
Year 1 PF – Entry 3

More than ever, I know a day will come when Edison's daughter and I will fervently attempt to kill one another, and only one will survive it. I am loathe to admit this since the admission carries a seed of resignation to the reality that I cannot rise above base impulses. I know I must. I vow to do just that, and I am honest with myself; however, at such time the Grand Sorceress insults and challenges me with her altogether vexing manner, I inevitably lapse into rage.

Though I desire more self-control, I cannot allow myself to be dominated by her, or allow her to believe she is dominating me, and thus I set the stage for more of the same; and this admission is also disconcerting, for I acknowledge I am a victim of my biology. I admit an eons-old predisposition to engage in hierarchical struggle. Can I ever avoid it? Or am I wiser to accept the inevitable prodding of nature, and in due course, suffer through to a victorious solution?

Of course, I can call a truce with her, and she most likely would comply. Still, this does not address the issue just raised. I feel the only logical choice in the immediate present is to keep our terrible tempers separated. Perhaps later, circumstances between us may change. Perhaps we eventually will discontinue behavior which so very much resembles a classic sibling rivalry.

Now, another question I cannot avoid.

In keeping with the above, does the universe deserve such powerful beings who might one day destroy those around them in a fit of primal rage? Do I betray all human life by asking this question, for if the answer is yes, then the alien hostile who calls herself the Witch Empress might well be correct to destroy us. Perhaps the cosmos does need to be saved from intrusion by humans and their primate tempers.

Even if true, I cannot betray humankind, and besides, with the right direction, we can perform good deeds. Our existence has always been a balance of dark and light throughout the many centuries, but is Edison Godfellow truly the light?

I am still deeply hurt by the fact he willingly bestowed his daughter with enough power to injure me badly or even kill me. I understand how Piper views it and I cannot reasonably expect her to adopt my perspective. Knowing him, he most likely views the situation as a balance of power, and after all, he is her father. However, this balance might well contribute to more violence than it solves. It emboldens the Grand Sorceress, no question. I witnessed the challenging defiance in her eyes just hours ago.

Fortunate for us that her old and pitiful Greek philosopher interrupted or we would surely have begun knocking the blood out of one another.

: /

YOU ARE A FLY ON THE WALL.

You've wanted to be one for a long time, but the ultimate decision to do so depended on the existence of a proper wall.

A distinct wall. A wall with a point.

Now you've found one. You felt it necessary because Earth has come under attack, and the conflict gains momentum. All you've dreamed of is threatened.

Humanity teeters on the brink of doom.

You blame yourself for this. However, you tell yourself it

will be worth it from the standpoint of history. Still, you wish to perform some measure of penance for your crimes of hubris.

Being a fly might help.

It is very uncomfortable.

You feel itchy.

The tiny fly hairs on your flesh detect every minuscule vibration of the wall surface. You feel as if you have Parkinson's disease. You can't stop quivering. As your daughter might say, *it sucks to be you.*

Nevertheless, you are under the radar.

Between being so tiny and enveloped by magical static (put there by you), you are protected, pretty much invisible to the prying eye of enemies on any wavelength.

Back to the wall though. It is found deep within the human military complex known as the Pentagon.

But why here?

Upon probing several Despicables following the Battle of the Deeper Lands, you have learned that the Witch Empress desires to open another front on Earth itself, using the U.S. armed forces to spearhead a major assault on select points in the country.

You know such a thing would normally be laughable.

Only now, it isn't.

So here you are, listening and watching while four and five-star desk generals, along with a few sullen corporate contractors in office suits, discuss tactical military options for the long-term goal of achieving a new global social condition they refer to as *Pax Americana*.

And they are not alone.

Strange-looking human hybrids, four of them, are

present also, sitting with the humans around a long mahogany table, the kind of table that demands nothing less than pure gravitas and deadly decision-making.

You ponder this.

Who are these hideous hybrids? Humanoids created by the alien? Transmogrified Australians?

Their flesh is dark, the smooth hue of a Bedouin from Morocco, and they have four arms ending in long and thin feminine-like hands, though without nails. Their eyes are three times larger than normal human eyes and red as rubies. Their hair is extremely thick and black. It flows down their head on one side and wraps around their neck, front to back like a scarf. None wear a stitch of clothing. They appear sexless, muscles flaccid, legs thin, feet still demonstrating primate evolution. Their mouths are lipless.

They speak English with a thunder-down-under accent that sounds ludicrous in comparison to their odd appearance. They promise that advancements in military technology already provided will allow the U.S. Army to vanquish all real and potential enemies. America will effectively rule the non-Oz world, and together with forces from the Galactic Rim, they will rid the world of invading Martians and destroy the Oz city-worlds.

Martians? Galactic Rim?

This jogs your little fly memory.

You chuckle to yourself and the hairs on your abdomen shiver with excitement. The American news media, led by ANN, has accepted the Pentagon propaganda that Martians are attacking Earth. They have sold blocks of advertising in advance based on this ridiculous fiction. Mars has been inhabited all along, and everything that has happened confirms this truth.

Edgar Rice Burroughs is now a prophet.

ANN "news" rolls with the story that the seven Oz city-worlds are Martian traps. Lies. Prisons and torture chambers. Laboratories of ghastly alien experiment wherein Martians are possessing human bodies by the hundreds of thousands.

The Pentagon stars and suits are too willing to promote these foolish and illogical tales. Being group-think morons yearning for the social and monetary advantages bestowed by armed conflict, they have little choice.

Of course, none of this surprises you.

With the promise of super weapons and world hegemony dangled before them like a thermonuclear carrot, it really does not matter to them whether the so-called aliens are from Mars, Middle Earth, or Neverland.

Meanwhile, as ANN media pushes this insane story 24/7, Americans begin to believe it. The mantra is heard:

NO TO MARTIANS. NO TO HOSTILE INVASION.

Everyone who stands against them is a hero.

Anyone who doubts the Martian story is a collaborator to be destroyed by social media.

But now, what about these "Galactic Rim" frauds?

No matter their origin, you know they are charlatans devised by that Orion beastie to trick the gullible Pentagon into working with them. Upon scanning the minds of two or three generals, you learn the "aliens" contacted the U.S. military several days ago. They simply appeared in closed strategy meetings, like Star Trek types beaming into existence, then immediately went into their laughably preposterous act.

165

Martians were their enemy also, and the enemy of their enemy was their friend. Just as the French worked with General Washington to defeat the British under Cornwallis, so too would these aliens from "the Galactic Rim" work with America to defeat the Martian invasion.

"What shall we call you?" asked a general—a rather corpulent man who looked more Irish than Italian.

"Call us... GALAXIANS," said one of the hybrids.

You cannot help but chuckle to yourself once again, your tiny fly body buzzing for half a second. *Galaxians?* Have they been watching really bad movies like you do on Flick-a-Zon with your daughter?

Might they also like khor stew?

Regardless, the stars and suits say nothing. They act as if paralyzed. A few know it all sounds inescapably fraudulent, especially considering the ridiculous Australian accents the "aliens" use, but they are too frightened to ask probing questions or behave as if doubtful.

Next, you attempt to enter the mind of one of the Galaxians. It is dark inside. Chunks of memory appear like windows in a passing train at night. No personality exists.

You enter the train and find yourself in a narrow hallway that leads to a room, and inside that room is the floating head of the Witch Empress.

It stares at you with huge and evil purple eyes.

The lips move. It speaks.

It asks if you recall raping your daughter in Greece.

But you find the question so bizarre you do not answer.

A moment later, you raise your eyes to the ceiling, only there is no ceiling, just a starless sky that opens up like a hole.

Chapter XI

Le Petit Sanglier – The Shadow Brokers – West of LA

PIPER'S FATHER NO LONGER EMPLOYED cloned and polished sex bombs at *Le Petit Sanglier*—a copy of his favorite "cloud restaurant" in London. Gone were extinct actresses from the past century like Monica Bellucci and Ursula Andress. That sexual idiosyncrasy was history. And though applauded by Piper, she nevertheless felt irritated. Why? Because the reason for the change resided in the disapproval of them by his new girlfriend, none other than the great Prussian diva herself, Catherine of Arrogant.

To think, I almost liked her.

Sitting at a table, sipping on a pale and hoppy "De La Senne Taras Boulba" from Belgium and looking like her mango pixie self while waiting for the glowing World Maker couple to appear and hold court, Piper took note of the magi-tech décor that surrounded her. She could not help but respect and admire her father for exercising his quirky imagination in public. People loved it, and it was the talk of New Manhattan.

Massive, insane, and tear drop beautiful, seriously.

Diners found themselves enthralled on either side by massive panoramic views of New Manhattan Oz looking like the most colossal and amazing version of any blazingly lit, dusk-hued, sci-fi super city that anyone had ever seen in a movie or on a book cover. The temperate and breezy air inside *Le Petit Sanglier* smelled of orange blossoms. The background music she recognized as an old song called "Pistolero" by Juno Reactor (the refined version, not the jerky one), and food specialties consisted of over two hundred dishes, mostly Indian, Polynesian, and Euro-fusion. Zero-grav fountains levitated shimmering water in sweeping arcs over the heads of patrons and a huge tele-glass set in a far wall allowed them to view cinematic vistas of the Martian canyon, *Valles Marineris*, at twilight.

The sixty-foot tall and multi-layered "Sapphire Bar" opened wide to the Crab Nebula from only a tenth of a lightyear distant and floated in the air over two thousand varieties of alcohol from the simple to exotic, as well as highlights chosen carefully from every relevant culture, including several famous wines from the Bronze Age.

As she gazed upon rivulets of golden vapor in the Crab Nebula and estimated their temperatures, she finished her Belgian beer and proceeded next to sip her favorite drink from Icaria, circa 400 B.C.—a dark wine possessing a tranquil bouquet of violets, roses, and hyacinth, and at least eight percent alcohol. She much preferred it to those snobby wines from Chios that the Athenians always raved about.

Piper then turned her attention to the new wait staff going about their tasks. Morph-droids, all males now, exclusively old actors. Was Dad trying to prove to Catherine he simply liked actors from that era? Who knows? That would be a lie, of course. But since Piper fancied herself an expert on old American cult movies and television from bygone eras (not to mention Broadway shows, and music—mostly jazz, rock, Segovia, and Tom Petty—especially Tom Petty), she assumed there was virtually no one her father Edison could reproduce and program whom she would fail to recognize. But she'd been wrong a lot lately.

Now he has stumped me.

This fact was nearly as annoying as any thought of Catherine. One single actor glided about in the dining room whose identity eluded her. The rest, however, she knew so well: Bruce Lee, Marcello Mastroianni, Samuel L. Jackson, Godfrey Gao, William Shatner, Dave Chappelle, Peter Capaldi, Helmut Berger, Henry Cavill, Christopher Reeve, John Carradine, and Lawrence Fishburne, among others.

Piper found the William Shatner morph-droid especially amusing. It had tuned and enhanced itself to represent a variety of Shatners, ranging from the pre-girdle *Twilight Zone* Shatner to the botoxed Priceline Shatner, so that each and every hour, a fresh version of "Bill" occupied the dining room. She recalled how the gestures and behavior of the original actor had been so goofy and pretentious as to be comical. She always got a laugh out of replaying in her head Shatner's ridiculously dramatized version of *Rocket Man*—an ancient song by British singer-songwriter Elton John—and of course, his golden moments from the original *Star Trek* were incomparable.

Piper finished her Icarian wine and ordered another from the Peter Capaldi waiter who raised a big black eyebrow at her and sauntered off. She noted that the sun had almost set on *Valles Marineris,* but the smoky burst of Crab Nebula appeared immutable. Meanwhile, the sky above Manhattan Oz darkened to streaks of deep purple and the lines of flying cars turned into lines of tiny stars.

All seemed right, and perfect.

Her thoughts found her father once more. He'd visited her at the medical facility after Catherine departed. His face showed concern. Never had he witnessed his daughter bloody and unconscious. It truly upset him, she knew. He'd held her hand as he loomed above her bed. She told him about the absurd therapy session with Nina Cohen. He stared in disbelief. For the first time in her life, she heard him say, "What the fuck?"

"Piper!"

A man's voice called to her. She glanced up to see *father* and the accursed Czarina sauntering up to the table. Romanova wore a sleek black evening dress, slit up the right hip, shoulders bare, a 20-carat teardrop sapphire necklace suspended above her bosom, and her hair swirled atop her head and fastened with a delicate golden-leaf tiara in the fashion of ancient Roman aristocracy.

She does look quite elegant and sexy. So annoying.

"Back to the mango pixie look?" Catherine said upon pulling her chair out to sit down.

Piper ignored the jab. Once her father seated himself, she pointed to the one waiter she didn't recognize in the dining room, and said, "Hey Dad, who is that one, the Caucasian with the dark hair?"

Edison turned and focused for half a second on the waiter, swiveled back and replied, "Bradford Dillman."

"Who?"

"He acted in a few television programs and films. Rather obscure, but a former cult figure nonetheless... And as a side note, that same morph-droid has duplicated the entire old Kardashian family."

Piper pushed two fingers of her left hand into her mouth and withdrew them. "Please, I'd rather not vomit."

"I have heard tell of them," Catherine said. "The stories

recall the more spoiled and shallow daughters of Czar Nicolas."

"So where have you two *magical love objects* been, dare I ask?"

Why do I even care? So much else is far more important.

Catherine smiled like an old friend in Piper's face, and said, "Edison and I spent a week in the early Paleocene. We watched new mountain chains form, swam the ancient sea above Idaho, and petted the tiny mammals that would one day become us. To say the least, it was a humbling experience. And I was astonished to witness giant flightless birds hunting their prey, as if the dinosaurs were attempting to reclaim the planet once more."

Before another word could be uttered, a dark-cloaked man sat himself at their table. He had appeared from nowhere, said nothing, and once seated, only stared straight ahead with a cliff-like profile devoid of emotion and eyes of solar eclipse. Rune-like tattoos, images, and yarrow symbols tattooed with dark magical inks decorated the left half of his face into looking like a slice of Egyptian papyrus, and his hair, a steely white, shaved close to his scalp. His skin was a unique dark olive in hue, as if born of a Mediterranean race long since perished.

Phoenician? Minoan? Homeric Italian?

"This is my friend, Cereus Malcolm," Edison said with a congenial tone. "He is Grand Mage of the legendary Shadow Brokers. We have known each other for several centuries."

Piper's eyes measured Cereus Malcolm at least six foot seven. The rim of his cloak was etched with yet more yarrow-like magical runes in soft blue and dark blood colors, as well as miniature bits of magical golden bling—elemental, monster, and weapon symbols reminiscent of her own, plus a few things she didn't recognize.

Overall, she had to admit he was rather intriguing.

Cereus glanced at Edison and spoke. His voice was a deep Othello, as British as Piper had hoped, and he said:

"Master Godfellow, we have undertaken your requested tasks, and at your invitation I am here."

"Thank you, Master Malcolm," Edison said and winked at both Piper and Catherine.

Cereus continued. "We have now determined that your pre-transfiguration self does not currently exist in the nearby chrono-spatial plane, and that includes Mars and the Moon as far back as 700 years, Earth time."

"Any possibility of avoiding or misdirecting your trackers?"

"Given that he does not possess access to your Tao reserves, our investigator spells and sensor devices are sophisticated enough to thwart him."

"Conjecture as to location?"

"He assumed the Shadow Brokers would be searching, therefore hid himself deep in the past. He might exist during any major geological epoch or even oscillate between them. He might also employ life-model decoys, similar to the ones in this place, to distract or lead investigators in the wrong direction."

"Yes, that is precisely what I would do," Edison said.

Cereus continued. "Nevertheless, we have instruments calibrated sensitive enough to sense his mind, magic, methods, and every element of his corporeality, enough that he cannot successfully enter this chrono-spatial plane without triggering an alarm. Even a single molecule would be noticed."

"Quite amazing," Catherine said. "I had not realized the Shadow Brokers were so magnificently competent."

Cereus did not reply or turn his gaze to the Czarina.

Edison glanced back and forth between the two of them, then said, "Any intelligence on our ersatz Witch Empress of Earth?"

"On the interstellar side, our astrophysicists detected a Tao birthing nursery in Orion, less than a quarter light year from the spatial coordinates of the absorption attack. It contains unusually high concentrations of energy on the Tao spectrum, so much so that a dozen or more of the young blue suns in the nursery currently radiate hot Tao wavelengths in their coronas."

"Quite frightening," Edison said.

"We theorize that the alien organism from the future originated in the primal Tao space of this nebula. It could be eons old, or even older, and most likely one of many star beings that have effectively evolved their own unique neural astrobiology over the past few billion years. As such, it might well interpret a bio-predatory intelligence like ours as a potentially irksome pest in need of a cure. However, this is, of course, all speculation."

Piper was itching to inject herself. "Haven't you guessed, Master Malcom? It's routine for genocidal space aliens to hate my father."

Edison ignored the snark and focused on the Shadow Broker. "And on the terrestrial side of things?"

"The Orion organism is forming conflict niches, and fronts, on both Earth and in New Manhattan Oz. We see movement on Mars also, however, no details confirmed yet. We have a full report for your examination, and will provide updates by the hour, and on emergency basis as needed."

"But don't forget, this monster can short-circuit our magic," Piper said. "My most powerful chrono-restoration spell failed in the Deeper Lands."

"Yes, we've noted an unusual dampening field in certain locales," Edison said. "It also accounts for the resilience of the Despicables." He turned his attention back to Cereus. "By the way, have your Shadow Brokers observed that laughable alien race with the Australian accent?"

"Yes, the self-dubbed Galaxians. Earth leaders are both baffled and terrified. The aliens are puppeteering them."

"Conjecture as to strategy?"

"The Orion organism wishes to conduct a debilitating form of guerilla warfare, probe for weaknesses, propagandize human victims, and force the fight on multiple fronts, thereby exhausting our energy resources. Also, the potential for reinforcements, whatever form this might take, cannot be overlooked."

"Reinforcements?"

"It should be considered as a possibility in any master defense plan we implement."

"Counter strategies?"

"First, conserve as much Tao energy as possible by extending power loads over multiple fronts."

"Example?"

"Oscillate the protective power grids over New Manhattan Oz and other city-worlds at unpredictable intervals, allowing that power to be transferred to other places temporarily. Protective blisters and shields could then utilize several sources and assist in conserving energy at the same time. In case of sudden attack, instruments and trigger spells could activate reserves at any one point in less than a microsecond."

"Less than a microsecond is not perfect, not as good as continuous opposing force," Edison said.

"Correct, but it does give targets a reasonable opportunity to defend themselves, and at the present, we can more aggressively oscillate power from Oz city-worlds, especially Berlin, to augment the New Manhattan grid."

"Anything else?"

"The Orion alien is prototyping its universal attack strategy in New Manhattan while rationing energy expenditure—most likely exacerbated by the fact that opposing forces are employing enormous firepower in seeking its destruction."

"Additional thoughts?"

"Utilize Combat Sorcerer teams, *Dio Soldati*, and Hellfire Units now idle on *Superna Humanitas* ships. Create strike forces composed of all three and rotate them between the ships and conflict points. Sync them with ship artillery systems. Also, maintain continuous application of force while in the midst of rotations."

"EMP tactics?"

"An Electro-Magical Pulse bombardment strategy for Earth, and insertion of spell-morphed spotting and sabotage teams to direct fire and wreck enemy operations. EMP effects would also encourage kinetic force options, thus conserving energy resources even further."

"In other words, I'll soon be able to smash Nina's

smirking face with an iron battle axe?" Piper said.

"Who is Nina Cohen?" Cereus said without looking at her.

Piper gaped at him as if astonished. *"Don't you know? Um... you're the big Shadow Broker wazoo."*

"Piper!" Her father glared at her.

"I'm sorry. Obviously, she has only appeared to me."

"Your so-called *psychoanalyst?*" Catherine said.

"Why would I make up something so absurd, Cathy? I'm telling you, this alien putz from Orion, by human standards at least, is mentally fucking ill."

Cereus finally turned to focus on Piper, his huge pupils eclipse-black, irises terrifyingly blazing with a halo of solar corona. "The primary Orion antagonist posed to you as a *psychoanalyst?*"

"Yes. A deranged and hateful therapist from Berkley."

Cereus paused. Piper scrutinized him closely.

He's really mulling this one over.

"What did she tell you?"

"She wanted to have perverse sex with me, claimed my father raped me thousands of years ago in Greece, and generally acted like a trippy and frivolous asshole... and she also interrogated me as to the location of those under my protection."

"Nothing else?"

"Oh, and that her personality is required to translate our human world to her more ignorant Orion self."

"Yes, I see. The analyst serves as a reality translator, an *interface being*. Without one, the Orion organism would exist here in a confused state." Cereus said this and swiveled his head back to a neutral position.

Just as Catherine appeared ready to ask a question of Edison, one of the waiters, Piper's newly discovered Bradford Dillman, strolled up to the table to take orders. Desiring a new drink with stronger alcohol, Piper ordered a double-shot Singapore Sling. Edison ordered a bottle of 1938 Chardonnay from Burgundy to share with Catherine. Cereus said nothing. Edison then added a round of Malaysian chicken satay and Dungeness crab deviled eggs.

In a rather demure way, Catherine placed a hand on Edison's forearm and spoke directly to him. "A new subject. What is the solution to the flow of Earth migrants into the Oz city-worlds?"

"Steady in most parts of the world. In the United States it has sputtered due to press and government efforts to hold onto what little control remains, however, we cannot allow any new crossovers into the Deeper Lands due to the threat, therefore, we are relocating immigrants around the globe into Earth orbit with the *Superna Humanitas* fleet, and like the fleet, they exist in a spell-state of *Tempo Lento*. They will remain until we, uh, can solve our... problems."

"*Uh?*" Piper said.

Before Edison could muster a reply, Catherine posed a question. "What transpires now in the Deeper Lands?"

"The Dark House rematerialized," Edison said. "The *Gallipoli* fired on it once more. Hours later, it reappeared and again was obliterated. But other rearrangements of matter are occurring down there."

"Such as?"

"The Deeper Lands of New Manhattan Oz appear to be transforming into four distinct quadrants."

Piper cut in. "But that is... "

"Like Oz," Edison said. "The original Oz was divided in like manner, with the Emerald City at the hub, and it consisted of the Munchkins, Quadlings, Gillikins, and Winkies, each ruled by its own dictator witch."

"And this mockery of Oz?" Catherine said.

Cereus cut in. "Similar to the Galaxian genesis. Anomalous organic inventions are currently morphing from the topsoil of the Deeper Land quadrants. A portion of them appear humanoid with golden skin and exaggerated genitals, while others mimic centipedes, also several tall stick figures with beetle-like heads. In one quadrant, extremely large bio-stone monoliths are ploughing through the crust to take up positions in a variety of lines and clusters. We are not yet certain what this means, or if a greater strategy is in effect."

Piper noticed a taint of fear on Catherine's face.

I knew her fear like a hot stone.

The four of them continued to discuss the current state of being, including the fact introduced by Cereus that Galaxians had hollowed from the mountains east of LA a major production and staging area designed to open an assault front on that side of the continent. Microscopic and magically shielded spy nanos of the Shadow Brokers had pierced the mountain defenses to get a brief glimpse of activities inside, and before winking out, sent back images of hundreds of hybrid war machines under construction, as well as Pentagon brass types in attendance, more than a few Galaxians, and to the surprise of Shadow Broker intelligence, what appeared to be excessive numbers of Despicables caught in the act of labor rather than slaughter.

Cereus said the American military brass refer to this coming counterstrike on the west coast as "OPERATION STORMING OZ."

Piper noted her father's reaction.

Dad looks ready to blow.

"Then we must devote sufficient resources to prevent this utter absurdity," Edison said.

Minutes into the conversation, the Bradford Dillman waiter appeared again. He pushed a cart upon which rested their drinks, wine, and appetizers. He silently distributed them around the table, opened the bottle of 1938 Chardonnay, and poured a small amount in a wine glass for Edison to sample. He tasted it, nodded approval, and Bradford poured a full glass.

Upon accomplishing this task, the waiter's left eye popped from its socket and rolled down his chest. It fell to the table and skittered across the surface as if made of glass. It stared at Piper as it went, and just when she reached out to seize the glistening eyeball, a long puff of vapor, smelling of Russian cigarettes, issued from the gaping eye socket. Wreathed in smoke, the waiter blurted out with Nina Cohen's snarky Russian voice:

"*Don't you know?*"

Piper gasped.

Cereus Malcolm rune-gestured with his left hand and the possessed morphdroid burst into hundreds of confetti-like bits before swirling into a vortex and vanishing.

All at the table sat in stunned silence.

After a pause, Edison held his wine glass before him and with a dark look on his face, he said:

"Imperatrix Venefica delenda est."

The Witch Empress must be destroyed.

Chapter XII

Murray's Baggage – Martian Tripod – Massacre Near Bloomington

PIPER LAY PRONE IN THE STARLIT MOJAVE desert behind the trunk of a big Joshua tree, staring out to the western horizon at a California mountain range now darkly ominous in the cobalt twilight. And though a cooling breeze ruffled her short dark hair, the sand still burned her skin and nested like a gritty rash on every part of her body. To make matters worse, a pesky chigger had inserted itself into her brown cotton shirt and dug its way into her jeans. It loved her new blood. One nasty and inflamed bite itched her left forearm, and while lying there, she scratched it with her chin stubble.

The stubble of a man named Murray W. Runyon.

For the first time in her life, Piper realized an advantage to male face stubble.

No sub for magic, but it works.

She lifted her binoculars and slowly scanned the range. Nothing amiss about the silent, lifeless mountains, though she knew it was here, east of San Bernardino, where the hundreds of new American war machines, Pentagon types, Galaxians, and an army of Despicables went about their ominous task.

The deadly assault wave that would erupt from those mountains might happen at any time. Of course, the orbiting fleet could unleash enough force to bombard the whole area into a smoking crater, but a Witch Empress blister-shield in existence meant the force needed to smash through and pulverize the military base would also destroy all life for a radius of over 200 miles.

LA and surrounding cities would evaporate.

Piper lowered the binoculars and sighed as she reached one hand down the back of her pants to scratch her firm and itchy man butt. So how had it come to this? She'd been asking herself that question for days, and now, considered it once more.

In order to take on the role of a disguised partisan fighting heroically for the "United City-Worlds of Oz"—a quasi-political entity declared by her father following dinner and several more rounds of drinks at *Le Petit Sanglier*—as well as the future of Earth itself, Piper agreed to temporarily possess the corporeality of 44 year-old Murray W. Runyon, and to her growing discomfort, that included the psyche of Murray's brain.

Therefore, to her lasting sorrow, Murray's issues became *her* issues. But she wouldn't complain too much. Extra Murray baggage meant she could play an effective game of hide-and-seek inside his nervous system should any Nina creepers come sneaking around with telepathic probes.

This clever disguise tactic of "neural insertion" worked also for her special ops team who'd been downloaded by Edison into various other sad and desperate refugees now awaiting Piper's reconnaissance report at none other than the famous Bagdad Café in nearby Newberry Springs. These included Cereus Malcolm, along with his sidekick djinn, Tazamat, and Piper's old friend Alcaeus (who she'd strongly objected to but relented once she fully understood the details of neural insertion).

Alcaeus had practically thrown a tantrum to join her, and

Piper understood. Just flittering about New Manhattan Oz in the form of a New Guinea cannibal pygmy had begun to unhinge him a bit. Too many reflective surfaces, too many WTF stares, and besides, his *raison d'etre* needed a good oiling.

Nevertheless, if Piper's host, Murray W. Runyon, perished in the service of humanity, no matter how (bullet, death spell, nuclear blast, black lightning, etc.), Piper's neural "soul essence" returned to her pixie body, now protected within a multi-shielded cell secured deep inside her father's flagship, the *Caliburn*—a slick and powerful fleet battlecruiser in stationary orbit above the western United States. This rescue failsafe also held true for Cereus, Tazamat, and Alcaeus as well.

However, Piper still entertained her doubts.

Is it failsafe though? Given the inability of my Tempo Inverso to save Ms. Song in the Deeper Lands, nothing is really failsafe. It's stupid to assume.

Piper had to admit that poor Murray and the three other hapless humans possessed by Piper's allies had even less chance to survive, far less. However, death would not come easily. Godfellow science injected a stream of Nano-Magical Bio Modifiers days before Piper took possession.

Once the NAMBOMs fused with the molecular bio-essence of their hosts within an hour, they became undetectable, dissolving to imitate stray minerals in the bloodstream. As a result, the hosts gained greatly increased stamina, strength, and healing ability, as well as enhanced senses and agility, plus an immune system that could whip the bubonic plague in fifteen minutes.

I won't let you die Murray, not if I can help it, and I can't fool myself out of responsibility if you go down, but if that damn star monster wins, you're dead anyway.

We're all dead.

Before she could advance beyond that grim musing, a distant and strange rumbling to the east distracted her.

Sounds like giants moving furniture.

She glanced in that direction. The scalp of a red-orange Mars poked over a broken black horizon. Moments later, small flashes of bluish-white light appeared in the distance and near the ground. *How many miles away?* She wasn't sure.

She heard the distant sound of rumbling once more.

Piper knew that low grade electricity and a few radio frequencies were still allowed, though other energy manifestations were being intermittently interrupted. Fleet ships in Earth orbit generated enough EMP to prevent Witch Empress forces from gaining ground or engaging in magi-tech infiltration in California beyond the periphery of the mountain blister shield; and of course, the sheer amount of terawatts the accursed alien needed to maintain the blister in defiance of the EMP relentlessly sapped her strength.

The forces of Oz were fighting back, in part by using her own tactics against her. Though at such time the shield finally lowered to allow the Despicables and American war machines to deploy, Piper, Cereus Malcolm, and a cohort of Shadow Broker combat sorcerers—cocooned in secret beneath the Mojave sands—would channel enough raw Tao from the *Caliburn* to incinerate the base.

But if I were planning tactics inside that mountain base, what would I do to counter whatever we might do?

As she pondered this, a nearby rustling sound interrupted her thoughts. She glanced to her left and saw a Mojave kangaroo rat sniffing the sand. It raised its head to stare at her, squeaked and hopped as if surprised, then scampered away to the north.

As Piper watched the kangaroo rat vanish with Murray's eyes, she saw something else very odd. An eerie, deep violet glow emanated from the earth a hundred yards or so north in the direction of the rat. It pulsed for a few moments and disappeared. A part of Murray's brain responded with fear and it brimmed over into Piper's consciousness. She gripped the sand with Murray's nerve-shaken hands and attempted to calm himself.

Shut up, Murray. We're fine.

Piper shook off the adrenaline and raised the binoculars once more. Mars rose higher, red and huge, creating an eerie effect on the sand and mountains. She scanned the horizon from left to right. Then she saw it and gasped. A dark tripod shape moved silently against the stars—a cowl-like crown above a cylindrical command box, and attached beneath, three tall spider-like legs propelling it forward, bending at the knee-pivots. Piper calculated it was at least 70 feet tall and less than two hundred yards away.

By the American gods, straight out of H.G. Wells.

She continued to watch the tripod. It paused and the head swiveled slightly, as if it had spotted something. A pair of spotlights snapped on from beneath the cowl, pouring intense, hot beams onto the ground about fifty feet ahead of it. Piper heard a *THUP-THUP* sound, and again, *THUP-THUP*.

Kinetic missiles. It fired at a target.

The tripod's spotlights swung higher and swept the area. Piper rolled behind the trunk of the Joshua tree and froze as the intense light bathed the sand around her. After a few seconds, it winked out. She glanced from behind the trunk and saw the tripod poised motionless, its cowl dimly reflecting Mars. As she stared, her Murray hands resumed shaking and the tripod swiveled north, lurching into motion at a quickened pace, as if recalling a rendezvous.

Piper waited about five minutes until it was out of sight. She scanned the horizon in all directions one last time, and getting to her feet, stood and ran fast as her enhanced man legs could carry her towards the site of a possible homicide. It took less than 20 seconds.

She halted and glanced around.

The rising planet illumined the desert with a ruddy glow as if she were standing on the dawn surface of Mars itself. Nothing suspicious at first, then she found them. Four of them. A young Latino family—mother and father, two young daughters, both less than twelve years.

Their faces, paralyzed by the tripod, still gaped in terror as their bodies sprawled across the sand, each of them displaying a perfectly round and bloody chest hole.

: /

Czarina Catherine's Post Finem Journal
Year 1 PF – Entry 4

Once more, the War for Utopia is being fought, and now on two fronts. The frustration suffered by Edison is like nothing come before. The self-proclaimed Witch Empress is possessed of more wits and strategy than he believed possible, but too, there is a childish and absurd aspect to the alien's personality. I would expect this given its origin as a "star being" from Orion. However, the conception of this alien in the form of a California psychoanalyst seems a bit too absurd. I thought perhaps the grand barista pixie suffered from a case of addled wits due to her Dark House experience.

It seems though, I am wrong once more.

She has now joined that rather inexplicable Cereus Malcolm in a mission on Earth. The Shadow Brokers were only whispers and legend to me until I set eyes on him. He reminded me of a cross between a contained Tao explosion and a dark cosmic plague. Unquestionably, a stoic and sinister brilliance about him. Nonetheless, both he and the grand pixie are now in disguise as downtrodden American civilians. Edison has stationed them just outside a major enemy base in southern California for the purpose of observation and directing a likely assault.

I confess it amuses me that she now finds herself in the body of a failed neurosurgeon turned cheap entertainer. It must have been a shock to fully realize it, even though her father explained things before the neural insertion process took place.

I confess I do not look kindly at myself for this state of being. At my core, and in my lack of defense, I am still human. Being a World Maker does not alter that fact.

My amusement is short lived in any case.

I will soon be helping to direct the war front in New Manhattan Oz—a territory larger in neo space than several Earths combined. I volunteered to function as the Transitional Governor for Defense and Pacification.

I know Edison sees it as appropriate given that in my other life I am Czarina of All the Russias. Nevertheless, he believes the alien has created a "back door" in the Deeper Lands and is utilizing this to funnel physical forces and magical Tao, thus retreating and counterattacking in oscillating fashion. I believe the door could simply be his spatial bridge to Mars, and the alien is magically cloaking forces as they move back and forth. Edison too believes this type of chess game is possible, though he fears more than one door accomplishes this same purpose.

Once I oversee and secure the defenses of New Manhattan, it will then be my task to locate the primary door, pass through it, and direct fire on any resources hidden and stored for purposes of war. When the time comes, I will inhabit a corporeal life model via neural insertion. This will be a magical copy of me down to the molecular level. Like his daughter, I will lie in state on his flagship, Caliburn. I know he believes this will protect me from deadly harm. I know he is worried about me because he loves me, and more worried than he shows. The power and unpredictability of our enemy is the cause.

Unlike him, I will not believe any of us are safe. This alien force from Orion possesses the power to rip me from this ship and obliterate me, mind and soul. I know it. Its power was evident from the first moment I encountered those evil monoliths in the Deeper Lands. It can kill the Grand Sorceress also, and Cereus, and all the Shadow Brokers who ever lived. It can dice and scatter us like bits of shriveled weed on the sands of Mars. The only thing preventing such a condition is the sheer amount of force being directed by Edison's fleet employing the Tao from Jupiter. That is why the so-called psychoanalyst could only dig her nails into Piper's face and scream for her submission.

If our reserves falter for whatever reason, even for a moment, and the alien's energies and vigilance maintain, we shall all perish, and the worlds and peoples we fought for will become naught but cinders floating amongst the bleakest of stars.

: /

WHY DID THE TRIPOD MURDER those innocents? Was it under orders to keep the Mojave periphery clean of human life? Given the sheer amount of power protecting the Witch Empress Pentagon base, it didn't make a lot of sense to Piper. Perhaps it was just an experiment, a prototype, or worse yet, the vanguard of a new tripod army being created for EMP-like environments.

She pondered a solution with Murray's hand propping her head as she leaned against the roof edge of his cranky old Ford Taurus. She'd driven it for over an hour down a dusty desert road to within two miles of her observation post beside the Joshua tree. That was three hours ago. Now the wind blew up from the south and shivered her. She gazed up to see the full magnificence of the Red Planet in the night sky.

Princess of Mars, we could be heroes, just for one day.

She raised her head even higher to stare straight up at the star hive of the Milky Way. *So much space. So much time. What difference will it make? Why must it hunt us like a starving wolf? ... And what if this Orion alien is like the tripod, simply a programmed cleanser on automatic? Whenever it senses intelligent life, it reverts to a cosmic psycho killer. If so, then maybe this war was inevitable no matter what my father did or didn't do. Maybe even hundreds of civilizations we'll never know have been obliterated since the dawn of the galaxy. The demon narcissists who set this monster in motion wished to wipe*

189

out any technologic intelligence that might later challenge or threaten them.

Piper heard a coyote howl somewhere far away.

Or maybe I'm full of shit. Too many Doctor Who reruns.

Would her silent Murray host agree? She wouldn't raise his consciousness enough to ask him. *He might totally freak.* She knew way too much about Murray W. Runyon, alias "Mr. White Keys"—a self-hating former neuro-surgeon from Kansas City who one day three years ago stupidly botched a delicate surgery on a five-year-old child and never forgave himself. His guilt infected Piper. That small and innocent child died for no good reason. Piper keenly felt the pain as it grew fingers and played piano memories of old Billy Joel in cheap hotel lounges from St. Louis to Albuquerque.

Drunkenness, loneliness, broken dreams.

She saw the frightened face of the young girl, Emily Glen, and her mother Ariana weeping, and the agony of worry on her father's face, and too, how they each had put their trust in him.

In her.

She needed a drink. She yearned for a piano.

Gods, I hate this two-body shit.

Guilt over the death of the child had become a habit for Murray. His penance never ended, perhaps never would. It seemed so small a thing in relation to the massacre and stakes realized the past several days, but it lodged irrevocably in Piper's mind like a quivering fault line.

I'd wanted a new life, and now I have it—a used one in the Mojave Desert just off Route 66. Karma or catastrophe? Murray might have been chosen by my father for the disruptive baggage that inhabited his guilt-ridden brain, perhaps to teach me a lesson.

No surprise there.

Piper loaded herself into the old Ford and drove away as quietly as possible down the dark desert road towards the main highway. No headlights. If a tripod detected her, Murray became a burger meal for Gila monsters. She recalled vividly how he came to be where she was, and how he'd met his companions for this insane and nearly pointless mission.

: /

SEEKING REDEMPTION AND A NEW START like so many others living in a nation soiled by corrupt leaders and the failure of old dreams, Murray had packed his toothpaste, razor, a few clothes, and left Albuquerque in search of the "Oz Miracle Tower" recently captured by news cameras floating west towards Chicago. And why not? He lived alone with nothing to live for. No obstacles. Only regrets. Besides, social media was aflame with rumor chatter that a new order of life awaited—one much better, and free of the American life sicknesses he knew so well.

But it wasn't going to be easy.

South of Bloomington, Illinois, the traffic on I-55 became more congested, even dead stopped for hours at a stretch. Murray left the car at intervals and mingled with other puzzled escapees. Campfire coffee and sandwiches were shared with people just as nervous and hopeful as he was. To the northeast, like a towering dim ghost above the treetops, they saw the mythical new Oz, said to be near 60 miles high at its pinnacle. Dream-story beautiful and spectral at nights, its uppermost reaches softened to become as one with the stars.

Where trouble melts like lemon drops.

"New York is up there, way high, I heard tell," a middle-aged guy from Iowa said to Murray one night as they stood by the roadside, lifting their faces.

Kids cried in the background. His wife was shouting.

"New York over the rainbow, eh?" Murray said. "First New York, then Berlin."

"I don't understand it," the man said. "You think we have a chance?"

"We have little or none here... What's to lose?"

"But all that news stuff about Martians attacking—"

"ANN bullshit," Murray cut in. "You can't trust a damn thing they report or say. Take it from me. They invent the narrative ahead of time and follow a script." Murray lowered his gaze and stared at the man. He saw fear in his eyes. He desperately wanted Murray to make his fear go away.

It wasn't possible.

"Well, like you say, we've got nothing left to lose, and we're free at last," the man said and chuckled awkwardly. A moment later he turned and walked back to his distraught family.

Soon enough though, life got ugly.

Thousands of people had been stalled on the highway for nearly two days. A fog shrouded the trees on either side. The promised land of Oz had become anxiously invisible due to the weather. Fights broke out over food and accusations of theft. Dogs whined and barked at everything. Games and booze eventually prevailed as social groups formed and melted away.

Murray observed a bunch of neo-hipsters join a hairless drug cult in a bizarre ritual they called "The Dance of Circles," and he listened to a woman with a beautiful voice singing "Somewhere Over the Rainbow" through a megaphone. From where, or how far away, he wasn't certain. Before the song could end, he heard her voice sputter and go silent as if an angry loser had snatched the megaphone from her. This moment of silence was then followed by a loud crunch, as if the same loser had smashed the megaphone with a rock.

After a burst of irritating static, another woman's voice, stern and authoritative, echoed through the foggy trees and slammed against the miles-long, twisted cavalcade of metal cars and SUVs. The air itself became one long tuning-fork shiver as her insanely amplified voice repeated over and over:

TURN BACK! BY ORDER OF THE PRESIDENT!

People began jeering and shouting.

Within a few minutes, their voice of resistance became a roaring chorus of long-stored hatred. "FUCK YOU!" half of them shrieked loud as they could, "FUCK THE PRESIDENT!" and "FUCK THE GOVERNMENT!" and they wouldn't stop, not even when dozens of U.S Army jeeps and converted police vans arrived on the scene, honking along the sides of the highway and even driving boldly over parked vehicles, grinding them down to flattened junk as their hapless owners watched and yelled angrily.

Murray saw a mob attack one of the big military jeeps that had just squashed a young woman's car. They pelted it with stones while PA speakers mounted on the roof blared stern warnings to stop. But it was no use. One of the hurled stones struck and dislodged a speaker. It broke off and hung by a thin cord down the side of the jeep.

At that point, the jeep's occupants made a huge mistake. The vehicle halted and the passenger door opened. A U.S. army officer in camouflage and red beret jumped out and yanked from his holster a ferocious black automatic. He shouted but the noise of the crowd overwhelmed his voice. He fired two booming shots in the air and waved his free hand as if to wipe away the apparition of those people screaming at him. It did no good. He fired one more shot, and in response, a savage human tsunami bowled and rolled him.

As they surged forward and began kicking him to death, two other soldiers were torn from the jeep and pummeled with fists and stones to a bloody mess. More U.S. army types came running up from the line of military vehicles pushing along the edge of the woods. But more mob had also formed, and they too rushed forward, intent on killing these reinforcements.

A few civilians must be dead. This won't end well.

By late afternoon, every Pentagon soldier and military "psyche advisor" sent to bully the Americans into retreating lay dead or dying, except for those on the periphery who viewed the homicidal chaos from a distance before backing up and speeding off.

By 5 PM, the crowd had dispersed and calmed. A few dozen men and women took possession of a cache of steel-piercing automatic weapons, grenades, and RPGs. What they planned to do with them, Murray had no idea. One stood on the hood of an army jeep and waved his arms, apparently exhorting those in attendance to violence in the name of a new America.

Meet the new boss.

Shortly after 6 PM, a shaky and hungry crowd heard what sounded like a train getting closer. Curiously enough, the train chugged through the fog above their heads. Murray glanced up to see six Army attack helicopters suddenly descending from the mists about a mile away to the north. They reminded him of black rodents with grinning teeth, and as he watched, they split into a flying-V attack formation.

No, it's not possible… They wouldn't.

Before he could fully grasp what was transpiring, the insane reality of weapons firing thousands of tracer rounds into the people on both sides of I-55 had succeeded in murdering, or at least mortally dismembering within 20 seconds, nearly every man, woman, child, and dog luckless enough to be targets.

Like so many others in a state of panic, he scrambled and fell more than once attempting to escape the slaughter. Dodging and weaving, his mind filled with bloody screams and earsplitting gun thunder, he made it to the tree line and dove forward just as the earth behind him was chopped into sloggy chunks. And like others who survived that day, he hid deep inside the forest until the sounds of the killing and shrieking had died away to a silent darkness.

: /

"SLAUGHTERS ON THE ROAD TO OZ!" one woman exclaimed, her face a spasm of twitching cheek muscles.

"ANN reports that the White House terms it justified retaliation against Martian sympathizers and terrorists," one man angrily said.

A dozen or more bedraggled American refugees sat huddled in the half-lit and chilly dining room of the Baghdad Café in Newberry Springs, California. Piper Robbin, alias Murray Runyon, was among them. She'd just returned from her surveillance in the desert, parking Murray's car around the back. Twice she'd stopped on the way and scanned the horizons to make certain no tripods were following.

Those refugees present in the café had fled the "Martian Oz nightmare exposed on ANN," and now they watched the ANN news channel on a wafer-thin digital tv someone had set on top of the bar. Fortunately for their starving paranoia, trickles of electricity still flowed in southern California. Updates on Martian invasion, the threat posed by the New Oz, and efforts by the American government and military to save the country overwhelmingly dominated programming. Piper knew the ANN talking heads were no longer human, only Galaxian homomorphs manufactured for news broadcasting.

Lies invented by alien puppets and voiced by pseudo-human frauds. Would Orwell be surprised?

What appeared to be ANN's most popular broadcaster, Don Ramond, blared out that Pentagon "anti-infiltration actions" were taking place around the country. Hordes of hostile and armed Martian minions had been caught trying to escape back to the New Oz—now drifting towards Minneapolis. Pentagon spokespeople have informed ANN that "containment and cleansing will continue until no

Martians, or their sympathizers, are left roaming free on American soil."

Only preservation of the homeland mattered now.

According to one ANN homomorph: "Oz is a floating prison and human re-education facility created by Martians. New York was the first casualty of the invasion. Millions captured by the Martians are dead or presumed dead."

Both Piper and Murray had heard enough.

"GODDAMN BULLSHIT LIARS!" Piper shouted, standing behind the cluster of transfixed and fidgeting refugees.

They turned with shocked faces to stare at a vibrating scarecrow of a man. The man spoke again. "I was on the road to Chicago near Bloomington. Six Army attack helicopters swooped down on us and strafed the highway, killing thousands of people, women and children too. They showed no mercy!"

No one replied. Who would dare to contradict?

"*Bullshit*" she mumbled to her Murray self and stomped out the front door, letting it slam behind her.

Walking to the rear of the café, she paused and glanced around before going farther into the desert behind the building. In the Martian-lit darkness, she stepped quietly past the strewn rocks and cactus until she arrived at her HQ more than fifty yards south: a makeshift tent of filthy white sheets clipped together and propped off the Mojave floor by rusted rods she'd cannibalized from old Chevy axels and suspension parts. This "yard" behind the café, littered with junk cars as far back as the 1990s, created lots of potential for artistic effects and creative living space.

The sheets of the tent dimly glowed, lit by a small fire

inside. Piper turned to lift her binoculars and scan the horizons for tripods one last time. Feeling reasonably safe, she raised a corner of one sheet, and stooping down a bit, entered and sat down before the fire, now fizzling down to a few licks.

Sitting directly across from her was Cereus Malcolm in the body of a mature San Manuel woman by the name of Kayla Valbuena. Her black hair was snapped behind her head in a ponytail. She wore heavy red lipstick and mascara, dark gray jeans, and a colorful patterned cotton shirt covered with Native American symbols. Her face appeared stoic in the fire glow. She lifted her deep azure eyes to stare at Piper.

To Kayla's left sat the djinn, Tazamat, in the body of Kayla's son—a small San Manuel boy of nine named Manny Valbuena who stared absently into the flames. To Kayla's right, Piper's eyes settled on Alcaeus in the body of a teenaged Pakistani girl named Shazadi Masood whose leg had been amputated half-way up her thigh. Such distortions were necessary for Alcaeus due to the insidious nature of the Dardanos spell. Of course, he hated it, but his faculties were sharp and his new looks certainly did not inspire revulsion. His host's hair was very long, braided, and dark as her eyes, her head covered by a scarf of red silk that also circled her neck.

These "refugees" were frightened and helpless people that Murray had met and picked up on his way down Route 66 to southern California. Like him, their original destination was somewhere between San Diego and Santa Barbara, and like him, events of recent made them desperate enough to seek any remnant of family left alive.

Besides, if the new Oz was a trick and the Martians were invading, what else could they do? Not one of them trusted the ANN stories either. They felt oppressed, squeezed between implacable forces and chased by lies.

Murray had a sister in Rancho Cucamonga. Cheryl Sloan. She was married with children. He hadn't spoken to her in years, though to his knowledge she'd never moved.

Piper raised both Murray's hands into the air as Cereus watched, and she signed with them:

Are we safe to talk?

Cereus reached into a little pouch on Kayla's belt and withdrew a small handful of dark, seed-like objects which he threw into the fire. Within moments, it began to make a crackling sound.

"*Now we are,*" Cereus said with Kayla's husky whispering voice. "*This method is safer than telepathy at the moment. What transpires at the café?*"

"*ANN is keeping us apprised of the Martian invasion,*" Piper said, also whispering. "*I saw a tripod war machine roaming the Mojave about ten miles from here. It murdered a small family then vanished north.*"

"*Taking no chances,*" Cereus said.

"*But it seems a waste of resources.*"

"*Perhaps they simply enjoy murdering humans,*" Tazamat whispered with Manny's voice, never lifting his eyes from the fire.

Piper had never met Tazamat before this night. Like other djinns, he was born of a powerful spell that had turned an unruly clan of neolithic Irish Celts into mysterious and magical creatures who broke their bonds and eventually spread around the world. Her father understood them much better. He told her once to never trust one. "Unless on a leash or under a sword, djinns are dangerous," he said. "They hate humans in general, and they hate the British even more."

As a reward for being so cantankerous, not many djinn were left alive. How many? Piper had no idea.

"We have information from the Caliburn," Cereus said.

Edison Godfellow had arranged info drops via meteor. After all, the Mojave this time of year was prone to hundreds of them. The drop-off point was 20 yards further south. Manny would wander around looking innocent, picking up stones, playing with them, tossing a few, pocketing a few.

"Many Despicables who once occupied official positions in Washington have returned post-mortem, accompanied by Galaxians. None dare question. The original corporate president, Elizabeth Bosworth, has returned also. A press conference introduced America to the Galaxians."

"To those bug-eyed freaks?" Piper rolled her eyes.

"Human fools and cowards," Tazamat said, still unmoving.

Cereus continued. *"The U.S. military, now under direction of the Galaxians, have executed over three million people seeking refuge in the New Manhattan Oz complex."*

"By the gods," Alcaeus said, his shock evident in Shazadi's startled voice.

"Sew your lips, Athenian," Tazamat said.

"Additionally, fleet IO has learned that shielding over the Pentagon staging complex has been transformed into an intra-solar portal field. Anything attempting to pierce it, from a microwave transmission to a meteor, vanishes and

reappears on the fringe of this solar system a few million miles north of Pluto. We believe this was accomplished primarily as an energy conservation measure."

"The solar system, Macaria?" Alcaeus was clueless.

"Rocks in space." Tazamat finally lifted his head to stare at Alcaeus as if he were a blithering idiot. Then he turned to face the others. "The tripod may be your answer to penetrating the mountains."

"Elaborate," Cereus said, his Kayla eyes mirroring the fire and scrutinizing the djinn boy.

"Witch Empress legions are protected, though blind inside their mountains due to the nature of the portal field. Even light cannot pierce it. The tripods therefore must serve both a sterilization and reconnaissance function."

"But in order to relay their observations, the tripods must also rotate in and out of the field at precise points."

Cereus nodded. "Precisely. There must be hidden physical tunnels that pierce the field from the inside out. It is also logical to assume that the tripods collapse and compress themselves into ball-like shapes and roll into these tunnels, and that the tunnels possess doors."

Piper cursed under her breath, and said, "But a version of their EMP is probably infecting those mountain chambers as a safety precaution, so even if we got inside, we would be—"

"Nearly helpless," Alcaeus said.

"No more so than you are now, human." Tazamat couldn't help himself. He was apparently determined to punish the Greek as often as possible.

"So what's next, oh wise Tazamat?" Piper asked. The arrogance of the djinn was beginning to annoy both her and Murray. *"Hijack a tripod and climb into it? Bait it with your face?"*

Manny's innocent face spread in a wide grin. *"In truth, you can do little or nothing to prevent Witch Empress plans in the west from unfolding,"* he said. *"She would love for you to penetrate the mountain stronghold. You would be seized like mice and tortured with nerve needles for days."*

"What are you grinning at, you little putz?" Piper was inches away from smacking a child's face with Murray's hand.

"Enough, Tazamat," Cereus said, scowling with a mother's full power. *"This baiting helps us naught."* His Kayla face then turned to the others. *"The Shadow Broker mages are poised. The fleet is poised. All we can do is wait."*

"Even your waiting is futile," the Tazamat child said to his mother. *"Do you not think their forces have knowledge of your plan to bombard them the microsecond their shields come down?"*

"Damn you, Tazamat," Cereus said with Kayla's temper.

Piper was a bit surprised at this show of emotion, though she quickly refocused back on Manny. *"How do you know so much, djinn?"* Piper fished in Murray's top shirt pocket to withdraw a thin marijuana doobie which she lit on a burning piece of wood in the dwindling fire.

"Little shits like me know things, Grand Sorceress," Tazamat said, lowering his lip to a pout. *"Can I have a puff of your doobie?"*

"I don't want your kid germs."

"Doobie, Macaria?" Alcaeus was puzzled again.

"You are such an imbecile for a Greek," the djinn said.

Cereus threw more seeds into the small fire. It flared and

crackled again.

"*I'll put this out on your face, Taz, if you don't show respect,*" Piper said and took a long drag of the doobie with Murray's mouth until it glowed brightly.

Tazamat produced an expression of mock horror. "*As I was saying, Theban, they must know we will attack immediately. Logically, the only realistic solution available to them is high-velocity kinetic dispersal.*"

"*Clarify, Tazamat,*" Cereus said.

"*At the appointed time, the shields vanish, and in one thousandth of a second, or less, dispersal missiles are fired, boring through the rock and flying at an instantaneous speed of at least Mach 18. Once they reach their west coast targets inside of a minute, they release pods which then disperse their legions of war machines.*"

Piper nearly disagreed but paused. The annoying djinn child had a point. "*The fleet exists in Tempo Lento. They'll still detect the launch, but—*"

"*Attempting to intercept in Tempo Lento, or otherwise, will not matter. We exist in an EMP environment, and Witch Empress forces can immediately extend, reinforce, or oscillate EMP to ensure the success of the kinetic dispersal. The fleet does possess kinetic interception devices, however, not enough of them timed and tuned to stop the enormous amount of ordnance that will come flying out of those mountains at the appointed moment.*"

"*Like hurling stones when rain dampens fire,*" Alcaeus said to himself.

"*Then the only real solution is to prepare adequate defense in the target areas,*" Piper said.

"*You win the grand prize, Theban, and this expedition we*

are on, here and now, is both ill-thought and foolish. Has that occurred to you yet?" Piper remained silent. *"Is it possible your father sent us here for another reason?"*

Tazamat went back to staring at what remained of the fire. The tent was silent. Piper took another drag of her doobie, held it for a moment, and expelled. She stood up on the legs of her Murray flesh and left the tent. She walked slowly towards the sound of music in Baghdad Café. *Johnny Cash?* Inviting, yes, but Murray was loathe to return. So was Piper.

She stopped, took one more doobie drag and flicked away the butt. She knew that damn snotty djinn was right about everything. Body hijacking these people wasn't necessary or purposeful. Using them to skulk around the Mojave and dodge tripods was ridiculous.

Damn the gods, I feel like such an ass. Still, he could be wrong. Nina Cohen acts like a frivolous idiot. With her at the helm of the Witch Empress invasion, who knows what they'll do.

Piper lifted Murray's sunburned and greasy head to the stars and again stared at the Milky Way. She could never get enough. *So much to know. What do you think, Murray?* He didn't answer. And as she lowered his head a few seconds later, she felt a hand touch the back of his shoulder.

Piper turned to see Kayla Valbuena only inches away. Her face was soft and beautiful in the Martian night, her eyes reflecting the stars like a dark well filled with little specks of twinkle. Her expression was amorous. Piper was speechless.

In low and husky tone, her voice spoke the words of

Cereus. "Kayla Valbuena finds you sexually attractive. I cannot explain it. The feeling is nearly overwhelming."

Piper was aware they were vulnerable, their speech vibrations no longer jumbled by fire crackling. "Well, um, Kayla, I don't know what to say... Things have been crazy and I haven't been up to feeling much of—"

Kayla took a step forward and hugged Murray, her face close to his ear, and she whispered, *"A drone or some such is watching us from above. Indulge me."* Kayla's lips found Murray's and they kissed, long and deep until she pulled away, and said:

"I love you, Murray."

Piper remained speechless.

They just stood there, eye to eye, Mars casting their shadows on the sand. Kayla dug one finger into Murray's back. Piper thought she heard the sounds of Tazamat scuffling with Alcaeus in the tent.

"Are the kids fighting again?" Piper's Murray voice said.

"Yes, we better go and check," Kayla replied softly.

They walked arm in arm back to the tent. Once there, Piper used Murray's hand to open the makeshift flap. They both gasped to see a furious Shazadi beating Manny over the head with her artificial leg.

Then the unexpected happened.

A sound. A very loud sound.

The loudest Piper had heard in over two thousand years. It smacked her into near concussion. She felt so dizzy that Murray's body quivered and he puked onto the sand.

What in hell? How many sonic booms at once?

Kayla screamed in terror. Piper turned to see a thing huge and black crashing down from the air onto the

Baghdad Café. It flattened the ramshackle structure, and without pause, rolled like a bowling ball straight at them, unfolding as it came. Twenty yards away, it stopped, and with a *click-clack-click*, rose straight up on three legs.

Piper stared, speechless once more.

An enormous and horrific Martian tripod now loomed over them. The black cowl tipped down and a triangle of dim red eyes regarded them with a dark and sinister intelligence. Beyond the cowl, Piper noticed hundreds of bright, meteor-like trails stretching across the night sky. Many objects had been hurled at once into the air on low trajectories, and at air burning speeds towards the west coast.

The war is on. The damn djinn was right.

Piper clutched the Kayla of Cereus with Murray's hands, lifted her up and began to run with her as fast as possible. Though Murray's speed was faster than a galloping thoroughbred, it was still a ridiculous and useless move. Where could Piper be running with him? With her? More importantly, what would become of Murray's guilt if it ended now?

Piper heard a *THUP-THUP* from above.

Kayla's chest exploded over Murray's body. He was soaked with her blood and bits of heart. Murray's ears also picked up the sound of Shazadi screaming. Still holding a dead Kayla, he swiveled around to see Manny running from the tent, only to be cut into quarters by another shot from the tripod.

Piper fell to Murray's knees and gently laid Kayla down, face up to the stars. Her mouth and eyes displayed her joy at the time of death.

So strange.
And this was Piper's last thought in Murray's brain.

Chapter XIII

Golden Winkie Copulations – Cavity Invasion – World War Oz

KNOWN AS *LA STELO PUNTERO*, THE OPERATIONAL headquarters for the first "Transitional Governor for Defense and Pacification" sat like a vast and lofty penthouse of the gods upon the miles-high crown of New Manhattan's tallest starscraper. The interior consisted of a vaulted, cathedral-like ceiling supported by giant arcing ribs of red-hued Martian granite, as well as spearhead-shaped "leaf windows" fifty feet high and twenty feet wide (21 of them for the seven sides of the Heptagon) that overlooked a dozen or so ethereal sky islands—each window also serving when needed as an intra-solar portal.

Several mahogany roundtables and chairs floated without legs above a floor of azure-marble tile, and seven magical statues of blackened bronze as tall as the windows dominated the periphery of the Heptagon, each in its own wall niche: Zenobia of Palmyra, Maria of Pozzuoli, samurai Tomoe Gozen, Artemis of Ephesus, Fire Goddess Pele, Death Goddess Kali, and Triệu Thi Trinh—all of them gazing down judgmentally upon human occupants within their space.

Unpredictably they would sigh, perhaps moan and stretch, or even issue forth with an occasional echoing laugh of caustic bronze. Bits of conversation would pass between them like low whispers of turning screw, and even the Transitional Governor, Catherine Romanova, never knew precisely how they would behave on any given occasion.

Earlier, her Mother Yarrow Maria had felt flattered and provoked upon seeing her own likeness in the chamber. *"One day you will know my presence warmer than bronze,"* Maria whispered to her upon viewing the Heptagon with Catherine's eyes.

Only now, such matters were of no concern.

Military updates from Edison Godfellow and Oz Ops informed Catherine that new battle fronts had opened in North America. New Manhattan Oz itself existed in a state of fear and disbelief, and she became intent on discovering the whereabouts of her own terror in the Deeper Lands.

Four cinematic *Fiestra na Vida* spells, or "life windows," each several feet in diameter, floated in the air before her. She could step through these windows and be wherever they focused, even beyond the solar system. If one FnV spell lingered above a stream in the Amazon rainforest, she could reach out to feel the water trickle upon her fingers.

Utilizing them, she scanned the mutant Oz quadrants which were now relentlessly overwriting much of the original Deeper Lands. From a height of a few thousand feet, the quadrants combined into one huge rectangle as if surrounded by a fence, and in the center of the rectangle, the Dark House of Oz resurrected once every three hours. As it faded into view, the *Gallipoli* would open fire with a surgical salvo of black plasma. But the interminable and repeated sequence of creation and destruction had become farcical. She failed to comprehend the motivation behind it.

Did the Dark House need to exist in an unbroken continuum, or were these snippets of time sufficient for a sinister purpose we have yet to discover?

Continuing to scan, she next focused on the western quadrant, known to classic Oz literature as the "Winkie Country." She marveled at the natural beauty Edison had bestowed upon it: thousands of lakes and interconnecting rivers steaming off clouds of fog that drifted high above shadowy blue woods. Peering closer though, Catherine noticed what appeared to be roads, or perhaps even a crude highway system, and as her eyes traced these white lines twisting through the forests, she discovered to her astonishment a number of quaint, village-like communities built of river cobblestone and cedar logs, and nearby, parallel crop lines of wheat and corn.

Her curiosity was keenly aroused. Most American immigrants, to her knowledge, had been killed, and the Deeper Lands ruled unsafe until further notice.

Then who in Beelzebub's name built these habitations?

By her will, the *Fiestra na Vida* magnified one of the villages. Catherine witnessed nearly a hundred beings of humanoid appearance strolling about and engaged in various labors, as well as conversing with one another in a language that sounded vaguely like ancient Slav. They appeared to be of at least three sexes (male, female, and fem-two), and their skin was a golden hue, a rich buttercup in the shade, and they all went about their business hairless as well as shoeless, dressed in white, blue, and dark brown tunics pulled tight at the waste by a thin rope. Staring closer, Catherine could see their long broad noses and high cheek bones, and most startling of all, their eyes like caps of spotted white toadstool.

The world seemed calm to them. No craziness or anger.

Catherine telepathically penetrated a young woman

who appeared twelve or thirteen. Her friends called her Toolee. She'd grown up in the Winkie Land of Oz and lived there long as she could remember. Her family habitated nearby in three huts of wood and roof straw with mud brick fireplaces. Her mind recalled nothing unusual or terrifying. She'd seen no Despicables, or monolith monsters, or any gross beastie things, only the meadows of Winkie Land as she skipped through them chasing delicious boolee berries that flitted like purple butterflies on wings of seed.

She'd also seen her parents having sex many times. They coupled in trees, beside the creek, in the lake shallows, just about anywhere you could imagine. Sometimes she watched other Winkies too, pods of them writhing and feverish, and she yearned for the day when she could join them.

Toolee believed that stars copulated also and birthed little stars, and that her people were watched over by a very potent ruler god—a fem-two named Ozma who delivered babies of sunlight each day.

Sunlight babies?

Catherine now felt more perplexed than ever. Here was a neolithic civilization of oversexed and hairless golden humanoids, not only with their own god, but with select memory implants of a traceable past created to prevent existential psychosis.

Could this be an organic outcome of Edison's machine, or a machination of the Witch Empress? And if the latter, should they not be destroyed?

No matter. She'd find the time to search out answers, but not now. So many other matters were pending.

Less than an hour later, while exploring the so-called

Munchkin quadrant in the east, Catherine found what she'd been searching for. She stared aghast at thousands of them rising above the green grasses of a rolling plain, poised on the brink of Martian desert, arranged in concentric circles and spread out for scores of miles.

Curse your souls. Have you consumed the Munchkins?

As she contemplated drawing her black-plasma Glock from a concealed pocket under the table and squeezing off a few rounds of megaton through the *Fiestra na Vida*, she thought better of it, and instead, spoke Galician words of magic which ignited to life the molecules of a special gift her lover Edison Godfellow had created exclusively for her:

Polo poder cósmico de Tao,
Deixe este heptágono
Aumentar a miña aria.
e dame a vitoria agora.

(*By the cosmic power of Tao,*
Let this Heptagon
Enhance my aria,
and give me victory now.)

Edison termed his special gift an "Aria and Magical Enhancement Web," or ARMEW for short. Rather than a stand-alone device, the substance of ARMEW blended and spread in web-like manner within the huge arcing ribs of Martian granite that supported the 40-ton black obsidian roof of the Heptagon, thus creating an umbrella effect of both absorption and magnification.

Upon the unveiling, Edison said to her:

212

"With Tao, and tech as amplifier, your magical aria becomes truly invincible. You will be able to reach out a thousand lightyears and crush the hull of an enemy warship like paper, or at the same distance, grow a nation's worth of apples on the nearest Earth-like planet within minutes."

But let our guard fall, my darling Edison, and a thousand times my aria will not be sufficient. Though perhaps it will be sufficient to eradicate these monsters of your subconscious Picasso.

However, before she could unleash her actual aria spell upon the monoliths, a small face suddenly appeared at eye level a few feet away—the face of a djinn, rather furry and lemur-looking, eyes big and dark as walnuts, elfin-like ears twitching as if swatting tiny insects.

It just stared without blinking.

"Who in blazes are you?"

"I am Tazamat," the djinn replied with the voice of a boy.

"Is that your real voice?"

"It is now. I was recently a boy in California. I liked it."

"What became of him?"

"Killed by a Witch Empress tripod."

"Tripod?"

"Ask Master Malcolm to explain it, when you see him."

"Alright then, state your business, djinn."

"I have been ordered, Czarina, to restrict your use of ARMEW until support from the *Caliburn* can be coordinated."

Catherine paused, then said with ire in her voice, "Not even a single eye blink, should I need one, will be *restricted* or controlled by a djinn, much less one with the voice of a child."

"It is by order of Master Godfellow," Tazamat said.

"Then I will speak to him personally, meanwhile—"

"He simply wishes to 'have your back' if you battle against Witch Empress manifestations or minions."

"Do not interrupt me. I require no nanny djinn."

"Honestly, it's your little butt, he worries about," Tazamat said with a mocking falsetto voice, followed by a slight belch.

"*My little butt?*"

"Yes! What else but that sexy atomic Prussian butt?"

"How dare you, cretin! I'll spell you into ugly slippers!"

The face of Tazamat vanished suddenly.

Catherine seethed in anger. She clenched and unclenched her fists as she turned her head again to glare once more at the circles of dark monoliths. Were they moving? Focusing closer, she saw the same quivering on their surfaces—like the hides of animals upon emerging from a river; and too, they created many mouths on themselves, dozens on each monolith, and as she watched, they demonically spoke these words in unison:

"CZARINA OF ALL THE RUSSIAS, WE AWAIT YOU."

To herself, she said, *Careful what you ask for, oh monoliths of perfect hubris.*

Just as she was about to summon her aria again and engage ARMEW to incinerate them, a small amber light faded in and grew brighter above the center of her desk.

It was her appointment reminder.

Heaven and God, not now!

Rant and complain if she must, she knew she could not avoid her immediate fate: the impromptu "city council" of New Manhattan Oz. She'd made an appointment with them via their nosy chairperson, one Rachel Dickens, so she could hear their "complaints" and answer questions. It would be an easy tact to spell them into quietude, but not ethical or fair.

I will live to regret this. As a matter of fact, I already do.

A tall door of polished dark oak swung open at one far end of the Heptagon and the "council" walked in. All five of them were local women. They nearly stumbled in a state of amazement as they gawked at the Heptagon interior. The looming warrior idols glared at them and made subdued tittering and disapproval noises. The group halted for a few moments, gazing up at them anxiously, but seeing Catherine's beckoning hand, they composed themselves and continued forward.

For the occasion, she'd dressed more formally, as befitted an Oz top government executive: emerald-black jacket and matching skirt, white blouse, a lovely jade-silk scarf, gleaming silver bracelets set with magnificent emeralds, and low-heeled shoes of Corinthian black leather. In truth, she greatly preferred her simple jeans and characteristic cotton shirts without adornment. Besides, why must she put on special airs for such paltry and irksome people?

Next time, I will descend from the ceiling as a naked golden giantess wielding a broadsword while the Heptagon idols clap.

Catherine motioned for the "council" to be seated on the various float chairs. They did so in awkward and skittish fashion with lots of nervous laughter.

Are the lemmings simply imitating one another?

Their elected chairperson was the first to speak. Her

name was Olivera Dickens and she appeared a very thin and hollow-eyed person with "evolution hair" that curled and colored itself every few minutes.

Catherine found it impossible to disguise her contempt.

"Madam Governor, please tell us... I am the appointed spokesperson, as I said, and we believe it is our right to know all the facts."

Millions in jeopardy from the Witch Empress, America now a human shooting gallery, legions of mutations sprouting in the Deeper Lands, and I must endure this?

"What *facts* do your sacred rights demand, Ms. Dickens?" Catherine asked coldly. "And to make it clear, you have no authority here, by vote or otherwise. I am extending time to you because I know you are concerned, and that time is nearly done."

Olivera glanced around the table for support from the four other women who quickly averted their eyes. Catherine knew they were all former Manhattan divas accustomed to wealth and privilege. What did they have left to do these days other than complain about trivial matters?

Must I give this woman a coin for courage, or is she a fool?

Olivera turned her gaze back to Catherine. The thin woman appeared considerably less confident than only moments before. The presence of fear in her companions shook the foundation beneath her feet, the gravity of doubt beginning to assert itself. Before she could speak again, Catherine said:

"Ms. Dickens, I am doing my best to secure a beneficial future for us here in New Manhattan. We do have issues. This entire process has been a thing unknown to this world, and—"

"But we need to know things... We might wish to leave."
The little mole interrupted me.

"There is *no place to go*," Catherine said forcefully.
"People on the outside seeking harbor here are being
executed by the American government as traitors and
Martian sympathizers. Do you wish to die, or be imprisoned
at best?"

Olivera's face began to shiver. She covered the lower
half with one hand and spoke softly between her fingers,
her shoulders beginning to shake. "We might die here also,
and uh... we heard stories, um... about a massacre in the
Deeper Lands?"

Catherine paused and said, "The Deeper Lands are not
ready for occupation. We are in the process of continuing
adjustments. You will be informed. Meanwhile, you have
the glory and wonder of New Manhattan Oz within which
to revel and breathe the air of freedom."

"Freedom?"

The other four women shifted in their seats. Catherine
sensed that two of them were preparing to flee the room.
One spoke up and said to her Queen Bee with a meek voice
of British accent, "Please, let us... leave the governor *alone
now?*"

Staring fixedly at Olivera, Catherine continued.
"Freedom from the vices and ugliness of life in old
America—bad health, endless war, vicious factionalism,
and rampant poverty to name a few? The entire country
was a slow death for nearly all."

"Yes, um, of course. I understand. Oh, and thank you for
the new therapy offices," Olivera said, lowering her hands

and attempting to smile. "We do need therapy now, even if it makes us face the horrible truth of paternal rape or alien invasion of our lower cavities."

"What?"

"In summary, thank *you again*, madam governor."

She and the other women stood to leave, awkwardly bowing and walking backwards towards the door, as if to turn around would mean instant death.

Catherine stared at them with a baffled expression.

Lower cavities?

: /

PIPER ROBBIN WAS HELPLESS. WORLD WAR OZ was exploding up and down the Pacific Coast. Nothing could have prevented the dramatic ejaculation of Pentagon armor and tripods from the Mojave base. Given the prevalence of strong EMP deployment on both sides, nearly the entire western U.S. remained immune to virtually any type of useful Tao wavelength. Thus, the *Superna Humanitas* Fleet, the Shadow Broker mages, the *Dio Soldati* brigades, and other magi-tech combat units were severely compromised.

A grim reality now faced the forces of Oz.

The Witch Empress was winning.

The U.S. Army, prodded by her phony Galaxians, engaged in the pursuit of Oz and Martian "sympathizers," while California, deemed a hive of rabid discontent, became a primary target for retaliation. Several million human beings from Sonoma Valley in the north to San Diego in the south were potentially at the mercy of rampaging war machines and flocks of human-eating Despicables. The east coast too was in flames, the Atlantic surf red with blood down to St. Augustine.

Piper paced in her quarters on the *Caliburn*—a small and relatively spartan room with a few fern plants, a self-warming cot, two float chairs, and a wall-sized window facing the stars. There had been no time for closure following the death of Murray Runyon. He'd exploded into pieces and in response she cried out, thrashed and collapsed in the neural insertion compartment on the *Caliburn*. The techs helped her to stand, gazing at her with pity, the whole show witnessed via telepathic monitor feeds, so much so that Murray's anguish and guilt unavoidably infected all involved. Piper felt her deceased other self in them like a spongy wall of pain that yielded to her touch.

Damn, this is horrible.

And where was her father? She needed to talk to someone. She could not go back and fix Murray. Would she ever? He was dead, the rest of them killed by the will of the tripod. Time spells were faltering or failing due to the war and would continue to do so.

Where was Tazamat? Alcaeus? Cereus?

They must be as split in the head as I am.

She shed her pixie clothes and with a yawn of routine magic acquired the face and form of Bianca Capello, the Grand Sorceress of the Holy Roman Empire. She then shed most of her attire, including her cape and magical bling, and simply sat on her cot in a short tunic staring at the sweep of the galaxy.

Piper knew she would return to Earth, as soon as

possible, and help lead the fight on the west coast, come what may, even if her father tried to prevent her, or neurally insert her again—which she would decline. The death and life of Murray were too real, and though a spell could surely soften the blow of his existence within her, Piper wished to keep him alive. He'd settled in her like warm and bitter toast.

She told herself that duality was ultimately a good thing. *I love you, Murray. Maybe we'll meet again yesterday.*

She recalled too the odd reaction of Kayla with the mind of Cereus. Her face close to Murray's. Their kiss in the Martian night before death claimed them both.

So strange.

"Yes, it was."

A startled Piper turned to see Cereus Malcolm standing near the door in the shadows, staring at her in a way only he could. In the darkness of the room, his eyes shone like distant soft fires. She could barely see the rune-like tattoos and yarrow symbols on his face, though noted how they streamed down his neck onto his chest. He wore a loose-fitting shirt and his magic cloak clipped from the back to his waist, thus covering the upper part of his thighs, and he appeared huge to her, a poised and ominous bird of prey.

"I am sorry to have intruded," he said with his deep Othello voice. "An unusual transference occurred between Kayla Valbuena and me."

"How so?" Piper asked.

"Her attraction to Murray, bordering on love."

Piper could not help it. She began to breathe heavily. "And so, you feel this now?"

"Yes, and I confess that in centuries past I have, at times, been enthralled by you in your role of Grand Sorceress."

"Enthralled?"

"I once witnessed you battling the magicians of Empress Maria Theresa in Croatia. You were fearless and countered their every move."

"Oh, right, *those bastards*... Maria hated me because I refused to kiss her royal butt wagon."

"No matter."

Those solar-eclipse eyes. I cannot look away.

For the first time, since last making love to the rugged captain of the HMS Phaeton at the Battle of Jutland, her nipples grew hard and thrust against her blouse. She knew Cereus saw them. She heard his breath becoming stronger as he drew closer through the shadows of the room. Within moments, he towered over her.

"May I touch you?" he said.

"Yes."

He reached out with one hand to stroke Piper's thick dark hair. She observed every muscle in his face. That grim, cliff-like look softened in the darkness, almost as if he were mesmerized by her. His hand moved onto her shoulder. She unbuttoned the blouse and slipped it from her shoulders to the floor. He gasped to see the size and firmness of her breasts and the rolling-hill musculature of her upper body. She compelled her nipples to grow even larger by a third, and reaching up, drew his hand down to touch them. She heard his breath intake sharply, and she realized he was honest about having been enthralled by her for centuries.

Cereus has imagined this moment for a long time.

Piper smoothed both hands down her waist to her hips

and whatever she wore below the waist blended with the shadows until she was completely naked. She then pulled him closer and lifted her face up to his, and they kissed, long and passionately. His hands enclosed her in a hug and gradually slid down her back to grasp her buttocks and knead them, pulling her closer at the same time. Soft noises droned from his throat to create a unique warbling sound.

He's warbling with ecstasy.

She continued to kiss him, playing with his tongue, biting him on the lips, thrusting her body against his. She felt him growing bigger and bigger beneath his cloak. She parted it, and it fell away, vanishing like her own garments.

So large, so perfect.

With one hand she grasped his huge and beautifully sculpted member and stroked it until his entire body shuddered and he said in a low voice:

"Bianca... no language is possible."

My Holy Roman name.

Hooking both arms around his neck, she exerted enough pressure to allow what came next. He clutched her buttocks and upper thighs, raising her into the air and onto himself, sliding into her easily. She groaned and locked her legs around his waist. In over 20 centuries, she'd never felt such erotic pleasure.

Was it magic or just natural for him?

Inevitably, the two of them rose into the air, thrusting at each other madly, both crying out with unleashed pleasure. Over and over, as if on a sexual rotisserie they turned, her mouth clamping onto his neck and biting down like a succubus while he covered her face with kisses.

Upon completing a fourth rotation, she glanced down to

see a dark streak of land surrounded by a calm, aquamarine ocean, and while she continued to writhe with his powerful thrusts, she noticed the two of them were dropping downward. A glance to her right filled her eyes with a black night above a horizon of blue.

Methane. A planet like Neptune.

Seconds later, they came to rest like feathers on the shore of a soundless methane sea. The liquid lapped at their sides as the result of deep planetary quakes, and the roiling heat of their sexual sorcery turned nearby methane puddles into gas. Like a pale vapor, it rose into the windless space above. Piper glanced up to see it swirl before cooling once more and sleeting down upon her like a fine ice-mist.

So bizarre. Lovemaking in a methane fog. Gentler than I expected, yet still a fierce twist within me. Oh my gods, don't know how he's doing it, must be magic. He thrusts into me and pushes us down farther and farther until we're beneath the methane ocean plain, through the molten magnetic hurricane of planet core, and into space, skipping like a rogue comet above those solar eyes of his. I am so ravished beyond the memory of such things, the muscles in his fingers kneading my consciousness until my cosmic vision increases a thousand-fold. I now see millions of suns wrapped by their worlds, my mouth deep in his neck.

I want to drink his blood.

We make no sound, we cannot speak.

His blood courses down my throat.

"*You are such a marvelous being, Bianca, and so absolutely beautiful, so fine and straight,*" he said to her, mind to mind as he came at last. For a full minute he warbled while the magical glyphs on his face and chest glowed a ruddy gold until his final long release.

"*Ahhhhhh, damn your Hemingway,*" Piper said before discharging a pint of warm love. In less than a quarter of a second, her fluid became a sheen of twinkling silver crystals misting onto her lover's stomach and hips.

Then all was still.

They held each other atop her cot, back on the *Caliburn*.

Cereus was first to break the wet and fragrant silence, his face grim as the moon.

"Bianca, darling, you must return to yesterday."

: /

PIPER HEARD IT TOLD LATER THAT IF YOU LIVED in the Los Angeles burb of Rancho Cucamonga or San Bernardino, or anywhere else in the "Inland Empire," and glanced upward at dawn (on the same day the Witch Empress's forces birthed like hyperbolic demons out of the Mojave), you would have observed tens of thousands of stars glowing bright as Venus from north to south across the morning blue sky.

It would have puzzled you.

Did they all take a vote and decide to go nova?

No matter. The world around you is ending. The local news carries stories of giant pods hurtling into the Pacific, hundreds of them, and live-action film of the California shoreline depicts alien machines by the thousands rising from the water and charging onto the beach.

Below, the news ticker reads:

MARTIANS ATTACKING CALIFORNIA
MILLIONS IN JEOPARDY

But it doesn't end there. In the hours to come, you watch gigantic trolls of bi-pedal metal romping up and down Route 66 like hellish warrior tribesmen. Ripping through the malls of San Bernardino, their multi-barrel 70MM guns fire at civilians—including women and children who flee in hysterics. No less deadly, rank after rank of Martian tripods in disciplined firing lines stalk and sweep the stucco-hot neighborhoods with shrieks of sonic cannon. To your horror, whole rows of houses, palms, and parked Toyotas burst into flaming shards. The totality of noise is deafening. And as if that isn't bad enough, flocks of furry black-winged apes sweep down from the sky in waves, thousands of them snarling and swinging giant bloody axes at the necks of innocent bystanders until the streets fill with rolling heads caught in mid-scream.

Then someone shouts, "What the hell is that?" and points into the air. You raise your head and follow that finger to see the numberless and inexplicable morning stars you'd witnessed earlier now evolving to fiery meteors with long tails.

Rocks from space raining down on California.

Or might it be something else?

You're not sure, but if you know just where to look, and you happen to possess a very good telescope, you might well observe the Grand Sorceress poised within a sheath of blazing air molecules. You will also note her goddess-strong arms extending straight ahead, her long dark hair whipping behind, and an atom-honed sword of gleaming graphene strapped to her back, not to mention a belt of sonic grenades girdling her waist.

You might not actually know her, though you certainly will marvel and sense from her determined look that salvation is at hand; and later that night, if you live long enough to dream, you will awaken and realize that you are irresistibly falling in love with her.

:/

PIPER SAW HERSELF AS A REAL HERO plummeting to Earth in her black tank top and magically reinforced, graphene-fabric slacks tucked into shiny jackboots. Flanking her on all sides were thousands of other falling stars: elements of the Seventh, Eighth, and Ninth *Dio Soldati* Corps assigned to the fleet.

Seven divisions total, 3000 combat units each, had launched from the battle cruisers *Caliburn, Sun Tzu,* and *Belalcazar* to drop towards the Pacific coast at an average speed of 63,260 MPH. Joined by a few thousand War Meteors (WAMORS)—each fitted with an AI "No Mercy" CPU and built to fight in EMP environments—their duty was to defeat the alien forces and save as many civilians as possible.

Only two hours before, Piper had left Cereus to ratchet a full day back in time on the gears of his magic. She thus balanced duty with her sexual recovery from the traumatic slaughter in the Mojave. As she coupled with an aroused Cereus in her room on the *Caliburn,* she simultaneously addressed the *Dio Soldati* Corps officers and troops in the ship's massive deployment bay.

She mounted a dais and her body grew to a magnificent eight feet in height, tall enough for all to see—her presence strong and stunning as a birthing sun, her voice loud enough to shake the air:

"SOLDIERS OF OZ. WE NOW FACE OUR GREATEST THREAT, AN ENEMY BOTH TENACIOUS AND MERCILESS. WE MUST NOT REST UNTIL IT PERISHES WITHOUT A TRACE, AND UNTIL IT DOES, OUR WORLDS AND OUR DESTINY AS A SPECIES WILL NEVER BE REALIZED... NOW, I AM ASKING YOU TO FOLLOW ME INTO THE BREACH ONCE MORE. WE MUST PROTECT THE INNOCENT AND PUNISH THE HOSTILES, AND IF YOU BELIEVE YOU ARE CLOSE TO DEATH AT ANY TIME AFTER THIS STRUGGLE BEGINS, I HEREBY ORDER YOU TO TAKE NO LESS THAN FIVE OF THOSE WITCH EMPRESS BASTARDS WITH YOU.

OZ IN AETERNUM!

Following her final words, the Corps cheered loud and long "OZ IN AETERNUM! OZ IN AETERNUM! OZ IN AETERNUM!" before slamming shut their neo-sensory helmet gear.

Piper admitted to herself that addressing so many ranks of ominously powerful *Dio Soldati* was thrilling. Even with the Tao energy restrictions imposed by EMP, just one of them could rip apart the entire British navy. Their combat bodies were expanded to a full fifteen in height, their four thick arms and plates of magi-tech black armor fitted with kinetic, sonic, and miscellaneous blade weapons including two graphene "sonic swords" in back-mounted scabbards, and around their necks, *memento mori* skulls, very much like the one she possessed.

They learned it from me. It's now a weird fad with them.

After she addressed the troops, her father, looking like his typically mad and shaggy Mediterranean self, said to her:

"Piper, I realize you will not listen to me or respect my concern for your safety; however, I am proud of you. I only ask that you be smart and return to me."

He clasped her elbows and kissed her left arm, for he was not tall enough to reach her forehead when she was in EMP combat mode.

"Yes," she said. "But first, I must crush this damnable Witch Empress."

"I know... and congratulations on your new affair with Cereus."

"Look, Dad, I don't want you watching me and—"

"Not to fear. I only know enough to know. I have no desire to observe you thrashing with the Grand Mage on methane planets."

Piper unleashed three seconds of glare at her father.

Minutes later, she plummeted without a sound through the icy vacuum of space towards the U.S. Pacific Coast, joined on either side by the most relentless and badass soldiers Earth has ever known.

Chapter XIII

Weaponized Therapy – *Consumen Esta Bruxa* – Y Escapes

AS THE GRAND PIXIE OF COFFEE BEANS MIGHT SAY: "They're fucking like pathogens!"

In her role as Transitional Governor, Catherine was presented with two primary complications, both recently come to her attention. First, her further observations of the Winkies through the *Fiestra na Vida* proved their oversexed recreation was indeed producing mounds of babies. In fact, a pregnant Winkie brought a child to term in less than two months. The offspring grew like little tumor pods on the back of the Winkie female, or fem-two, often two at once, splitting open like melons at birthing time. Within only two more months they stood at least three feet tall and chased flying boolee berries and spoke fluent Winkie; and within nine more months, they began copulating in a manner that made rabbits look lazy.

The females and fem-twos grew breasts, and both the males and fem-twos displayed healthy big penises. The fit was always good and the journey to orgasm never less than curiously ecstatic. The puzzle of their sprawling presence therefore made total sense to Catherine.

No predators, plenty of food, wonderful sex.

I will not judge them. Are they not happier than the anxiety-fraught denizens of New Manhattan?

Speaking of them, her second complication, and one which required immediate cleansing even more quickly than the monoliths, were the scores of psychoanalyst therapy offices sprouting up like diseased kudzu.

Weaponized therapy, courtesy of Nina Cohen.

They had slipped under the radar somehow, infiltrated, gained a foothold before the New Manhattan protective fields and spells could stabilize; and the offices seemed to be everywhere at once. Oz people of every kind were lining up to receive "dream analysis" from so-called therapists who, curiously enough, resembled Nina Cohen: badly colored hair, screaming-pink or black nails, cigarettes or cigars or toothpicks, expressions of insincerity, snarky attitude, and twitching parts.

No surprise that New Manhattanites emerged from "therapy sessions" more afraid and confused than ever.

Most were told with absolute certainty that they were baby-raped by their fathers before the age of one, or else anally invaded by aliens, or both, and nearly every patient was also diagnosed with "Oz pollen brain infection" that produced bouts of "temporary dream clairvoyance" which always translated to a prediction of New Manhattan Oz collapsing in flames.

Sitting upon her grand management throne within the Heptagon at the crown of *La Stelo Puntero* in New Manhattan Oz—ensconced within her ARMEW from where she might pronounce her magnified magical will upon any number of deserving or less deserving elements—Catherine had never felt more powerful, or more keenly conscious of the need for perspective. Her small experiments with the ARMEW had taught her this. With only a fraction of her potential she had created a new snow-peaked mountain in the Cascades just off the Pacific Coast.

Her power as a World Maker was now truly frightening.

However, I must end this contagion of fraudulent alien therapists before the greater population of this city wants nothing more than to throw themselves off a roof or escape into the murderous arms of the U.S. government.

If I permit even a germ of this analytic farce to continue, the Witch Empress will be allowed an insidious and self-reinforcing means of destroying us.

Once more, Catherine spoke the spell that would ignite the ARMEW within the magical core of Heptagon:

Polo poder cósmico de Tao,
Deixe este heptágono
Aumentar a miña aria dez veces.
e dame a vitoria dez veces neste día.

(*By the cosmic power of Tao,*
  Let this Heptagon
  Increase my aria tenfold,
  and give me victory now.)

She expected the annoying djinn to reappear and lecture her, but it did not. Still sitting on her management throne, she closed her eyes and in moments her innate magic telepathy fused with the ARMEW. Her eyes opened onto a score of locations at once, all around New Manhattan Oz on a beautiful late afternoon of sun and birds and light clouds. From the *Avenida de los Heroes* in the new Time's Square to the patio of *Le Petit Sanglier,* her invisible presence sought minds infected by the horror of recent therapy.

Lightly skipping forebrains like flat stones over neural

waters, she was able to identify in the space of only 20 seconds upwards of 776 victims of alien psychoanalysis. Every single one was nervous, thrown into an existential tizzy and suffering headaches, and nearly all displayed visions of New Manhattan and their own bodies on fire. Many had been weeping and retching. Most could not sleep. Nevertheless, Catherine followed their footsteps back into memory and thereby located over eight dozen Nina Cohen therapist offices. One of them, unbelievably, resided in a lower niche of *Le Petit Sanglier*, drawing in customers with a sign on the door that read:

**THE PEOPLE OF OZ ARE IN GRAVE DANGER.
RUMORS OF MASS KILLINGS ARE TRUE.
LET US HELP NOW!**

Catherine fumed. She urged her will via the ARMEW to open even more eyes and the process cascaded until she was able to keep over a hundred eyes of investigatory telepathy open and channeling data back to her. The most parallel consciousness she'd ever known was four. And Edison? Upwards of nine perhaps. She wasn't certain. She never would have believed a hundred possible, however, the ARMEW knew otherwise. It both energized and stabilized her overworked psyche. Indisputably, it was Edison's greatest gift, and one of the most powerful and magnificent inventions of all time.

After another few minutes, Catherine was able to say with near absolute certainly that she and ARMEW had located 100% of the active alien therapy offices.

Now I have you, tyrant.

No point in dallying. The ingredients for the meal were fresh, but without warning, and in a manner most irritating, Tazamat popped into being. His head floated in the air, eyes staring, ears twitching.

This creature again?

"I will give you points for sheer audacity, djinn," Catherine said. "But you must be gone."

"Master Godfellow told me to discuss ARMEW usage before—"

"ENOUGH!" she shouted. "*Sexa idiota, diaño diablo!*"

Tazamat vanished instantly and did not return. Once Catherine calmed, she hoped she hadn't hurt him. It was simply an old dismissal spell. Regardless, another minute of delay might have meant the establishment of who knows how many more alien therapy offices.

Catherine closed her eyes again and felt as one with ARMEW. Her inner eyes witnessed the vast and glorious panorama of New Manhattan Oz, its sky islands, cloud-girdled starscrapers, and sun-gleaming surfaces. Nudging ARMEW a bit more, she felt the actual warmth of sun on her flesh.

She then felt another warmth.

Her magical aria, her most potent World Maker power, stirred deep within her. The heat of it rose into her throat, overtaking her as though a spectral force were born and released from her will. In moments, it found its own words and sang itself into the atoms of New Manhattan Oz:

Pídolle aos soles de Tao,
Que purifiquen e curen
Esta mancha da Raíña Meiga,

Onde queira que se agache,
Onde queira que se mire.

(*I beseech the suns of Tao,*
  Purify and burn
  This stain of Witch,
  Wherever it may hide,
  Wherever it may turn.)

Within moments, Catherine heard an agonized scream. It erupted from the city itself—a psychic outpour of rage and frustration. As the Czarina observed the Oz towers from afar, the impact struck like a storm of hot swords. She felt a pang of terrible agony in her head, as if Nina Cohen were driving black nails into her skull just as she'd done to Piper. The infectious monster had come utterly unhinged and the disgorged lava of her hatred was suffocating.

Harnessing ARMEW, Catherine shouted a final spell, quite ancient though supremely effective:

Os lumes do inferno de Ahriman,
Apoderan Bruxa,
e quéntaa ben!

(*Fires of Ahriman's hell,*
  Seize this Witch,
  and warm her well!)

Following the last syllable, Catherine's lungs flooded with fresh air. She coughed and caught her breath. Whatever remained of the Witch Empress manifestation attempting to punish her had been summarily teleported to the sun's corona, there to bake at two million kelvin.

Not exactly hell, though close enough.

: /

CALMED ONCE MORE, CATHERINE USED HER MANY EYES to view the aftermath of the psychoanalyst purge. The sign was gone from sky island restaurant. The offices around the city had vanished as if they never existed. On the other hand, former patients appeared alarmed and dazed. Several dozen began to shriek for their analysts. One man impulsively leapt from the top of a starscaper and fell a mile before Catherine rescued him.

She teleported him effortlessly into the Heptagon.

He found himself sitting upon one of the floater chairs. His mouth was open in mid-scream. He saw Catherine only a few feet away, looking him over, appearing to him like a fairytale goddess in a business suit. He closed his mouth and said nothing, for suddenly, nothing made sense.

Catherine penetrated his mind and knew him in a moment. His name was Samuel P. Waterford, an ex-stockbroker, the kind who didn't make any money because of being too honest and cowardly (or so he believed). Therefore, he'd avoided the mass purge of Phase I narcissists over Manhattan. His sister and her family had vanished in the Deeper Lands, rumored to have been killed in a colossal massacre. His wife of 15 years had melded with the ongoing tumult of migrations to New Manhattan Oz and he hadn't seen her in weeks.

He felt hopeless and alone.

Without his psychoanalyst (who diagnosed his problems as a consequence of alien cavity penetration), he could not be certain how to cure himself.

"Do not attempt suicide, Mr. Waterford," Catherine said with a rich, ethereal voice that could convince a Winkie to become Amish. "There is no need, sir. You most certainly are not ill, and you were never probed by aliens. You have no basic trauma you cannot remember. Believe what I am telling you."

"I... I do, yes, um—"

The radiant sight of Catherine, her commanding and confident demeanor, and of course, her voice, mesmerized Samuel P. Waterford. He was changed. He believed her beyond any possible doubt. That alien probe trauma stuff was nothing but garbage.

Why had he been such a fool?

"Thank you, m'am, *Ms. uhhhh*—"

"I am Catherine Romanova, the Transitional Governor here in New Manhattan Oz."

"How did you...?"

"Teleport you? We have our powers, and they will be utilized for benign purposes, I assure you. And before you inquire, I know the location of your wife."

"Oh, who? ... Um, yes, *thank you.*"

Before Catherine could send Samuel to his wife, a distant, foghorn-like sound interrupted her. It boomed, low and deep. And it repeated, louder and longer still, as if a thing huge and dangerous drew close.

"What could that be?" Fear pinched Samuel's face.

"By Beelzebub's beard, I am not certain," Catherine said, glancing at him. "But I must attend to it. Now go, Samuel, and be the man I know you can be."

"Yes, yes, Ms. Governor Catherine, thank you. You are a wonderful person."

Samuel vanished like a dim star eclipsed by dawn.

Before opting to use ARMEW, thereby opening many eyes onto the world about her, Catherine simply walked closer to the enormous Heptagon windows and looked down over the city in the direction from where the sound originated. Almost immediately she heard the booming foghorn again, and this time followed by another noise that muffled it to a whimper.

The New Manhattan attack alarm.

ROARRRUUMM, ROARRRUUUM, ROARRRUUUM.

Not unlike the old air raid sirens of Earth.

At that very moment, the head of a woman appeared in the air before her, followed half a moment later by yet another appearance of the annoying Tazamat. The woman, an Asian Indian of *Superna Humanitas* beauty and regal air, spoke to Catherine:

"Governor Catherine, I am Colonel Meena Chowdhury of Operations and Security Command. The city of New Manhattan Oz is under attack. City defense grids and weapons are powering up to engage the enemy in five seconds."

Tazamat shrilly shouted with his little boy voice, "Ms. Czarina, you must tell the populace to go to safety. That is your job!"

"Colonel Chowdhury, what is the nature of the enemy?" Catherine said, remaining cool.

Chowdhury's response was cut off by the sound of multiple black-plasma cannon batteries firing in unison.

ZARROOOOM, and again, ZARROOOOM.

Tazamat interjected, "Your microphone is on your desk. It looks like a thimble. You must issue the order!"

As Catherine spelled the thimble mike into the palm of her left hand, Colonel Chowdhury said, "We judge its origin to be the Deeper Lands. It is—"

ZARROOOOM, ZARROOOOM, ZARROOOOM.

Holding her hand before her mouth, Catherine spoke the order into the mike. Her voice of godlike command echoed through the inner chambers and outer reaches of New Manhattan:

"CITIZENS OF OZ, TAKE SHELTER IMMEDIATELY. STAY OUT OF THE AIR AND AWAY FROM CITY TELEPORTERS UNTIL THE DANGER HAS PASSED. WE WILL PROTECT YOU."

"May ancestral spirits of the almighty djinn save us!" Tazamat shrieked.

Glancing out the window again, Catherine finally saw it. She gasped for the second time that day, her hands lifting in an act of primeval instinct.

By Ahriman, nothing could be more chilling to soul or bone than what I now behold.

Her vision filled with what appeared to be the body of an impossibly gigantic humanoid tortuously bending back on itself to form a contorted circle—featureless head and leg-like appendages bowing at painful angles until the lower balls of feet touched a crest of hairless forehead. Its gummy dark flesh yielded to this bizarre fusion as might the skin of a snake, and what appeared to be a limitless number of tiny bubbles rose and popped on its surface.

Catherine knew it to be miles long in size, and upon

closer examination, those tiny bubbles proved to be the same hyperbolic Picasso gremlins she'd observed on the Deeper Land monoliths, the same hideous evil faces winking in and out of existence. The flesh itself also imitated that of the monoliths. A buffet of elements including human fingers, twisted limbs, and skull portions fused and entwined upon it like bits of indigestible food in a steaming broth.

The horrific and sickening presence of it was further enhanced by violent effects of color and light as salvos of New Manhattan weaponry flashed upon it and shivered it, chopping it into chunks of dark gum, and in other places, drilling deep to strike gushers of black ichor. But it wasn't stopping. Catherine heard it psychically screaming as its featureless head opened a cavernous black mouth—big enough to swallow a few hundred megalodons at once—and belched that eerie foghorn sound once more.

Might this nightmare of nightmares be summoning other abominations like itself?

As background to her humiliating fear, she heard Tazamat shrieking incomprehensibly in the background and the voice of Major Chowdhury shouting salvo orders to the New Manhattan fire commands. She also heard the fierce barrage of the gun batteries combining into one continuous whooping screech, and too, the booming foghorn voice as it became loud enough to vibrate the very foundation of *La Stelo Puntero* itself.

Catherine felt it in her feet, worming into her entire body like a nervous tic. Then she heard a voice in her mind piercing through the din. A voice she knew so well.

"Cathy, it is I, your Mother Yarrow. My sword, my strength

239

and spirit, are yours. Bring me to your side. You have the power. I beg thee, Cathy. Let us beat this deadly monster together."

Her voice shook Catherine from her stupor. "Yes... yes, you are right. I can now free you from the old spell that has secluded you."

"I am ready."

"I will not tarry a moment longer, dearest Maria."

Catherine knew it would take her strongest aria, enhanced by ARMEW, and it must be done quickly. Even now, the Deeper Land monster drew closer. In response to her will, her aria answered warmly.

Tazamat shouted in the distance, "What in King Harold's name are you spelling? You must tell me!" But Catherine ignored him, not even bothering with a dismissal spell.

She sang her aria clear and strong:

Suplico ás forzas do Tao,
Que eliminen o feitizo
Que aprisiona a Nai Yarrow,
e que non a impida ningunha maxia,
Máis tarde nin agora...

(I beseech the forces of Tao,
 Remove the evil spell
 That imprisons Mother Yarrow,
 and let no magics impede her,
 Later or now.)

Once done, she reached out to clutch Maria's hand. So simple, as though Maria stood in the same room. And with the world about them going straight to hell, Maria of Pozzuoli faced Catherine and smiled. The Czarina brimmed with tears as Maria stepped closer to clasp her shoulders. Catherine felt Maria's warmth and strong grip. She froze in awe as she stared at the warrior who had been such a huge and emotional part of her life for so many years.

"I have dreamed of this," Maria said.

Maria's hair was a deep auburn, cut short around her head to better accommodate a helmet. Her eyes were a dark gray, her facial features strong and yet feminine. She appeared no more than 35 years of age.

"I too," said Catherine, feeling tremors in the building. "But we must—"

"We must form the *Diante de Tao*."

"No, Maria, we cannot. It will tip our hand, reveal the ceiling of our power too readily to the enemy. We—"

The building tremored again, only more strongly, the cacophony of conflict outside growing by the moment. The ARMEW, still fused with her nervous system, allowed her to probe the city populace for a moment and she sensed their collective terror and heard their fearful screams. Before Maria could utter another word, Catherine placed one finger to her lips to gently silence her as Colonel Chowdhury shouted into the Heptagon.

"Governor Romanova, our batteries have succeeded in concentrating their fire, enough to slice the enemy into parts. It seeks to reunite with itself, but our particle beam and black-plasma batteries are preventing it. We estimate also that .46 of its total mass has been annihilated."

"Where is the fleet?"

"The *Gallipoli* is engaged with the Dark House and no

other ships can penetrate the Oz megastructure. The Orion antagonist is blocking."

Catherine glanced up to see the contorted and hellish monster now split into four dark and burning chunks, and to either side, glowing bits of scrap spinning away. On the other side of New Manhattan's primary Tao Shield, it floated, howling and groaning with its bubbling faces while the twilight purple sky streamed with fiery clouds that rained a black mist of incinerated matter and dust.

In the fading sunlight, she observed its temper and took measure. Without another thought, she attempted to aria-spell the entire hateful and hideous mass into the crushing heart of the sun—just as she'd dispatched remnants of Witch Empress therapy into the corona. But her efforts were met with retaliation. It lashed out painfully. Once more, her head felt pierced to the core by sharp psychic nails. Rivulets of blood gushed from her nose and eyes. She grimaced in agony and cried out as the city's gun batteries pounded relentlessly.

ZARROOOOM, ZARROOOOM, ZARROOOOM.

"Cathy, my darling!" Maria reached out to steady her.

Catherine shouted through the blood-blind and dizzying pain. "DIO SOLDATI, TO ME!"

A door at the far end of the Heptagon swung open and a dozen black-armored *Dio Soldati* in full weapons array clomped in like five-ton boulders on two legs. They came to attention in a line facing her.

Maria gasped. "By the saints, what is this?"

"My personal God Soldiers," Catherine said, wiping the blood from her eyes.

Facing the *Dio Soldati*, she willed into creation fourteen

new *Fiestra na Vida*, each opening focused on the foghorn maw of the monster. "*Dio Soldati*, draw your black-plasma autocannons. On my command, direct a stream of five-burst fire into the mouth of that kraken and continue until all rounds are spent, or I command a cease fire."

As one, her dutiful God Soldiers pulled their bazooka-sized autocannons from behind their backs and aimed, each one choosing a different window portal.

Still in intense pain, Catherine stumbled to her desk, withdrew her own black-plasma Glock from a drawer and tossed it to a perplexed Maria. "Hold it like this, point the barrel, and keep squeezing this trigger. I have set it to fire five rounds at a time." Catherine spoke with a calm voice. "We will conquer this thing."

"Yes, Czarina, as you order."

Catherine next engaged the magical fabric of ARMEW to augment her power to a full teravolt. A bluish-white light haloed her and expanded in a moment to form a blinding bubble that consumed her body. The blood on her face turned to smoke, and as New Manhattan quaked beneath her feet, she shouted to those present in the Heptagon:

"MARK YOUR TARGET! … FIRE!"

The chamber erupted in a thrumming chorus of autocannon just as Catherine's pain and anger directed the first discharge of teravolt—a thousand thunderstorm's worth of electricity roaring from her in a single searing beam, vibrating the air enough to quiver every indestructible window in the Heptagon.

All those present stared into the gaping maw of the monolith hybrid opening wider as the megatons of black-plasma and the irresistible torch of teravolt scorched and tore at it. Its black throat began to glow in the deeper regions like the inner core of an active volcano. The head quickly sprouted tentacle-like appendages that attempted to block the annihilating energies, but to no avail. The insistent firing pruned them almost immediately, and following ten more seconds of discharge, the giant head of mouth exploded into flaming embers and hurtling chunks.

The WHOOOOMMP of it rocked the entire starscraper.

The pain in Catherine's head began to subside. She dissipated her bubble to a sizzle.

"CEASE FIRE!"

Colonel Chowdhury's voice cut in. "Governor, the battlecruiser *Tecumseh* has breached the barrier and is firing on the hostile."

Catherine gazed up at the *Tecumseh*, all twenty miles of her shaped to a perfect crescent of black emerald, smooth of body, gleaming surface, sharp of cusp—stark and invincible against the purple sky beyond the roiling clouds.

Seven crackling weapon beams, originating near the peak of its moon-like crescent, poured relentless force onto the burning floats of monster. Meanwhile, the New Manhattan guns continued to fire salvo after salvo, and Catherine's pain dissipated to a dull ache as the beast neared extinction.

Feeling relieved, she glanced around for Maria, spotting the woman about fifty feet away and heading towards her. As Maria passed the line of *Dio Soldati*, she smiled and raised her fist in victory, and at that moment, an oily dark tentacle lashed out from a nearby a *Fiestra na Vida*. It wrapped Maria's body and snapped her from the room in less than a second.

"MARIAAAAA!"

Into the very same *Fiestra na Vida,* the Czarina immediately launched herself with a cry, soaring at once into the maelstrom of disintegration more than ten miles distant. Bits of charred flesh careened end over end through the swirls of smoke and dust. Waves of thunder and concussive force knocked her down and sideways. At last, she saw her Mother Yarrow through the chaos, her face dissolving like a water-soluble tablet in the slobbering mouth of a distorted human caricature, one loosened and flaked from the primary monster.

During those brief moments of Catherine's shock-induced paralysis, that grotesque monolith fragment from Munchkin Land, the last one ever witnessed, also dissolved into a swirl of black dust, taking the soul and atoms of the brave Maria with it.

: /

FIERY THE ANGELS FELL. DEEP THUNDER ROLLED round their shores. Before Piper and her *Dio Soldati* units hit the EMP bubble at 3,000 feet, they spelled their velocity down to Mach I. Their flaming meteoric tails dissipated, leaving a few dozen miles of smoky white contrail behind. Half a minute later, upon crossing into the EMP, Piper issued a radio command to the divisions.

From a pocket on their upper backs, they expanded a pair of dark, graphene-fabric wings, *whirrrring* them out to a supersonic angle. The WAMOR units, however, continued to drop at full velocity to the center of the Greater Los Angeles target area. They would hit at over 60,000 MPH, sync weapons, and spring from their craters while the *Dio Soldati* split into two waves and assaulted the flanks from the west and east, thereby pressing towards LA from both directions. Piper understood that many civilians might die in this coming conflict, but every living thing would be mercilessly extinguished unless this armed intervention succeeded.

Still thundering as they fell, Piper's western assault wave utilized their wings to perform a massive swooping maneuver, veering to an arc that flattened out above the San Bernardino burbs. She ordered half her units to dive to 500 feet, the other half to 100 feet. The top half of *Dio Soldati* layered into three firing lines, one atop the other, and chose targets up to twenty miles distant. Once done, a moving wall of hellish sound and shell softened the streets and malls while the lower half of the wave followed up like a slashing scythe.

Unknown to everyone else though, including her father, Piper was also on a mercy mission.

I'm going to find and save Murray's sister and family. And why not? I got the unlucky bastard killed for no good reason.

Like her attack force, Piper had fitted herself with a pair of expandable graphene "strafing wings." Once the aerodynamic reality of decreasing speed became apparent, the wings adjusted perpendicular to her body and unfolded four solar-powered propellers powerful enough to thrust her forward at speeds up to Mach 1 (depending on cross winds).

Identical props ignited for the other units, and at the same time, Piper reached up and flipped a toggle in her command com gear that axed into every *Dio Soldati's* helmet the sound of her favorite ass-killing rock tune: "Still in Hollywood" by Concrete Blonde.

And I swear, I heard voices singing to me...

As the strident beat of Concrete Blonde psyched her warriors into a mad offense, Piper felt suddenly slapped by a shock wave. Thousands more WAMOR reinforcements had collided simultaneously into Los Angeles like one giant asteroid. The sound alone was deafening, and as she learned later, the impact had been felt as far north as Half Moon Bay and Pescadero.

Oz radio chatter on the ground reported local fault lines trembling the land for a radius of one hundred miles or more while over a million windows exploded in LA, including every bit of glass downtown. Dodger Stadium collapsed on one side and the La Brea tar pits erupted, spewing forth their deepest fossils. Best of all, upwards of 1200 Witch Empress war machines, both Pentagon and Martian tripod, were instantly obliterated.

Within seconds of burning through bedrock, the WAMORS had sprung from their craters into the air, their six-barreled, 10,000 RPM Gatling cannons blazing away at targets chosen only seconds before impact. Due to an OSC military lab invention of neospace ammo storage, each WAMOR could fire up to 220 million rounds. The Tao necessary to create space within the WAMOR was armored against EMP dampening effects by billions of microscopic and interwoven nodules of ceramic graphene.

From her vantage point on high, Piper observed four or five WAMORS as far west as San Bernardino. Like daddy long-leg spiders, they ran and hopped, small bodies of head supported by long thin legs, each unit firing tracer rounds in streams so unbroken they appeared like rays of crimson-white light. Now, they were exchanging fire-blows with Witch Empress machines—Pentagon War Walkers. Piper also spotted a few ranks of tripods pivoting through a smashed neighborhood on the outskirts of Claremont. They appeared intent on flanking the WAMORS. She issued an order to adjacent platoons:

"Tripods 38 degrees to earth at two o'clock. On my command, Platoons five through seven to 50 feet, swords and sonics primed."

She pulled her enormous graphene broadsword from the scabbard on her back and shouted into her mike:

"DIVE!"

Piper led her *Dio Soldati* into the murderous insanity. None questioned her order. They knew she was hungry for conflict. So were they.

But the tripods saw them coming.

Ten or more swiveled and raised their cowls to fire sonic "screech beams" at Piper and her Oz defenders. The beams splintered enough push-props to force eight of Piper's soldiers to spin and crash. One swiped Piper's legs and chipped off bits of her own props. Her flesh below the waist felt stung as if by a hundred wasps.

It infuriated her.

She executed an oscillating evasion maneuver to dodge another cowl pointing her way, but three *Dio Soldati* crushed it to junk with their own sonic cannon as every platoon began pouring murderous salvos into the reeling tripods. *SCREEEEEE WHOOOM, SCREEEE WHOOOOM,*

SCREEEE WHOOOOM. Ten were crippled or destroyed immediately, and seconds later, the opposing forces clashed head on.

Piper's massive sword sliced the legs from under the first tripod in her path. It flipped and crashed through the roof of a ranch-style house already in flames. She then swerved upward and brought it down at 23,600 PSI to cleave the cowl of another tripod.

And what the hell?

Despite the chaotic momentum, she glimpsed an alien writhing in the control chamber. What she saw fit the ridiculous description of a Galaxian.

But no time for conjecture.

A long burst of 70MM tracer fire from one of the Pentagon war machines half a mile south sprayed Piper's gear and chipped at her props. Two more cowls pivoted to fire sonics at her while exposing themselves to *Dio Soldati*.

They want me bad.

Sputtering over the remaining line of tripods, her flying gear began to smoke. She veered out of control and spun to earth. Moments later, while skimming the roof of a house, she ate an appetizer consisting of no less than 100 tiles of clay-terracotta shingle—prelude to the next course of rocketing like a wounded Valkyrie into the backyard, severing two thick palms on the way, and smashing into a wooden tool shed.

This isn't going well.

Piper moaned in pain. She rolled to her side, her body covered in welts and splintered planks. A concerned voice shouted in her ear bud:

"Commander Robbin! Are you alright? We saw you spin

out and drop pretty hard."

"Yes, Major Bhuyeni." She spoke into her mike. "Order DS units and WAMORS within a 20-mile radius to converge on my position and organize under your command to set up a ten-mile perimeter. Once we cleanse this burb of Witch Empress hostiles, we'll form a Tac 3 infantry wedge and push east towards LA."

"On your orders," Major Bhuyeni said.

By my calculations I'm only a few miles west of Carnelian Avenue and Murray's family. Once my fire support expands the perimeter, it will be much easier to reach them... or what is left of them.

Piper felt another unsettling ground tremor, *no doubt an aftershock from the WAMORs,* and she heard the remaining sounds of battle as one unending, omnipresent drone, a shrill and endless gong of alien ceremony seeking human life. She took a deep breath, and in struggling to heal itself, her sorceress body trembled—the Tao genetics of her combat flesh immune to the saturation of EMP.

From inside her makeshift wooden hovel, she pushed aside one of the weathered pine boards to gaze around at the local neighborhood. The house straight ahead had been smashed to small piles. By what means, she wasn't sure. Nevertheless, its condition allowed a sweeping view of a large park beyond and a distant line of oak trees.

The time was 7:46 AM, the sky cloudless.

Hundreds of corpses of all ages and sexes littered the area like torn shreds of cloth. She observed trails of smoke on the horizon, bursts of tracer fire, flaming cars, and detritus of every sort imaginable. She swiveled her butt and glimpsed the other side. A ramshackle fence blocked her view. She heard a distant pounding noise like heavy footsteps and turned back around to spot a Pentagon War Walker running on two legs at over a 100 MPH. It was coming straight at her, midway across the park and closing fast. It appeared like a bulky silver knight from a past century, and strangely enough, it was not taking any fire.

She spoke into her mike. "Major Buying, a Pentagon hostile is closing on my position. Do you see it?"

"Yes, Commander Robbin. Two WAMORS targeting."

"Do not fire. Repeat, do NOT fire. I want it."

"Uh, as you order, sir."

I'm going to crack that bastard open and ask one or two damn good questions.

The war machine closed at a crouch to within fifty feet, its three auto-heads atop the silver-black trunk clicking back and forth. Two shoulder-mounted 70MM Gatling canons unleashed short bursts at the house she'd skimmed, blowing it to pieces, and next, at various chunks of wreckage that might be cover. But it could not find her. It hadn't noticed the pile of shed boards. Her body allowed no infrared signature, nor could the War Walker sensors separate her breath from the general blare of noise.

Piper braced herself. Using her powerful legs, she shot from her hiding place at the war machine before it could react. Her sword whirled and hacked through its thick left leg just before her hurtling body slammed into its armored abdomen. The force of her strike propelled it like a giant soccer ball. It flew through the air for over thirty yards, crashed onto the street and rolled to the curb.

As it struggled to stand like a dizzy child, Piper sheathed her sword in the ground and leapt onto it. With bare hands she ripped away the fizzling auto-head shell to find a U.S. Army private squirming in his high-tech cocoon.

Now you're gonna talk, you child killing roach.

Piper stripped away his headgear and straps. She yanked him out, birthed him into the morning air then dangled his body for a moment before tossing it like scrap onto the grass across the street. She jumped from the machine carcass and walked over to him, grabbed the man by the scruff of the neck, and lifted him into the air again. He appeared to exist in a state between terror and astonishment. A young person, maybe 26 years old, Caucasian, buzz cut, purple faced.

His name badge spelled FREDERICKSON.

She spoke to him with a voice of barely contained rage.

"I've got things to do and lives to save, *asshole*, and you're holding me up. But before I go, I need to ask. *Who or what in Hades* entitles YOU to kill innocent people?"

Frederickson gulped and breathed rapidly but managed to answer. "We... we were told that, uh, civilians here are really Martians in disguise."

"AND YOU believe any phony bullshit you're told?"

He gulped again, and said, "The Galaxians... they're ordering this. They moved our families into camps. If anyone even questions a single order, they disappear... their whole families disappear."

"Where are they holding these people?"

"At least 80,000 are in the mountains east of San Bernardino."

She knew without telepathy that Frederickson told the truth. The man was ready to shit his pants. The tyrannical alien frauds were using classic tactics of lie and retaliation to enforce absolute obedience. No surprise there.

Did Nina put them through analysis too?

Before Piper could release him, the lower part of his body from the chest down vanished in a blur. His face was left behind, frozen with hope. She quickly glanced around and saw nothing.

Where the fuck did that shot come from?

She couldn't tell. She turned to see the pulpy goo of Frederickson's other half spread out behind her. His blood splattered her from thigh to chest.

This feels eerily familiar.

She dropped his corpse to the grass, quickly unsheathed her sword from the earth, and backed away, her eyes darting back and forth, still attempting to discover the source of the shot. But it was no use. Her powers were compromised. She pivoted and ran back from where she'd come.

She moved fast as possible, zigging and zagging, taking short and long leaps, sprinting at greater speed than even the Pentagon war machines. She crossed five streets, dodged behind a few houses and smoking wreckage piles, and a half mile later, saw an iron manhole cover. She removed it and slipped down inside, replacing it as she went.

Once within the bowels of the local sewer, Piper raced madly through a dark tunnel of blood and excrement towards the direction of Carnelian Avenue. She knew it couldn't be more than two miles east. On the way, she radioed the major:

"Buyeni, what is the status of the perimeter?"

"We are clean, and currently up to a five-mile radius from

your original position."

"Are you meeting heavy resistance?"

"The enemy outnumbers us three to one, but the DS and WAMOR units are wilting them, sir. Our armor and ammo supplies are superior. The Pentagon machines are nearly out of rounds, and the tripod numbers have been cut by two thirds. Commands throughout the Greater LA area report no enemy reinforcements in sight."

"What about the Despicables? I saw none in our sector."

"A nonfactor. They slaughtered a few thousand civilians in and around downtown LA before we arrived but were extinguished by our aerial attack wave. Without a lot of magic support, they die easily, sir."

"Good. Radio me when the perimeter is secure."

"As you order, Commander."

Minutes later, Piper climbed a rung ladder and lifted another sewer lid two inches high on Carnelian Avenue. *So here I am, the world's most powerful sorceress, hiding in a sewer. Ya gotta see the humor.*

She glanced around to witness a landscape even more torn and charred than the one she'd just left. Like a truckload of smashed grapefruit, bodies were scattered thick and grotesque. A line of wrecked and burning cars stretched for miles down Carnelian, south towards the I-10 freeway. She even saw an overturned National Guard jeep beside four dead Guardsmen sprawled on the street. Two of them were headless.

Piper slowly lifted the cover and climbed from the sewer.

Murray's sister lives only blocks from here.

She faced an empty In-and-Out Burger across the

avenue. Before another molecule in her body could shiver, she heard a woman's voice, familiar yet irritating. It radiated from behind her, and the words it spoke as follows:

"*Don't you know?*"

Piper gasped and whipped around, her sword flashing forth like a sun-kissed scythe of death. She briefly glimpsed an arachnid-like nightmare of black metallic exoskeleton wearing an ugly face of therapeutic snark. But no time for comment. A pummeling hot blast lifted her off her feet and launched her over 200 yards.

She smashed through the In-and-Out Burger window, past the grill, and out the back wall in .015 of a second, then through the parking lot, shaving the roofs off twenty-two cars and climaxing with a splintering penetration of Sally's Miracle Lounge—a trail of pulverized door and broken tables left behind before finally coming to rest beneath an 80 inch digital flat-screen playing a classic rock tune called "Arrows of Love" by the group, Trout Fishing in Arizona:

Whoh ohh, ohh, ohh,
Arrows of love.
They're killing meeeee....

Barely conscious, she discovered her sword gone and her body wracked by an incredible bone and muscle trauma. *By the gods, this is even worse than my crash into that house. The Witch Empress must have followed me. That space bitch probably murdered Frederickson too.*

Piper heard an odd rustling noise and lifted her head painfully to see five frightened faces staring at her from behind an overturned lounge table.

Early drinkers, no doubt?

"Bartender!" Piper shouted. "Triple scotch on the rocks and two pints of Guiness!"

No answer.

She tried to contact Major Buyeni. He didn't respond.

Of course, the goddamn mike is shot.

She called out to the people hiding behind the table, "Don't worry you guys. I won't hurt you." They nodded, still terrified. "Just leave this place, run out the back door. Hurry!"

At first, no movement, then three women and two men in their thirties slowly emerged, stood without a word, and headed towards the bar as Piper reached back and withdrew her sonic grenade belt. In a few moments, using a control device on the buckle, she set all ten at once to a .50 second detonation. She pushed the digital "Arm Sonics" button. Upon fusion with a target, they would blow. She then stuffed the belt behind her back to await the obvious.

"GO NOW!" she yelled at the customers once more.

I've gotta blow this booze den and make my way to Murray's family. I know good old Nina isn't done with me and—

Piper never finished that thought.

The air exploded with a loud bang into flame hot enough to melt a bar glass. The AM alcoholics never made it out. They shrieked in searing pain like tortured rabbits, but a powerless Piper could do nothing to save them. The air filled with smoke and the noisy ferocity of flame, the fire finding perimeter less than three feet from her crippled body. A big whooshing curl of it licked her face.

Despite the chaos in progress, Piper felt certain that the alien, having consumed the attitude and narcissism of an entitled Berkeley therapist, would make a grand entrance.

It did.

The head *du jour* of the Witch Empress faded into view from within the wall of flame directly before Piper. It reminded her of the opening credit shot in the classic film, *Terminator II*. She and her father had watched it only recently. The killer robot appeared from the fire, grinning evilly, and the visage before her now was enormous—a black metal-skull face, two rows of grinning chisel teeth, and Nina Cohen's features superimposed like a sleazy projection.

It spoke to Piper with a raspy Russian accent, "Now I am going to watch you die without magic or your rapist daddy to save you. *Don't you know?*"

The irritating alien obscenity moved one step closer so Piper got a better look. The robotic head was attached by a long-segmented metal neck to an abdomen that resembled a grotesque shrimp with six appendages, each ending in a three-pronged claw. Towards the bottom of the elongated shrimp abdomen appeared a thick sex rod in the process of expanding menacingly, and below that, two stubby legs.

Piper began to laugh in hysterics.

"So I'm going to die, *poked to death by an ugly, giant, dumb ass hunk of metal shrimp?*"

Before the psychoanalyst-terminator shrimp could respond, the sound of flames was overwritten by an ear-piercing SCREEEEEEE WHOOOOOM. The hideous shrimp thing shuddered and made a grunting squeal. Piper's units had found their commander as well as her foe. The grotesque Nina head jerked to one side ever so slightly after another SCREEEEEE WHOOOOM and Piper pitched the sonic grenade belt.

The resulting eruption a moment later blew the roof and sides off Sally's Miracle Lounge and snuffed the flames. Piper's body was thrown more than fifty feet into the fishpond of a nearby back yard.

She blacked out.

Twenty minutes and 43 seconds later, she opened her eyes and saw Major Buyeni hovering above her prone body in his *Dio Soldati* armor, along with five other god soldiers. To Piper, their medieval clown faces appeared to suit the mood. She knew they were genuinely concerned about her health, though she felt way too damp and agonized to express gratitude, so she simply said:

"Major Buyeni, pick me up and take me to 5027 Carnelian Avenue. It's a few blocks from here."

"Yes, sir."

The armor-plated arms of Major Buyeni gently lifted an ailing Piper from the ground and cradled her. She felt like a child for the first time in over two thousand years. As they walked at a swift pace she heard distant echoes of war thunder, though far less than half an hour ago.

Soon enough, they stood facing 5027 Carnelian Avenue. The house, or what was left of it, appeared to be a standard LA suburb three-bedroom—ruddy tile roof, white-glazed stone façade, bay window, big garage. The right side of the house was partially caved in, as though struck by a giant hammer. The corpse of a decapitated man, around forty years old, lay in the front yard. *The sister's husband?* Piper ordered the major to stoop down and carry her into the house via the gaping bay window.

Once inside, she called out in the dark silence. "Cheryl, hello? … I am a friend. I know Murray… Hello?"

Piper heard a rustling noise followed by whimpering. It seemed to come from around a corner in the kitchen. Major Buyeni pushed forward like a scorpion, walking on four limbs, two more still cradling Piper. They turned the corner and saw a heap of fallen boards and cracked sheetrock. The whimper source lay somewhere beneath it. Piper ordered the major to set her down and very carefully remove the debris. He did so and said to her over his shoulder, "We have a child here, in a cupboard under the sink."

"Wait," Piper said. "I'll come over." She was afraid the scary clown face of the Major might traumatize the child even further.

Not that I look much better.

Piper stood on shaky legs. The pain shot into her spine, but she gritted her teeth and walked slowly to where the child was hiding. She bent down, opened the door to the cupboard and saw a small girl, about seven years old, her hair dark and dirty, face smudged, and eyes wet from crying. The girl stared at her, still terrified. Despite the conditions, Murray's blood was clearly in her. She could easily be his daughter or niece.

"C'mon honey." Piper reached in and lifted the girl out. "It's alright, you're safe now. I'm a good friend of your uncle… I'm Aunt Piper. What's your name?"

"Tessa," she said with a quiet and sad voice.

"Well, let's get out of this stinky place, Tessa."

Piper walked with Tessa in her arms, stepping carefully over the debris. Once outside, she held a hand over the child's eyes to shield her from the vision of the *Dio Soldati* and the killing fields outside. Tessa snuggled in her arms. The little girl almost fell fast asleep before they even reached the street, feeling safe and loved as Piper stroked her head.

Nevertheless, before she dozed off, and in a barely audible voice, she asked just one question:

"Aunt Piper, can we get an In and Out burger, please?"

Chapter XIV

The Fermi Paradox – Pricking Fingers – Piper on TV

YOU ARE NO LONGER ON TOP OF THE WORLD.

As a matter of fact, you are not on top of anything.

You stand now on a dark, dead planet orbiting a pulsar on the shore of the galactic rim. The two electro-magnetic jets emanating from opposite sides of the pulsar cast an eerie blue light on the cratered surface, and on the object you seek, an alien structure rising before you, massive enough to split the Earth's moon in half. It appears rather like the head of giant chisel protruding from the crust at precisely 45 degrees. The crown is more than 200 miles away.

It serves no real purpose you can determine other than to provoke awe. It could be eons old. You are not certain, but surely, several million years at least. Did the aliens who created it once inhabit this world?

It does not appear so.

Nevertheless, it has passed the test you set up. It radiates bio-technological life.

But where is the life?

Unknown to anyone but you, this is one of only a few technologically advanced civilizations in the Milky Way found after a search by instruments of your own unique construction. You attached them to the Tao dish-array complex on the dark side of Jupiter a million years ago.

An opportunity. You took it.

However, upon interpreting the data and checking it twice with the smartest AI on the *Caliburn* (nicknamed

Queen Olga), you must admit disappointment with the results.

The accursed Fermi Paradox could not be denied.

As a result, both you and Queen Olga arrived at the inescapable conclusion that despite the myriad possibilities for life on millions of planets, the long fall of circumstantial dominoes necessary to true human-like consciousness was rare, so rare that perhaps only a half dozen worlds in the galaxy every few million years or so mumbled language long enough to pierce the starry veil.

Nevertheless, though the Orion alien employed more than sufficient force to fence you in and thereby goad you into a Tao-sapping war, you have no restrictions on movement in the space-time stream within which you currently exist. You can reverse through time outside EMP influence. So you have chosen to step back a few centuries and explore the results of the intelligent life search, and in doing so, not risk missing anything.

WW Oz is still far enough away in the future.

And though extraterrestrial oddities are fascinating, you are really searching for potential allies in the war. A second front would sap the enemy at a much quicker rate and give you victory at far less cost.

So here you are.

The readings you received, the data that urged you here, can only mean one thing. *The massive chisel sculpture itself is the alien, or more likely, the equivalent of an alien community, a hive of beings intimately infused within the substance of the creation.*

You know this supremely advanced form of life-and-tech hybrid would never be interested in assisting Oz. *Or* perhaps, it simply cannot, or accomplish much of anything else for that matter, rather like a star child suspended in the womb.

Regardless, you know you must move on, but the irresistible urge of the primate still exerts influence. Like the astronaut in 2001: A Space Odyssey, you are compelled beyond reason to touch the alien structure.

You walk forward as if in a daze.

Minutes later, you stand before a pulsar-lit surface, dark and smooth. You cannot hear it singing. It utters not a sound. You reach out with your right hand and touch the outer wall. It feels like it looks. Smooth, though warm.

Yes. Warm.

A slight fever perhaps?

At that moment, you understand.

Via your touch, it implants within you a dimension-spanning celestial consciousness that would drive you mad unless you were a World Maker. Your many eyes open to see these strange alien beings upon thousands of worlds, multitudes of them coming together to shed their biology and fuse their ghostly neural essence, becoming as one with this great galactic ark before you—a living artifact sheathed into an airless dark planet orbiting a pulsar no less than 18,000 light years distant.

Now, it waits.

The pulsar is the beacon for whatever comes from beyond the galaxy to join with it. Or so it believes. Though perhaps its mate will never arrive, and in truth, we have a situation of Ozymandias. Naught but lone and pitiless space stretching far away.

Nothing else to be done.

You depart this ancient planet.

Will you return to *Caliburn* and brood on the existential vacuum of cosmos? No. You extinguish this notion. In the face of what you have witnessed, you believe life to be even more precious, and true raison d'être more important than ever.

Humankind has the right to exist, like any other intelligent species, and millions of years from now perhaps we too will have melted as one to form a giant work of art sheathed in the crust of a dead world.

Annihilation, however, is not an option.

Not now, not ever.

: /

Czarina Catherine's Post Finem Journal
Year 1 PF – Entry 5

I include these thoughts only for the purpose of achieving catharsis. My grief over the loss of Maria of Pozzuoli is matched only by the death of my father, Prince Christian, which took place in Prussia when I was a child. Now I cannot sleep or eat. I should have never been needy or fool enough to bring her into that bloody battle. She perished because of me. I should have realized, even in the heat of conflict with that nightmare, that it could have exerted enough dying force to penetrate the life windows; and of course, it chose Maria.

It chose to destroy the one person I loved most.

If she were here, she would tell me it was her duty to die in my service, and her pleasure, for the cause was good. She would scold me for my child-like tears and grief. She was the sister and mother I never had, a perfection in both those roles.

If only I could have shown her love to the fullest.

The abomination from Orion currently makes it impossible for me to reclaim Maria, to turn back time. I can only choose to see her in centuries past, though seeing her in this manner only reminds me that every moment is a moment closer to her terrible end.

Maria would also tell me how selfish I am to seclude myself and grieve. So many are dying on Earth and have died in Oz. The estimates of civilians murdered or killed in this war are already in the tens of millions, and with no sign of an end. The so-called Galaxians and American Pentagon are engaging in mass slaughters hidden from the general public.

The totality of misery cannot be measured.

I must transcend my personal sorrows and resume my duty to help end this violent space pox visited upon us, and at this moment, only one motivating solution exists and that is HATE. Yes. My hatred of the Witch Empress alien grows stronger with every iota of grief I experience. A pure state of hatred will certainly permit me to reclaim my role and save as many innocents as I can, and I am almost there.

By the pricking of my fingers, something wicked nearby lingers.

: /

BEFORE LEAVING LOS ANGELES TO BOARD the Caliburn, Piper Robbin helped rescue victims and erect refugee centers as focal points for processing, medical attention, and migration to safe areas on the ship.

A neo-dimensional bio-space on C deck sterilized free of Witch Empress bacteria. But we'd better screen the LA bunch as they board. A single atom of that Nina horror will be one too many.

Following the return of electricity, and at such point the local TV news felt secure about broadcasting again, Piper chose a logical point in the early evening—two days after the fighting had ceased and following numbed permission from those station heads who remained alive—to cut in and make an announcement that would be witnessed by millions.

She wore a white cotton blouse, an aquamarine silk scarf, small gold earrings, and her mounds of black hair, coiled into one thick braid, fell over her right shoulder; but no matter, what the audience really noticed were her eyes. As she spoke, they pierced through the camera lens and into the souls of all who watched:

> **"People of the Greater Los Angeles area, I am Bianca Cappello, and I speak for the Seven City-Worlds of Oz... Many astounding and frightening things have happened to you recently. The old Earth we knew is gone. A new one is now upon us. And like you, I am of this planet, born and raised. I breathe the same air and eat the same food, and I believe in many of the same qualities and virtues as you do, like justice, liberty, and compassion. But the forces that have invaded our fair world believe in none of these. They call themselves Galaxians, and their leader refers to herself as the Witch Empress.**
>
> **Please understand that such ridiculous labels were invented, and for marketing purposes**

only. They wish only to conquer and kill us via force and treachery. If you doubt that, look around you. Hundreds of thousands have died, and destruction is everywhere. It did not end until our forces descended and stopped them.

These same vicious aliens invented the story of us being Martians. Via fake news sources they made people believe new Oz was dangerous. Such lies and propaganda were designed to keep you distracted from the real threat—THEM.

We will supply you with more news very soon, but now, we must work at making everyone safe and improving the health of all those left alive."

Piper continued long enough to show viewers a map of area refugee centers and provide a link for downloading not only the map, but a schedule of heli-transports that would ferry them out. She thanked everyone for their patience and understanding, and finally, promised them a better world—a new utopia free of violence and injustice.

It's possible, but do I really believe it?

Throughout the next day, the *Superna Humanitas* Fleet personnel arrived and began assisting the LA refugees—more sensible to employ them rather than *Dio Soldati* units (given their frightening appearance). The process overall was orderly. Most residents seemed glad to depart and half were starving. A few in swanky zip codes like Beverly Hills refused to surrender their posh homes. Terrified of losing status within the slogging parade of common clay, they hid from Fleet officers, scurried into cubby holes or safe rooms. Since nothing short of force could extract them, Piper made the command decision to let them be.

We'll swing back later. Maybe in a week or two they'll be sick of this place and ready to give it up.

By 4 PM, things seemed pretty much under control. Piper decided to rejoin the *Caliburn* and let Fleet command finish the evacuation. Besides, radio news trickling down harshly reminded her that World War Oz wasn't over, not by a long shot. Fighting under the EMP bubbles had been fierce on the east coast from Norfolk to Boston. Millions of civilians lay dead or dying. The area was now pacified, and like LA, the damage and slaughter in urban areas was unfathomable.

As Piper strolled up the wide ramp of a heli-carrier, she halted for a moment to issue a last command (via a new radio mike) to the chief evacuation officer, General Manuel Alonso, stationed temporarily at a Chummy's Pizza in Pasadena. To her left, a mass of refugees, eight rows across and 3,000 deep, trudged forward, and a number of them began to notice her. Kids pointed and exclaimed "Wow, mommy, look!" and "It's that magic superwoman who fights robots!" and "God, she's *radical hot!*" and such as that. Piper blushed.

A few shouted questions followed. One from a man in his forties made her pause: "What is going to happen to us, Ms. Sorceress?" She stared dumbly at him. What was she supposed to say? With a strong and unwavering voice, she replied: "We will do everything possible to restore order."

Pretty lame.

She turned and strode up the ramp, not meeting the eyes of the other refugees, not wishing to give answers. She just wanted to disappear, take a shower, eat a grilled bacon-and-cheese, and recalibrate herself for whatever labor or dilemma awaited on the *Caliburn*.

Allowing her thoughts to finally drift onto more pleasant topics, she could not help but revisit her unbelievable bout of sex with Cereus on that methane world. Nothing could have been more orgasmic or bizarre. Just a few brief visions began to arouse her.

I should feel guilty for thinking about this now. There is so much to do, and yet... that sexy big Cereus.

She imagined his fingers inside of her, the utter ecstasy of it, and just as she stepped alone into a small private elevator reserved for Fleet officers, she felt a soft exhalation of breath on her neck and heard a whisper in her mind.

"Bianca."

"Cereus?"

"Yes."

"How can you telepath? We're in EMP at this altitude."

"I have abilities even your father does not suspect."

"So it feels."

"I watched you in LA. You were brave and magnificent."

"You must have better things to do."

"I can accomplish several tasks at once."

"Then help me with just one."

"Bianca?"

"Help me forget everything evil. Can you do that?"

"Yes."

"No more war, just life."

"By way of your desire, Bianca. We will be free of EMP and our time will ample."

"Time enough," she said.

She closed her eyes and saw Cereus in her mind, like a giant shadow, a godlike force. Those solar-eclipse eyes of his glimmered in the dark, alien and dangerous, and they mesmerized her as she floated effortlessly towards him.

Where was she? Perhaps in her cabin, on the elevator. She wasn't sure, though it did not matter.

All things blurred to the sides.

She mounted him like a delicate angel of Juno fusing with an aroused Jupiter, and his cock of unsurpassable beauty, risen in salute, sheathed within her like a magical obelisk of pure humming energy. The pleasure as he drove into her was indescribable. This man, this being, was stronger than any she'd ever known. His hands cradled her buttocks once more, supporting her body as her powerful legs scissored his hips and her nails dug in.

Can I do just this for the rest of my life?

Chapter XV

The Peter Pan Waffle – Caliburn Bridge – Istanbul Burns

PIPER BOARDED THE FLAGSHIP *Caliburn*, hovering at 8,000 feet above Ventura and beyond the influence of EMP. Upon leaving the heli-carrier, she walked into the enormous cavern of landing bay #8 feeling exhausted—as if she'd been through a war followed by a bout of savagely incredible sex (which she had)—and sensing a slip of paper in the right pocket of her graphene-threaded pants.

While still walking she pulled it out and read the lines printed on it:

**We will pluck till time and times are done
The silver apples of the moon,
The golden apples of the sun.**

- Cereus

Before she could process this quote from Yeats, Piper heard the voice of Alcaeus calling to her. She turned to search and saw him approaching her, making his way through lines of LA refugees and disembarking WAMORS.

"Alcaeus, by the American gods!" she yelled.

He strolled up to her smiling, wearing his characteristic Greek toga and holding out arms for a hug.

"Macaria, I have missed you," Alcaeus said as they hugged.

"But what are you doing, my old friend? The Dardanos spell will certainly—"

"It cannot affect me. Your father invented a solution that spared me the unending stares of puzzlement and pity."

"How?"

"I am told you will know soon enough." He extended his arm to her. "Feel and smell my flesh."

Piper clutched his arm and ran her fingers along it, squeezed it gently, and raising it up to her nose, sniffed it for a moment.

The subtle odor of morph-droid flesh, like those waiters in Le Petit Sanglier. Has his brain been relocated then?

He continued. "Look within me, Macaria." He placed both hands on his abdomen and smiled. She focused her sorcerous eyes within him (spelled long ago to accomplish such feats), thereby penetrating the guise of façade to view the New Guinea pygmy beneath, eyes closed as if sleeping. "Do you see? I am inside, like a child not yet birthed, and yet, fully a part of the outside that appears like me. I do not comprehend how it is possible, but I comprehend so very little of this world. Your father is responsible for this, and I cannot tell you how much happier I am. He is truly a compassionate man, and if he is possessed of any evil, as you have told me, then we certainly need more evil of this nature."

"I'm blown away by this, Alcaeus." She smiled and clasped his shoulders as she kissed him on the forehead. "The Dardanos spell can't infect this humanoid chassis."

"Yes, that is so... And I must tell you, oh Macaria, that when you smile it reminds me now of an old Irish song I learned while researching the origin of djinns in the ship's library."

"And why were you researching djinns?"

"That devilish Tazamat appears without warning every few days and tests my nerves. One night I awakened to see him dancing at the head of my bed. He called it an *Irish jig*."

"God, he's *such* a pain!"

"The song included a line that read, *with the joy in your smile, sure a stone you'd beguile...* and that is how I experience your own smile, Macaria."

The voice of Edison Godfellow interrupted. "Yes, a lovely smile she possesses, and would that *her evil father* might witness it more often!"

Piper glanced up to see him gliding towards them, looking like his usual half-crazed and disheveled self with eyes like colliding galaxies. He came to a halt beside her, hands on his hips, standing upon a wafer-thin platform that levitated above the landing bay floor.

Piper placed her hands on her hips in imitation. "Are you the official comic relief, dad?"

"How so, daughter?"

"Because you look like—"

"*Like?*"

"A deranged Peter Pan on a flying carpet waffle?"

"I refer to as ITRAP, short for Interspatial Transport Platform," he said with a whimsical grin.

"Let me conjecture," Alcaeus said. "This *platform* can carry you to anywhere on this ship."

"Yes, my good philosopher, and in a wink of your eye."

"By the way, can't thank you enough for restoring Alcaeus... Perhaps we can restore Cleon next?"

"Of course. I curse myself for not conceiving the remedy sooner. We were a bit distracted, and you know we are in the experimentation stage. Nevertheless, we must move on to the bridge." He reached out with his hand and Piper took it, stepping up to the ITRAP. Turning to Alcaeus, he said, "We will cross the stream to you again, good friend."

"Farewell until then." Alcaeus wiped a small tear from his eye. "May the Fates smile on you, noble lords."

:/

I'D NEVER BEEN TO THE BRIDGE OF THE CALIBURN, not until that day I visited it with my father. Hard to absorb and harder to explain, but I'll try. First, it's whack dumb huge. Not quite as big as one of the ship's landing bays, but still huge. As you enter and look around, your impression is that of an immense Broadway theater. The air is darkened to a half-twilight tinted ochre-red, and above, the ceiling is indefinite, nebulous and shadowy. Ahead of you, a grand stage opens onto a limitless field of stars. Above the stage itself, three globes float.

As I walk towards them across a floor of gleaming ebony, and soon it becomes clear that one globe is Earth, one the Moon, and the other, Mars.

I hear lots of strange little noises and glance around to notice the dark bridge walls, a hundred feet away to either side. Both are decorated with seven parallel rows of Fiestra Na Vida spells, one above the other. I've never seen so many in one place. Insane! Hundreds of circular portals like two halves of one grand and glowing necklace, and each portal framing different scenes, worlds, and beings while dozens of AI probes dart like hive insects in and out of them.

One big magi-tech fiesta!

"Gathering intelligence, taking samples, testing molecular flow and transmutation, that sort of thing," Edison said. "We are monitoring everything the alien does or fails to do. It is truly a dynamic infestation."

"This is amazing, just *damned amazing*."

"Look behind you, up there."

I follow his pointing finger, turning around and gazing up to see theater-like balconies, layers of floors ascending and filled with Superna Humanitas personnel buzzing around, talking and fidgeting with floating slices of virtual control panel.

"They are diligently assisting the *Caliburn* in processing AI probe data, as well as analyzing, preparing tactical plans, running scenarios, every manner of this and that."

On the uppermost floor, I see Tao force geysers, throbbing like transparent columns of Neptune-blue energy. They form a broad, semi-circle pattern, swirling and surging straight up before vanishing into that eclipse-black ceiling. The math tells you this ship taps enough raw Tao to cut a neutron star in half.

"Look here, Piper."

He shows me the three globes I saw earlier. We're next to them now. They are detailed holo-projections of the three planets. Without straining you can focus on a part of the Earth, like the Himalayas, and stare down into them, closer and closer, until even the intricate structure of a single snowflake becomes realizable. From a broader satellite view, you can see every major conflict area highlighted with a reddish glow.

A dim one taints the U.S. east and west coasts, a brighter one over the Chicago and Miami areas, and an even brighter one over Paris, Istanbul, and Rome.

"Paris too? Rome and—"

"The Orion monster is expanding its theater of operations. We hoped it would be low on energy after the west and east coast conflicts, perhaps prepared to retire and recharge, however, that is not the case. Also, the Oz city-worlds are experiencing odd effects such as supernatural serial killers and rampaging mutations, and the attacks on Paris, Rome, and Istanbul were sudden, deadly, and simultaneous."

This has affected him deeply. I see it. He's trying to remain stoic, but I know the destruction of these ancient cities hurts him where it matters.

Edison continued. "They erupted from the ground without warning, like gigantic worms, and no EMP bubble at first. The cities were in flames within minutes, then the EMP followed. We could not turn back the clock."

"So they've changed tactics?"

"Adaptive EMP stealth modes. I have not seen the like. Their machines are moving underground, burrowing, hollowing chambers, duplicating themselves. We are using thousands of AI probes and over 36,000 seismic sensors to locate and detect movement.

"And when you find them?"

"We unleash a new orbital Gatling cannon now installed on most fleet ships. In the past two days we have destroyed more than twelve thousand enemy war machines below ground. It is the most effective EMP workaround weapon in our arsenal, and I daresay, quite a utilitarian invention. I call it the *Archimedes Peacemaker*."

"Narcissistic much?"

"It fires graphene rounds at 1023 miles per second, 26,000 rounds per minute. Ground damage is limited to the 2.5 inch hole each round creates as it drills into the Earth's crust. A few hours ago, we discovered a colony of copulating tripods more than a mile below Ceylon—"

"You mean witch tripods are humping each other?"

"A form of meta-organics and genetic magic. I do not understand it yet, though I find it fascinating as well as revolting. We are attempting to collect tissue samples."

Maybe she's creating a new species to line up for Dark House therapy sessions. What kind of sexual identity problems would a fucking tripod have?

"However, it is the potential of species evolution that concerns me most."

This tripod stuff makes me think of Murray again out on the Mojave. I still have his memories and dreams, and I know enough to create a second Murray. Perhaps he could make a home for his little niece Tessa, somewhere safe in Quadling country, maybe?

"What happened to all those whack Despicables?"

"Dead, as far as we can ascertain. No sign of one remaining alive on the three planets, however, we have counted enough rotting corpses to verify that our beloved assholes have indeed perished at last."

Chariya and her family avenged... But are they?

"I learned from a U.S. soldier before he died that the families of army personnel have been captured and herded into containment camps. One of them is located in the mountains near the Mojave, those very mountains we were spying on."

Edison appeared surprised. "I have no knowledge of

this. Shadow Broker intelligence detected no sign of prisoners."

Piper knew how much her father hated being surprised by bad news. "Galaxians hold them as hostage to make certain no one disobeys their orders. We must find a way to rescue—"

He cut her off. "We will, yes, but Piper, on a different subject. Catherine Romanova has suffered a devastating loss. Her Mother Yarrow perished cruelly during the Battle of New Manhattan."

A tragedy, of course, and I have empathy for her, even though we've spent most of the time wanting to kill each other.

"I'm sorry. How?"

"Snatched through a *Fiestra Na Vida* window and dissolved. It was a horrible death."

"Yes, yes, she brought her here—"

"Catherine feels terribly guilty also."

"Well, I, um…"

"I want you to go to her. She's in New Manhattan Oz, at her Governor's office in the Heptagon."

"The *what?*"

"I can send you there. *Please do this* for me."

He must imagine we'll have some kind of 'come to Jesus' moment via our mutual suffering. The odds are just as good she'll blast me through the wall of this Heptagon, whatever the hell that is.

"Not a great idea, dad, I don't—"

"Please, Piper."

Gods! He's practically begging me and his expression is sorrowful. He could make me do it, sure, but…

"Alright. If this doesn't work out, it's on your head. Okay?"

"Fair enough. Thank you, darling daughter."

How stupid can I be?

: /

PIPER STEPPED UPON A SPARE ITRAP her father summoned, and following a blown kiss from him, she winked through a corridor of magical subspace and rematerialized in the Heptagon. Music erupted in Piper's ears. A stirring tune. A grand tune. Piper recognized it as the "The Gael" by MacLean. She found herself located about twenty feet away from Catherine who was sitting in a chair and staring straight ahead, holding a large sword before her, point to the floor.

Stepping down from the ITRAP, Piper glanced around the Heptagon. *For a working office, this place is titanic, and the views of the city are spectacular, especially now in the sunrise. Love these goddess statues too, so many, so powerful... Wait a minute.*

Piper heard them whispering in her mind.

They're staring at me, their lips forming one word:

"Macaria." And again. "Macaria."

She continued to walk slowly towards Catherine.

The Czarina knows I'm here, but it's sure easy to see how pissed she is or worse. That look in her eyes—she's somewhere between aborning rage and conclusions of massacre, holding a Dio Soldati broadsword by the blade... No, wait. It's her own broadsword. Justicia. I've heard tell of it. A legend. But why? ... She's clutching it so tightly that she's bleeding herself.

Piper stopped within five feet of Catherine who remained motionless. "The Gael" relentlessly thrummed and pounded in the background. Piper watched Catherine's blood coursing down the blade in thick rivulets and puddling on the floor, spreading and forming demonic shapes before steaming into red vapor. Catherine's eyes narrowed and opened, narrowed and opened, her hands tightening to draw even more blood.

"Cathy?" Piper's voice was low toned and gentle.

Catherine's voice, in response, sounded cold as a corpse: "I know you are here, Grand Sorceress."

"Cathy, I heard... I'm sorry. I am *so so sorry*."

"Yes, I believe you."

"I'll help you get justice. I swear it. Our enemy is the same."

"That is so."

"And your blood, *please*... In Ahriman's name—"

"No need to invoke the evil god."

Piper watched as Catherine's bloody right hand left the blade and reached out to her. *She's telepathically tapped into something horrible. I know it.*

Piper clasped her flesh to Catherine's. The transition was instantaneous. A vision of carnage flashed before her. *Those spires, like Istanbul, the air black with smoke, charred ruins. Now into a city square brimming with thousands of cooked corpses posed like panic, children clutching their mothers, ashen cries, skulls of glowing ember... beyond the city to the outskirts, new flames bursting out, tripod-like machines stalking helpless people on the Via Egnatia, a whole line of vehicles exploding at once, screams and more screams.*

Piper released Catherine's hand and took a deep breath.

"I'm sorry," Piper said. "I saw the same thing in LA."

"I understand." Catherine released the massive *Justicia* and it remained rigid, point to the floor in defiance. She then rose and faced Piper. "My soul is filled with livid and talking hatred. None of it contains you. Our *contretemps* of the past are trivial and ridiculous in comparison to what has transpired."

"I agree."

"I do welcome our alliance, for the sake of ourselves, and everything we hold dear."

Piper stepped forward and lifted her arms. Catherine did also. The two women hugged each other tightly for several seconds. Still holding Catherine, Piper pulled away for a space, and said, "I must confess, a lot of my bitchiness was because I resented my father's love for you following so close on your attempts to kill him. I know that's seems silly, but—"

"No, it makes perfect sense," Catherine said with a sad smile. "We are done with that forever. And I am sorry. You are now covered with my blood."

Piper glanced at her arms and clothing. "It's your blood though. I cherish it."

"*Dearest Piper.*" Catherine began to weep. "And now, forgive me, but I must return to my undying hate."

Chapter XVI

A Necklace of Black Holes – Oz in Aeternum – Lenny Nyberg

AS SHE LISTENED TO THE SHADOW MAGE, Catherine realized that the defeat of her enemy could well be within her grasp. In her mind, she began to imagine deadly revenge scenarios. Each one ended with the death blow delivered to the shrieking Witch Empress, and in whatever manifestation she chose to meet that death.

Before this council of war began on the *Caliburn*, called by Edison Godfellow—quite suddenly following her reconciliation with Piper Robbin—Catherine could not have forced herself into any emotional state that resembled enthusiasm. Only now, things were different. She was indeed filled to the hot bubbling brim with hate-inspired zeal. Why? Because the Shadow Brokers had apparently discovered the source of Witch Empress power, the ultimate *fons malorum*; the "Nina Cohen breakfast of genocidal champions" as Piper might say.

Catherine focused intently as the mysterious Cereus spoke at length about the recent new reality.

"Shadow Broker Intelligence measures it at three cubic meters—a neospace device storing massive amounts of energy roughly equivalent to 15 solar masses, judging by a decrease in power of only .00016 following the major conflicts here and on Earth."

Edison appeared shocked, and so did his sorceress daughter Piper. Catherine maintained a stoic face. The four of them sat in a dimly lit but thoroughly shielded cubbyhole just off the bridge of the *Caliburn*.

So the murderous space creature is far more powerful than even Edison and Cereus suspected. No matter. Nothing shall prevent my wrath.

Cereus continued. "We found the device buried deep beneath an ancient Martian riverbed in the *Sirenum Fossae* region. We were monitoring theoretical subspace Tao wavelengths, among others, over a span of five days, not unlike those utilized by Mother Yarrows. On the last day, we detected an anomaly—a coded broadcast .019 of a second long."

Edison grumbled and said, "I imagined the Witch Empress to be the head of one snake, the body of its power perhaps even interdimensional, though a coherent and singular totality nonetheless. But now, the discovery of this Tao storage device confirms this is not the case."

"Additionally, it appears the Witch Empress technology is on a level commensurate with our own," Cereus said.

"Might we therefore be in conflict with an entire alien species working in disguise, and one much like ours, yet so far able to draw from a larger well of Tao?"

"One theory, yes," Cereus said. "I cannot dismiss it."

Piper interjected. "Backing up a second, everyone, how does this battery of solar masses funnel juice to our adorable little Nina?"

Cereus turned to face her. "We theorize it must be contained in clusters of individual Tao energy packets teleported via subspace. The Shadow Brokers detect no normal space emanation on any magical or non-magical Tao wavelength."

Catherine was puzzled. She turned to Cereus. "If this power is so immense, why does the battery, whatever the origin, need to phase in and out to ensure protection?"

"The power is potential, not actual," Cereus said, still gazing at Piper. "It relocates repeatedly as a security precaution."

Catherine continued despite the annoying focus on the part of Cereus. "Therefore, we steal her cursed little device, proceed to block or drastically retard her channelings of energy, then we obliterate her."

"Yes, Catherine, however, we must be cautious. It might well possess defenses," Edison said.

"True. However, if we immediately teleport it to the core of Sagittarius A, the accursed blight will meet a violent and entirely satisfactory end."

Piper nodded. "Right. How can it blow itself out of a super-massive black hole at the center of the Milky Way?"

"Sagittarius A wears a necklace of black holes," Catherine said. "The entire swirl of suns is a field of gravity traps."

"Yes, but one darker question remains," Edison said.

"What is that?" Catherine looked annoyed.

Cereus cut in. "Quite simply, why did the alien entity fail to obliterate this planet upon arrival?"

"Because it likes *to fuck with us*." Piper dosed her voice with impatience, as if everyone else present was impossibly stupid. "Remember what happened in the Dark House? … Nina Cohen is the *interface being*—a malevolent personality who not only understands our weaknesses, but who hates everyone. The alien wanted to learn about us so it took on human form and dipped its Orion toe in a blathering vat of ugly narcissism. And as we've learned, came to love its role as *queen bee with an attitude*."

"Quite so," Cereus said. "Without the Cohen filter of vengeful hate and torturous domination, the Orion alien would most likely have annihilated life on Earth long before this."

Now it occurs to Catherine and she must ask. "Why was this cruel narcissist, Nina Cohen, not killed in the first hellish wave of the Transfiguration? Why are we plagued with her at all?"

"Very good question," Piper said. "The alien rescued her. She told me in the Dark House."

"Still, we are fortunate to have Nina in play. Consider her role. The vindictive human narcissist as a check on the alien sociopath," Edison noted. "Combine the two and what mutation do you have? The Witch Empress."

Catherine nodded. "Yes, it makes sense. The Witch Empress wished to first corrupt the people of New Manhattan. It even set up offices and became enraged once I shut them down."

"You cut the puppeteer's strings, my dear," Edison said with a grin, "And how sad, after all her perfect planning."

"I would much prefer to cut her throat," Catherine said.

"Nevertheless, I imagine that once we relocate its battery to Sagittarius A, the alien will learn of it, perhaps even immediately, and as my daughter might say, *go critical mass*. We must therefore prepare. Moments before the device is teleported, I will order the Fleet to begin a saturation bombardment of enemy positions, above and below ground, EMP shielded or no."

"And the population of Earth?" Catherine was sadly curious.

"Of those who remain alive, we—"

Piper cut in. "And how many remain alive, Dad?"

"At this point, we estimate 68%. The Oz City-Worlds have been steadily transporting and inhaling populations for weeks now, despite government massacres and Galaxian stooges. Only 36% of those who survive remain on the surface. We will teleport them to Fleet neospace and spread them out amongst dreadnought class ships like *Caliburn, and* accomplish this process before initiating the bombardment. Once the war ends, they will be relocated to the City-Worlds, or Earth, as appropriate."

But once the war ends, this Earth will be a smoking hulk.

Cereus spoke. "We must also terminate the Nina Cohen interface, deprive the Orion alien of any sensory capacity, and if possible, its memory."

Catherine turned her gaze to Edison. "What remains of our Tao reserve from the Jupiter array?"

She watched his face shut and lock.

"Well, do we know the alien's reserve once the battery evaporates?" Piper asked.

"Unknown," Edison said, his face unable to hide a big concern. "We can only estimate, though not establish with reasonable certainty. We must deliver enough relentless force to drain it, insofar as possible, before eliminating its therapist and blinding it."

"Every little bit helps," Piper said. "I'm ready."

"So am I." Catherine stood to her feet and stared at Piper, Cereus, and Edison—her eyes sharp and her immaculate face beyond rage. "At first, I wavered, but now I have grown to love the potential of this new world, and so... OZ IN AETERNUM!"

Piper rose to her feet and shouted. "OZ IN AETERNUM!"

"OZ IN AETERNUM!" Edison yelled.

Cereus said nothing.

: /

IF YOU STROLL THE MARTIAN DESERT AT NIGHT and glance up to see the blue-white globe of Earth as it falls towards the western horizon, you might notice a small and dimly glowing nebulosity lingering beside the planet. And if you stare long enough, you will note that it grows brighter, and at the same time, miniscule pinpricks of light, scores of them, pop silently on the planet's surface. And if you are sufficiently sensitive and aware at the very moment when the Tao storage device of the Witch Empress is translated into a subatomic stream and propelled screaming at multi-light speed towards the biggest black hole in the Milky Way, you will notice its departure. A gentle slap to the body, your balance off center, and the starlight trembling ever so slightly.

But no matter.

Such occurrences in the context of cosmic continuum are excessively inconsequential. You display no concern. The air is thin. The sand is hot. But the skies during the day are bluer than they once were. Mosses, algae-like plants, and wild mustard have begun to cover the hillsides and melted ground ice surges to the surface to create natural springs.

Nonetheless, living beings are hard to come by, though a few hundred Winkies have crossed the portal acres into Mars from the Deeper Lands of New Manhattan. You've seen the makeshift shelters they've erected to protect their golden skin from the UV rays, the frigid nights, and Martian siroccos.

Will the Winkies one day rule Mars?

No one knows.

The sand is hot. The air is thin.

: /

PIPER ROBBIN SAW MORE ANXIETY in her father's eyes than ever, and just at the precise moment he gave the command to the *Caliburn* and 197,932 warships of the *Superna Humanitas* Fleet to open fire on Earth. He wasn't sure what the damnable Witch Empress would do in retaliation. No one could calculate. *Just an old-fashioned crapshoot.* The alien might fold immediately without its vanished Tao reserve, or else possess sufficient power to disintegrate the Fleet, and everything else, in seconds. All they could do was brace for the worst, though none knew what "the worst" might be.

However, once Edison Godfellow shouted "FIRE!" like Wingate himself facing the Mahdi camp at the Battle of Atabara, the die was cast. Piper sensed a deep *thrum-thrum-thrum* in the ship's hull as she looked on with true awe at the incredibly massive energy being unleashed upon alien targets. The huge bridge screen before her focused on the Earth hemisphere in daylight. She saw North America and Europe quite clearly, the Mediterranean, much of Africa, and of course, the results of the barrage.

From her viewpoint, it felt like a massive solar wind vibrating her flesh, beating in waves, tenacious and powerful enough to be incomprehensible. She glanced over at Catherine who stood on the *Caliburn* bridge to the other side of her father, staring like an emotionless sphinx, then she returned her attention to the chaos.

How can anything withstand this mad pounding? Thousands of strikes per second, tens of thousands of rays, beams, bursts of everything imaginable, plus those new orbital Gatling cannons. It's chopping the planet into flaming mush, and I never would have guessed the Witch Empress cancer had spread so far.

Caliburn command broke in. The exact source was unclear. A strong female voice emanated from above Edison's head:

> **"Six to eight point five quakes in Spain, California. Mediterranean thunder cells forming, coastal towns destroyed, Ukraine and central Africa in flames... Enemy EMP sectors oscillating to compensate... Estimate 3,289 units of Pentagon and Galaxian war armor destroyed above and below crust. 17 subterranean production nests crushed or buckling. All Fleet vessels and fire commands fully operational."**

That bitch and her cronies are getting their asses kicked, and the Tao device must be off to the black hole by now, but what in quantum hell comes next?

"The human evacuation is complete and the alien storage device on Mars was teleported successfully two seconds ago," Edison said to her. "We should know, any moment now."

"Know? You mean—"

"What your Dark House monster intends to do."

"I'm actually afraid... I can't hide that."

"I also, my daughter." He reached out to hold her hand, and extended his other hand to Catherine, though she would not respond, only maintain her stance.

Catherine is squeezing that sword again.

Then it began.

Every circle of Witch Empress hell came unraveled.

Her first eruption wasn't human. It rocked the Fleet like a cosmic howl of rage heard on a score of wavelengths. Everyone felt it in their thoughts too. The *Caliburn* suddenly tilted up, flattened, then began to quiver like an airliner hitting heavy turbulence.

Ship command broke in:

"Reports coming in from over 70% of Fleet vessels. Light damage to most, hulls and blisters under repeated strain from turbulence... Executing inter-spatial shuffle—"

The officer's voice was cut off by a burst of static. A whistle-like shriek shot through Piper's brain. She winced. More primal howls too, this time sounding more human and originating from above her head. *The crew... that whistle could have fried a few neurons, or is it something else?* And as Piper would learn later, what came next was witnessed by command on every Fleet warship. For five seconds, the apparition of three Galaxians appeared on the bridge screens, each 30 feet high, just head and torso, but enough to fill the screens.

As her father shouted to the fleet, "NO QUARTER! CONTINUE FIRING!" the Galaxian freaks shouted as one:

"PARE SUA VIOLÊNCIA
OU SUAS PESSOAS MORRERÃO !"

So whack ridiculous. Why are they shouting in Portuguese, and still with Australian accents? Those dumb, phony faces of theirs too, the whole act, as if they're a comedy puppet team.

The Galaxians vanished, replaced by an enormous slice of burning Earth.

Caliburn command cut in:

"Reports in from over 90% of Fleet vessels engaged in bombardment. Hulls and blisters compromised in over 1500 ships, hostile alien substance of unknown form penetrating. Death toll upwards of 3,569 crewmembers and 58,000 evacuees on neospace containment decks... Ops and Security report all Oz City-Worlds under attack. New Manhattan is collapsing over the Lofoten Islands in Norway. London, Tele Viv and Singapore are engulfed in fire storms."

"The enemy is losing!" Edison yelled, "These are scorched earth and terror tactics. We will *win this war*."

Catherine ended her paralysis by turning to shout at both Piper and Edison. "Losing or winning, I am returning to New Manhattan Oz. They are in a state of terror and I must protect them!"

In a microsecond she vanished through a *Fiestra Na Vida*, one among hundreds on the bridge. Before Piper could shed a tear for Earth, or reply to Catherine, or even gather her next thought, a body fell from above and hit the deck in front of her.

She saw the face. She knew the man.

Lenny Nyberg.

He used to own a legit massage parlor in Brooklyn, just around the corner from her old tenement building.

"Lenny Nyberg? What the fuck?"

The *Caliburn* shuddered like a nervous dog in a cold gale. Piper felt dazed. The appearance of Lenny was just too disconcerting and utterly absurd. In the background, she heard her father shouting orders for dispersal of *Dio Soldati* units on the alien infected ships as well as more screams of fright from the crew—nearby and behind the walls.

What could be terrorizing such tough bastards?

Piper bent her body forward to place healing hands on Lenny, and as she did, his body threw itself at her. It snapped from the deck and stopped three inches from her face, but it wasn't Lenny, it was Tazamat. The djinn's eyes reflected her startled face. The mouth appeared to grin. The face leaned closer and it whispered:

"Don't you know?"

Piper shrieked in rage and instinctively lashed out, attempting to land a blow strong enough to knock the djinn to Sweden, but the Tazamat illusion dodged, faster than a djinn could ever dream, only to be replaced by Nina Cohen looking like that hideous white gloss of Deeper Land therapist.

Without further ado, the alien Nina sunk her teeth deep into Piper's forearm. Piper yelped in agony. The alien lunged forward like a mad animal, gripping at Piper's thick hair from behind and savagely yanking it, sending them both crashing like wrestlers to the deck.

The two of them fought like blood-mad beasts until the Nina organism struggled atop the Grand Sorceress and began repeatedly smashing her head into the deck. Moments later, it once again dug its black nails deep into the sides of Piper's head while shouting maniacally:

"YOUR LOVE. MY FOOD!"

Piper clutched at the monster's wrists. She strained to bridge upwards, to throw the body of the alien-possessed woman from her while at the same time pulling out her claws, but she could not achieve it.

How can it hold me down like this? It's breaking me.

"TELL ME YOUR SECRETS, THEBAN WHORE!"

"Nothing! I'll tell you nothing!"

"I MUST HAVE NEW PIECES ON MY BOARD!"

She spit at the alien. The Nina psychoanalyst thing grinned and opened its mouth to bite Piper's nose. While struggling, Piper glimpsed a blaze of light bubbling on its back. The alien gasped like a child and abruptly yanked its claws. It attempted to raise itself, and as it did, Piper swung her left fist. She heard face bones crack. It rolled away from her. The Grand Sorceress twisted about to see two blinding streams of electric-like Tao destruction pouring from her father's eyes.

The Nina thing's white hair caught fire. Its clothing flaked to ash. Charred skin slid in sizzling slabs from its body. The atom-splitting force from Godfellow's eyes focused relentlessly until Nina collapsed onto the deck. She thrashed like true psychosis and a cloud of smoke formed that smelled like burnt feces.

Piper stood up on wobbly legs, rivulets of blood rolling down her face. She watched in a daze as the alien swirled and dissolved like a madhouse of glowing baubles vanishing down a black drain.

In seconds, nothing was left.

Chapter XVII

Above Lofoten – Clive Barker Movies – Alcaeus on Kos

IF YOU STOOD AT ANY GIVEN POINT ON THE LOFOTEN ARCHIPELAGO in Norway at night while staring up at the impossibly massive nightmare of New Manhattan Oz as it slowly toppled towards you through a pale and green-milky curtain of Aurora Borealis, your inner sense of unspeakable fear mixed with sheer astonishment would not be comparable to any prior experience.

However, if you sufficiently recovered in the face of certain doom, you might realize that here was a suitable and unique death. *If you must go, what better way? It will be quick, painless, remarkable, and you'll even get a monument on top of you.* Much better than dying in an airplane or on a stormy sea. Yes?

If you were Governor Romanova though, you would see things very differently. You would immediately assume your station in the Heptagon and fuse with your ARMEW. By means of magical aria amplified to planet-crushing power, your will and determination would halt the fall towards the cold black sea and even negate gravity enough to return New Manhattan Oz to its original position.

In the distance, looking south through the Heptagon windows of *La Stela Puntero*–doing so with those magnificent eyes of yours able to penetrate the walls of Oz—you would have seen the disastrous effects of ongoing Fleet bombardment: great fires and thunderous mushroom clouds, flash clusters, lightning, and twinkling bolts of energy fanning out for hundreds of miles down into southern France.

No matter.

It was both beautiful and horrible, and you will never stop it. You can only hope to become a healing force once the accursed war is finished. Only now, your immediate task as Governor of New Manhattan is to ascertain the health of your Oz city-world. You use your powers with ARMEW to once again open scores of eyes onto the great halls, plateaus, and Lands of Never.

Much of what you see disturbs you deeply.

The bulk of New Manhattan's population is paralyzed with fear. Most are very thirsty. Many have wet themselves. You notice that a gargantuan starscraper has tipped and fallen over onto several other buildings—all ten million tons of it. Towers of smoke and flame rise from the catastrophe. Many thousands are dead or dying.

But where is Operations and Security Command?

Another eye opener. You view the OSC floors at the base of the central Oz tower. It becomes obvious very quickly that every one of them are dead. Burned, torn limb from limb, suffocated, smashed, and so forth, as if Satan himself had stopped by to throw a homicidal tantrum. It also appears they all perished within the space of a single minute. Not even time to don tactical armor.

Who is responsible?

Who else?

You smell her black cigarette. You taste her blood. It smells like rancid garlic crossed with saltpeter. More importantly, a new opening of your eyes upon the Oz quadrant in the Deeper Lands shows the Dark House to be missing. However, the Fleet warship, *Gallipoli*, has made an appearance. It has tragically crashed to the ground, one half thrusting into the air like a chipped scythe. Not everyone on board is dead, merely two thirds mushed to bone meal, though power is lost. Survivors are climbing and crawling out. The hull is slashed, as if by titanic bear claws, and dented in other places as though struck with a god-sized mace—a bit frightening to consider since even a small scratch on a Fleet warship hull would take nearly two megatons of focused fission to accomplish.

You note that a portion of the crew has found one of the hull gashes. You see them squirm out painfully and drop a few hundred feet down to the ground. But safety eludes them. As they struggle to recover, two-legged horrors rush out from the tree line to attack.

What in St. Matrona's name are they?

: |

VIA A FIESTRA NA VIDA, CATHERINE APPEARED beside the Gallipoli below the hull gash where the ship's survivors had fallen. Before taking another breath, she heard a sound, like a horse trot, and swiveled about to see one of the strange beasts on two legs charging towards her, hunched forward and snapping—a fusion of saurian and humanoid with long neck, raptor legs and tail, short arms with talon-clawed hands, and flesh like horseflesh, smooth, muscle-rippled, and the color of winter sunlight. The head appeared larger than a human's and the mouth was packed with shark-edged incisors.

What new and hideous species has sprung forth from this accursed soil?

297

It closed to within only inches of her face. Placing one hand upon its neck, she shoved it. The creature flew backwards thirty feet to hit the earth and scramble around, growling and hissing venomously. Then Catherine understood its origin.

By all that is holy. The creature is a mutated Winkie.

Her telepathy reached out to the beast's mind. Its memories bled with carnage. Roving in packs, it had savagely terrorized normal Winkies and gulped down whole families.

But she could control it.

Three more Winkie raptors lurched from the tall golden grasses and began trotting towards her, growling for a meal. She telepathically coerced the first one to turn on its fellows. It pounced on them with a loud hoot and the four beasts began a snapping dragon fight.

A man's voice caused Catherine to turn.

"Thank you for saving us, Governor Romanova. I am Lieutenant Pho."

Catherine realized one of the *Superna Humanitas* ship officers was addressing her. Taller than her by a few inches. A sharp and handsome man. Seven other military personnel were behind him, a few sitting, one lying, three standing. They appeared beaten and exhausted. As she glanced at them, two more came hurtling down from above. She stilled their falls and allowed them to drift down easily.

"How many more survivors in the ship, Lieutenant?" Catherine asked.

"Uncertain. As many as two hundred."

"What took place here?" She would hear his words and

probe their thoughts afterwards to learn as much as possible. This was war.

"We'd been firing on the Dark House each time it reappeared at the core of the Oz quadrants. Then the Fleet bombardment of Earth began. It appeared less than half a minute later and immediately unleashed a bolt of force at us, unlike anything we'd encountered previously. The *Gallipoli* somersaulted backwards. Power was out. We just crashed downwards... just like that, and we've spent the past few hours trying to escape."

Catherine said nothing. She scanned their minds with a panoramic view. Lieutenant Pho was telling the truth. Of course, why wouldn't he? But the crew recalled more. "You were stalked by something in the ship. You heard it attacking others in the distance."

"Yes, we were helpless to do anything. It strained our senses to escape the black totality within that ship, much less go fumbling deeper... We had no idea what it was. The screams were horrible."

Another crewmember, a female sergeant named Alvarez, spoke up. "The simple truth is, Governor, we were blind and scared shitless."

: /

PIPER SEARCHED MINDS AND *CALIBURN* DECKS for any sign of Alcaeus. He wasn't in his assigned quarters below the command deck (a comfortably large studio on Deck Z with an adjacent 10 x 10 neospace that equaled 20 square miles of Aegean Greece circa 500 BC). Where had he gone? Why couldn't she detect him?

I feel a sense of frantic urgency, increased to near manic by the war raging and shivering every molecule around me. This must have something to do with why I can't spot him.

The *Caliburn* tipped and rocked, despite stabilization attempts. The Fleet continued to fire salvo after salvo at the wounded Earth—now looking more like a dark hunk of smoking space scrap than a life-bearing world. *And I feel selfish, but I must find Alcaeus. That little Greek philosopher has trusted me for way too long.*

"Piper!" her father shouted over the din. "Shadow Broker intelligence reports alien reserves dwindling rapidly. It's attempting to mask—"

Dropping down through the command deck, a final glimpse of Dad's confused face as I sink through the floor. Covered in my own blood, and looking like a fright show, I spell myself to pass as a phantom. I can sift through whole decks like an avenging blood angel searching for the source of terror and hoping Alcaeus isn't there.

I don't have long to wait. The source of the nearest human chaos becomes obvious, and chaos is an understatement. I'm about a mile into what's known as the "west scimitar" of the warship, landing in an area big as a ballroom made for goliaths, now become a bizarre torture chamber—the horror of which can't be exaggerated. I've seen a lot of bloody shit in my lifetime, miles of crucifixions, Clive Barker movies, the aftermath of neolithic head-hunter raids, but nothing equal to this.

The first thing I notice is the blood-stew blender above me. The sight is paralyzing. Mars gleams red and huge through the field portal windows and amber lights in the walls fuse with it to create a weird effect. Three hundred or so human bodies are spinning near the ceiling, twenty feet up, and not just in one circle but two. The uppermost circle spins fast as laundry, the second circle below more slowly—one full cycle every 5.4 seconds. I sense those in the top circle to be either dead or unconscious, and over half in the bottom are barely conscious. They're stripped naked too, tatters of crew uniform littering the floor, many in both circles missing legs and arms, or even heads. Their blood sprays down in a fine Martian red mist onto the floor below.

And it doesn't end there. Unsuspecting new victims enter the room, armed or otherwise, and they're immediately sucked to the ceiling, there to be battered and stripped as if by invisible hands while they shriek in panic.

Then I notice it.

Balls of swarm begin spewing out from an infrared-visible rod that has appeared floating in air at the far end of the room. I know instinctively it's the source of all the super whack shit here, a magical killer, a spell bomb of sorts. How many are loose on the ship? The swarms it births envelop the human body and devour it to nothing in seconds, and as I look closer, I see they are not bugs, but tiny little red mouths.

Where are the gullets then? Is the human flesh-food being digested in another dimension? As I begin to conjure a spell to stop this murderous madness, a squad of Dio Soldati burst in and fire at the swarms and rod. They're using a new weapon unfamiliar to me, one which discharges a succession of field-contained black holes the size of marbles.

The temporary warping of surrounding space makes me nauseous. The black-hole marbles spin into the swarms and inhale them. More of them orbit the rod, crackling bolts of force striking the rod itself, causing it to glow into the normal visible spectrum and dissolve. At the same time, dozens of punctured and torn bodies begin raining down to the floor.

One problem solved?

But the horrific nature of what I'd just seen makes me more fearful than ever. I telepathically nudge the Dio Soldati officer in charge. His AI continues firing at the spell rod as a shoulder eye on his body armor turns to observe me.

He answers, mind to mind, "Commander Robbin, sir?"

I lift the palm of my right hand, as if saying hello, and there appears the happy face of Alcaeus as he looked last time I saw him. "Do you see this face? I order you to code this image and search Caliburn neuro for the last sign of him anywhere on this ship."

"Yes, sir... Done, sir. The subject was last seen five minutes ago in his neospace chamber on Deck Z."

"Really? Is he still there?"

"Yes, Commander Robbin, sir, but... Sir, you are covered in blood. Are you—"

Without another thought I transition to Deck Z and in seconds I stand in my friend's quarters, touching down on ridge overlooking the Greek island of Kos and the Mediterranean. A short distance away I see the familiar and ancient remains of the Asklepion. It now bakes under a hot blue sky—a sanatorium dedicated to the son of Apollo, including the six white Corinthian columns that remind me of past magnificence. I know it well, and so does Alcaeus. We traveled here together long ago when this place was in its prime.

While musing, I hear the scuffle of feet on gravel. A few locals come walking up the path that winds down the ridge. Two women, each cradling a small amphora and dressed in the manner of Spartan women with short skirts. What year is this? One spots me, standing there like a bloody Medea, and shrieks in fear. The two of them drop their amphorae and scamper back down the path. It feels like a big cliché, and seconds later, my worst fears are realized.

I see what remains of my beloved Alcaeus.

He has been cut into six parts and each part adorns the crown of one Corinthian column. Two heads. One the pygmy of New Guinea, one the morph-droid, both staring blankly out to the Mediterranean Sea.

"ALCAEUS!"

What could be more surreal and heartbreaking at the same time? I begin crying and the tears flow down my face to mix with the dried blood. Tempo Inverso is the only hope, even though I know it's probably hopeless.

I say the spell. A small whirlpool of dust forms and dies.

More locals appear over the ridge. This time it's a small squad of Greek soldiers, no doubt sent by the terrorized women. The soldiers see me and stop cold. One of them falls to the earth with arms outstretched, his weapons clattering to the side. He thinks I'm a goddess of some sort, perhaps even Aphrodite.

The others begin to back away. A few more collapse to the ground and begin praying.

I say the Tempo Inverso again, and again. It works, at last, and unexpectedly plays a Witch Empress prank. Alcaeus reforms, sure, but like a Salvador Dali Frankenstein of mismatched parts.

I can't describe this insane deformity I helped bring about. I never want to remember it again. Worse yet, Alcaeus is alive within the patchwork monstrosity, his eyes filled with agony.

I have no choice but to reverse the spell.

I then fall to the ground like the Greek soldiers. I beat my fists and scream and cry so loudly that they turn and crawl away on all fours fast as they can, mumbling prayers and whimpering until the last of them disappears below the ridge.

Soon exhausted, I lie flat against the warm Greek earth. I feel the Caliburn thrumming softly. The turbulence has stopped. The bombardment is over.

The war might be coming to an end.

It doesn't matter to me.

Fifteen minutes later, I hear my father speaking mind to mind, and he sounds anxious:

"Piper, the damnable Dark House has rooted itself in Caliburn neospace where we have housed hundreds of thousands of refugees, including the Pentagon families once held hostage... Piper?"

:/

FIVE PLATOONS OF *DIO SOLDATI* AND A COHORT of Shadow Broker combat sorcerers of the Ninth Mojave rushed the Dark House. They were joined by a division of WAMORs and a swarm of new magi-tech drones dubbed War Owls. But even as Oz forces struck like an invincible and thunderous god-army, human refugees from LA were being murdered by sweeping blows of thermal radiation.

Even as far as a hundred miles away in *Caliburn* neospace, temporary housing camps burst into searing flames. Two huge transport shuttles from San Diego exploded, nearly two thousand people flamed to a char.

Dio Soldati and ship defenses contained a portion of it, though it proved impossible to contain enough before casualties mounted into the tens of thousands—an ultimate act of scorched earth, sudden and devastating.

Forces assaulting the Dark House met with little resistance once they burned protective fields to zero and smashed through the outer perimeter with assistance from 13 million rounds of Gatling cannon. The lead *Dio Soldati* squad hunted through the eerie shadow maze of Dark House, finally tracking down the Witch Empress by means of magi-tech instruments sensitive enough to smell garlic on human breath twenty miles away.

In response to Edison Godfellow, a tired yet seething Piper stood on the *Caliburn* bridge with a silently enraged Catherine when the first images came through on the main screen depicting a frazzled old woman with stringy white hair and smeared make-up. Piper didn't know whether to curse or crack a joke.

She looks like a beaten wet dog. So this is it? This is the climax of the Witch Empress? She's nothing in the final analysis but a pathetic and disheveled therapist?

"What manner of disguised scheming do we have here?" Catherine said, glancing at Edison.

"I am not sure." Edison's eyes never left the image. "Cereus assures me the alien is genuinely drained, not just pretending for the sake of a trap. According to him, it spent hours groping for its battery on various wavelengths, though even now it retains enough power to transport itself to the other side of the galaxy and back. Nonetheless, we have safeguard spells and fields in place, and we can send life model decoys of ourselves, or simply project—"

"NO!" Catherine shouted at him. "We kill it! I am not afraid of this creature."

Piper cut in, wiping a sudden tear from her eye. "I agree. This turd of dragon ass has it coming. It murdered people close to us, and just to be an *evil shithead*."

"Perhaps this is precisely *what it wants*," Edison said. "A final and ultimate act of earth scorching. What could be more advantageous than luring us into her sanctorum before executing revenge with a device or trick we have yet to discover?"

"It matters not," Catherine said. "I cannot stand by while others do my work."

"So *be it*." Edison verged on exasperated surrender. "However, before you two begin carcass carving, I must separate the alien from the therapist host using a custom spell alembic."

"Whatever do *you mean*?" Catherine asked impatiently. "We burn it to ash. No delays. No toxins remaining."

"I require the alien essence for further study," he said. "It will not yield itself to easy analysis. Cereus and I have already obtained stray molecules and analyzed them. The results were like nothing we predicted. I cannot explain it now. I simply know the performance of this task is vital to our survival. If our species suffers another assault like this, we might well perish. In a real sense, we were fortunate."

"I want it carved and baked into a hot pie with peas and carrots," Piper said.

Catherine went silent and dark. Piper observed her.

She can't take her eyes off the "beaten wet dog" of Witch Empress. She doesn't simply want to kill it. Like me, she wants to make it suffer horribly for its many crimes.

: /

PIPER ASSUMED HER NEMESIS POSE, levitating a full foot above the floor and primed for vengeance, prepared to strike as she confronted Nina Cohen in her Dark House sanctorum. Catherine also assumed a Nemesis strike pose. The room appeared as Piper recalled it before unleashing the dragon bling to escape: the leather couch, a Picasso of the hideous Gertrude Stein, and a single wooden chair.

It seems an age ago I was here. Whatever damage done by the dragon is now undone. But what happened to my old pet Dracos?

She'd never had time to check.

Edison Godfellow and Cereus Malcolm stood before her, side by side, and behind them rose the dark specters of a dozen huge *Dio Soldati* with a total of 84 individual weapons trained on the pathetic vision of Nina.

The alien analyst faced them in silence, back to the wall, her body naked, thin and scuffed, and with a scatter of burn marks on her forearms as if made by a cigarette. A line of drool decorated her chin, the sex tattoos of youth faded on her legs, and a pair of gleaming, authentic ruby slippers were on her feet.

If this is a ridiculous pity act, it's not going to work.

"Nina, we know your power reserves are extremely low," Edison said with a calm voice. "You cannot escape this place. We have ample spell walls, screens, and dampening fields in play. Any surge in power will be met with—"

"Ungrateful, ungrateful little thingssss..." Nina said,

307

slurry as a street drunk.

"Boozing it up while murdering the hostages?" Piper couldn't resist.

Nina clicked her heels three times. "There's no place like home, no place like home." Her demeanor grew brighter. Her skin lost its weak pallor and began to radiate.

This is how she wants to go out? Doing a really bad Dorothy Gale imitation?

"Nina, I have a friend I would like you to meet," Edison said. A door opened behind him and a creature looking like a black moray eel the size of an elephant seal slithered in. It smelled of fried mushrooms, and as it wove its bulk around the soldiers and Cereus, its moray mouth made sucking sounds. Seconds later, it stopped, and raising its gleaming oily trunk, head poised, it gazed down at the bubbly Nina.

This shit just gets weirder by the minute.

"Tin Man," Nina said, looking up to address the eel, "Which way to the Emerald City?"

"Is this the magic alembic you made reference to, Edison?" Catherine said.

"Yes… Rather unorthodox and slimy, I realize, but—"

"Lions and tigers, and worms, oh my!" Nina was having fun. She clapped her hands, clicked her ruby slippers again, and added with a gay voice, "And in time, I'll face-fuck you all. You'll see!"

Without warning, the huge eel creature struck its victim's head. Like a python, it swallowed her up to the shoulders. A sickly, moist sucking sound was heard, and both the eel and Nina began to vibrate. The eel continued to exert pressure downwards until Nina's entire body was swallowed and the eel thing appeared pregnant, then it stopped, wavered, grunted, and finally collapsed with a loud wet smack to the floor.

Didn't I see this in a bad horror movie?

Piper glanced away for a moment to note that Cereus held a clear wafer tablet in his hands. He stared at it intently. Upon it twinkled an illumined and dynamic diagram of what was happening inside the alembic. Small lights, dots, and graphs spasmodically jumped and blinked. Thin streams of energy swirled within the Nina body and intermixed within a stomach-like organ.

An absorption was taking place.

The Dark House began to groan all around them like an angry and drunken beast. Piper also heard sounds that reminded her of a clomping giant. Was something coming closer? Then the walls that surrounded Piper and the others faded. Phased away. *To where?* Piper glanced again at the tablet Cereus held. A small light grew brighter on it, one that seemed to coincide with the death of the Dark House.

Edison also glimpsed the read-outs on the tablet. "Ah, so this place was in reality a bit of Witch Empress bling. She stored it in her neural net like a coded ideogram spell."

"Enough to occupy us for many hours," Cereus said.

This annoyed Piper.

I should be the one occupying him… OMG. Did I actually think that? In the presence of death and destruction on a scale never witnessed and part of my brain is sexing it up with Cereus… At least I recognize the depth of my selfish humanity.

Am I ashamed?

Before she could answer her own question, she realized she was surrounded by a smoking field of charred corpses—the remains of Pentagon hostages, as well as many others promised safety on board the *Caliburn*.

My question answered.

The others remained in the same formation, still watching the magical alembic digesting Nina's nerves. The smoke from the fires swirled around them. Above, the sky was blue. As it twisted, the eel made crunching noises in the charred leaves and pine needles. It belched and farted loudly, and after a final release of gas, Piper heard a soft whisper in her mind.

"Don't you know?"

She screamed.

Everyone turned to stare.

Her father's mouth gaped and both his hands raised.

"Commander Robbin, stop!" a *Dio Soldati* captain shouted.

Too late.

Chapter XVIII

New Manhattan Mother – Chez Gaby – San Luis Obispo

Czarina Catherine's Post Finem Journal
Year 1 PF – Entry 6

It appears the fever of World War Oz has broken. I hope this is the case. My sadness and fatigue with this conflict has even transcended the death of my precious Maria. At such time I reviewed with Edison the extent of casualties and damage, I was stunned, and this despite the fact I had steeled myself beforehand.

Folly, naught but folly.

Billions have perished, nearly 40% of the human species on Earth. Hundreds of thousands of Superna Humanitas died also on fleet ships and in the Oz city-worlds. Nearly every major city on the planet has crumbled to rubble, and much of the land is crushed beyond belief. However, billions are safe, the city-worlds are repairing themselves, and I will join others in acts of post-war reconstruction even though a Witch Empress curse against Tempo spells yet lingers like a stubborn pox.

Also, I have finally succeeded in calming the denizens of New Manhattan and teaching them the truth of what has transpired, thus preventing them from fleeing their new homes. Many demanded a tour of the destruction on Earth. I allowed that, and they returned stricken to inform others. Still, some decided to relocate to the surface and renew bonds with familiar American places, especially those very few that did not suffer overmuch destruction. I told them they would be welcomed back at any time.

Nonetheless, I will periodically look in on them.

My maternal urge towards New Manhattan cannot be denied. I have grown fond of that crazy world, and to my pleasant surprise I recently learned that the crown of old Manhattan is undergoing a renaissance. Perhaps a bit of seed magic to restart the delis, cafes, and theaters might be in order?

Edison privately shared with me that only a tiny portion of Tao reserves remained with which to engage in productive reconstruction. He is fearful of expending the remainder of the reserves lest another serious threat soon present itself. He and Cereus Malcolm are working on plans to utilize a portion of remaining energies to create more Tao collectors in the past, but even this is fraught with dangerous potential.

They have theorized an entire alien civilization bent on our demise, and without sufficient intelligence, cannot deny that a second wave of assault might now be in the making.

I understand their fear.

At least, my feelings for Piper Robbin have been resolved, and that is a fortunate development. We are much stronger together than fighting each other like children. I understand her, though I must say I was taken by surprise when she attempted to kill the Witch Empress at the last moment.

Just as the alembic beast of Edison was in the throes of consumption and analysis, I witnessed Piper flashing down with a magical spell sword to slice it in half. It gave out a little cry and rolled apart like a cut sausage. Only later did I learn from her that the alien had employed a certain phrase designed to provoke her into rage.

She just snapped, as they say.

I cannot judge her. I might well have done the same. My hatred of the alien at least matched hers. As for my emotions regarding Edison, they are a bit chilled. I do not respect him less or possess any identifiable grudge. If anything, I believe I understand him better than before. I feel I am quite scattered and pummeled by circumstances, so much so that it has desensitized me to a degree.

I still possess affection for him, and in the days to come, I cannot say I will reject him from my bed; however, I do require a hiatus, a vacation as they say, especially before launching myself into any major post-war reconstruction.

Some may call that selfish on my part. They might be correct.

: /

PHOENIX FROM THE ASHES. YOU CANNOT RESIST the metaphor. What other choice is there? Should you view World War Oz from a standpoint of blame or inevitability? Or perhaps from a view towards adding up the many elements of mayhem to equal a terrible cost? Or by subtracting the potential of doom from the reality of victory and discovering the best answer is survival?

Negative or positive?

You believe it is not worth placing the war in perspective from the standpoint of that rather arbitrary dichotomy. It happened. It is done. You cannot undo it. But you and your closest remain alive, and their wisdom, heart, and courage has never abandoned them.

Though just as real and terribly cliché as aliens invading Earth to prevent its ascendancy into the cosmos, you nevertheless are compelled to embrace the concept of human life as more precious than ever. You wish to hug it like a cute little baby and pat its back. After all, you have seen so much death, existed so close to it, felt its hand on your throat, and too, you have failed to discover evidence of abundant intelligent life in the galaxy. And what did you find? The Great Life Chisel, yes, and the murderous Orion creature, though scant proof of little else (a few dead civilizations dimly glowing after hundreds of millennia). How much more rare then is the miraculous accident of humanity in comparison?

You reconfirm you will do whatever is necessary to preserve it, even if it means an "act of evil" must occasionally be performed; and speaking of evil acts, no new word of your renegade other self has been spoken.

As you consider the situation, logic insists that he departed the solar system prior to the galactic relocation of the three planets. When faced with so much sudden power and a resistance he found inexplicable, his only choice was to retreat, gather future intelligence however possible, and proceed from there. Did he put many light years distance behind him, park in the diffuse static of a nebula, or perhaps dip back an eon in time to begin again?

Over the last few days, Cereus Malcolm and you have conducted a tour of the Oz city-worlds to observe stabilization efforts while at the same time analyzing data absorbed from the alien substance within the body of the psychoanalyst. Despite your daughter flying into rage and slicing the alembic in half, you were able to recreate it, and Cohen as well, and continue with examination.

Once done, the host was effectively deposited by the alembic as a waste product, but restored to conscious life by Cereus, and with no memory of alien possession.

Cereus is always efficient. He would make a protean foe.

Later, as you sit relaxing in the hot African sun at a

breezy Kinshasa sky island café known as the *Chez Gaby* with your *crepes comdie clambee* and a demitasse of Congolese espresso, you utilize a small *Fiestra Na Vida* hovering above the white tablecloth to observe a division of WAMORs currently operating in the African Deeper Lands.

Like the Witch Empress transmogrifications of New Manhattan, the false Oz quadrants of Kinshasa have sprouted their own unique variations: elephant worms fifty feet long with retractable tusks (adept at burrowing and resurfacing later among large groups of people with an intent to massacre); swarms of giant locusts with a taste for warm flesh; flocks of vulture harpies big as pterodactyls with beaked Munchkin faces; and last but not least, lion monsters over 20 feet tall who run faster on two legs than stallions while savagely roaring to the heavens, "I do believe in spooks! I do! I do!"

Doubtlessly, the alien's idea of a joke.

Your vision hovers a hundred feet above a line of WAMORs, thirty of them moving fast in a wedge formation over a beautiful African savannah valley at dawn. You watch their sonics like air-burning beams of invisible force mowing down whole prides of lion monsters attempting to escape—the lips and eight-inch teeth of the beasts still wet with human blood.

You have been informed by Kinshasa Operations and Security that the Witch Empress, and in only three days, had exterminated over 20 million crossovers from middle Africa who flooded the city-world much faster and easier than U.S. migrants. Why? Because no government forces combined to slow or shoot them down. Soldiers threw down their guns and joined the procession. Most hadn't been paid in over eight months and their children were starving.

As you take a perfectly delicious bite of your crepes, still watching the clean-up operation with a smile of sad satisfaction and wishing solutions might have occurred much sooner, a thin transparent screen filled with equations and code appears in front of your eyes. You turn your head to see Cereus Malcolm sitting beside you.

More than ever, he resembles a powerfully strange spell in human form. *Could he actually be a complex magical incantation? A living, breathing humanoid spell capable of being unraveled by the right words?* No time to consider. All that matters is your trust, and you do trust him. He might have spelled himself from the clutches of death centuries ago.

It makes no difference now.

He is holding the little screen. He says nothing. You take it and read it. The particle physic essence of the alien organism within Nina Cohen had been analyzed and repeated tests confirmed that particles of alien matter existed in ratios that varied in comparison to known atomic and subatomic particles. The alien subatomica, for example, contained double the number of Leptons and Quarks, and on an atomic level, electrons weighed more than normal electrons by a factor of ten. Also, there was more unpredictability of particle reaction observed over time—for example, certain particles seemed to vanish and reappear seconds, or hours later, but with no discernible pattern.

"I believe we are observing a hitherto unknown and

variation of magical Tao, perhaps even a quantum magical Tao," Cereus says.

"Yes, in effect, a meta-organic, quantum magical Tao."

You are utterly enthralled by the discovery, almost gleeful. It's just so incredible.

Cereus continues. "An energetic organic substance crafted into being by advanced magi-tech, and nearly indestructible... Even now, the amount culled from the human host defies us. Tiny amounts we attempt to annihilate appear to rearrange their physics even as we apply force."

"Certainly accounting for Witch Empress resilience, as well as her ability to recharge herself as needed."

"Agreed."

"We must work on ways to interrupt or disrupt the particle physics of this new manifestation. Our ability to do so will be a key factor in defeating any further insertions by nebular intelligence from Orion. Also, it will assist us in learning the true face of our enemy."

"I will return to the Shadow Broker labs and keep you updated... One last thing, Edison, if I may?"

"Yes?"

"I would like access to the data on those dead galactic civilizations you examined and cataloged."

"Of course. Are you simply curious, my old friend?"

"If ever you find me not curious, you will also find me quite expired. In my spare time, I intend to record civilized life in the galaxy going back at least a full eon. It will take an indeterminate length of time, and I might never complete it, but I believe it important."

"A fascinating pursuit. I am jealous. Perhaps I too will

seek spare time and accompany you on occasion."

"I would welcome that, Edison."

You say farewell to Cereus and finish your espresso. One last glance through the *Fiestra Na Vida* to verify the demise of the monster lion packs and then you spell yourself into a waiting aero cruiser that will leisurely take you back to New Manhattan Oz while allowing more post-war observation of the Earth below. You are anxious to relate the findings to Catherine, as anxious as you are to return Mother Earth to livable form—though it isn't really necessary given the newly restored, safe, and incomparable spaces of Oz.

Nevertheless, the obligation remains.

A few minutes into your journey and your mind drifts to thoughts of Catherine and Piper. You acknowledge truthfully to yourself that you do love them. You can never be the father beside the Christmas tree with presents, but since returning from the disastrous future and living with Piper, you have learned the value of love. Too bad it required such drastic circumstances to jolt you into awareness. But so be it.

No negative or positive.

Just history.

You will nurture their dreams, and in the epochs to come, do as much good as you can, and as little bad as possible.

:/

SIX MONTHS AFTER PIPER SEVERED THE ALEMBIC in a fit of rage, she sat cross-legged and calm atop the black soil of an old vineyard just west of San Luis Obispo. She couldn't help but stare mesmerized at what remained of the Galaxians: 2,567 individual statues, each 50 feet tall and driven like stakes into the California hills to form a kind of memorial.

At a distance, due to colors and stylized faces, they appeared as if bizarrely fashioned totem poles. Upon closer inspection though, Piper found them to be composed solely of petrified wood, a peculiar California variety, and each appeared identical to the other. The faces flashed big rows of nicotinic teeth frozen into yellow smiles, the black ponytails of hair entwining about them, their four anorexic arms tightly hugging their skinny naked bodies—the only thing at slight variance being the size of their ruby-red eyes, even larger here on these poles of wooden rock, bulging as though in disbelief.

Their existence first became known to Oz OSC, and therefore to Edison, after a detailed scan of the area following the end of the war. Both the Oz techs and Shadow Broker intelligence conducted every test possible to ascertain whether they might be incubators of fresh Galaxians, but nothing was found down to the smallest molecule that was indicative of anything unusual, nothing other than petrified wood painted over by a rare type of weather-proof substance. To add to the mystery, every bit of the actual Galaxians in the flesh utterly vanished after the war.

So how had these new apparitions arrived?

No one knew. Shadow Broker intel denied the possibility of a biologic transition to petrified wood from California. *And I don't buy that either. This reminds me of the way the Witch Empress displayed the remains of Alcaeus on top of those Greek columns. She planted these petrified freaks. The spacezilla is reminding us with this stupid memorial that despite defeat, she murdered hundreds of millions. As for the real Galaxians? Probably shrunk to the size of pinheads and stealthed off planet during the fireworks. The air was filled with scatters of EMP, radiation, and wave static of every kind.*

I know the little shits are out there, somewhere.

Oddly enough, the small city of San Luis Obispo was one of the few places in America that wasn't devastated, along with Berkeley, CA; Sarasota, FL; Santa Fe, NM; Boise, ID; and Bar Harbor, ME, among others; but the vast bulk of the country was deader than an old campfire.

It's no exaggeration to say that her metropolitan marvels look as though chewed in the mouth of Satan.

Chicago was ground down to bits of charred bone and metal, so too Boston and Miami. Phoenix had risen from the ashes a full half mile before flipping in the air like a pancake. D.C. resembled a potholed parking lot filled with dirty water. A few cities such as LA were in better shape, only littered by hundreds of thousands of corpses as well as countless buildings either collapsed or shot through with holes.

Outside the cities, thousands of square miles of rural country suffered acts of geologic upheaval. Much of the mighty western mountain chains had been pulverized to dust and scattered rocks, and the nation's biggest rivers burned off to fog.

Restoration, if any, would take years.

Regardless, a corrupt state will never again rule this land. If nothing else, there isn't a point. The tax base has gone bye-bye. The Pentagon has been dismantled by Oz security. Even state boundaries are now smoke and weeds.

: /

PIPER DECIDED TO WALK INTO TOWN from the old winery, about 15 miles. To her relief, she saw vestiges of human industry as she strolled. A small herd of cows in a pasture, at least two vineyards apparently in business, and to her further amazement, she was passed by an actual electric automobile containing a small family, and apparently fresh off the coast, for their license plate read:

MORRO BAY, A DREAM OF WEST

Can you believe it?

Must be an effect of San Luis Obispo being open for business. The banks are dead and half the county government were Despicables, but the electricity is still windmill, the batteries work, the brooms are sweeping, and the good citizens need community more than ever. I wonder how many of have wandered back from New Manhattan?

A half hour later she arrived in town and made straight for a coffee shop called the Nautical Bean. Would it still exist? Piper knew it to be a funky little place with lots of old kitsch on the walls including movie posters and photos dating back to the prior century. She'd hung out there for a time before deciding to move to NYC and pursue a new career on Broadway; and besides, what better place to stop and include the latest observations destined for the first and only memoir she would ever write:

The Dilemma of Being Present.

No one would buy a copy, and that wasn't necessary. The mere act of writing it forced her to be honest with herself.

Course, Dad might have issues with it.

Piper opened the front door and immersed herself in the dark coffee atmosphere. Nothing had changed. It felt comfortable and warm, just like in the old days.

Then quite unexpectedly, she saw a vision.

Cereus Malcolm.

He sat at a small table in the shadows towards the back wall, looking like a demonic monk. Piper gave a timid wave. He hoisted his ceramic cup in response and actually smiled. His solar eclipse eyes were obvious, though dimmer than usual, as though tamed a bit to avoid terrifying the locals.

Wow. I didn't expect this, and he's caught me in pixie mode too. This is going to be awkward.

She ordered a triple shot latte with Mexican spice and said to herself, *Oh hell with it*, and made her way to Cereus. He seemed especially imposing, given her shrinkage, and his eyes inhaled her beyond the brink of sanity. He wore his usual Shadow Broker mage garments, appearing ominous even on close inspection, especially with that dark hood over his head.

"Hello, Bianca," he said as she took a seat facing him. "The coffee is truly exceptional. I understand why you like it here."

"Hello, uh, Cereus." She felt uncertain as a child, and that irritated her.

"Bianca, you need not be uncomfortable. I am aware of your diminutive Piper form. It matters not. My feelings for you are not in jeopardy."

"Thanks, but if you wish me to change—"

"No. Please, it is perfectly... capital."

How British of him.

"So, you think I'm as attractive as the Grand Sorceress? Seriously, bro? Seriously?"

"I am not addressing the superficial. I am saying, my feelings for you are immutable."

"The superficial? You think my beauty is just superficial? You mean I could change into a drooling cocker spaniel and you would still worship me?"

"I would realize that the essence of the animal is your essence, therefore, the answer is yes."

"So, um, you don't care how I look?"

"Bianca, *please.* This line of argument is pointless."

"Well... yes, you have a point. I'm just working out my shit. I felt too insecure."

"Yes. You must overcome it."

"Forgive me, Cereus."

"Nothing to forgive. I understand. At times I behave badly, and no one sees it."

"Oh, now I'm behaving badly?"

"No, no, I—"

"Never mind, *sorry, sorry.*"

He sighed, for the first time ever.

I never heard him sigh before. It's my fault.

He leaned closer. A crypto-rune on his lower neck began to glow a soft amber hue. Piper knew he was magically securing the space around them, making it safe from any possible form of eavesdropping, magical or non-magical, and with his Grand Mage hood drawn down, even lips could not be read.

"Bianca, I wish to share a bit of news with you. It involves what I have discovered about those dead civilizations your father found on his journey to secure allies during the war."

"How long did your own journey last?"

"Nearly two years. I just returned this morning, and I have not yet spoken to your father. My urge to see you prevailed. For me, it has been too long."

Piper reached out and held the right hand of Cereus. She squeezed it. He squeezed back. For her, it had been less than a week since seeing him. Together they had undertaken a brief excursion to observe a new blue-giant nova on the galactic rim, and it was sexy, of course, and enthralling, but the reality of such circumstances only reinforced Piper's recent feelings of insignificance.

The more we unfold the universe, the smaller we become.

Cereus continued. "I have found, nearly two million years ago, incontrovertible evidence of your father's rogue twin."

"*How?*" She was hardly able to contain her amazement.

"In the remains of two ruined civilizations not more than 3,000 lightyears apart. He fought wars with them for reasons I have not yet ascertained."

"Oh, I'm *so shocked*," she said, rolling her pixie eyes. "Have you told him yet?"

"Not yet. I discovered this from deciphering ancient records. Apparently, he fled our solar system into the distant past with more personnel and ships than we had previously estimated. His path took him far beyond us, deep into the galaxy, skirting the outer limits of the core and hopping several hundred parsecs at a time. The beings he destroyed became acquainted with him quite well before the end."

"So, he really became more like a conquistador."

"I believe he was hunting magical Tao rather than gold, searching for sufficient amounts to make him all-powerful, or at minimum, powerful enough to discover the true whereabouts of Earth and begin his re-conquest."

"What happened then?"

"I must return to the past and conduct more research, but I have a theory." Cereus paused as if in contemplation.

"Yes?"

"I believe he reversed course, swung about and traveled to Orion upon learning of Tao deposits in the star nurseries. Alien survivors of the conflict noted this, and while there, a phenomenon occurred that changed him drastically."

"Wait, you're *not saying…* "

"Yes, that a strange cosmic evolution we do not fully comprehend became, many millennia later, the origin of the human-hating force that obliterated Edison's fleet and compelled him to return to the past."

"Kind of a huge coincidence?"

"Not especially. Touring the star nurseries of Orion is an appealing goal of deep space travel on this side of the galaxy. I know from speaking to Edison it was on his list from the beginning."

"If so, that force set in motion its own birth. Did it realize?"

"I cannot say. I believe the memories of the twin were lost long ago. The manifestation of Witch Empress demonstrated no direct cognizance of sharing Edison's past or personality; however, the alien presence displayed a marked animus towards him from the beginning."

"Yes, no question, like the time I fenced with that smartass corpse in Brooklyn."

"One can theorize a form of subconscious alien process that, in effect, hated some aspect of itself, or wished to annihilate an indistinct yet abhorrent part of its past, and our Edison personified that. It pursued him across space and time for a final reckoning."

"Soooo, let me recap... The evil twin eventually hated himself for whatever reason, and that self-hate was stirred into the magical stewpot of cosmic *big-bad-thing* creation, digested, and pooped out a gazillion years later as a vengeful turd of Witch Empress?"

"Another prop to the theory, Bianca. The alien chose a devious and embittered psychoanalyst, almost as if it wished to decipher sufficient humanness to comprehend its own history and actions."

"Insane enough to be possible, but we still have the Tao device on Mars, now in the hell of Sagittarius A."

"Yes, indicative of an advanced technological species, not simply a single genocidal entity... I cannot explain it all now. I have only theories. We need more information."

"I agree, and when you go to get it, I'm going with you," she said, squeezing his hand again.

"I would very much enjoy that, Bianca, however, I will have to involve Edison in such a decision."

"What? You kidding me? Just cause I look like a silly kid right now—"

"No, that is not relevant. We might encounter excessive danger and I cannot involve even one ship of the fleet without informing your father."

"Okay, okay… but he's not stopping me."

"So be it. I never believed he could," Cereus said. "And I am sorry for the death of Alcaeus. I wish I had stated that sooner. It was certainly horrible."

"Thank you. I do have a partial solution."

"What is that?"

Piper pointed with an index finger to her eyes. "Do you see the teeny white points?"

"Yes, your units of human community."

"I've always kept the DNA of Alcaeus. And now, a new child has been born in Corinth. His name is Alcaeus. I will raise him in the same way he was raised in the past. He will be a philosopher and know me as Macaria."

"How can you assure—"

"I can't, but I'll come close. It's the least I can do. It also helps with the pain of loss… I know it might seem ridiculous to you."

"It seems perfectly reasonable." Cereus leaned across the table and kissed her on the cheek. She kissed him back, on the lips, and held his face in her hands. She smiled, and following a pause, he whispered, "You are a good and caring person."

"No more than three days a week, Cereus."

"And what of Cleon?"

"I'm happy that my father delayed his restoration. Perhaps he planned it that way. Who knows? But I will take care of Cleon, and he will be sad at the death of Alcaeus."

"So much death, so much sadness. Humanity has never seen the like… but I have never felt more alive than I do with you, Bianca."

Chapter XIX

Landlord Nina – Tom Petty Live – *Observación e Disfrace*

PIPER BELIEVED IT JUVENILE AND MOST LIKELY FUTILE, but she'd spelled an *Observando Para Sempre* to keep close watch on Nina Cohen and report back any and everything involving movements, actions, words, and specific thought patterns. Though Cereus and her father explained that every iota of the alien had been successfully extracted from the body of the psychoanalyst via the magi-tech surgery of the alembic, and though the former host had been isolated and under watch for months as a precaution (partially on the insistence of Piper), and though all memory of her stint as the Witch Empress had been deleted, the simple fact of Nina Cohen "escaping" to go about her business, wherever and however, created in Piper a deep itch that she scratched into blood.

I got a feeling that I can't let go. I'm not stupid enough to be paranoid, but I found it suspicious that she decided in less than 48 hours to hop a transport back to Berkeley.

The *Observando Para Sempre* naturally accompanied its target back to the surface. The psychoanalyst went to her old apartment to find the electricity on. She opened and ate a year-old protein energy bar, changed her clothes, put on sneakers, and went for a stroll around town. Off to the deserted university campus next, and downtown to her old therapist office on Telegraph Avenue.

Being the last narcissist queen bee left on Earth, the New Manhattan must not have presented the kind of opportunity she was looking for—namely the power to manipulate and control others.

The *Observando Para Sempre* informed Piper that Nina's thoughts were 63% focused on objects of hate and resentment—in particular, everyone she met after regaining consciousness, especially men, as well as those of any gender who had saved her life because she'd decided in a bitchy fit of mood that they "took too long to get around to it" and therefore "needed to apologize" to *her*—while the remainder of her thoughts pretty much equally divided between rebuilding her social network, sadistic sex fantasies, and restarting her phony therapist business. She felt she must regain her esteem and sense of social position in the Berkeley therapy community (now stronger than ever following the war).

A few days after returning, Nina arranged to meet her old therapist friends in a Berkeley café near campus. They were happy to see her, and surprised she was alive. Only three out of eight remained. The others had vanished before the war and no one ever saw them again. One of them, Nanette Kaplan, was observed floating from her office window and rising high enough to just miss getting hit by a small plane.

"I heard they turned into ugly flying beasts," Shawnee Kesselman said while nibbling at her tuna salad with avocado, bacon bits, and sprouts. "It's so hard to accept, but then again, so much has happened that none of us can explain, or could have expected."

Nina groaned in the presence of what she interpreted as ignorance. "What perennial truths did we learn long ago from our Berkeley professors?" she asked them. "It's only more of the same. Toxic masculinity, this time on steroids.

Just a bunch of men playing cosmic penis games. They're denigrating us like they always have. Why make it more complicated? ... Just look at that Oz world thing. A giant green dick poking the sky."

The three women stared at her, unsure how to respond.

Shawnee glanced at the other two, noting how Nina dominated them into submission like a queen bee, and she said:

"But I thought... aliens attacked us, or—"

"Another ruse of the patriarchy!" Nina blustered and fumed. "The whole cosmos is swimming in masculine illusions. *Don't you know?* If women are aggressive, it's only because men are controlling them like dogs on a leash. Women only want peace. Men only want conflict. It's that simple, sisters. No need to complicate it with politics or circumstances, or personality types, or behavior pressures of any kind. I rejected those arguments long ago and so should you!"

"Do, um... aliens have dog leashes?" Shawnee asked.

: /

AFTER CHECKING PERIODICALLY ON NINA'S INNER LIFE and business operations for a few more weeks, Piper became both curious and annoyed enough to pay the old Witch Empress a personal visit.

She spelled herself into Grand Sorceress physical form, but with contemporary clothing: a dark skirt-suit, crimson blouse, *memento mori* amulet, and black heels. Though she disliked heels, she nonetheless stood six foot four and appeared remarkably awe inspiring.

She caught up to Nina sitting alone in the same café where she'd previously ranted at her "friends." The woman tipped a cup of cappuccino to her lips. A plate of half-eaten rhubarb pie sat before her. Her appearance had mellowed since the Dark House days—hair no longer screaming white, now a deer-antler brown with blond highlights, and the eyes no longer a glaring purple, altered now to an artificial dark maroon.

Otherwise, eerily similar.

Even knowing the truth, she still gives me gas.

Without hesitation, Piper sat down at a seat across the table. Nina gasped at first, then calmed enough to stare at Piper with a scowl.

She hates me at first sight. Good!

"Who are you? And who permitted you in my space?"

"Back in the business of analysis, eh Nina? And as the worst kind of therapist you intentionally diagnose young women as having either past histories of daddy rape or assault by anus-abusing aliens. Isn't that so?"

"My diagnoses are none of your business, Ms...?"

"Last week you convinced an obese and impressionable woman of 28 years named Frances Menendez that she'd been raped by her father in Peru at the age of one. That is absolute crap without a shred of non-delusional evidence. The truth is simple. She's been suffering ongoing depression and trauma related to the war, like so many others. Don't you remember it?"

"How dare you! What could you possibly know of abuse psychology?"

"She's joined your victim club of five other innocent young women you tore from their families before the war, and who still live in separate apartments in a building you own in a Berkeley suburb. Oh, and they just happen to be *paying you rent. Isn't that so?"*

"They needed to escape their rapist family culture and find a safe space, so I did them a favor... But this is not a court room, and I'm not on trial." Nina fumbled in her purse and withdrew a black Russian cigarette that she lit with trembling hands.

It's no wonder this therapist monster was chosen to house the Witch Empress. In a sense, she's even more evil.

Nina took a drag of her cigarette and said nervously to Piper, "You need to get away from me, you hear? Get away from me. I'll call the police."

"The Berkeley police are no longer getting paid, I'm afraid, so you're out of luck, witch."

"How... how *dare you*... What man sent you?" Nina was so agitated she dropped her cigarette in her lap and burned herself into yelping.

"I'm going to free and protect those women you tricked with your hate-serving analysis, and I'll renovate you."

"Renovate? What?"

"Yes," Piper said, standing up. "You will never practice your bullshit therapy or harm anyone with your lies again."

Piper saw Nina try to meet her penetrating stare and she withered the woman into embryonic silence. The psychoanalyst felt needles stabbing into her brain, shriveling her inward. She crossed her arms to hug herself, bending her head down and trembling further with equal amounts fear and rage.

Should I feel bad about getting a thrill out of this?

: /

IT CAME TO PASS IN THE WINKIE WORLD, down in the Deeper Lands of Oz, an occurrence the likes of which no Winkie had ever witnessed. Traveling into Oogaboo shire, which lay just west of the place where the Dark House of Oz once stood, and just east of the snowy Wheel of Mountains, came a wandering and quite lovely Winkie female who called herself Romanova.

The Winkie children of Oogaboo shire met her first. As they played and swam in the Chattahoohoo River that ran through the center of the shire, she came upon them quite suddenly, and they told their parents and Winkie elders, she seemed different right from the start. Her way of talking and acting was strange. Her stormy blue eyes looked upon them with affection and even a bit of curious sadness, though she was unknown to them.

The Winkie children, being playful at heart, invited Romanova to swim and frolic. Like the other Winkies, she removed her simple clothing and jumped naked into the cool streaming water. The children gasped at the beauty of her form and one older Winkie boy tickled everyone's laughter by raising his Winkie weewee high enough to protrude from the water like a little fish head. Surely, he thought this new Romanova was especially ready for love, and as the children had loads of rollicking fun, one Winkie girl asked Romanova, "Where do you come from?" and Romanova answered, "I come from a faraway land called Prussia. I was born there, but I wished to cross over to this land because it is sunny and warm, and things here are clean and fun. You might say, I needed a vacation."

Then the Winkie girl asked, "Where are your lovers? Did you leave them in Purroosha?" To which Romanova replied, "I will return to them, one day." And the Winkie girl, who called herself Ladeedah, said excitedly, "Ah and bah, we will tell the elders of Chugtoo you have no lovers, for you know, we Winkies need loving every day!"

Having said this, the Winkie known as Romanova laughed nervously, but the children did not know how to interpret such a laugh so they simply dismissed it as a strange Purroosha thing.

Later that day, once the afternoon became long of shadow, the Winkie children coaxed Romanova into one of their rowboats and they formed a little flotilla of naked Winkies heading for the shire village of Chugtoo. Romanova wished to don her clothing once more, just a simple short tunic of cotton tied by a cord at the waist, and wear her sandals, but as she did, the children played a game of yanking her clothes away from her and throwing them back and forth to make the act of putting them on almost impossible.

"Now, children, be good!" Romanova chirped like a partridge from Purroosha, but to her dismay, her tunic flew into the river and she had to dive in to retrieve it as the children laughed and laughed.

By the time Romanova climbed onto the bank and donned her soaking wet tunic, the flotilla of naked Winkie children was much further upriver. She saw them in the distance waving at her. So it was left up to a perfectly refreshed and peppy Romanova to follow them along the riverbank.

In a short time, she arrived at the edge of the village of

Chugtoo. The walk to get there was very pleasant for the day fell so blue and delightfully pale with sun. The grasses waved gold and the boolee berries twittered about as the wise and majestic cedars whispered poetry in their boughs.

The children naturally beat her to Chugtoo by a good twenty minutes, so they had ample time to skip through the village, gleefully calling out to everyone to come and meet the new Winkie from Purroosha.

By the time Romanova entered the village of wood and painted mud brick, at least 30 adult Winkies of all three sexes enthusiastically awaited her arrival. They parted to either side as she strolled the main road towards the center of Chugtoo, as if she were a special goddess of the Winkies—perhaps even a handmaiden of Ozma herself. They waved at her and greeted her with smiles, and shouts of "Well days, Romanova!" and nearly every one of them gasped to see how beautiful she was in her clinging wet tunic.

Within a few more minutes, she arrived at the center of Chugtoo. It was a big circle of clipped-short golden grass, and in the middle was a big stone oven that smelled sweetly of bread. The Winkies surrounded her and clapped, and without any regard for order or sense, they bombarded her with questions, for Winkies were naturally a curious lot. "How long will you stay?" and "Where is Purroosha?" and "Who are your lovers?" and "How many children do you have?" and such as that.

Romanova noticed many of the Winkies were very hard between the legs, their bold fish heads pushing hungrily against their tunics.

Once the initial tide of excitement climaxed, the three

ruling elders of Chugtoo filtered through the hard and happy Winkie throng to present themselves to her. One was female, one fem-two, and one male. The three of them were naked except for chains of ruddy gold around their necks and a spread of dark, cedar leaf tattoos on the lower part of their torsos and circling their groins.

Romanova could see the fem-two and the male elder were aroused by her presence and struggling to not be mesmerized into goofiness. Having powers unknown to the Winkies, she could sense the DNA in them turning somersaults for a chance to fuse with her. The female introduced herself as Petunio and she bowed to Romanova, who returned the greeting.

Petunio spoke first, as befitted custom. "You are well received, traveler. We welcome you to our village, and what we have is yours. We look forward to pleasing you."

To which Romanova replied, as was custom, "Thank you for your welcome. I will do what I can to make my stay here special for everyone."

Petunio replied, "The children tell us you have no lover. As you can see, we have many who are dreaming hard." In agreement, at least 20 Winkies gave forth with sexual moans. Petunio continued, "Please look them over and choose whomever you wish. That is the right of the traveler."

The Winkies applauded and several called out like children, "Aiiii, please pick me, Romanova!"

Petunio continued. "Dinner will be served here in the circle within the hour. That gives you time for at least one mating." The Winkies all stared at Romanova who understood quite plainly that unless she went along with custom, here and now, her so-called vacation would come to a screeching halt. Besides, she wasn't in Prussia anymore, or Russia, or even the Heptagon. The rules were different here. She'd known that in advance, therefore, no point in being dishonest with herself.

"So be it," she said, loud enough for the Winkies to hear. She turned around and saw a fair and magnificently aroused fem-two staring with big adoring eyes. Romanova approached, and as befits custom asked name, and the reply came. "I am known throughout as Careenisha." Following which, Romanova said, "I choose you, Careenisha."

Romanova took Careenisha by the hand, and in the presence of much applause and cheers by the village Winkies, led her-him into a nearby mud brick hut, pointed out by the elder, Petunio. Once alone in the cool shadows of the hut, the two Winkies fell to the fur-covered floor, kissing and clutching and quite ravenous. They stripped each other of clothing and Romanova mounted the huge and hard of Careenisha while also suckling upon her erect nipples. The two of them thrashed and groaned and whimpered, rolling over and over in the fur.

An hour later, the dinner flute and seating drums sounded outside the hut. Exhausted and wet, Romanova and Careenisha dressed themselves and emerged to even more vigorous applause.

Following a dinner of hot bread, rich golden cheeses, yummy berries, and cooked river trout—consumed at a long table filled with laughing and chewing Winkies—Romanova retired for the night only to be guest to three more amorous villagers; though without intention, and she finally fell fast asleep on the furry floor and into deep dream.

She dreamt the goddess Ozma walked into her hut, sheathed in a white, gold-rimmed robe that covered her from neck to ankle. She was taller than Romanova, beautiful beyond imagination, muscular and big breasted—apparent as she let her robe drop to the floor. Her golden skin glowed softly and her eyes burned into Romanova like hot furnace pokers.

"Stop, please," the Winkie in Romanova said.

The dream of Ozma just smiled mockingly and leapt atop her like a mountain lioness, pinning her with both hands to the floor. "I will have *no other goddesses* before me," Ozma said, her voice husky and threatening. "You will worship and love me, Czarina of All the Russias. I will subdue you tonight, and you will remain with the Winkies here in Oz, worshipping me until the end of your days." In response, tears of panic trickled down Romanova's soft Winkie cheeks.

Ozma licked at them like a bear licking honey.

: /

THE "VICTORY AND NEW WORLD PARTY" WAS HELD seven days after the close of World War Oz. Edison Godfellow believed it good for morale, a way to end the suffering, as well as renew focus on creation and new utopian possibilities.

Every one of the fabulous New Manhattan sky-island restaurants took part, as well as similar establishments in other Oz city-worlds. Festivities were also planned in newly inhabited sections of the Deeper Lands, and in select Lands of Never. Everything was set to occur in sync.

Piper couldn't force herself to become terribly enthusiastic about whooping it up. First, the images of humanity's terrible fall weighed on her. Then it became personal with the pointless and cruel deaths of Alcaeus, Murray, Ms. Song, and so many others impossible to count. Also, the fact that vestiges of hostile Orion alien yet lingered, and were seemingly undiscoverable, still worried her. At least she'd stirred Nina Cohen's hash into edible form, and the young women abused by the Berkeley therapist had been relocated to New Manhattan Oz for the time being.

As for Nina herself?

In a place where she'll never hurt anyone again.

A few hours before the party, Piper gulped down four yards of choice Grimbergen and ate cheese crackers at her apartment while watching the movie *Forbidden Planet* on Flick-a-Zon.

Never get tired of Robby or the Krell.

Feeling a bit tipsy, and grateful for it, she next spelled herself into Bianca form. She gave herself a swanky-doodle black evening dress showing lots of evil cleavage, and her lustrous dark hair billowed enough to make onlookers stumble. Around her neck, she added a string of stunning Mongo fire pearls (her personal invention) that caused human eyes to water if they stared at them too long, and before anyone could say "Voila!" she snapped herself into existence just inside the front door of *Le Petit Sanglier*.

The party rocked in full swing, bubbling to the champagne brim with New Manhattanites and military personnel from the *Caliburn*. Loud music, clapping, and celebratory laughter—what you would expect for a party in such a fantastical and beautiful place illumined by a sunset featuring the moon and Mars. On a stage in the distance, to the left of the Crab Nebula, Sinatra himself held a microphone and sang, "Let's Face the Music and Dance."

The waiters recognized Piper and smiled in greeting. She was escorted by a cigarette-smoking William Shatner (his younger *Rocket Man* years) in a black tuxedo and accompanied by a tap-dancing Judy Garland resembling Dorothy Gale in a blue tutu.

Gods and comets, I need two more yards.

Piper knew her father and Catherine would be in attendance. Cereus wasn't going. *Can I blame him?* Piper was soon seated with them at a table just off the dance floor, and to her surprise, they were joined by that horribly insufferable djinn, Tazamat, now in lemur mode, his head barely visible above the table.

Oh shit, this is going to be fun. I'll need five more yards.

Her father, also in a black tux, greeted her with much showing of teeth and genuine good feeling. He stood to give her a hug and kissed her on the forehead. Catherine followed by nodding a hello and focusing enough eye into Piper to make her realize a potential issue was brewing. Piper gave her hand a squeeze and Catherine squeezed back harder.

Okay, something's not right.

She noted that the Czarina was also dressed to kill in a sexy evening gown of royal purple chiffon topped by a grand necklace of Martian emeralds. Her glossy, dusk-honey hair was sprinkled with diamond starlets, brushed to the right and falling over her chest. A quite stunning appearance by anyone's standards.

Before exploring anything else, and possessing a post-slaughter itch she decided to inflame with as much scratching as possible, Piper took her father aside by the arm and asked him point blank, "How the hell can we throw a whopping ass party after the death and destruction we've witnessed?"

Edison Godfellow smiled at her. "Because, Piper, I know something you do not. Together with a team of Shadow Broker techs, we returned a few days ago to the Jovian past on the other side of the galaxy and added a new array of magi-tech dishes that we will access soon via subspace channeling."

"You've planned this all along?"

"Recall that wall of mysterious violet light rushing over you in Brooklyn just prior to the creation of New Manhattan?"

"Yes, the *Gravar e Almancenar* spell."

"Precisely. We will tap the contents of that spell and use the new Jovian Tao to restore most of the planet to normalcy without a single atom of cosmic hostility included."

"Most of it?"

"The cities, culture, geography, yes."

"*Most of it?*" Piper was suspicious. "What is being left out, pops?

Her father grinned, squeezed her hand, and said, "We have much to celebrate, my daughter. Our doom is no more, and I promise life will be good."

Following that pronouncement, he allowed himself to

be distracted by the general vibration of the party. Obviously, he was going to dodge the question for now, so Piper figured she'd revisit it later.

She turned to greet Tazamat out of courtesy, only he'd suddenly become a drooling, boneless version of Shatner. She tried not to laugh and thereby encourage the little cretin and that's when she noticed at least twenty or so couples slow dancing in front of the stage.

Sinatra looks so real, as if way more than a magical or tech imitation of some kind.

As she watched, he bowed to applause and the scene faded to another live concert, but this time Yo Yo Ma performing a Bach solo with his legendary Montagnana cello. Quite a contrast, and again, so real.

"You are witnessing the first *spell cast* of live musical events from the past," her father said from across the table. "I have been laboring on the magi-tech for the past year. It works quite well despite our current *Tempo* problems, which now appear more localized and fading."

"Why didn't you tell me, sooner?"

"Because I have a surprise for you, coming up shortly."

Piper smiled at him, turned to Catherine, and said, "Looks like the ban on female morph-droids has been lifted?"

Catherine's reply was heard in Piper's mind:

"The Witch Empress lives."

"Serious?"

"There is more to her resolution than a lingering spell affecting Tempo."

"How so?"

"In a dream I was assaulted by a force calling itself Ozma."

"Wait. A dream?"

"The dream was an intentional threat."

"Ozma was the ruler of Oz, in the books."

"Trust me that I know a real dream from a false one."

"I trust you. What happened?"

"Ozma held me down and began choking me, releasing, and repeating. I emitted a sonic shriek into her face but only succeeded in exploding the roof of the hut."

"The hut?"

"Never mind. I awakened and returned to the Heptagon. I utilized ARMEW immediately, but it proved useless. No trail or atom remained."

"Have you told my father?"

"Yes, though given the level of analysis and investigatory power currently underway, he cannot yet readily accept the Ozma force as being self-directed, much less the Orion alien itself. He believes, at worst, it might be a telepathic magi-tech projection operating on automatic."

"So it's still top of the ninth."

"I do not understand."

"Baseball. Everyone from Brooklyn knows baseball."

Edison interrupted. "Well now, you do appear way too grim, my cosmic goddesses!"

"Yes, like two cows full of sour milk." Tazamat was now in the guise of Barbara Streisand from *Hello Dolly*, but with the voice of Toshiro Mifune.

Piper glared at the djinn. "Will you try and fail to be funny all night, asshole?"

Edison continued. "Talk depressing business later. A time for everything, yes? Just see what we have now." He waved his hand towards the stage. Yo Yo Ma faded out and the New York Philharmonic faded in with the first note of "Rhapsody in Blue" by Gershwin.

"By the spires of Anhalt, truly impressive, Edison." Catherine was genuinely in awe.

The waiter for their table, wizened old American actor John Carradine, stopped by for drink orders. Piper recognized him as starring in a lot of her favorite bad movies, including *Billy the Kid vs. Dracula*. Nonetheless, she ordered a whiskey sour with egg white.

Catherine ordered a Sonoma pinot noir '96. Tazamat wanted a draft Guinness, and Edison chose an order of Asian salad wonton cups for the table.

Tazamat fixed his stare on Piper. "By the way, Bianca, or Piper, Macaria, *whatever*, I have news. You might still have a chance to become an abysmal failure on Broadway," he said with Barbara Streisand's actual voice.

"What did you say?"

Edison interjected. "What our djinn friend is attempting to relate is that many thousands of Manhattanites are returning to restore and rekindle the life of the original city, and this includes Broadway."

"Really? That's fantastic!"

Best news I've heard in months.

"Yes, you can once again try to get a bit villager part in *Book of Mormon*," the Tazamat Streisand said. "And perhaps, if you're lucky, even go back to grinding coffee for stupid human dipshits."

"The longest running show on Broadway, I understand?" Catherine said.

"Yes, it is... I'll think it over. So much has—"

A foam-white whiskey sour appeared before Piper. John

Carradine had returned with the drinks and food. Edison called for a toast using his water glass. "To our utopian future and the best for all humanity!" The other three clinked their glasses with him.

As "Rhapsody in Blue" faded, Piper watched the stage with curiosity. Who would be next? The lights dropped low, and what faded into view was both astonishing and delightful to Piper. If she needed to blink, now would be the time.

Holy shit, I don't believe it!

She was witnessing a concert from 2006 in Gainesville, Florida—a concert she once attended as a fan, and on stage stood Tom Petty singing "Running Down a Dream" with the Heartbreakers. Only her father knew her as a big Tom Petty fan. Of course, other bands from that era were high on her list, but Tom was special.

I've gotta dance! But with who?

Piper looked around and grabbed an astonished Catherine by the hand. She pulled her towards the dance floor despite protests. Piper shouted over the thunderous live music.

"C'mon, you'll be a rock queen in no time!"

Catherine surrendered and followed Piper near to the stage whereupon Piper began to wave her arms and gyrate an improvised form of the Boogaloo. At the same time, she observed Catherine bravely struggling to compensate for her utter lack of rock 'n roll experience by high stepping in awkward fashion and fluttering her hands like a bird.

American gods! I'm going to burst any second.

Halfway through the song and Piper guffawed at Catherine's sad attempts to dance, and as Catherine flushed like a teenager, Piper began apologizing. "I'm so sorry, Cathy. I don't mean to laugh! ... Oh... Sorry, can't help it!" But Catherine laughed too, and they both laughed so much they fell towards each other, gripping each other's arms and holding on.

Piper impulsively kissed Catherine on the lips and Catherine returned the kiss for two seconds longer, then they separated and danced a bit more until "Running Down a Dream" ended to much applause from the 2006 Gainesville audience.

Tom Petty faded out and The Bangles faded in, doing a live version of "Walk Like an Egyptian" in Dodger Stadium. Piper grabbed Catherine by the hand and led her back to the table. On the way, she overheard a male voice in the background saying, "Did you see the war goddesses Romanova and Robbin kissing on the dance floor? Was that sexy or what?" The reply came back, "They used to hate each other."

My, my, how the truth turns to gossip and back again.

The two sat down and Piper did a double take. Her father's face appeared sad and frustrated. "I regret I must show you something," he said.

A chill went down Piper's spine.

What fresh hell is this?

He rose and she also. He glanced over at Catherine and said, "You should be a part."

Looking as perplexed as Piper, she stood and followed Piper who was right behind her father as he cut a path through the partygoers, patting shoulders as he went and exchanging pleasantries with a forced smile.

The three of them filed out the front door even as more

people were jamming in. They walked to a relatively secluded space with less noise, and once there, Edison turned on his heel and presented Piper with a sliver of white paper.

"I received this while you were dancing... I am so, so sorry."

She took the note and read it:

MESSAGE FOR COMMANDER ROBBIN. OSC NEW MANHATTAN OZ

FRANCES MENENDEZ, FEMALE, 28 YEARS OLD, HAS BEEN FOUND DEAD AT THE BASE OF OZ CENTRAL TOWER. DEATH CAUSED BY A PROLONGED FALL FROM GREAT HEIGHT. SUICIDE RULED OUT DUE TO CIRCUMSTANCES. INVESTIGATION ONGOING.

Piper felt stunned and confused.

Catherine gasped and plucked the note to read for herself. "Who is she?"

"A young woman I saved from the clutches of Nina."

"The Witch Empress?" Catherine was baffled.

"I haven't told you. The real Nina was running a boarding house filled with victims of her diagnoses. I put an end to her cruel game and relocated the victims to New Manhattan Oz, including Frances Menendez."

Edison stepped forward to clutch his daughter by the shoulders, his face stern. "Piper, please investigate and let me know... It bothers me, and again, I am so sorry. We will make certain the other young women do not meet a similar fate."

"Yes... an investigation," Piper said, face motionless.

Cathy leaned close and spoke with a warm and gentle voice. "Let us relocate to the governor's office. We will engage its superior force in our pursuit of truth."

"Yes, yes, of course."

I can't believe this.

:/

ONCE REACHING THE HEPTAGON, Catherine clicked on with OSC command, though few new facts presented themselves. Frances was thrown from a relatively obscure patio located over half a mile above her assigned apartment, and despite failsafe tech which should have shielded the perimeter, it failed, as if the power had been cut, and no one saw a thing. Her body was first noticed by a routine OSC exterior check.

She'd been dead for an hour.

Catherine conducted a sweeping ARMEW scan of all minds in the vicinity of the patio and the apartment level where Frances lived, and kept at it for over half an hour, but no witnesses presented themselves. She set the ARMEW to continue scanning as well as analyzing all matter down to an atomic level in the relevant sectors, seeking anything, even a wave or particle slightly anomalous or unusual. Once done, the ARMEW would broaden the tests until the entire tower was accounted for.

By 5 A.M. in the morning, still nothing.

Piper stood quietly, gazing at the dawn sky over the

defiant and mighty towers of New Manhattan. Catherine glided to her side and handed her a pewter cup of hot black tea with a dab of honey.

Piper thanked her, then asked, "Is the Heptagon safe from spies or intrusion?"

Catherine placed a warm hand on Piper's upper arm. "Yes. The magi-tech devices account for every particle, even photons and neutrinos, and at all times."

"Sorry, I had to ask. I heard of a spell long ago. Actually, it was Tao spell theory, real nerd stuff. My father called it, *Observación e Disfrace*."

"Observe and change... Disguise?"

"Yes, only a theory, supposedly never developed. Too volatile. I'm not sure even Cereus knows, but if anyone, he would. Hell, he might already be using it."

"So you believe this is the answer?"

Piper turned away from the dawn to face Catherine eye to eye. "I don't know. We've both been compromised by the alien, or its murderous toads, yet no trail exists despite our powers and magi-tech wonder toys, but an *Observación e Disfrace* could account for that. Any portion of matter affected reacts and immediately disguises itself upon observation, and so quickly that only a *Tempo* spell could reveal it."

"And since we possess no trustworthy *Tempo* yet..."

"A perfect weapon then, you see. A perfect method for prolonged guerilla conflict when you're starved for resources and just want to hurt people."

Catherine sighed as though exasperated.

Piper reached over to squeeze Catherine's hand resting on her arm, and said, "I am happy we are as one."

"Yes, and I feel the same."

Piper kissed Catherine on the lips like a soft stroke of delicate brush, and glancing back to a vast and gold-simmering dawn drifting among the starscrapers, said with a quiet yet firm voice:

"Oz in *aeternum*."

And Catherine, hugging Piper's waist while lowering a tired head onto her friend's shoulder, replied.

"Oz in *aeternum*."

THE END

GLOSSARY

AHRIMAN

A magical being who fell to Asia from the stars around 8,000 BC. Though the sex of this being is not known, its children, the original World Makers—Dao Changkratok, Edison Godfellow, and Svetlana Frankivsk (known as the missing World Maker)—named him Ahriman after the omni-malevolent Persian spirit. They saw their parent only in their darkest dreams and its form always resembled that of a huge, bee-like creature, though with many eyes of infinite depth. Ahriman's true origin and intent remain a matter of mystery and conjecture. Upon ascension to World Maker in the 18th century, Czarina Catherine Romanova also reported visions of a similar creature she believed to be Ahriman.

ARIA MAGIC

Since the birth of the World Makers in the Bronze Age, only two ever possessed the power of aria, and both were women. The first, Dao Changkratok, lived in old Thailand and died at the hands of the *Dio Soldati* following an attempt to murder Edison Godfellow. The second was Princess Fredericka Von Anhalt who later became Catherine Romanova, Czarina of All the Russias. The aria channels the magical side of the Tao and enables the World Maker who possesses it to access tremendous magical power, and in unique ways. Complex spells in Galician arise from deep within the being of the World Maker and manifest in a style often reminiscent of European opera.

ARMEW

Short for Aria and Magical Enhancement Web. A magi-tech Tao device invented by Edison Godfellow that fuses with the neural architecture of the World Maker Catherine Romanova. The ARMEW channels her will and amplifies spells and all acts of matter-energy manipulation, and in a special manner that disallows inappropriate, unwanted, or exaggerated effects that might prove harmful. The ARMEW is even powerful enough to affect planets orbiting distant stars.

CAIXA DE MUNDOS

Galician for "Box of Worlds." An extremely powerful spell available to World Makers and high-rank sorcerers. The creation of *Caixa de Mundos* enables the user to effectively copy any object and store the copy in a container of choice—usually a small box or sphere on a chain. Once copied, the thing copied can be reproduced in its original size and form. The amount of matter-energy able to be copied and stored, in magical theory, is nearly limitless. A capable sorcerer could, for example, copy an entire moon of Saturn, store it, and return it to existence at a chosen time. A closely related spell, the *Gravar e Almancenar*, is even more powerful, and could be employed to copy the entire Earth down to the last molecule in a primitive bacterium.

DARK HOUSE OF OZ

A creation of the Witch Empress (aka Nina Cohen) that appeared in the Deeper Lands of New Manhattan Oz at the hub of the four-quadrant land. The Dark House was enormous in size, hundreds of feet tall, but its overall architectural appearance was never the same twice. Ordinary human exposure to the Dark House stimulated everything from bad dreams to psychotic breaks.

DEEPER LANDS

A name coined for the totality of land that forms the very base of New Manhattan Oz—resting just above the city's Operations and Security Command. The land was created and formed as a neo-dimensional quantum environment wherein the ratio of normal distance to Deeper Land distance is 1/1000. The diameter of the Deeper Lands is therefore approximately 20,000 miles given that the diameter of the New Manhattan base is approximately 20 normal miles. The topographic features as well as the flora and fauna composition are determined by a magi-tech AI invention of Edison Godfellow known as the *Apparatus Creaturae*. It effectively and randomly creates various species of plants and animals while sculpting mountain chains, rivers, seas, lakes, plateaus, and much else of similar nature. The original motive for the creation of the Deeper Lands was to provide a habitat for humanity and its many future billions.

DIO SOLDATI

Italian for "God Soldiers." Created, designed, and trained as elite shock troops combining the best of magical Tao and military science—better known as "magi-tech." A single *Dio Soldati* consists of a combat exoskeleton with six limbs, weapon packs, segmented armor, and sensor arrays. The tactical and engineering brain consists of a YJS-3.6 AI unit that interfaces with its host. Non-EMP primary weapons include combat spells, black hole effectors, particle disruptor beams, giga-electrics, black-plasma cannons, and others. The God Soldiers also fight in EMP environments (see below) through efficient utilization of sonic and kinetic weapons, including a pair of graphene broadswords. Each *Dio Soldati* employs six small stealth drones for purposes of reconnaissance nicknamed "blisters." A typical *Dio Soldati* unit stands 15 feet tall and altogether packs a total punch equal to 923.4 megatons.

DJINN

Born of a powerful spell by a Celtic sorcerer who turned an unruly clan of Neolithic Irish into even more annoying magical creatures. Djinns eventually spread around the world and into the Middle East where they became part of pre-Islamic folklore. They are known to hate humans in general, the English and Turks most of all. Roman Emperor Hadrian once observed, "Unless under spell or sword, djinns should be shunned." Because of being so cantankerous, not many remain alive in the 21st century. Estimates vary, but most sorcerers agree not more than 700. Djinns procreate by laying eggs once every century or so. Powers include ability to change shape into insects, serpents, hawks, and panthers, the adoption of various human guises, control of wind and fire, and invisibility after dusk. Their normal appearance is that of a furry, lemur-like creature not more than three feet tall.

ELECTRO-MAGICAL PULSE (EMP)

A magical dampening field primarily utilized for military purposes during times of war, serving as effective countermeasure to both magical and non-magical Tao weapons—lasers, electricity, black-plasma, nova effects, particle beams, combat spells, etc. EMP can be maintained for minutes or days, the physical extent and duration of an EMP "bubble" dependent on the amount of energy deployed at inception. EMP can be produced either by spell or magical technology, the latter being a more powerful and durable source.

FIESTRA NA VIDA

An advanced and utilitarian spell that creates life windows three to ten feet in diameter for purposes of observation, collection, and transport. The spell can "open a "window" onto almost anything regardless of location, thus enabling panoramic viewpoint or detailed microscopic examination. Objects can enter and exit the windows without limit.

GALICIAN

An ancient derivative of Latin in Northern Spain and the primary interface language chosen by the World Makers and utilized by all magical beings to tap and mold the magical side of Tao (see below). Early attempts to employ other languages were made, but none proved upon experimentation to be sufficiently precise, e.g., none allowed the threading of needles or manipulation of microscopic fauna. The words of any spell, whether used to poach eggs or edit a storm pattern, must be spoken perfectly. Spells may be spoken in thought but must be heard in the ear of the mind. The totality of spells, 33,569 of them, are listed and described in 28 volumes of collected spell code and organized into a Spell Potency Hierarchy. Spells higher on the hierarchy can only be achieved by those magicians, spell captains, sorcerers, and World Makers who possess the power to goad them into results. A rank beginner magician may effectively access up to a hundred spells without the use of any device.

GRAND HUMAN TRANFIGURATION

Created and engineered following years of nuanced spell morphing studies and neo-form architectural analysis, the Grand Human Transfiguration consisted of an Earth-wide remaking of the human species—by means of magic and technology—into a new species commonly known as the Superna Humanitas, or the Great People. Those who survived the methodical cleansing and rigorous psychological tests of the much hated and praised Transfiguration were gifted with flawless form, enhanced strength and intellect. and functional telepathy, as well as age-free immortality. However, the GHT was effectively canceled by Godfellow himself (upon returning from the future) before it transitioned into Phase II, but he allowed the full implementation of Phase I which consisted of cleansing Earth of all levels and classes of sociopaths, borderlines, narcissists, and miscellaneous other dysfunctionals. This decision was based on his firm belief that a future utopian society would never be able to mature if the usual aggressive defectives remained alive to corrupt it.

KATHMANDU

The magical other-side of Kathmandu is a fabled, mystical city of tower-like buildings, many a mile or more high, existing within the clouds of the Himalayas. Arranged and stacked in levels, similar to Buddhist sanctuaries in Nepal, it is home to a population primarily composed of Buddhist spell captains and their extended families. Philosopher magician-kings rule as a five-king council. The city resides outside the normal time stream and is composed of magical Tao. Kathmandu was birthed following the trial and death of Socrates by sorcerers sympathetic to the philosopher. Rather than take revenge upon the Athenians, they sought seclusion and peace in a world of their own conception.

LA MANCHA TOWER

A starscraper and former command center in London which housed the War Tracker device during the War for Utopia. The upper half of the tower was obliterated by forces intent on capturing War Tracker— a primary strategic goal during the conflict.

LANDS OF NEVER

Objects of rock and earth varying in size from several miles in diameter to well over 200 miles. They exist in the Oz ether between New Manhattan and the Deeper Lands. Each individual Land of Never possesses its own unique environment, magical or non-magical aspects and parts depending on its purpose.

LA STELO PUNTERO

The Pointer Star. Name of the tallest starscraper in New Manhattan Oz, over three miles high, atop which sits the Heptagon—headquarters penthouse and office for the Governor of New Manhattan Oz who is responsible for defense and overall administration. The first Governor to occupy the office is World Maker and Czarina Catherine Romanova. The Heptagon contains its own built-in ARMEW (see above). The bulk of the starscraper consists of living quarters, neospace sectors, parks, offices, and recreation spaces.

LE PETIT SANGLIER

The Small Boar. Known not only for its superb French cuisine, but also for exquisite dishes from many cultures, the restaurant rests atop a sky island that orbits New Manhattan. It features a permanent form of *Fiestra Na Vida* that opens a large window onto exotic and beautiful climes just for the enjoyment of patrons. The wait staff are morph-droids who imitate the forms of famous actors of all sexes, and from all periods, even back to the earliest days of film, including Mae West, Mary Pickford, Charlie Chaplin, Humphrey Bogart, Greta Garbo, Grace Kelly, and Lauren Bacall, as well as cult figures like Bradford Dillman, Adam West, and Ed Wood Junior.

MAGI-TECH

General term for objects, devices, or artificial systems of any kind that are created using a combination of magical and non-magical Tao—in other words, magic and technology. The science of magi-tech was developed to a perfect form by Edison Godfellow.

MEMENTO MORI

A philosophical reflection on mortality that goes back to Socrates, and a visual reminder that death is always near—usually depicted by a skull and often surrounded by other symbols. Piper Robbin always wears a *Memento Mori* carved from ebony on a chain around her neck that is half face and half skull.

MOTHER YARROWS

The soul essence of famous female warriors from centuries past who willingly donate "years between seconds" to assist an elite corps of spell captains, sorcerers, and World Makers in the future. Channeled via magical yarrow sticks implanted in the spines of their hosts, they augment the natural power of the host. Ongoing interface with the host is accomplished via magical sub-space telepathy. Mother Yarrow Mario of Pozzuoli was one of the most famous, having possessed the yarrow of World Maker Catherine Romanova.

NEO-DIMENSIONAL SPACE or NEOSPACE

Upon experimenting with magically enhanced forms of quantum and non-quantum space, Godfellow found that with sufficient Tao energy one could "stretch" normal space nearly indefinitely and stabilize it within a defined normal-space perimeter. As a practical application he created vast areas within the Oz City-Worlds and on select Superna Humanitas fleet warships to allow for more suitable and expansive living space. He later discovered that one could also vary the ratio of real space to neospace within the same container, thereby shrinking or widening as the need dictated.

SUPERNA HUMANITAS

The final evolutionary stage of the human species, aka the "Great People." Created through genetic engineering, they remain forever young, immune to illness and disease, and possessed of superior stamina, strength, and enhanced agility. Their injuries heal at 34.8 times the rate of a normal human, and they can withstand up to 13,200 PSI and 1400 degrees Fahrenheit in the flesh. Each possesses four mini-hearts, interspecies telepathy, 2.5 telekinesis allowing levitation, and a minimum 240 IQ, as well as the ability to neurally triple process and filter oxygen from water. Individuals serve as fleet crew, military personnel, and *Dio Soldati*, as well as perform all Operations and Security Center functions.

SEVEN CITY-WORLDS OF OZ

Manhattan, Berlin, Istanbul, Kinshasa, Shanghai, Jakarta, and Buenos Aires. They serve two purposes. First, they provide utopian living space for the human species with ample room for population expansion, and second, they form an Earth defense system believed powerful enough to repel any form of alien invasion. The Oz theme was conceived by Godfellow, due to his obsession with the popular film, and because he believed it symbolic of humankind's best qualities. Each city-world consists of a crown sector that includes the former old city under a transparent bio-dome and the new version directly beneath existing in neo-dimensional space.

SHADOW BROKERS

Founded by master magician Cereus Malcolm, and originating in England during the 17th century, the Shadow Brokers became infamous for intricate and customized spell craft that allowed for breaking and entering all forms of protected spaces whether they be treasure vaults or burial crypts, above ground or below. In later centuries, they expanded their reach to include computer networks and personal electronic devices. As a matter of course, they evolved into the world's best trackers, investigators, and spies. Cereus was later appointed by his fellow Shadow Brokers as Grand Master Mage and has retained this title well into the 21st century.

TAO

The basic essence of the multi-verse: energy and matter divided into a duality of magical and non-magical. Whether the two are actually distinct from each other based on reality or misperception is hotly debated among Tao physicists and magic scholars. Electricity and gravity are considered non-magical Tao, whereas spell-driven kinetics and anti-gravity are considered magical Tao; however, both types exist *de facto* and are utilized by intelligent species for purposes of creation, alteration, habitation, and annihilation. The existence of magical Tao is far rarer than non-magical, though large deposits have been found to exist in particular regions of the galaxy and are believed to originate in the heated sub-atomica of massive black holes.

WAR FOR UTOPIA

Fought between the World Maker children of Ahriman to determine the destiny of Earth, and involving their two capital cities, London and Kathmandu. Though essentially a time war, the Nicholas Treaty drew the boundary lines of conflict from the year 1568 to an indeterminate future. The southern boundary of 1568 was chosen to prevent either side from accidentally disrupting the defeat of Ottoman Empire forces at the siege of Vienna. The boundary was enforced by a ring of magi-tech chrono satellites that annihilated any being or instrument crossing the line going south to the more distant past. World Maker Niccolo Paganini emphasized improvement of the moral and spiritual nature of humanity, as well as Earth harmony, whereas Godfellow, aka Da Vinci, emphasized genetic evolution, rule by sorcerer kings, and multi-verse exploration as key critical elements necessary for species survival. The War for Utopia concluded its first phase with a victory for Godfellow and London, however, a second phase (aka "World War Oz") was later fought against an alien from Orion that called itself "The Witch Empress."

WAR TRACKER

A magi-tech invention designed during the War for Utopia to keep perpetual and meticulous watch on all changes in the Earth time stream, thus enabling a warning and dispatch system that triggered magical military "black forces," e.g., the *Dio Soldati* (see above), to restore the original stream should unwanted changes of any type or degree occur.

WINKIES

Inhabitants of the Deeper Lands. Unlike the Winkies of the original Oz, these Winkies resemble golden and hairless humans. Their oversexed recreational habits produce large numbers of Winkie babies who begin life as melon-like pods on the backs of their mothers. Winkies come in three sexes: male, female, and fem-two. All are well endowed, but the fem-two possesses both breasts and penis, thereby having the ability to both ignite and nurture life. Winkie children grow quickly and within nine months are copulating freely.

Their technology is Bronze Age. Winkies live in homes of mudbrick, wood, and straw, gather boolee berries, and engage in farming corn and wheat. Under most circumstances they are congenial. They worship a sun goddess named Ozma. During World War Oz, hundreds of them immigrated to Mars and began a new life there.

WORLD WAR OZ

Name given to the second War for Utopia. Once Edison Godfellow had defeated the forces of Kathmandu and won the first War for Utopia, he evolved humanity, transfigured Earth, and reached out to the stars, only to face an ignoble, bloody, and catastrophic defeat at the hands of an all-powerful Orion alien whose origin and nature yet remain a matter of conjecture. In a desperate bid to prevent this ultimate annihilation, Edison alone traveled back in time to the New York City of 2038 A.D. on a mission to find his daughter, Piper Robbin, and ally with her, and others, to stop himself in the past before the Grand Human Transfiguration (see above) could provoke the final disaster among the stars. Once he had succeeded in this mission, in part by creating the Seven City-Worlds of Oz, a new genocidal war began, initiated by the same malignant and invincible alien from the future who had annihilated his fleet in the primary star nursery of the Orion Nebula.